9

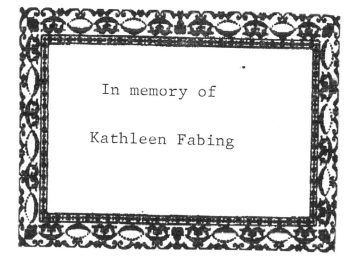

In memory of

Kathleen Fabing

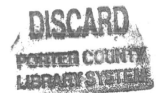

A
PERFECT
CRIME

G·K
Hall
&Cº

This Large Print Book carries the
Seal of Approval of N.A.V.H.

A
PERFECT
CRIME

PETER ABRAHAMS

G.K. Hall & Co. • Thorndike, Maine

Published in 1999 by arrangement with Ballantine Books, a division of Random House, Inc.

G.K. Hall Large Print Core Series.

The text of this Large Print edition is unabridged. Other aspects of the book may vary from the original edition.

Set in 16 pt. Plantin.

Printed in the United States on permanent paper.

Library of Congress Cataloging in Publication Data

Abrahams, Peter, 1947–
    A perfect crime / Peter Abrahams.
        p. cm.
    ISBN 0-7838-8476-1 (lg. print : hc : alk. paper)
    1. Man-woman relationships — Fiction.   2. Adultery — Fiction.   3. Large type books.   I. Title.
    [PS3551.B64P4   1999]
    813′.54—dc21
                                                    98-48258

This book is dedicated
to Alan Cohen.

Many thanks to Ron Lawton for his information on chain-saw sculpture, to Peter Borland and Judith Curr for their excellent editorial advice, and to my wonderfully supportive agent, Molly Friedrich.

The scarlet letter was her passport into regions where other women dared not tread.
— Nathaniel Hawthorne

1

Thursday, the best day of the week — the day of all days that Francie was predisposed to say yes. But here in the artist's studio, with its view of the Dorchester gas tank superimposed on the harbor beyond, she couldn't bring herself to do it. The problem was she hated the paintings. The medium was ink, the tool airbrush, the style photorealist, the subject slack-faced people in art galleries viewing installations; the installations, when she looked more closely, were neon messages fenced in with blood-tipped barbed wire, messages that though tiny could be read, when she looked more closely still. Francie, her nose almost touching the canvases, read them dutifully: *name that tune; do you swear to tell the truth?; we will have these moments to remember.*

"World within world," she said, a neutral phrase that might be taken optimistically.

"I'm sorry?" said the artist, following her nervously around the studio.

Francie smiled at him — gaunt, hollow-eyed, twitchy, unkempt — Raskolnikov on amphetamines. She'd seen paintings of slack-faced people looking at paintings; she'd seen neon messages; she'd seen barbed wire, blood-tipped, pink, red-white-and-blue; seen art feeding on itself with an appetite that grew sharper every day.

"Anything else you'd like to show me?" she said.

"Anything else?" said the artist. "I'm not sure exactly what you . . ."

Francie kept her smile in place; artists lived uneasy lives. "Other work," she explained, as gently as she could.

But not gently enough. He flung out his arm in a dramatic sweep. "This is my work."

Francie nodded. Some of her colleagues would now say "I love it" and let him learn the bad news in a letter from the foundation, but Francie couldn't. Silence followed, long and uncomfortable. Time slowed down, much too soon. On Thursdays, Francie wanted time to behave as it might in some Einsteinian thought experiment, hurrying by until dark, then almost coming to a stop. The artist gazed at his shoes, red canvas basketball sneakers, paint-spattered. Francie gazed at them, too. *Do you swear to tell the truth?* Even bad art could get to you, or at least to her. She saw something from the corner of her eye — a small unframed canvas, leaning against the jamb of a doorless closet, went closer, to end the shoe-gazing if nothing else.

"What's this?" An oil painting of a plinth, cracked, crumbling, classical, bearing a bunch of grapes, wine-dark, overripe, even rotting. And in the middle ground, not hidden, not flaunted, simply there, was a lovely figure of a girl on a

10

skateboard, all poise, balance, speed.

"That?" said the painter. "That's from years ago."

"Tell me about it."

"What's to tell? It was a dead end."

"You didn't do any more like it?" Francie knelt, turned the painting around, read the writing on the back: *oh garden, my garden.*

"By the dozen," said the artist. "But I painted over them whenever I needed canvas."

Francie kept herself from glancing at the busy pieces on the wall.

"That's the last one, in fact. Why do you ask?"

"It has a kind of . . ." Something. It had that something she was always looking for, so hard to put in words. To sound professional, Francie said, ". . . resonance."

"It does?"

"In my opinion."

"No one liked them at the time."

"Maybe I'm just a sucker for overripe fruit," Francie said, although she already knew it wasn't that. It was the girl. "Caravaggio, and all that," she explained.

"Caravaggio?"

"You know," she said, her heart sinking.

"A kind of grape?"

"He said that? A kind of grape?" Nora, having finished her lunch — a very late lunch, eaten on their feet at a coffee place in the North End — helped herself to Francie's. "Soon the past will

11

be completely forgotten."

"And life can begin," said Francie.

Nora paused in midbite. "You feeling okay?"

"Why do you ask?"

"How's Jolly Roger these days?"

"Why do you ask?"

Nora laughed, choked slightly, wiped her mouth. "Can you play for me tonight?"

Nora meant tennis: they belonged to the same club, had played together since eighth grade. "Not on Th— no," Francie said.

"I hate to cancel on her."

"Who?"

"Anne? Anita? New member. Shy little *frau*, but she has a nice game. You should meet her."

"Not tonight."

"You said that. What's tonight?"

"Work," Francie said, not without a twinge inside. "And you?"

"Got a date. He called me this morning."

"For tonight? And you said yes?"

"He already knows I've been married twice — do I have to simper like a virgin for the rest of my life?"

"Who's the lucky guy?"

"Bernie something."

Francie picked up the check — Nora's settlement from marriage one had gone the other way the second time — and got her car from the parking garage. She turned on the radio, found Ned, drove out of the city.

12

"And we're back. I'm Ned Demarco, the program is *Intimately Yours*, our beat marriage, love, family in this increasingly complex world. It's Thursday, and as our regular listeners know, Thursday is our free-form day, open-forum time, no studio guests, no set topics. We talk about what you out there want to talk about. Welcome to the program, Marlene from Watertown."

"Dr. Demarco?"

"Ned, please."

"Ned. Hi. I really enjoy your show."

"Thank you, Marlene. What's on your mind?"

"First, can I ask you something?"

"Shoot."

"That voice of yours. Do they do anything to, like, enhance it?"

Ned laughed. "Lucy, in the control room: Doing anything to enhance my voice?" He laughed again, easy and natural. More relaxed with every show, Francie thought. "Lucy says she's doing all that science possibly can. Anything else, Marlene?"

"It's about my husband, I guess." The woman paused.

"Go on."

"He — he's a wonderful father, an excellent provider. Even helps out around the house."

"Sounds ideal."

"I know. Which is why I feel so guilty for saying this, even having it in my mind."

"Having what in your mind, Marlene?"

She took a breath, deep and troubled, audible down her phone line, over the air, through the speakers in Francie's car. "Lately I've been daydreaming a lot about this boy I went with back in high school. And nightdreaming. I'm talking about all the time, Dr. — Ned. And my question is, Would there be any harm in looking him up?"

Ned paused. Francie could feel him thinking. She drove into a tunnel and lost him before the answer came.

The city dwindled in her rearview mirror until there was nothing left but the tops of the two big towers that gave downtown its distinctive look, intruding on a cold, silvery sky. Francie crossed the New Hampshire line, drove north on roads of less and less importance, entered the wilderness beyond the last bed-and-breakfast, and came to Brenda's gate at dusk. She got out of the car, unlocked the gate, drove through, leaving the gate closed but unlocked, as she always did. The rutted track, thick with dead leaves, led up over a hill, then down through rocky meadows to the river. Most of the light had drained from the sky, but the river held on to what was left, in odd blurred streaks of red, orange, and gold: like an autumnal Turner seen through a fingerprint-smeared lens. Francie stopped in front of the little stone jetty, where two dinghies — red *Prosciutto* and green *Melone* — were fastened to the lee side. Climbing into one, she discovered

14

the cause of the odd blurring — a skin of ice lay on the river. So soon? She rowed out to the island, oar blades slicing through the fiery glaze, sheared ice scratching against her bows.

Brenda's island, two or three hundred feet across the river, almost halfway, was a fat oval with flattened ends, no bigger than an acre. It had a floating dock, five huge elms, isolated from disease, thick brush that hadn't been cleared in years, and a flagstone path leading up to the cottage. Francie unlocked the door and went inside, closing the door and leaving it unlocked, as she always did.

The cottage: pine-floored, pine-walled; all that old, deep-polished wood made it almost a living thing, like a fairy-tale tree house. There was a south-facing kitchen, looking down the river; an L-shaped dining and living room facing the far shore; and upstairs two square bedrooms, each with a brass bed, one unmade, the other covered with pillows and a down comforter. A perfect little cottage that had been in Brenda's family for more than a hundred years; but Brenda, Francie's former college roommate, was the last survivor, and she lived in Rome. She'd asked Francie to keep an eye on it for her, using it whenever she wanted, and Francie had agreed, long before anything ulterior came along.

Francie switched on the generator, lit the woodstove, poured herself a glass of red wine, sat at the kitchen table, and watched night swallow everything — riverbanks, river, floating

15

dock, great bare elms — leaving only the stars above, like holes pierced through to some luminous beyond. The skateboard painting — *oh garden, my garden* — drifted into her mind. Could she properly buy it for herself if the price was right? The artist would probably be glad of the money, but a sale to the foundation would do more for his career. Francie debated with herself for a while. The answer was no.

She threw another log into the stove, refilled her glass, checked her watch. The first feeling of anxiety, like a thumb pressing the inside of her breastbone, awoke within her. Perhaps some music. She was running Brenda's CD collection through her mind when the door swung open and Ned walked in.

"Sorry I'm late," he said.

"You scared me."

"Me?" he said with surprise. He smiled at her; his face was ruddy from the cold, his black hair blown by the river breeze. The atmosphere in the cottage changed completely: the night lost its power, lost its grip on the cottage, withdrew. "You all right?" he said.

"Totally."

They faced each other in the kitchen of Brenda's cottage. The expression in Ned's eyes changed, dark eyes Francie had learned to read like barometers, meteorologist of his soul.

"You know what I love?" he said. "When you're waiting here, the only light for miles around, and I'm rowing across." He came closer, put his arms around her. Francie heard herself moan, a sound that happened by itself, in which she heard unambiguous longing. She didn't care if he heard it, too, couldn't have kept the sound inside in any case.

"I missed you," he said. His voice vibrated against her ear; and yes, what a voice it was.

"What did you tell Marlene?" Francie said, her face against his chest.

"Marlene?"

"Who wanted to get in touch with her old high school boyfriend."

"You caught the show?" He leaned back a little so he could watch her face. "What did you think?"

"You're getting better and better."

He shook his head. "Thanks, but it was flat from beginning to end — and just when this syndication thing is in the air."

In the silence that followed, Francie felt his mind going somewhere else. She repeated her question: "What did you tell her?"

He shrugged. "That she'd be playing with fire."

A little chill found the nape of Francie's neck, a draft, perhaps; it was an old dwelling, after all, with almost no insulation. The very next moment, Ned put his hand right on the spot, right on the chilly part, and rubbed gently. Then the voice, in her ear again: "But sometimes fire is irresistible."

Francie felt her nipples hardening, just from

the words, just from the voice. *And life can begin.*
They went upstairs, Francie first, Ned following,
as they always did.

Brenda's cottage was their world. In truth,
their world was even smaller than that. They
spent no time in the living room, except to feed
the stove, had the occasional drink in the
kitchen, but not food — Ned never seemed to be
hungry — and they both showered in the upstairs bathroom; other than that, their time together was spent in the made-up bedroom on the
second floor. It was not much bigger than a
prison cell, a prison cell where the sentence was
never long enough.

There was no sound in the made-up bedroom,
other than what they made themselves under the
down comforter. Sometimes Ned moved very
slowly; sometimes he just reached between her
legs with no preliminaries, as he did now. It
didn't make any difference: Francie, who had always responded slowly in sex, or not at all, responded to Ned no matter what he did. She
started moaning again, and the moans turned to
little cries, and rose in volume, so loud they
could surely be heard outside — or so she
thought, although that didn't matter either: they
were alone on an island in the middle of the
river, with no one to hear, and then she was
coming, just from the touch of his fingertip.

After that, they moved together, not like
dancing partners, or old familiar lovers, or any of

18

those other similes, but more like a single organism rearranging its limbs. Their world shrank still more, smaller now than even the bedroom, down to the space under the comforter, a warm, humid, gentle world where the ancient connection between sex and love was at last clear, at least in Francie's mind. She stared into Ned's eyes, thought she saw into him to the very bottom, thought he was doing the same to her.

They came together — how Francie disliked the vocabulary that went with all this — could reach this supposed goal of lovers whenever they wished, and Ned settled down on her.

"It's different every time," he said after a minute or two.

"I was thinking the same thing."

They lay quiet. Francie pictured Ned rowing across in the darkness, herself in the cottage, both hearts beating in anticipation. "It's like 'Ode on a Grecian Urn,' " she said, "except the anticipation is met." He was silent. "At least in my case," she added, not wanting to speak for him. But Ned had fallen asleep, as he sometimes did. Because of the way he was lying on her, Francie couldn't see her watch; she would let him sleep for a little while. They breathed together, noses almost touching. In a way, this was best of all.

Sometime later, Francie heard a sound outside the window, a sound she couldn't identify at first, then realized was the beating of heavy wings. An owl, perhaps. There was at least one on the island; she'd watched it, flying by day, minutes before she saw Ned for the first time: August, only a few months earlier.

Francie sat on the floating dock, her feet in the river's flow. She spent an hour or so studying slides before putting them away and lying back, eyes closed to the sun. The slides lingered in her mind — images of cold-hearted children, alienating and unsettling — then faded. Francie was close to sleep when she felt a shadow pass over her body. She opened her eyes and saw, not a cloud over the sun, but an owl flying low, something white in its beak. The owl spread its wings, extended its talons, disappeared in the high branches of one of the elms. Turning back to the river, Francie caught sight of a kayak, gliding upstream.

A black kayak with a dark kayaker, paddling hard. As he drew closer, Francie saw he was shirtless, fit without being muscle-bound, hairy-chested, gleaming with sweat. He didn't see her at all: his eyes were blank and he seemed to be paddling with all his might, as though in a race. He flew by, into the east channel of the river, and vanished behind the island.

Francie lay back on the dock, closed her eyes. But now they didn't want to stay closed, and she didn't want to lie down. She rose, toed the end of the dock, dived into the river. The water was at its warmest, warmer than she liked. Francie swam a few strokes, then jackknifed her body as she'd been taught long ago at summer camp, and kicked easily down into the cold layers beneath.

Francie had always been good at holding her breath. She swam on and on close to the bottom, ridding herself of sun-induced lassitude before rising at last, clearheaded, to the surface. She broke through, took a deep breath — and saw that the kayak, having rounded the island, was now bearing straight down on her, only a few strokes away.

The kayaker was paddling as hard as ever, eyes still blank. Francie opened her mouth to yell something. At that moment he saw her. His body lost its coordination instantly; his blade caught a crab, splashing water at Francie's head. The splashed water was still in midair, a discrete body, when the kayak flipped over.

The paddle bobbed up and drifted beside the upside-down kayak, but Francie didn't see the man. She dived under the kayak, felt inside; he wasn't there. She peered down into the depths, saw nothing, came up. A second later, he burst through the surface, right beside her, gasping for breath, bleeding from a gash in his forehead.

"Are you all right?" she said.

He looked at her. "Unless you're planning to sue me."

Francie laughed. Their legs touched under the surface. He called her — at work — the next day. She hadn't been looking for love, had resigned herself to living the rest of her life without it, and perhaps for that reason had fallen all the harder.

Ned awoke. Francie knew he was awake right away, even though he hadn't moved at all. She was opening her mouth to tell him about *oh garden, my garden* when he stiffened.

"What time is it?" he said.

"I don't know."

He rolled over, checked his watch. "Oh, Christ." In seconds he was gone from the bed, gone from the room, and the shower was running. Francie got up, put on the robe she kept in Brenda's closet, went down to the kitchen, finished her glass of red wine. All at once, she was hungry. She let herself imagine going out with him, having dinner somewhere, feasting, then coming back, back to the little bedroom.

Ned came downstairs, knotting his tie. A beautiful tie — all his ties, his clothes, the way he wore his hair — beautiful.

"Hungry?" she said.

"Hungry?" he answered with surprise. "No. You?"

She shook her head.

He leaned over, kissed her forehead very lightly. "I'll call," he said.

She tilted her face up to his. He kissed her again, this time on the mouth, still very lightly. She licked his lips, tasted toothpaste. He straightened.

"Rowing back is another matter," he said.

Then he was gone, the door opening and closing softly. The draft reached Francie a few seconds later.

Driving fast toward the city, Ned realized how hungry he really was. Had he eaten at all since breakfast? He considered stopping somewhere along the way but kept going, one eye on the radar detector; he liked eating at home.

Ned switched on the radio, found their only affiliate, a weak AM station that replayed the shows at night. He heard himself say: "What do you mean by looking him up?" a little too sharply; he'd have to watch that.

"You know," said the woman — Marlene, or whatever her name was. "Finding out where he is. Giving him a call."

"To what end?"

"To what end?"

He should have gotten rid of her right there; he had so much to learn about the entertainment part. "For what purpose?"

"I guess to see what happens."

"Marlene?"

"Yes?"

"In your description of your husband's good points, I think — correct me if I'm mistaken — you omitted any mention of your sex life."

"I've tried, Ned. To make it more exciting. Nothing works."

"What have you tried?"

The car phone buzzed and Ned missed the

23

woman's answer; he didn't recall it being interesting anyway, although he suspected the question was the kind the syndicators liked.

"Hello?" he said into the phone.

"Dad? Hi, it's me, Em."

"I recognized the voice."

"You think you're so funny. Where are you?"

"On my way."

"There's no dessert."

"What would you like?"

"Rocky road."

"Consider it done. Love you."

"Love you, too, Dad."

Ned stopped at a grocery store near his house, bought two pints of rocky road, a jar of chocolate sauce, almonds. At the cash register, he noticed some nice fresh flowers: irises, always a safe choice. He bought some for his wife.

2

His mind on those moans and cries that Francie made, Ned parked in the garage beside his house, sat for a few moments in the darkness. There had to be some evolutionary purpose for those female sounds, some reason important enough to outweigh the risk of attracting predators in the night. Did it have anything to do with the bonding of the couple, its positive consequences for the next generation? Ned rubbed the spot on his forehead, an inch above the right eyebrow where the headaches began, as one was beginning now, picked up the grocery bag, went into the house.

Em was at the kitchen table in her pajamas, busy with her paint set. The next generation. "Guess what this is going to be."

"The solar system."

She nodded. "Guess how many moons Saturn has."

"A lot. Ten, maybe."

"Eighteen. Which one's the biggest?"

"That's a tough one. Triton?"

"Triton, Dad? Triton belongs to Neptune. I'll give you one more chance."

"Rocky road?"

"You're not funny."

Ned scooped ice cream into two bowls —

three scoops in his, he was so hungry — spooned out chocolate sauce, sprinkled on almonds. He raised his first spoonful. "Here's looking at you, kid."

Em rolled her eyes. "Why do old people always fall for that stupid movie?"

"Old people?" He took a bite and almost winced at the pain; ice cream was the fuel his headache had been waiting for.

Anne came into the room, carrying an empty laundry basket. "You're late tonight."

"It's Thursday, Mom," said Em, before he had to reply. "When Dad stays late to plan next week's shows."

"I forgot," said Anne.

Ned turned to her. "You look tired."

"I'm all right. How was the show?"

Did she never listen to it? "Not bad." He reached into the grocery bag, handed her the irises.

"These are lovely," said Anne. "What's the occasion?"

"No occasion."

"For God's sake, Mom," said Em, "where's your sense of romance?"

Ned flossed his teeth, brushed them, took two ibuprofen and a Nembutal, and went to bed. His brain shut down, compartment by compartment, until finally there was nothing but the headache between him and sleep. Then it was gone, and he sank into a dream. A cottage dream: he was lying in the red boat but somehow looking out the window of the little bedroom; Francie reached around him, ran her fingers, those soft, beautifully shaped fingers, up the front of his thigh, higher. He was hard at once, groaned, rolled over, reached for her, almost said, "Francie." But it was Anne; his hands had known right away, had saved him. The dream broke up in fading pieces, the image of the red boat last of all.

She fondled him. It was nice, familiar, homey. But Anne coming on to him? This was unusual. He tried to remember the last time — her birthday? his? — but couldn't. As though reading his mind, she said, "I do have a sense of romance, you know."

That got to him. "I know." The words thickened in his throat; he almost confessed everything, right there. But he mastered himself, said no more; she misinterpreted the catch in his voice, taking it for lust; slipped him inside herself without ceremony; moved her hips in lithe comma-shaped motions, efficient and pleasing; ended in a silent shudder, like an express elevator reaching the top floor.

She lay on his shoulder. "Was that good?" she said.

"Of course."

And after a minute or two: "Did you come?"

"What do you think?" He squeezed her arm.

She said nothing. Not long after, she rolled over and went to sleep. The compartments in

Ned's brain reopened. The headache returned. His eyes stayed open.

Francie showered, dressed, made the bed, went downstairs. She washed her wineglass, corked the wine, turned off the generator. Then she stood unmoving in the darkness. The silence was complete, Brenda's cottage under a spell, as it so often was.

Francie opened the door, letting in the river sounds, then closed and locked it behind her. Brenda's key hung anonymously on her key chain, one of many. The moon had risen and in its light she saw mist along the bank, rising with the temperature; the ice had melted away. Francie climbed into the dinghy, cast off, rowed across the west channel to the stone jetty, reflected moons bobbing in her wake. She tied up, redid Ned's knot — he'd taken *Prosciutto*, as always — substituting two half hitches for his series of lubberly grannies, and glanced back at the cottage: a geometric shadow under the free-form shadows of the elms. The owl rose into the sky, its white wings flashing like a semaphore in the night.

She drove to the gate, got out, locked it, went on. For five or ten minutes she was alone with dark woods rising on either side, shutting out the sky. Then headlights of another car appeared. That broke the spell; she stepped on the gas like any other exhausted commuter hurrying home, although she wasn't tired at all.

The house — on Beacon Hill, but heavily mortgaged and in need of sandblasting and a new roof — was dark, except for the light in the basement office, a big, private space that would have made a perfect bedroom for a teenager, if one had ever come along. Francie let herself in, turned on the lights, checked the messages, checked the mail, opened the fridge, found she was no longer hungry, drank a glass of water. Then she went downstairs, through the laundry room, and stopped outside the closed office door.

"Roger?" she said. No reply. Was he sleeping on his couch? Francie thought she heard the tapping of computer keys but wasn't sure. She went upstairs, got into bed, and was almost asleep herself when *oh garden, my garden* took shape in her mind, with those rotten grapes and that skateboarding girl. A teenager, of course. She tried to stop herself from going on in that direction but failed, as she always did. To come into the house, to see a skateboard lying in the front hall and a backpack slung over the banister, to hear strange music rising up from that basement room. Think about something else, Francie.

Em. She thought of Em. Em would soon be a teenager, although Francie wasn't sure of her exact age, didn't know her birthday. Ned almost never talked about her, never at all unless Francie asked, and of course Francie had never seen her, not even a picture. From the absent picture of Em back to *oh garden, my garden* wasn't a big jump, and from there to an idea: what a present the painting would make for Ned! Was there any way of giving it to him? In some ways they were like spies, governed by the rules of their trade. She was never to call him, he called her, and only on her direct office line; no letters, faxes, E-mail; they met only at the cottage. Preserving his marriage was the reason, and Em was the reason for that. Francie understood. She could keep a secret, in the sense of not telling another person — and in any case had no desire to shout her love from the rooftops — but she hated the spycraft.

Still, presents were a gray area; he did bring her flowers once in a while when he came to the cottage. Always irises, probably because she had made such a fuss about them the first time. She didn't particularly like irises, although it didn't matter much. They had usually wilted by the next time she saw them, the following Thursday. Francie fell asleep, turning over schemes for getting *oh garden, my garden* into Ned's hands.

Roger knew she was there, outside the door. He glanced at the time on the upper-right-hand corner of the screen: 12:02 a.m. Was it gratitude she expected for working these late hours? He was the one who had paid for the M.F.A., those summers at I Tatti, the accumulation of all that useless knowledge she had found a use for. He went back to his résumé.

Exeter, first in his class. Harvard, summa in economics, captain in tennis. Twenty-three years with Thorvald Securities, beginning as an analyst, ending as senior VP, number three man. Number three on the chart, but the brains behind everything, as everyone knew — everyone with any integrity. "Wow is all I can say," as the counselor at Execumatch had told him at their first meeting. "Let me guess — you got sixteen hundred on your SATs."

"Correct."

"And in the old days yet, before they started monkeying with the numbers."

"Old days?"

"Sure. Now you can make mistakes and still be perfect. Is that indicative or what? But this" — tapping the résumé — "this is the real deal."

Then why was he still looking for something suitable a year later?

Roger loosened his tie, closed his résumé, clicked his way onto the Web, logged on to the Puzzle Club.

>*MODERATOR: Welcome, Roger.*

Roger made no reply; he never said anything on the Web. The next day's *Times of London* crossword was up, and beside it in the Puzzletalk section some live-time discussion was taking place. Roger checked the time — 12:31 — and began the puzzle. One down: a six-letter word for disorder. He typed in *ataxia*. Two down:

31

seven letters, pugilist — *bruiser*. Three down: nine letters, to cut an X — *decussate*. So one across must be *abduct,* and four down . . . he tapped away at the keys, completing the puzzle at exactly 12:42. Not his best.

Roger scanned the discussion in progress.

>*MODERATOR: But what do you mean, Flyboy, by a quote perfect crime????*

>*FLYBOY: One they cant finger you for it, of course.*

>*MR.BUD: Finger you? Sounds like a bad EdGRobinson flick.*

>*REB: No such animal. But perfect crimewise you cant be anywhere near the scene, not w/DNA and all that shit. Flake of dandruff falls off your head, you fry.*

>*MODERATOR: So you get someone to do it for you, is that it?*

>*FLYBOY: Right = and they get busted for some other caper and rat you out rotb.*

>*MR.BUD: You are a bad movie Flyboy.*

>*MODERATOR: rotb????*

>*FLYBOY: right off the bat.*

>*MR.BUD: Jesus.*

>*REB: But he's right. A perfect crime = it's got to be absolutely unconnected = like someone in China pushed a button. Click. You're dead.*

>*FLYBOY: Or a penny drops off the Empire State Building. Goes right through your skull to the sidewalk.*

>MODERATOR: A penny drops off the Empire State Building????

Roger left the Puzzle Club, switched off the screen, removed his tie and shoes, lay down on the couch, pulling a blanket over himself. He laughed aloud. The vulgarity, the ignorance displayed on the Web for everyone to see: had they no self-awareness at all? He closed his eyes, called up the image of his completed *Times of London* puzzle, word for word, perfect, done. Ataxia: that was the problem with the world these days. Perhaps he could slip it in during his breakfast interview.

A window table at the Ritz.
"Roger?"
"Sandy?"
"You haven't changed a bit."
Roger made himself say, "Neither have you."
"That's a crock," said Sandy, sitting down. Roger hated that expression, hated when men patted their paunches and said "What do you call this?" as Sandy was doing now, especially since he didn't have much of one. The waiter poured coffee; Roger left his alone, afraid that his hand would shake.
"Still playing?" asked Sandy. Sandy had been number two on the tennis team, thrashed by Roger in challenge matches every spring. Now he ran the third-biggest venture capital firm in New England.

"Infrequently," said Roger. Perhaps he should ask Sandy whether *he* still played, but that might lead to some sort of loathsome rematch twenty-five years after the fact, so he reached for his coffee cup and said nothing. The cup clattered against the saucer; he put it down.

"Can't remember the last time I had a racquet in my hand," Sandy said. "Fact is, we've taken up rock climbing, the whole bunch of us."

"Rock climbing?"

"You should try it, Roger. It's a great family activity."

Roger had nothing to say to that. He tore his brioche into little pieces.

"How's Francie, by the way?"

"You know my wife?"

"Slightly. She gave a talk a few months ago on this new sculpture we've got in the lobby. I don't pretend to understand the sculpture, but your wife had us all eating out of her hand."

"Did she?"

"That combination of looks and brains, if I can say so without being politically incorrect . . . but I don't have to tell you, do I, you lucky devil?"

Roger picked up his butter knife, dipped it into a bowl of raspberry jam, spread some on a scrap of brioche, trailing a glutinous spill on the white tablecloth. Sandy gazed at the red stain for a moment, then said, "I hear there've been changes at Thorvald."

"Yes." How to explain it to Sandy? Sandy

wasn't very bright; Roger retained a memory of him frowning over some tome in the Widener Library. No doubt best to say something vague and diplomatic, and move on. Roger wiped the edges of his mouth with the napkin and readied something vague and diplomatic. But the words that issued were: "They were very stupid."

Sandy sat back. "In what way?"

"Isn't it obvious? They were such idiots, they —" He smothered the end of the sentence: *fired me.*

"They what, Roger?" Sandy asked.

It occurred to Roger that in the past year Sandy might have begun doing business with Thorvald, have his own sources inside. "It's not important," he said. *What's important is giving me a job, if you're not too dim-witted to see how much I can help you.*

Sandy sipped his coffee in silence. Did Sandy resent him for those weekly drubbings, so long ago? Was it possible he didn't understand that there'd been nothing personal, that it was simply how the game was played? This was a negotiation to be handled with care.

"Sandy?"

"Yes, Roger?"

"I could use a job, goddamn it." Not what he'd meant to say at all, but Sandy was one of those pluggers — a baseliner, as he recalled, with no imagination — and pluggers exasperated him.

And now Sandy was giving him a long look, as

35

though he were sizing *him* up, which was ridiculous due to the disparity in their intellects. "I wish I could help, Roger, but we've got nothing for someone of your level."

That was a lie. Roger knew they were looking or he wouldn't have set this up. But too tactless to say; Roger substituted: "You know how many times I've heard that?" His orange juice spilled, perhaps because of a convulsive jerk of his forearm; he wasn't sure.

After the waiter was done mopping, Sandy said, "None of my business, Roger, and please don't take this the wrong way, but have you ever considered early retirement? I know that Thorvald gave — that Thorvald usually does the right thing with their packages, and with Francie doing so well, maybe —"

"What's she got to do with this?"

"I just thought —"

"Do you know how much she grossed last year? Fifty grand. Barely enough to cover her hairdresser. Besides, I'm too young —"

"We're the same age, Roger. I stopped thinking of myself as young quite some time ago. The promising stage can't last forever, by definition."

Roger felt his face go hot, as though reddening, although surely no change was visible. He composed himself and said, "I wasn't aware that stage had occurred at all, in your case."

Sandy called for the check soon after. Roger snatched it from the waiter's hand and paid himself. Sandy met someone he knew on the way down the stairs, stopped to talk. Roger went out alone. On the street, he realized he had forgotten to leave a tip. So what? He had the feeling — strange, since he had been going there since boyhood — that he would never eat at the Ritz again.

Roger bought a bottle of Scotch in a shop where they called him *sir,* although not today — there was a new clerk who could barely speak English — and took a taxi home. The driver had the radio on.

"What's on tap, Ned?"

"Thanks, Ron. Male infertility is the topic today on Intimately Yours. *In the studio we'll have one of the foremost —"*

"Mind turning that off?" Roger said.

"Pliss?" said the driver.

"Radio," said Roger. "Off."

The driver turned it off.

In his basement office, Roger drank Scotch on the rocks and played Jeopardy! on his computer. The first European to reach the site of what is now Montreal. The economic unit of Senegal. The largest moon of Neptune. Who was Cartier, what is the C.F.A. franc, what is Triton? All too easy. He tried to get into his old computer at Thorvald but couldn't pass the firewall.

He refilled his glass, had another look at his résumé. Too bad, he thought, that IQs weren't standard CV material. Why shouldn't they be? What better measure? He rose, opened a file drawer, dug through press clippings, photographs, ribbons, trophies, down to a yellowed envelope at the bottom, addressed to Mr. and Mrs. Cullingwood. He read the letter inside.

Enclosed please find the results of your son Roger's Stanford-Binet test, administered last month. Roger's intelligence quotient, or IQ, as measured by the test, was 181. This places him in the 99th percentile of all those taking the test. It may interest you to know that there are several schools in our area with first-grade programs for gifted children which may be appropriate for Roger. Please do not hesitate to contact us for further information.

Roger read the letter again, and once more, before putting it away. He topped off his glass, logged on to the Puzzle Club. The *Times of London* crossword hadn't appeared yet, but there were others, including *Le Monde*. That one took him almost an hour — his French was rusty. When he had finished all the puzzles, he gazed at the on-line discussion that had been scrolling by the whole time.

>*MODERATOR: How did we get onto cap-ital punishment????*
>*BOOBOO: The Sheppard Case. What they based the fugitive on.*

>*RIMSKY: Yeah, yeah. But how about it when it works the other way = coldblooded killers on parole?*

>*MODERATOR: I don't think that happens very often, do you????*

>*RIMSKY: Let me tell you something I'm a corrections officer down here in Fla.*

>*BOOBOO: So?*

>*RIMSKY: So I know what I'm talking about when it comes to coldblooded k's.*

>*BOOBOO: :)*

RIMSKY: :) yourself. Ever heard of Whitey Truax, for example?

>*MODERATOR: ????*

>*FAUSTO: What's this got to do with the $ of apples?*

>*MODERATOR: Let Rimsky tell his story. Rimsky = what's w/Whltey Truax?*

Roger followed the discussion until footsteps overhead made him take his eyes from the screen. Francie. He was surprised to see night beyond the little window high in the basement wall.

And the bottle almost empty, although he was sober, complctely. Sandy's worst moment had been his salivating over Francie. There had been lust in his eyes, beyond a doubt. What a complete — what did the Jews say? Putz. That was it. He didn't even want to work for — with — a putz like Sandy.

But something about that lustful look,

39

Francie, Jews, and the word *putz* itself — a lubricious mix — gave Roger a sudden urge to sleep upstairs tonight, something he hadn't done since . . . he couldn't remember. Donning his crimson robe, he poured what remained of the Scotch into his glass and a second one, and carried them upstairs.

"Francie?" he called. "Is that you, dear?"

3

His first day in the halfway house, Whitey Truax went looking for whores. This was nothing he had planned: no one planning would have considered it, since the job they'd found Whitey — spearing trash on the I-95 median — ended at five, and he had to sign back in at six.

Just before dawn, the DPW pickup began dropping off the crew one at a time, stringing them out a few miles apart. Whitey was last. Riding alone in the back, he saw the sun coming up between two high-rises, and started trembling. He'd been facing west for seventeen years, or maybe it was just the morning chill.

The pickup pulled over on the north side of exit 42, Delray Beach, and Whitey climbed down. Then it drove away, and there he was on dewy green grass, a free and unsupervised man. He shrugged on his reflective vest, stuffed the tightly folded orange trash bags in his pocket, stabbed a Mars bar wrapper with his steel-tipped pole.

Stab, stab, stab: Whitey was full of energy. By four, he had filled a dozen bags, all they'd given him, and worked his way almost down to exit 41. With nothing more to do, he stood leaning on his pole, sweat slowly drying, and watched the cars go by, most of the models unfamiliar. Was this a bad way to make a living? Too hot — he'd never liked the heat — but otherwise not bad at all. No watching your back, no taking shit: cake.

Rush hour now, and traffic was stop-and-go. A woman in a convertible looked at him, not twenty feet away. She had a ponytail, damp at the end, and wore a bikini top — must be coming from the beach, thought Whitey; but he wasn't really thinking, just staring at her tits, heavy, round, mesmerizing. The combination of visual overload and complete tactile deprivation made him start trembling again, just a little. He opened his mouth to say something to her, but the only word he could think of was *fuck,* and he knew that wouldn't work. Traffic lurched ahead and she was gone, leaving him with the memory of those big tits. Her shoulders had been heavy, too; in retrospect, it was possible she was fat, even grossly so, but this realization barely surfaced in Whitey's mind. Retrospection wasn't one of his strengths.

Instead his mind wandered, not very far, to those sounds women made when they got excited. He'd heard them in movies. No X-rated stuff allowed inside, of course, but even in normal movies women made those sounds. Melanie Griffith, and who was that other one he liked? Whitey could see her face clearly, mouth open, but he was still fishing for the name when he felt something stir against his ankle. He jumped back — he was very quick — thought *snake,* thrust the steel tip at the reptilian head, right through, pinning it wriggling to the ground. Hadn't lost his quick, not one little bit.

As it turned out, the creature was not a snake, not a reptile at all, but a bullfrog. Too late to do anything about that. Whitey watched it die, blood trickling into a crown pattern over its eyes, wriggling becoming sporadic, those pop eyes growing dim. Whitey felt bad, but not too bad: the frog's own damn fault, after all, for making him panic. Whitey panicked sometimes, especially if he was surprised. That was simply the way he was — didn't make him weak or anything. But the syndrome — word he remembered from the testimony, so long ago — combined with his quickness, could lead to trouble, as he knew well.

Which was why he had to stay calm. He took a few deep breaths to settle down, placed his foot on the bullfrog's back, withdrew the steel tip. The bullfrog hopped up on its hind legs.

"Jesus fucking Christ," Whitey said, and let him have it again. The frog lay still after that, facedown, legs spread flat on the ground. That was when the possibility of whores arose in Whitey's mind, whores that very day.

A DPW truck picked him up a few minutes later, left him outside the depot at five.

"Hey, you."

Whitey, walking off, stopped and turned.

"Where you think you're goin' with that?"

Whitey thought fast. "No place."

"No place is right. Equipment stays here."

43

Whitey came forward, tossed the steel-tipped pole onto the truck bed. "No harm intended."

The guy just looked at him.

A bus drove up, number 62. He checked the social worker's handwritten instructions: his bus; it stopped a block from the halfway house. But Whitey didn't get on. Instead he set off toward a neon-lit intersection he could see in the distance, the kind of intersection where there might be liquor stores, bars, women. Whitey felt in his pocket. He had thirty bucks, plus four hundred and some in the bank account the social worker had helped him open the night before.

What would thirty bucks buy? A Pepsi, for starters. They hadn't had Pepsi inside, just Coke, and Pepsi was Whitey's drink. He went into the first convenience store he saw. "Wow," he said to himself, or maybe out loud. There was so much stuff. He went to the cooler at the back and found the Pepsi. They'd changed the design on the can. He liked the old one better. Had they fooled around with the taste as well? He remembered hearing something about that.

Whitey took a six-pack, went to the front of the store, laid it on the counter next to a cigar display. "With you in a sec," said a voice a few aisles away.

Whitey eyed the cigars. Weren't cigars in these days? He'd never smoked a cigar, not once in his whole goddamned life. Whitey glanced around. There was a video camera, but it hung loose from the ceiling, all askew. Whitey boosted the biggest cigar in the box, slipping it up his sleeve in the familiar motion of a man patting his hair in place.

The clerk appeared. "Anything else?" he said.

"Matches," said Whitey.

"Matches are free."

Whitey took two packs. "Thanks a bunch."

He walked another block toward the neon intersection, stopped, cracked open a Pepsi, tilted it up to his mouth. Christ, it was good, even better than he remembered. He swallowed half of it, then lit the cigar, filling his mouth with a thick ball of hot, wonderful smoke, slowly letting it out, curling through his lips. He was alive. Standing outside an electronics store — a banner on the window read: ARE YOU READY FOR HIGH DEFINITION? — Whitey sipped his Pepsi and puffed his cigar. A gorgeous weatherwoman on a big-screen TV was pointing at flashing thunderclaps on a map of some European country, France, maybe, or Germany. European weather: this was the big time. Whitey watched transfixed until he happened to notice the price sticker on the TV. And that was the sale price. He walked away.

Cigar in his mouth, the remaining five cans of Pepsi dangling from the empty plastic ring, Whitey reached the intersection. Liquor stores, yes. Bars, yes. Women, no. He went into Angie's Alligator Lounge and sat at the empty bar.

"What can I get you?" said the bartender.

Alcohol was out: halfway house rules.

"What've you got?" said Whitey.

"What have I *got?*"

"Beer," said Whitey, first word that came to mind. "Narragansett." That had been his beer.

"Narragansett?"

"Bud, then."

The bartender served him a Bud. "Buck and a half."

Whitey gave him two bills, waved away the change, just waved it away with his cigar, very cool.

"I'll level with you," Whitey said. He waited for the bartender to say something or change the expression on his face. When none of that happened, he continued, "The truth is I been away for a while."

The bartender nodded. "Narragansett is kind of a collector's item."

"And a little company would be nice, you know? Someone to talk to," he added, but the bartender had already picked up the phone. He spoke into it quietly for a few moments, not looking at Whitey once, hung up. Less than a minute later, a woman walked through the front door, sat down beside Whitey; the bartender found something to do among the bottles. Whitey laughed, more like a giggle that he modulated at the end.

"What's funny?" said the woman.

Whitey took a hit off the cigar. "Inside you get shit," he said. "Out in the world all you got to do is ask." He turned to her. She was stunning. He could smell her. That was stunning, too. What sounds would she make, coming and coming? His mouth dried up.

She was watching him, squinting just a little, possibly from the cigar smoke, or maybe she'd forgotten her glasses. "You're the one wanted a date, right?"

Whitey swallowed. "A date," he said, liking the sound of that. "Yeah."

"You wanna finish your beer first?"

"Beer's a no-no."

She rose. He went with her to the back of a lounge and out a back door. "We're leaving?" Whitey said.

"Know what a liquor license costs?"

She led him into an alley, around a corner, and into a hotel. The sign said HOTEL, but there was no lobby, just a beefy guy behind bulletproof glass, his head on a desk. The woman went by it, up a flight of stairs — oh, following her ass up the stairs, that was something — into a room with a bed and a sink in it and nothing else.

"Mind washing off?" said the woman, nodding to the sink. "Can't be too careful these days." She was still stunning, despite the harsh strip lighting in the room. Her pimples or whatever they were didn't bother him at all, and he was used to that kind of lighting.

Whitey washed off. When he turned to her, she was sitting on the bed, yawning. " 'Scuse me," she said. "Okay. Suck is twenty-five, fuck is forty, suck and fuck fifty."

47

Whitey didn't know what to say, couldn't have spoken anyway, his mouth being so dry. He tried some calculations. Suck and fuck was clearly a deal, but fuck alone was what he wanted — to be deep inside her, to make her make those Melanie Griffith sounds — and all he had was thirty dollars, minus what he'd paid for the beer and the Pepsi. Christ! He couldn't even afford suck.

"But since you look like a nice guy," she said, breaking the silence, "I could maybe do you a little discount."

Whitey tried to say something, could not, put all his money, even the change, on the bed. She stared at it. He leaned over her, smoothed out the crumpled bills.

"Oh, hell," she said, scooping it all into her sparkle-covered purse, "let's not . . . what's the word? Starts with *D*."

Whitey didn't know. He just knew that he was going to get laid after all. The knowledge turned on a kind of buzzing inside him, a buzzing he hadn't heard for a long time, not since — but best not to think about that. He put his arms around the woman and pulled her close, knocking her head awkwardly against his belt buckle.

"Easy," she said. "Take your pants off."

But Whitey didn't have time for that; he made do with just pulling them down below his knees. Meanwhile the woman lay back on the bed, hiked up her skirt, pulled off her panties, and he saw that other sex, the lips and hair, all real, right there, as the buzzing grew louder. She stuffed the panties down the side of her boot. Whitey fell on her, shoved himself inside.

Not quite inside, perhaps against her thigh. She reached down between them, took his penis in her hand — "Dicker," she said, "that's the word I was looking for" — and guided him in.

"Oh, God," Whitey said, "oh my God." He thrust himself in and out, almost drowning in the buzz, about to come any second, when suddenly he remembered Melanie Griffith. Slow down, big guy, slow down, he told himself. He had to hear those female sounds. He slid his hand down her stomach, into the wetness, found her clit, or something, and started thrumming it back and forth, fast as he could.

"Knock it off," said the woman.

Whitey froze. His hard-on went droopy inside her, just like that. The buzzing stopped. In the silence he heard some little animal behind the wall. The woman made a hitching motion with her hips.

"You stupid bitch," Whitey said.

"Huh?"

Everything was going sour, like the last time. Where were the smart women? His needs were simple and this one was supposed to be a professional, for God's sake. It made Whitey so angry, he hit her, not hard, only the back of his hand against her pimply face.

Whitey realized almost right away that he had to make it up to her. "Okay, so we both made

mistakes," he said. "Don't mean we can't —"
But she writhed around under him and jabbed at
a button on the wall that he hadn't noticed.
"What's that about?" said Whitey. "Look, we
were getting along pretty good there for a while.
No reason we —"

The door burst open. All fucked up, like the
last time, but things that hadn't happened before
were happening now, like this beefy guy coming
in with the baseball bat. But the panic inside
Whitey was the same: a screaming gusher from
deep in his chest, boiling up and spraying red in
his brain. It took away visual continuity, leaving
Whitey with a few strobe-lit impressions: the
beefy guy going down, the bat now in his own
hands, blood here and there, *are you ready for
high definition?* And then he was out the door and
in the street.

Whitey returned to the halfway house at 6:05,
signed the clipboard. "Sorry I'm late," he said.
"Got off at the wrong stop."

"Everyone does, first day," said the social
worker. "But don't make it a habit."

"I brought you a Pepsi."

"That was thoughtful of you, Whitey. I've
been going through your file. Seems you were
quite the stickman up north."

Silence. "Stickman?"

"Isn't that the term? Hockey player. I don't really know the game."

"That was a long time ago."

"What I'm getting at, we're big on recreation here at New Horizons. Physical activity helps to take the edge off, if you know what I mean. Ever considered maybe getting into jogging, for instance?"

"I'll think about it," Whitey said.

"That's all we ask."

4

Francie, in her bedroom, stripped off the heavy brown wrapping paper and had a good look at *oh garden, my garden* — the best kind of look, alone, private. She'd bought it on her way home from the office for $950, unable to resist, now that it was for Ned. The artist hadn't cared at all whether the buyer was Francie or the foundation. His only request had been for payment in cash. Francie hadn't anticipated that, but on reflection it suited her fine. Standing at the foot of her bed, with the painting propped up on the pillows, she liked it more than ever.

There was a knock at the door. She almost said "Who is it?" but who else could it have been?

"Dear? Are you awake?"

Francie slid the painting under the bed, kicked the wrapping paper in after. "What is it?" she said, thinking, *dear?*

"Can I come in? Into the matrimonial chamber?"

"It's not locked, Roger."

The door opened. Roger came in, wearing a Harvard-crested robe over his shirt and tie and carrying two tumblers. "You're in your nightie."

"I'm going to bed."

He sat down on the end of it, held out a tumbler. She noticed that his feet were bare; legs under the robe, bare, too. "Care for a drink?"

"Thank you, Roger," she said, laying it on the dresser. "But I'm a little tired."

He gave her a long look, as though he was trying to communicate some emotion. She had no idea what it could be. "Is something the matter?" she said.

He laughed, that single bark he'd been using for laughter the past year or so. "We haven't played tennis in some time, have we, Francie?"

"No." *He* hadn't played in years. But they'd met on a tennis court: Francie, on her college team; Roger, a few years out of Harvard, helping the coach after work. Francie was a good player, if not in Roger's class, but good enough so there were boxes of mixed-doubles trophies somewhere in the house. Had he come to set up a match? She almost laughed herself but lost the impulse when she saw him staring at her thighs.

Roger licked his lips. "I understand you know Sandy Cronin."

"We've met."

"I had breakfast with him today."

"How did it go?"

"Quite well." Roger took a sip from his glass, a sip that became a long drink. Silence. Then: "Do you know the word *putz?*"

"Yiddish for *prick.*"

His eyes glazed at the word, or maybe the word coming from her mouth. What was going on? He touched her hand. "Let's go to bed."

That would have been her last guess. The perfect reply, the honest reply, came to her immediately: *I'm a one-man woman, Roger. I don't sleep around.*

"Is something funny?" Roger said. His hand was still touching hers, not holding it, just touching the back. An odd gesture — not friendly, not warm, not erotic.

"No."

"Sit down, Francie."

"Why?"

"Is that a lot to ask?"

She sat down. His hand covered hers, stroked slowly up her arm: a hard, horny hand, like that of a manual laborer, which Roger was not.

"Have you been drinking?" she said.

"That's not a very nice suggestion," said Roger. "And inaccurate. I'm feeling uxorious, if you must know."

His hand reached her shoulder, jerked quickly down, took possession of her breast. Francie recoiled, but he hung on to her nipple, manipulating it in various ways, as though hoping to stumble on some combination that would change her mood, like a safecracker fiddling with a lock.

"Roger, for God's sake." She tried to push him away. He fell on her — was much bigger and stronger — and as he did she noticed for the first time that although there wasn't a single white hair on his head, his nostrils were full of them. His Harvard robe fell open, his penis pressed against her, and at that moment — unbidden, ill-timed, insane — the image of Ned's penis appeared in her mind.

Roger's, almost a schematic in contrast, butted against her rigid body.

"Stop it now," she said. And then his mouth was on hers, his tongue probing. This wasn't him at all. She twisted her head, tried to roll away, but Roger got his hand under her ass, pulled her close, forcing his penis against her. At the same time, she felt his finger moving behind her.

"What the hell are you doing?"

"Spicing up our marriage. You are my wife."

"You're sick." Francie struck out at him, barely aware of what she was doing.

He stopped moving, stopped pressing, raised himself. Four scratches ran across his cheek, blood welling in the deepest. Their eyes met. Roger's eyes: but behind them could have been anybody, and the face was the face of a man who resembled Roger. It reddened under her gaze; at the same time, his penis dwindled, as though all the blood had drained to his head. He got off her, rose, straightened his robe; his tie remained perfectly knotted. He went to the door, opened it, turned.

"You may fool other people, *dear,* but you don't fool me. Never have. And now you're a dried-up cunt as well, no matter what anyone else thinks." He went out, closing the door softly, never touching the wound she had made.

Francie didn't start crying until she was in the

shower, hot as she could stand, scrubbing and scrubbing, bathroom door locked. Crying: from not being able to stop, to realizing it wasn't doing any good, to stopping. Getting out of the shower, she saw her wretched face, fogged in the mirror, and turned away. She dried herself, brushed her teeth, brushed her hair, but stopped abruptly in midstroke: *no matter what anyone else thinks*. What did that mean? She thought back, searching for some mistake in her spycraft, found none. Then who was *anyone else?* Sandy Cronin? Was his behavior tonight some form of sexual competition? With a noncompetitor, of course, and still he had lost. Clear in her mind theoretically, the disconnection between sex and rape had now been demonstrated as well.

Francie put on a fresh nightie — flannel, to her ankles — and went to bed, curled up in a ball. She tried to keep her mind from doing anything, but failed. It went right to her most vulnerable spot. Why wouldn't it, after what had just happened on the bed, and with the skateboarding girl underneath?

Francie's most vulnerable spot, in three acts. Act one: the months of frequent, if not passionate — how could it be passionate when it was regulated by doctors, ovulation calendars, thermometers? — fucking that had preceded the discovery that it was Roger's fault. Not fault, but contained in his body: low sperm count, and what sperm there were, deformed. Act two: sex in a petri dish, forcing the coupling of her eggs

56

with the best of the deformed sperm — also a failure. Act three: a conversation repeated many times in different words, but first held as they left the doctor's office for the last time. Francie: *I guess that leaves us with adoption.* Roger: *What would be the point of that?*

That same act three might have done double duty as the beginning of the last act of their marriage as well, a long, attenuated denouement with this twist of Roger's job loss at the end, and a second twist after that, if you counted Ned. Roger's question — *What would be the point of that?* — had illuminated some long-concealed but essential difference between them, masked by Roger's early dominance: his intelligence, education, worldliness, and his good manners, which she'd perhaps mistaken for kindness. Would a child have made it all better? Francie didn't know; she just knew she had wanted one, wanted one still. Roger, in the end, had wanted to pass on his genes.

Francie thought again of Em: how she would like to meet her, even see her from a distance. Her mind moved on to Ned and quite abruptly, like a heat-seeking detector, to that earlier inappropriate mental image of his penis. Magnificent, like those on a Grecian urn — or were they too mannered? The comparison was probably to some simpler art, more robust, more iconic, even primitive: the Sumerians, perhaps; a Babylonian stone carving, for example.

My God, she thought suddenly. *How can I be*

thinking of sex? But she was. Ned drove everything else out of her mind; he was deep inside her, and not even there. After a while, her body unfolded, her hand came up under the flannel nightie, and she found herself as ready as she'd ever been. What was this all about? The power of love, she decided, strong enough to keep Ned with her all the time, Roger reduced to nothing. A calming thought, but the glowing numbers on her clock kept changing, and still she didn't sleep. She picked up the phone and called the only person she could call at that hour.

"Hello?" said a sleepy-sounding man.

"Bernie?" Francie said.

"Yeah?"

"What's your last name, Bernie?"

"Zymanzki, with two Z's. Do I know you?"

"Put Nora on."

Rustling sounds, fumbling, a grunt. And Nora: "Francie?"

"Yup."

"What's wrong?"

"Tell me about divorce."

"I'm a big believer; you know that. I believe in it more than I believe in marriage."

"And in my case?"

"Unless I'm missing something, it's long overdue. Stop it, Bernie."

Nora paused for a moment, long enough for Francie to supply the missing piece. She remained silent.

"Francie?" said Nora. "Are you crying?"

"Why do you ask?"

Pause. "I've got a court on Tuesday, sugar, five-thirty. We'll talk."

Francie lay awake all night, got up at dawn. She dressed, packed her briefcase, went downstairs to Roger's door. She knocked. No answer. She opened the door. The room was dark, except for the glow of the computer screen. Roger sat before it, his back to her.

"Roger?"

No reply. No sound but the tapping of his fingers on the keys.

"It's time to talk about divorce."

No reply. The tapping didn't stop. Perhaps he bent a little closer to the screen. Francie closed the door and left.

Roger stopped typing, leaving twenty-nine across — hell, in ideal form — blank. He went upstairs, into her bedroom — their bedroom — suddenly felt dizzy, sat on the bed. As the dizziness passed, Roger noticed torn wrapping paper sticking out from underneath the bed, investigated, found a painting. He studied it for a few moments — an amateurish effort — and put it back.

Divorce: unthinkable. Loss of job, breakup of marriage, what a hideous cliché. And he'd devoted most of his adult life to Francie, was certainly responsible for that polish of hers that so impressed the Sandy Cronins of the world. Plus they'd done so much together — at that very moment, he remembered a gorgeous running topspin lob she'd made to win a key point in the Lower Cape mixed-doubles championship ten, perhaps fifteen, years before. Those legs of hers, like a dancer's, and she was still beautiful, in some ways more than ever, as the Sandy Cronins pointed out. The bastards envied him. Corollary: she was an object to be proud of. Perhaps they'd hit a bad patch, but didn't every marriage? As soon as he landed a suitable job, everything would be all right. Until then, that fifty grand she brought in was essential. No, divorce was out of the question. He would be ready with an apology the moment she got home. He could swallow his pride, up to a point, even though denied his marital rights. And perhaps there'd been something wanting in his approach last night, probably due to rustiness. That, too, could be fixed.

What kind of flowers did she like? He thought of calling one of her friends to find out, but he didn't really know her friends. Except Nora, whom he didn't like, and Brenda. Where was Brenda? London? Paris? Rome? All easily reached by phone. He found Francie's address book in her kitchen desk.

Brenda. Rome. He dialed the number, heard a female voice: *"Questa è la segretària telefònica di . . ."* Roger had no Italian and wasn't aware that he'd reached an answering machine until he heard the beep. He hung up without speaking.

Tulips? Petunias? Gladioli? Probably not gladioli — weren't they associated with funerals? Roger's mind leaped to another thought: what if something happened to Francie? The fifty grand would be gone, and while he had life insurance, she did not. Who was that insurance peddler — Tod? Tad?

Roger put on a suit and tie and went out to hunt for flowers. It was snowing, fluffy snow that quickly spread a thick carpet on the sidewalk. Roger's ankles were cold; he glanced down, saw he was still in his slippers. He stepped back inside, put on his L.L. Bean boots, decided to try Brenda again. God was in the details: the flowers had to be right.

"*Pronto,*" said a voice, again female, but not the answering machine. He felt a change in the way his luck was running.

"Brenda?"

"*Si?*"

"This is Roger Cullingwood."

"Roger?" Pause. Then: "Is Francie all right?"

"Very much so. I'm having a little dinner for her tonight, in fact."

"I can't possibly make it on this kind of notice, Roger."

He laughed and heard the echo of the laugh in the line — a strange barking sound, surely distorted by the Italian phone system. "I know that. The problem is I can't remember her favorite flower."

"And you called me in Rome? Aren't you

61

sweet. Lilies, of course."

"Lilies. Thanks very much." He was about to say good-bye when she asked,

"How's the cottage, by the way?"

"Cottage?"

"You know — Francie looks in from time to time. I hope."

"I wasn't aware."

"On the Merrimack. In it, rather."

"In it?"

"I've got another call, Roger. My love to Francie."

When Francie came home from work, there were lilies on the hall table and in the kitchen, lobsters steaming in the pot, champagne on ice. The dining room, unused for at least a year, maybe longer, was lit with candles, the table set with the Sèvres that had belonged to Roger's grandmother.

"My apologies, Francie," said Roger. "I don't know what got into me. I was drunk, as you said, but that's not an excuse. I'm deeply sorry."

Francie was speechless. She hadn't even expected to find him upstairs.

"No need to say anything." He sat her down, filled her glass. The scratches on his face were invisible. Francie saw he'd covered them with face powder, probably from her drawer, since it was too dark for his complexion. "Recognize this champagne?" he asked.

Laurent Perrier Rosé: they'd drunk it to celebrate the end of the hiking trip he'd taken her on in the Cevennes, following the route of Robert Louis Stevenson. That had been years ago, not long before the petri-dish phase. Francie was amazed that he would remember, amazed by the candles, the lilies. It was all perfect, and unreal, like a Cary Grant movie; and pathetic, which Cary Grant never was. That — the pathetic part — and the secret fact of Ned, undermined the righteousness of her anger.

He cracked a claw. "Remember that summer, Francie?"

"Of course." She saw that he was without a tie, almost the first time she'd seen him that way since he'd been fired.

"We had fun, didn't we?"

"Yes."

"You're not eating. I didn't overcook it, did I?"

"It's just right." She took one bite, could barely get it down.

"That's better," he said, beaming. "Here's to France. And Italy, too, for that matter."

They drank to France and Italy. "What's this all about, Roger?"

"Just dinner," he said. "No agenda. A quiet marital dinner."

"Did you hear some news today?"

"News? What sort of news?"

"About work."

Roger kept smiling, but his eyes no longer participated. "Everything's going to be just fine."

"What did you hear?"

"Nothing definite. But I'm optimistic."

He went back to the hiking trip, bringing up details she was sure he would have forgotten: the shepherd with the steel teeth, the one-eyed dog that had followed them for days, the blue-black cherries they'd picked off a tree, eating until they could eat no more, cherry juice dripping off their chins. All true. But what had become of that Roger, and how responsible was she? Too late to go back — or even think about it — but would there be dinners like this in some future with Ned, candlelight in his eyes, melted butter on his fingers, time?

"And now for dessert," Roger said.

"None for me."

He came in with a pecan pie, her favorite. "Just try it," he said.

Again one bite. Had she ever tasted better? But still she could hardly swallow.

"I went heavy on the butter and added a little maple syrup," Roger said.

"You baked this yourself?"

He nodded.

"But you don't bake."

"I followed the recipe in one of your books. It's really not that complicated, is it?"

He tilted back his head, waiting for an answer. The candlelight illuminated the patch of face powder and the white hairs in his nose. All at once, Francie felt she was about to vomit. She pushed back her chair.

"If you've got work to do or something, don't let me keep you," Roger said. "I'll clean up." He swirled the champagne in his glass, forcefully, into a tiny pink-and-golden maelstrom. "And Francie? About this divorce business — could you give it some thought?"

"I'll give it some thought."

"That's all I ask." He raised his glass to her, champagne slopping over the side.

5

Nora had a 5:30 court, but Francie got stuck in traffic and arrived ten minutes late. Nora was already in the bubble, hitting with the assistant pro against a woman Francie didn't know. Nora hadn't said anything about doubles, Francie preferred singles — and weren't they supposed to have a talk? Francie changed and hurried onto the court, stripping the cover off her racquet, apologizing. The women met her at the net.

"It turned into doubles," Nora said. "Why don't you play with Anne? Anne Franklin, Francie Cullingwood. Francie, Anne."

They shook hands. Anne was pretty, slim, fine-complected, and didn't quite look Francie in the eye: no doubt the shy *hausfrau* Nora had mentioned. "I've heard such good things about you," Anne said.

"Who's been talking?"

Anne blinked. "Why, Nora."

"Don't believe a word she says," Francie said. "What side do you like?"

"Forehand," Anne said. "But if that's your side, I could . . ."

"Not a problem," Francie said, going to the backhand, swinging her racquet lightly, trying to make her arm feel long. She always played better if her arm felt long.

"Hit a few, Francie?" called Nora from the other side of the net.

"Serve 'em up," Francie said, not wanting to delay the game any more.

The assistant pro went to the net and Nora got ready to serve. "Better stay back on the first one," said Anne. "I have trouble with her serve."

"Tell me about it," said Francie, backing to the baseline.

Nora boomed in her big serve, the jamming one that spun nastily into the returner's hands. To Francie's surprise, Anne stepped away — fast and light on her feet — and chipped a low forehand crosscourt. If Nora had a weakness it was getting down for the low volley; she could do no more than float Anne's return back down the middle, two or three feet above the net, and Francie, closing, put it easily away.

"Beautiful volley," said Anne.

"Your setup," Francie said.

Nora's next serve kicked out wide on Francie's backhand. Francie didn't quite get around on it and the assistant pro picked off her return, angling it at Anne's feet from point-blank range. Somehow Anne dug it out, bunting it down the alley for a clean winner.

"Partner," said Francie.

They broke Nora at love, something Francie didn't remember seeing before, won the first set 6–2. Neither did Francie remember the last time she'd played with a doubles partner whose game so nicely fit her own, Anne's speed and steadiness matching her power and shot-making.

"What've you guys been smoking?" asked Nora on the changeover.

They toweled off, drank water, changed sides. "New in town?" said Francie as she and Anne walked toward the baseline.

"No," Anne said. "Just getting back into the game now that my kid's a little older. I didn't realize how much I'd missed it."

"Boy or girl?" said Francie.

"Girl."

"What's her name?"

"Emilia."

"Pretty."

"And what about your kids?" said Anne.

"Don't have any," Francie replied, handing her the balls. "Your serve."

Francie didn't play as well in the second set, but Anne played even better, and the assistant pro, frustrated, lost her cool a little and started blasting the ball with all her might, usually out. Six–one.

"Thanks for putting up with me," said Anne as they went to the net to shake hands.

"Putting up with you?" said Francie. "I was on your back the whole second set." She tapped Anne's behind with her racquet. "Nice playing."

After, they sat in the bar, Francie, Nora, Anne. The club had a new microbrew on tap. Nora ordered a pitcher. Francie signed the chit. "You like microbrews, Anne?" Nora asked, filling their glasses.

"I'm not sure I've ever tried one."

"Live a little," said Nora. She raised her glass. "Here's to fuzzy balls."

The bartender, used to Nora, didn't even turn, but Anne's face, still a little pink from tennis, went pinker. She took a tiny sip, said, "It's very good," put down her glass.

"While on that subject," said Nora, downing half of hers, "I may be getting married this spring. Or next week."

"Congratulations," Anne said.

"She's just being funny," Francie said.

"Not true. Bernie wants to marry me."

"Did you ever get his last name?"

"Does it matter? I'm not going to use it anyway."

"I kept my maiden name," Anne said. "My parents weren't too happy about it."

"Maiden name," said Nora. "Can you believe an expression like that? If you ever started really thinking about things, you'd want to shoot everybody." She refilled her glass. "With the exception of Bernie. He's kind, sweet, and gentle. He does have that toenail thing, though."

"Fungus?" said Francie.

"Whatever it is turns their nails all hard and yellow." Nora went to the bathroom.

Anne, still pink, turned to Francie. "Nora mentioned your husband was quite a tennis player."

"He was," Francie said. "And yours?"

"He doesn't play. I — I've tried to get him interested, but he has no free time."

"What does he do?"

"He's a psychologist." Anne took another sip of beer, bigger than the first, as though fortifying herself. "Can I ask you something?"

"Sure."

"I hope it's not too pushy."

"We'll never know at this rate."

Anne went pinker still, and Francie felt a little ashamed of herself. "Are you and Nora playing in the tournament?"

"What tournament?"

"The club doubles championship."

"We don't play together anymore. Not in tournaments."

"But you won it a bunch of times — I saw in the trophy case."

"We finally decided to preserve the friendship instead."

"I know you're joking. You're both so supportive on the court."

"Not of each other. The last tournament we played they called the police." Anne's eyes widened. "Now I am joking," Francie said; how delicate this woman was. "What's on your mind?"

"First," said Anne, "I'd better confess I don't usually play as well as I did tonight. Not nearly."

"And second?"

"I wondered if you'd like to be my partner in the tournament."

"How could I say no?"

Nora was back, Anne gone. "She's not as fragile as she makes out," Nora said. "See the way she went right at me with that overhead in the second set?"

"She probably assumed you'd be moving to cover the empty court."

"Is that your way of saying I'm fat?"

"No. 'You're fat' is my way of saying you're fat."

"So you're not saying it?"

"My meaning is clear."

"Because even supposing I'd put on three or four or fifteen pounds — did you notice how hard I'm hitting the ball?"

"You've always hit hard."

"Not like this. I'm going to write an article for *Tennis Magazine* — 'Eat Your Way to Power.' Just a little beefy hip rotation and pow — F equals MA."

"You're working on the M?"

"That's what's revolutionary about it."

Nora ordered more beer; Francie signed. "Ready to talk about Roger?" Nora said.

"As I'll ever be."

"Does he have that toenail thing, by the way?"

"You'll have to ask him."

"Meaning you don't know?"

Francie said nothing.

"Meaning you're not occupying the same bed? Of course. And that would be your Byzantine way of telling me. How long has this been the case?"

"Some time."

"That would be months."

"Many."

Nora shook her head. "One month is my limit when it comes to abstinence — must be tied to the cycles of the moon, something tidal. After that, I need life support." She studied Francie's face, quite openly. "Can't be good for you, either," she said. "Someone like Anne, that's different — modest sex drive at best."

"How would you know something like that? Maybe she's in bed with her husband as we speak."

"Ironing his shirts is more like it," Nora said. "Can I ask you a personal question?"

"No."

"When was the last time you had an orgasm? In the company of another human being, that is."

"What difference does it make when I had an orgasm? Nuns —"

"You're not a nun. Answer the question."

The true answer was last Thursday, and not only one. Francie came very close to saying just that: her lips parted, the tip of her tongue curved up to form the *L* of "last," and after that the whole tale — cottage, kayak, little bedroom — would come spilling out. Francie clamped her mouth shut, held it all inside; she could keep a secret.

"What?" said Nora. "What?"

Francie tried to think of some breezy diversion, some bridge to another subject, but nothing came to mind. Nora's eyes narrowed. "This divorce can't come too soon."

"I don't know about that," said Francie.

"Why not?"

"Maybe if he had a job again, Nora, but right now it wouldn't be fair."

"Fair? You said fair?"

"Yes."

"Then maybe it's time to consider a boyfriend."

"And that would be fair?" Francie asked — very close to the first question she would have asked if the real story had come spilling out.

"You're asking me if cheating on Roger would be fair?"

"If you want to put it that way."

"That's the way people put it." Nora thought, drank more beer, thought again. "Got anyone in mind?" she said.

"No," said Francie, feeling Nora's gaze and not even trying to meet it.

A long silence followed. Nora poured the rest of the beer, looking at Francie from the corner of her eye. "Did I ever tell you about my grandmother?" she said.

"Rose? I knew her."

"But did I ever mention the time I called her number, six months after she died?"

"Why?"

73

"Because there was something I'd meant to tell her." Nora rose. "Good luck, kiddo."

"Good luck?"

"With Anne," said Nora. "In the tournament."

Francie went home. The phone was ringing. She picked it up.

"Francie? Anne Franklin. Hope it's not too late. They just called me with the draw — we play Friday at four-thirty, if that's all right."

"Fine."

"And I was thinking maybe we could set up a practice match before that."

"Sure."

"I've got a court Thursday at six."

"Thursday's out," Francie said.

"I'm sorry — that's the only time they had."

"We'll just have to wing it," Francie said.

Francie went to bed but couldn't sleep. She kept thinking of Nora's grandmother, kept hearing the chill in Nora's voice when she wished her luck. That was unbearable: candor, as they said, was the soul of friendship, and she had let Nora down. There would have to be at least one change in Ned's rules.

6

Thursday. Francie spent the day in her office, preparing a report (negative) for the acquisitions committee. ". . . menstrual performance, coupled with an installation consisting of outsize Tupperware (e.g., casserole dish — 10 ft. diameter) suspended from a . . ." She found she'd already typed that sentence, not once but twice, as a quick scroll through the text revealed. She couldn't concentrate at all. This often happened on Thursdays, but this Thursday more than ever.

The phone rang. Francie reached for it with dread. Once before Ned had called to cancel, at about this same time. But it wasn't Ned.

"Francie? Tad Wagner here."

"Yes?" She'd heard the name but couldn't place it.

"Your insurance agent — classmate of Roger's."

"Oh, yes."

"How're you doing?"

"Fine, thanks."

"So I understand. I saw a nice article in the *Globe*."

"That was really about the foundation. I wasn't even supposed —"

"I'm impressed. But the reason I'm calling — now that this career of yours is taking off, have you given any thought to a term policy in your own name?"

"A term policy?"

"That's the instrument I'd recommend in your case."

"Are you talking about life insurance?"

"That's my forte." He pronounced it correctly — at least Harvard gave you that.

"I have no dependents, Tad."

Pause. "What about Roger? Word is he's . . ."

What about Roger? Roger had supported her for years. And if they did end in divorce, she could change the beneficiary: *to Em*. "How much does it cost?"

Tad described different options. Francie settled on a term policy for $500,000 with Roger as beneficiary and hung up. Tad must have been desperate for business: that *Globe* article was six months old.

Ten to four. Enough. She saved and printed her report. Then she wrote *To Ned, with all my love, Francie* on a plain sheet of paper. She stared at the words. They seemed alive on the page.

Francie folded the paper, put it in an envelope, taped it to the rewrapped painting leaning against her desk. She'd never written Ned a note before — written communication was out — but this was special. He could destroy the note if he wished. The pleasure of writing it had been exquisite: it made their relationship real. Francie packed her briefcase, picked up the painting, took the elevator down to the garage.

She drove out of the city under a low and fast-darkening sky, planning what she would say about Nora. It was just a question of making him see how close they were, how trustworthy Nora was. Francie was sure he would understand. Her heart grew light and buoyant — she could feel it, high in her chest, like a bird about to fly. She felt as happy as she'd ever been, at least as an adult, until just across the New Hampshire line, when the car phone buzzed. She realized immediately that she'd forgotten to send the goddamn report upstairs to the acquisitions committee.

"Hello?" she said.

But it wasn't the committee. First a faint background voice, female, said, "Three minutes to air," and then Ned came on. "Hello," he said.

"Ned."

"Hi." He never spoke her name on the phone. There was a pause, and in it Francie thought: *Say you'll be a little late.* He said, "I'm sorry, but I can't make it today."

"Oh."

"Two minutes to air."

"Really sorry. Something's come up; I'll explain later."

"Something bad?"

"Nothing bad, but I've got to go."

"Bye, then."

"I'll call."

Too late to go back to the office, and Francie didn't want to go home. She kept driving, wishing she hadn't said *Bye, then* like that.

77

Something coming up had to mean something involving Em — a parent-teacher meeting, a dance recital. Em came first. Em was the reason Ned couldn't get divorced; Em was the reason for secrecy. Francie understood that, accepted it. If she had a child, she would be the same . . . Francie didn't finish the thought. A competing one had risen in her mind, obtrusive: *If I had a child, I would never take the risk, not for anyone.* She shoved this second thought away, back down into her unconscious or wherever it had sprung from. She didn't have a child: she couldn't know. And how unfair to Ned. He loved her, he loved Em. Did that make him bad?

Francie was almost at Brenda's gate before she remembered the show. Switching on the radio, she caught Ned in midsentence, the signal weak and scratchy with static but audible: ". . . pain will ever go away? Maybe not — that's the truth of it. But it will change into something else, something more manageable. Time may not be a healer, but at least it turns wounds into scars, if you see what I mean."

"I think I do, Ned." The woman was crying. "Thank you."

"Rico from Brighton. Welcome to *Intimately Yours.*"

"Hey. Great show. Can we switch to something different for a second?"

"Thursday, Rico. Anything goes."

"I'd like to talk about the Big A."

"The Big A?"

"The A-word, Ned."

"Adultery?"

"You got it."

"And what's your angle?"

"The scientific angle."

"Which is?"

"You know," said Rico. "Nature's law. It's in a man's best interest to get his genes out there as much as possible and it's in a woman's best interest to have a man around to help with the kids. I mean, that's a contradiction, right?"

"And the implication?"

"That it's not about morality. You do what you gotta do."

There was a long pause, full of static. Then Ned said, "Why don't we throw that out to the listeners — the Big A, a question of —"

Francie lost him completely. Night had fallen now. Her headlights glinted on Brenda's gate. She unlocked it, drove through and up the hill. At the top, she tried the radio again, and Ned came in clearly. ". . . reduce this to a bunch of genes? Let's take another call."

All at once, Francie had a crazy idea. She had a phone, it was a call-in show, she knew the number. Why not call him? He'd never said not to call the show. Free-form Thursday. She picked up the phone and dialed; no chance of getting through anyway.

"*Intimately Yours*," said a voice. "Who's this?"

"Iris," said Francie. "On a car phone."

"And what did you want to talk about?"

"Genes."

"Mind turning off your radio? You're next."

Francie waited, her heart beating its Thursday beat again. What was the saying? Hide a tree in the forest. Did it apply to what she was doing? Maybe not. Maybe this wasn't such a good —

"You're on."

Ned spoke, right in her ear, but with a tone he never used with her: "Iris on her car phone, welcome to the show. What's on your mind, Iris?"

Maybe not a good idea.

"Iris? You there?"

Francie said, "I just want to tell you how much I like your show. Thursdays especially."

Silence. It seemed endless. Then the line went dead. She turned the radio back on, felt herself blushing like a schoolgirl.

". . . lost Iris. Let's take another call." Ned, his voice pitched higher than she'd ever heard it. Not a good idea, not well executed, not funny. Francie pounded her hand on the steering wheel.

Early retirement: an infuriating suggestion. On the computer in his basement office, Roger opened the file containing his résumé and made a single change, adding *IQ — 181 (Stanford-Binet)* on the line below the date of his birth. He printed the résumé, read it over. The new entry didn't look bad, no worse than a long list of specious awards, for example. Quite professional. He prepared a mailing list of potential employers for the revised résumé.

After that, Roger logged on to the Puzzle Club, started the *Times of London* crossword. Where was he? Hell, in ideal form: that would be *dystopia*. Seven across, six letters: ugni, sylvaner. He typed in *grapes*. Ten down, nine letters: loss. Roger paused, sat for a few moments, then went up to Francie's bedroom; their bedroom. He bent, looked under the bed. The painting of the grapes and the skateboarding girl was gone.

Roger grew aware of Francie's clock radio, broadcasting to an empty room; she was like that, leaving on lights, running the tap the whole time she brushed her teeth. "Genes or no genes, Ned," a woman on a phone line was saying, "it'll always be cheating in my book."

"Sounds like the first line of a country hit," said a studio voice, gentle and sympathetic: the kind of male tone suddenly common in broadcasting, a tone Roger hated.

"Let's take another caller," the man said as Roger moved to shut him off. "Who have we got? Iris on her car phone, welcome to the show. What's on your mind, Iris?"

A long pause. Roger was unfamiliar with Francie's clock radio; he fumbled for the switch, found the volume instead, turning it louder.

"Iris? You there?"

"I just want to tell you how much I like your show," a woman said. "Thursdays especially."

Roger froze. Time seemed to freeze with him.

The radio went silent, until at last the smooth-voiced man cleared his throat and said, "Oops, looks like we lost Iris. Let's take another call."

"Hi, Ned. Can we get off this adultery thing for a minute? I'm having a problem with my —"

Roger turned off the radio, stood motionless by the bed.

Francie. Beyond doubt. What had become of her, calling any talk show at all, to say nothing of a smarmy, prurient one like that? To let herself be used by them, like one of those pathetic big-haired women on television? He left the room, closed the door, stopped. And why would she call herself Iris?

Car phone. What was the number of Francie's car phone? Roger didn't know, had never called it. He went downstairs to the kitchen desk where Francie kept all the household accounts. He found the latest cellular phone bill, noted her number, and dialed it, leafing through the bill as he waited for a ring.

"The cellular phone customer you have called is not available at this time," said a recording.

Roger wondered where she was.

Francie drove down to the stone jetty, printing fresh tire tracks in unbroken snow. The snow should have warned her of what lay ahead, but not until her headlights shone on the river, white instead of black, did she realize it was frozen. She got out of the car, stepped onto the jetty, looked down into the dinghies: five or six inches of snow on their floorboards, caught in the ice.

Francie gazed across at the island, the tops of the elms white against the night sky. She hadn't anticipated this; a New England girl, and she hadn't foreseen winter, the changes it would bring for Ned and her. Now she saw them very clearly — motel rooms, dark parking places, furtiveness. Her mind recoiled, and Ned's would, too. Without the cottage, they had a relationship entirely mental, like some Victorian exercise in frustration. How long could that last?

Francie walked to the end of the jetty, sat down. Her feet took charge, lowering themselves to the ice. Then she was standing. Nothing cracked, nothing split; the ice felt thick and solid. She went back to her car for the painting, then moved out onto the ice, one step after another.

Francie walked across the river. She wore leather city boots, not even calf-high, but high enough. The snow on the river was only an inch or two deep, the rest blown away by the wind. This was easy — good traction, and no rowing, no tying up — with Brenda's wintry island more beautiful than ever. A moonless, starless sky, but she could see her way easily; the snow brightened the night. A shadow stirred in the elm tops, rose high above. The owl. Francie paused to watch, lost it in the darkness, took another step. The next moment she was plunging to the bottom.

Down she went in complete blackness, icy

water bubbling around her, so cold it made her gasp, swallow, gag. Her foot touched something: the bottom? She pushed off, a panicked, reflexive kick, and frantically kicked toward the surface — or what she hoped was the surface, because she could see nothing but bubbles, silver on the outside, black within. But the surface didn't come. Was she moving at all? So heavy: she struggled with her coat, freed herself from it, tried to get rid of her boots, could not. She kicked, wheeled her arms, felt pressure building in her chest like an inflating balloon, and always the never-ending shock of cold. Her head struck something hard and she sank.

As Francie sank, she had a strange thought, not her kind of thought at all. She wasn't religious, certainly didn't believe in any kind of quid pro quo, deal-making God. But still, the thought came — *If you let me live, I'll never see Ned again* — as though she were guilty, and this the punishment.

Francie kicked again, once, twice, the bubble about to burst from her chest. Her head had struck something hard: the underside of the ice? She raised her hands in protection, and her fingers reached into night air. Francie broke through the surface, choking, retching, but alive. She floundered in a pool of black water, no wider than the top of a well.

Francie commanded her hands: on the ice. They obeyed. Pull. They pulled, but the ice broke off. Francie tried again, and again, and again, hands, face, body numb, teeth chattering at an impossible speed, breaking off chunks of ice, breaking, breaking. She heard a terrible cry, her cry, and then the ice held for her. She flopped onto it, drew herself up, inches at a time, to her chest, her waist, and out.

Some shivering mechanism now controlled her body. She staggered across the ice, onto the jetty, into her car. The keys? In her coat: gone. But then she saw them glinting in the ignition, left by mistake. What was happening to her? She turned the key, switched on the heater, full-blast. The engine was still warm. It had been only a few minutes. She clung, shaking, to the steering wheel, and remembered *oh garden, my garden*: gone, too.

It was after midnight when Francie got home. From his basement office, Roger heard her footsteps overhead. He waited an hour by the clock and went upstairs.

Francie's boots were on the mat by the front door. They looked wet. Roger went closer. They were wet. He picked one up. Soaked, inside and out, and it was too cold for rain. Had she gone for a walk on the beach, strayed too close to the surf? He sniffed: no salty smell, but to be sure he gave the leather a lick of his tongue as well. Freshwater, then, and at least a foot deep. Freshwater: ponds, lakes, rivers. He gazed up the stairs, thinking.

Roger put the boot down, aligned the pair

neatly. He went into the kitchen. Francie's purse lay on the table. He looked through it: wallet, with driver's license, credit cards, forty-two dollars; zinc lozenges, tissues, vitamin C, a key ring. Key ring. Not like her. She always left her keys in the ignition when she parked in the garage, no matter what he said.

There were seven keys on the ring: car key; two house keys, front and back; a key to her locker at the tennis club — he had had one just like it — a small key that would be for luggage; and two he couldn't identify. These two he removed from the ring and laid on the table.

Roger went to Francie's kitchen desk, found paper and a pencil. He placed the keys on the paper and traced their patterns. Then he pocketed the paper, put the keys back on the ring, left the purse the way he'd found it, went downstairs to his basement room. The crossword waited, unfinished. One down, nine letters: loss. That would be *ruination*.

7

"Good show this afternoon, Ned," said Kira Chang, vice president of Total Entertainment Syndication, raising her glass. "Here's to *Intimately Yours.*"

Sitting at the table in Ned's dining room, they drank to the show: Anne, at the far end; Trevor, Ned's producer, on her right; Lucy, the director, next to him; Ned at the end; Kira Chang on his right; Trevor's assistant next to her. Ned didn't like the wine at all, wished that Anne could have done a little better. And he wished she could have done better with the whole dinner, despite the late notice.

Ned had called at 3:30, and Anne had said, "I wasn't planning any dinner at all — isn't it Thursday?"

For a moment he found himself holding his breath. "Meaning what?" he said.

"Thursday, Ned. When you stay late to plan the shows."

"Yes. Normally. But Kira Chang's in town."

"Who's she?"

"I told you. Sweetheart. The syndicator."

"I thought that was next week."

"The meeting's next week, but she happened to be in town today and she dropped in. Trevor says it's a good sign, so we should take advantage of it."

"I'll do my best," Anne said.

Her best: the oyster stew, the lemon chicken with snow peas, the tiramisu from Lippo's. And this maroon-colored wine, possibly Romanian — he couldn't read the fine print on the label.

"Delicious, Anne," said Kira Chang. "And I hear you're quite a tennis player, too."

Anne smiled nervously. The light in the dining room was a little too strong; it made her look washed out, or was that just the effect of Kira's presence?

Trevor refilled his glass — not for the first time — and said, "One thing we've never discussed, Kira, is the name of the show. What do you think of it?"

Kira looked at Trevor across the table. "There's only one answer to questions like that — I'll let you know after we poll the audience."

"To see what *it* thinks, you mean?"

"That's right."

"Isn't that leading by following?"

Kira smiled at him. "This isn't art, Trevor. It isn't even politics. It's just entertainment."

"Total entertainment," said Ned.

Kira laughed. "Bingo."

She left soon after. Ned walked her out to the waiting taxi. A cold wind blew down the street, ruffling her glossy hair. She turned to him.

"Thanks for dinner," she said. "And don't forget to thank Anne again for me. I hope I didn't upset your routine."

"Not at all," Ned said. Their eyes met. He said what was on his mind. "Did you really like the show today?"

"Not much," Kira replied. "But that's what I like, right there. The way you asked that question. You're good with women, Ned. That's your strength. And it goes a long way in this business."

"But the show?"

"Too early to say. I hope you understand that when we green-light something like this we often bring in our own people on the production side."

"The show was Trevor's idea in the first place."

"The cast-iron sincerity in your tone — that's part of the appeal, for sure," she said, opening the door of the taxi. "But the metaphor to keep in mind, if you want to make it big in broadcasting, in anything, is the multistage rocket."

"Meaning the booster falls away?"

"Good night," she said, closing the door. The taxi drove off.

"Did it go all right?" Anne asked when they were in bed.

"Fine."

"What a relief. She made me so uncomfortable."

"How?"

"She's so poised, so . . . everything I'm not."

"Don't be ridiculous," Ned said. The booster

falls away: that meant ruthlessness, and he wasn't the ruthless type. He rolled over and tried to sleep; the headache awoke over his right eye, unfolding like a flower.

"Francie?"

Francie opened her eyes. Roger was standing by the bed, looking down at her. A jolt of adrenaline rushed through her, washing away decaying fragments of terrible dreams.

"Hope I didn't scare you," he said with a smile. "Not going in today?"

Francie started to speak, but her mouth was too dry, her throat, her whole body, hurting. She tried again. "What time is it?"

"Nine-thirty. You slept through the alarm."

Francie glanced at the clock radio.

"I shut it off," Roger said. "How can you bear that station?" He smiled again. "Coffee?"

"You've made coffee?"

"Should be just about done." He reached out as though to pat her knee under the covers, thought better of it, went out. Francie sat up, saw her damp clothes lying in the corner. She rose, aching in every muscle, kicked the clothes under the bed, got back in just as Roger returned with a tray: buttered toast, marmalade, steaming coffee.

"You should stay home," he said. "You don't look at all well."

"I'm fine."

Roger pulled up a chair, watched her sip the

coffee. "Working late last night?" he said.

"Yes."

He nodded. "I hope you're appreciated," he said. "Some *especially* important project, is it?"

"I don't know what you mean by especially important. The acquisitions committee meets next week — it's always a busy time."

"Seen anything you like recently?"

"What do you mean?"

"Objets d'art. What else could I be referring to?"

"Nothing." But it had been years since he had discussed her work. "I'm recommending a few pieces."

"Such as?"

"There's a photographer in Providence. She does old people under streetlights, in black-and-white. Mostly black."

"Any paintings?"

"No paintings," Francie said.

Roger dressed warmly: turtleneck, chamois shirt, thick corduroy pants, ski hat, Gore-Tex gloves, his L.L. Bean boots. He went into the garage, opened Francie's car, looked in the glove box, found a wrinkled envelope with a map drawn on it jammed at the back, as he'd been sure he would — he knew her, and nothing she did could change that. *Directions to B.'s,* she'd written in her neat hand. He studied the map for a minute or so, replaced it. Then, putting a shovel in the back of his car, he drove to a hardware store. The clerk made keys from the two patterns. Roger filled his tank and headed west, out of the city. His car had four-wheel drive and good tires, but the sky was low and dark and snow was in the forecast. He switched on his headlights and set the cruise control prudently to fifty-five.

Snow was falling by the time Roger stopped in front of Brenda's gate — marked *wrought-iron g.* on the map, as he recalled — falling, but falling hard enough to have obliterated any trace of tread marks? Roger's eyes followed the track that rose up the hill beyond the gate, white, smooth, unbroken. He had his first moment of doubt.

The gate was padlocked. Roger got out of his car, took out the two keys. The first one worked. He drove through, his wheels spinning slightly as he came to the top of the hill, and cautiously down the other side, foot on the brake the whole way.

He parked by a stone jetty, covered in snow, and looked out at the island in the river. Snow, clean and pure, lay deep on everything: the trees, the roof of the cottage, the river. Roger remembered going out in the Adirondack woods as a boy to cut down a Christmas tree with his father's man, as they called him, Len; how Len had pretended to chop off his own foot, having brought along a Baggie of ketchup to complete the illusion: red stains in the snow, Len laughing his toothless laugh, a drop of mucus quivering from the tip of his hairy nose. Roger's father had fired Len that very day for putting such a scare into the boy.

Roger stepped onto the jetty, saw no sign of tracks across the river. Doubt again. Was he seeing ketchup and thinking blood? He gazed down onto two dinghies, filled with snow. It was falling harder now, the flakes bigger. Roger reached into the nearest dinghy, picked up an oar, and jabbed it on the river ice. Solid. He lowered himself onto the river and started across, testing the ice with the oar at every step.

Roger walked onto the island, past the giant elms, also reminding him of his boyhood, up to the front door of the cottage. Snow on the porch, snow on the glider, even a little mound of it clinging to the upper hemisphere of the doorknob. Doubt. He took out the remaining key. It worked. Roger went inside.

He closed the door, took off his boots, took off his gloves. Kitchen: a wine bottle on the table, half full. Roger reached for it, stopped. *Flake of dandruff falls off your head, you fry.* Strange, how the mind worked. He put on the gloves, drew the cork, tilted the bottle to his lips, not quite touching, and tasted the wine. Still good, although not much of a wine. He stuck the cork back in, left the bottle in the same spot on the table.

Roger opened the refrigerator, empty, and the cupboards: dishes, glasses, the expected. He went into the living room, ran his eyes over the books, mounted the stairs. He glanced into a bedroom with a bare mattress on the bed, moved into the bathroom: bar of soap and a bottle of shampoo in the shower. He picked up the shampoo with his gloved hand. Principessa was the brand, and the writing on the bottle was Italian. A towel hung over the rail; he could see it was dry.

Roger went into the last room, another bedroom, this one made up. He checked the closet: two life jackets and a terry-cloth robe on the rail, something silver glinting on the high shelf at the back. He reached for it, a box, a silvery slippery box that he almost dropped. Lancôme face powder: would have been messy. He put it back. Then he knelt, peered under the bed, saw dustballs. He pulled back the duvet, checked under the pillows, stared at the sheets. White sheets, spotless. He bent over the center of the bed until his nose was almost touching the bottom sheet and sniffed. He smelled nothing.

Ketchup, instead of blood. Had he built a huge construction on a foundation of nothing? Then, straightening, Roger saw brown-tipped flowers in a glass vase by the window, dying but not dead. Irises? Yes, but even if they were, what then? Nothing certain. A foundation of very little. If he had made one mistake in his life, in his work, it was letting his brilliance speed him along too quickly. *Homo sapiens* was a jealous species.

Roger smoothed the duvet, went downstairs. He stood in the kitchen for some time, watching the snow fall. Then he put on his boots and went out, making sure the door was locked behind him.

Roger walked back across the river, poking ahead automatically with the oar, his brain rearranging the few pieces — irises, wine, wet boots, call-in show — and projecting the shapes of missing ones that might not even exist. He almost didn't notice the bump in all the white smoothness of the river, a protrusion like driftwood covered in snow.

Bending over it, Roger dusted off the snow. Underneath he saw not driftwood but a brown-paper-wrapped package, frozen stiff. He got his hands on it, pulled; the package didn't budge. Clearing away more snow with the blade of the oar, he saw that the package, tilted at a forty-five-degree angle, was stuck in the ice.

Roger went to his car, returned with the shovel, chipped away carefully. After a few minutes, the package came free. Then he was down on his hands and knees, tearing at the frozen paper.

A painting. One half blurred and damaged, all murky brown and green. But the other half showed a crumbling plinth, a few dangling red grapes, the front wheels of a skateboard.

The wind began to blow at the wrapping paper. Roger scrambled around, gathering it up. He came upon a white envelope, threw off his gloves, ripped it open. Inside a note: *To Ned, with all my love, Francie.*

Roger stood in the middle of the river, snow falling harder, wind whipping icy flakes at him from different directions. His mind was the same — a turmoil of thoughts, racing by too fast for even him to examine. *Must clear, must clear, must clear,* he thought, and with great effort he forced his brain to stop, his mind to go blank. He stood panting, his head empty, feeling nothing, not cold, snow, wind.

And into this calm, a meditational calm, although he'd always despised the idea of meditation, came a first brief thought, or rather, memory. *A perfect crime: it's got to be absolutely unconnected — a penny drops off the Empire State Building, goes right through your skull.*

8

Roger drove back to the city, still at a prudent fifty-five, but his mind was racing. He was used to the speed of his mind, had known it to run far ahead of him before, but never in this super-charged way. His whole body was shaking slightly, like a shell that could barely contain the forces within. *Hold on to one thought,* he instructed it, or at most a single train of thought. He settled on one right away, a simple syllogism. Major premise: F tries to make a fool of R. Minor premise: R is not a fool and will not bear it. Conclusion: question mark.

Not quite a question mark, because he knew that some action was required. She had come into their house — his house, his ancestral house — with another man's sperm inside her, perhaps many, many times. Another man's sperm: a vulgar, dirty, contemptuous betrayal, almost slimy, like a plot development in one of those movies about alien beings in human shape. Another man's sperm — what a primitive fixation she had with the substance, on reflection — inside her, and she talking and smiling away at him. Smile and be a villain, Francie. There was no fixing anything now, no going back. And what was society's answer? No-fault divorce. If this were Sicily, or Iran, countless other places, he could now — what? *Kill her with impunity.* A crime of passion, almost expected. Divorce implied nothing more than absence of affection, lack of feeling. Therefore divorce did not apply. He felt. He felt the opposite of everything husband should feel for wife. She was his enemy, had proved him wrong in one of the basic decisions of life, whom to marry. What action was appropriate? Question mark.

Not quite a question mark. Deep in his mind, did he not already know the answer must be related to that penny dropping off the Empire State Building? *Yes.* The conclusion awaited, long before the thinking was done. But slow: this was not Sicily or Iran. America, land that had deteriorated so much as he grew older, had failed him so badly. Slow: there would be many steps along the way, down and down toward that coppery glint. And every step must be a careful step, all planning, all preparation thought and rethought.

For example, on the front seat beside him sat the damaged painting and Francie's note. *To Ned, with all my love, Francie.* His mind writhed away from the words. *Get back on track, one thought, one thought.* The painting, the note. Too risky to hide them in the house and he no longer had an office. Was there any other space over which he held exclusive control? The answer came at once, probably because of the morning's business with the keys: his locker at the tennis club.

Step one, then. There were two kinds of lockers at the club: full-size metal ones in the locker room, and half-size wooden ones lining the thickly carpeted hall that led to the courts. Because of his dislike for showering at the club, Roger had taken a locker in the hall. He walked to it now, the painting wrapped in the scraps of brown paper he'd salvaged, note tucked inside, and unlocked the door with his key. Inside he found equipment he'd forgotten about — racquets, cans of balls, tennis shoes, towels. No room for the painting. He put the painting down, the brown paper unfurling, glanced around, saw no one, took everything out of the locker, picked up the painting, rewrapped it imperfectly, one corner protruding, and was just placing it inside when a female voice spoke right behind him. "Roger?"

He slammed the door shut, wheeled around, saw a big woman in a purple warm-up suit, a pair of racquets slung over her shoulder. "Oh. Nora." Not very smooth, perhaps, possibly lacking in friendliness, so he added, "Hello. Nice to see you."

"Likewise. I didn't know you were playing again."

"Playing again?" How to handle this situation? He looked at her: only Nora, after all, a jock, not very bright; he'd never understood what Francie saw in her. "Thinking about it, in any case," he said. "Come to reintroduce myself to the gear. Shake hands with my racquet." A witticism —

shaking hands with the racquet was the age-old introduction to the forehand grip. He laughed.

Nora didn't. Her brow, in no way noble, or even intelligent, wrinkled. *Must I explain the god-damned joke?* Roger was thinking, when three women came down the hall on their way to the courts, talking woman-talk. "Say hi to Francie," Nora said, joining them.

"Will do," said Roger with a smile, turning the key in his locker, then trying the handle twice to make sure it was locked.

Driving home, Roger fought the urge to stamp down on the gas, to smash the cars around him. *On track, stay on track, use your brain.* He used it to think about crime.

Roger knew that people sometimes got away with crime, but did any of them *necessarily* do so? Or did they simply rely, tacitly or explicitly, on sloppy police work, nonexistent police work, luck? He considered luck. A person could be taken on a cruise ship, for example, invited for a glass of champagne on a deserted stern deck at night, pushed over the rail. It might work, but was it teleologically guaranteed to do so? Of course not. Someone might be sitting in the shadows, obscured by a lifeboat, and witness the whole thing. Or the falling person might cry out, attract a quick glance through a porthole or from someone on a lower deck, leading to alarms, searchlights, rubber boats crisscrossing the wake. The person might even fall unnoticed but then happen on a piece of driftwood, cling to it until dawn, be rescued by a fishing boat. Therefore the cruise ship scenario, attractive because no body and therefore no evidence is found, required luck, would not succeed of necessity, was far from perfect.

Calmer now, Roger was in no way downcast by the negative result of this speculation. Quite the opposite, if anything, for all at once he was hungry and thirsty, his appetite keener than it had been for a long time. He pulled into a suburban steakhouse, the kind of place he would never enter — wagon wheel by the door, cowboy pictures on the wall — and ordered a big steak and a double Scotch on the rocks. What was this strange feeling bubbling up inside him, strange but not quite forgotten? He put a name to it: enthusiasm. And in the next moment he realized with a shock — ironic, unsettling, but finally pleasant — that he had found a job at last.

"I'll have another," he said to the waitress.

"Another drink, sir?"

"Another of everything."

"Including the garlic bread?"

"Pourquoi pas?"

"I'm sorry?"

"Yes, garlic bread by all means."

Accidents, he thought, chewing his food with relish, trying to keep pace with his mind. Tampering with brakes, with steering rods, with ovens, with furnaces, with ski bindings all required technical knowledge; all carried the risk that evidence of tampering might remain. And if tampering was suspected, the first suspect would be the spouse.

Roger removed the round paper napkin from under his glass, wrote on it:

poison — no — expertise, traces
contract killer — no — in his power
arson (house) — no — evidence — accelerant
infection (injection?) with some disease —

"Care for anything else, sir?"

Roger slid his hand over the napkin. "Just the check."

The waitress went off. Roger raised his hand slightly to peek at the napkin, like a poker player checking his hole card. The disease idea. Pro: like an accident, it provided a credible noncriminal explanation for death. Con: it required expertise, a disease not readily contagious yet fast-acting and certain. *No*, he wrote beside it, but reluctantly. He paid his bill, went into the bathroom, tore up the napkin, flushed the shreds down the toilet, got in his car, started home. He had gone a few blocks when he made a sudden U-turn and sped back to the restaurant. What if some scrap of the napkin was still floating in the toilet bowl? He hurried inside — "anything the matter, sir?" said the waitress — strode into the bathroom, peered into the toilet. Nothing but water; he flushed it again anyway, just to be safe.

"Francie?" he called, entering the house on

Beacon Hill; their house, under the laws of the Commonwealth, but his by moral right, since he had inherited it from his grandparents. No answer. He went into the kitchen, saw her purse still on the table and a stack of mail, some opened, on the desk. He riffled through it, found a letter from Tad Wagner: *Please find a copy of your coverage statement. Once again, thanks so much, and if I can be . . .*

Roger checked the coverage statement. Amount: $500,000. Beneficiary: himself. Yes, he had found a job, and it came with a suitable performance bonus. Had his mind somehow known about Francie even then when he'd first thought of Tad and arranged to run into him on the street? A reunion that had led to a drink, talk of Francie's success, proud exhibition of the *Globe* clipping — but no explicit discussion of her possible insurance needs, unnecessary with the Tads of the world. The human mind had unplumbed powers, his especially. He heard Francie moving about upstairs, left the desk the way he'd found it.

Roger was putting cookies on a tray when Francie came into the room: the sight of her. Her face, once such an appealing mix of elements — bright eyes, strong features, soft skin — was nothing but a mask. How clearly he saw that now. Despite all the thinking he had done that day, despite the need for long and careful preparation, despite that glinting coppery goal sometime in the future, he wanted to beat her head in, then and there. "Care for a cookie?" he said, offering the tray.

"No thanks," she said.

"Feeling better?"

"Yes."

She was wearing a coat: an old one, he noticed, unworn for a year or two. "Going somewhere?"

"Didn't I tell you? I'm playing in the tournament."

"Mixed?" he asked.

"Women's doubles, Roger," said Francie, taking her purse and moving toward the door that led down to the garage.

"Good luck, then." She went out. He waited until he felt the vibration of the opening garage door under his feet before calling, "Don't forget to bend your fucking knees."

"God, what fun," said Anne. Still sweating slightly, they sat at a corner table of the tennis club bar, overlooking the courts. Seven–five, two–six, seven–five: they'd knocked the number one seeds out of the tournament. "That backhand down the line you hit at five all ad out — unbelievable. I wouldn't have the guts to try that, not in a million years."

Francie just smiled.

"And then your two best serves of the night, right after. Bang bang. I could have kissed you." Beer came, and water, lots of water. Pink with exertion and victory, Anne talked on and on, reliving the match, her words sometimes tripping over themselves. Francie hadn't seen her like this, suspected it didn't happen often. She wondered about Anne's husband.

Anne paused for breath, took a big drink of water. "Was it Jimmy Connors who said that tennis is better than sex?"

"Maybe his tennis," Francie said. "Not ours."

Anne glanced at her, and in that glance Francie saw her realizing she'd been talking too much, at least in terms of some inner code. Her mood changed, the blood draining from her face, leaving her pale. Her eyes took on an inward look: something was on her mind, something unrelated to tennis. She tried some beer, started to speak, stopped, and finally said, "Can I ask you something, Francie? I hate to be too personal, but the truth is I find you so easy to be with — like someone I've known for a long time."

"Ask away," said Francie.

Anne said, "Are you a good cook?"

"That's the question?"

Anne nodded.

"I have two surefire appetizers, two surefire entrées, one dessert," said Francie. "The rest is silence."

Anne smiled, an admiring smile that made Francie a little uncomfortable. "I thought my lemon chicken was surefire, too," she said, "but I guess I was wrong." The inward look again. Francie waited. "Does your husband ever bring people home for dinner at the last minute?" Anne asked.

"He's actually been doing the cooking lately," Francie said.

"Aren't you lucky."

Anne added something else that Francie didn't catch. She was thinking of their own dining room, and the happy sounds that used to fill it. At one time she and Roger had entertained a lot, then less, and since the loss of his job, not at all. Plotted on a graph, she wondered, would those dinners track the health of their marriage? Down, down, down, with upturns here and there: a stunted marriage, like a tree growing in the face of an impossible wind.

"Thursday of all days," Anne was saying, "when he usually works late. It was going to be a McDonald's night, and then boom. So I threw together the lemon chicken, but they hardly touched it. And I suppose the wine wasn't very good either, although that didn't stop them from drinking plenty of it. I'd read an article on Romanian wine, goddamn it." Was Francie imagining it, or had Anne's eyes filled with tears? Tears, yes: and Anne saw that she saw, and tried to explain. "He cares so much about his career. The least I can do is put a decent meal on the table."

Francie could imagine Nora at this point, saying, *Your husband sounds like a jerk.* She toned that down. "I don't see the connection. And if he's any good at his job, a failed lemon chicken won't make any difference."

"You think? He's so ambitious."

"I do. Lighten up, for God's sake."

Anne's eyes cleared. "I'm sure you're right," she said. "You're so clearheaded, Francie, so in control."

Francie, suddenly picturing herself under the ice at Brenda's cottage, her breath escaping in silver-and-black bubbles, said nothing.

"Can I ask you a favor?" Anne said.

"But first do me one," Francie said. "Stop asking if you can ask and just ask."

Anne laughed. "With pleasure." She reached across the table, touched Francie's hand. "Give me one of those surefire recipes of yours."

Francie took the paper napkin from under her glass and wrote:

Francie's Roast Lamb, serves 8
7 cloves garlic, 1 halved, rest chopped
2 pounds baking potatoes, peeled and . . .

She came to the end, added the reminder to keep the gratin warm while waiting to carve the lamb, handed the napkin to Anne. "Enjoy."

"Oh, I'm sure I will," said Anne. "The very next time we have company." Her face brightened with an idea. "Maybe you and your husband would like to join us?"

"That sounds nice," Francie said.

9

Anne, having checked her watch and said "Oh my God, the sitter," left in a hurry; Francie sat alone at the corner table in the bar. Looking down on court three beneath her window, she watched the second seeds playing their match. They were good, but nothing like the pair she and Anne had just beaten, nothing like the pair she and Anne had so quickly become. Francie couldn't remember playing this well at any time in her life. How was it possible, with so much on her mind? Her near-drowning, her stupid on-air phone call, the loss of *oh garden, my garden,* Roger's attempted seduction, to put the kindest light on it, and his subsequent attentiveness, just as disturbing. Some of it had to do with Anne, of course — they fit together so well — but was the rest simply chance? Or was it one of those Faustian bargains, her life falling apart while her tennis got better and better? She wanted no part of that. Tennis was her game, but just a game. In any case, her life wasn't falling apart — not with Ned in it, no matter what happened. Francie paid her bill, went downstairs to her car, started for home.

Roger sat before his computer. The Puzzle Club was up, but he was not really attending. In fact, he was staring through the words on the screen, into a translucent beyond, his mind working out the possibilities of planting a bomb in an Israeli consulate, having first ensured that a visiting art consultant would be inside at just the right moment. A wretched idea, he concluded: messy, inelegant, leaking evidence, guaranteed to provide a full-scale investigation, and he knew nothing of bombs, bomb-making, bomb-planting. He leaned his head against the screen and thought, *What am I doing?* The computer hummed quietly against his brain.

Perhaps he was wrong about everything. All his evidence was circumstantial. Even her note and the call to the radio show could be logically explained: maybe she had developed one of those fan manias for a celebrity, maybe it was all taking place in her head, maybe she and the smooth-talking poseur had not even met. Did that sound like Francie? No. But there was a basic instability to her character — indeed, in the character of every woman he had ever known — so nothing could be ruled out. For his own peace of mind, if nothing else, he required eye-witness evidence. For example, was she really playing in the tennis tournament, or was that a lie to cover her presence somewhere else?

Roger pulled into the parking lot of the tennis club just in time to see Francie come out the door and walk to her car. She was wearing a warm-up suit and tennis shoes, didn't look his way, and probably wouldn't have noticed him if she had. He could see in his headlights that she was lost in thought, no doubt had fumbled away a close match, probably choking on a big point. No matter: she hadn't lied about the tournament. She drove past him, out of the parking lot, turned north, toward Storrow Drive and home. He followed. Once inside, he would offer her a drink, perhaps make a fire, if there was any wood in the storage room. From there he knew he could find some subtle way of bringing the conversation around to call-in shows. He needed hard evidence.

Francie's car phone buzzed. She answered.

"Are you on speaker?" Ned. He had never called her on the car phone before.

"No."

"Are you alone?"

"Yes. What —"

He interrupted. "What's that sound?"

"I don't hear anything." She checked her rearview mirror: two rows of double headlights winding back toward the western suburbs.

Silence.

"I'm at the place," he said.

"The cottage?"

"Don't say that. It's a cellular call, for God's sake." Pause. "Can you make it?"

"Tonight?"

"Tonight. I'm here tonight."

"Is something wrong?"

"Just can you make it."

"Yes, but —"

"Good." Click.

"— the ice." But the ice. Would he try to cross before she arrived? No. Not having the key to Brenda's, he would wait in the warmth of his car. But what if he didn't? Francie didn't know Ned's cell phone number; the rules made it unnecessary. She tried information — unlisted.

Francie exited at Mass. Ave., crossed the Charles, drove north. But what if he didn't wait in the warmth of his car? Was she willing to let him die to follow the spycraft rules? No. She called information, asked for Ned Demarco in Dedham — she didn't know the street — found the home number, too, was unlisted. She stepped on the gas. Some time passed before she realized Ned wasn't in danger: she'd locked Brenda's wrought-iron gate and he had no key to that either, couldn't drive down to the river. But she stepped on the gas anyway.

Francie drove north into winter. The roads were bare but lined with snowbanks that rose higher and higher as she crossed into New Hampshire, the tree branches sagging lower and lower, weighted down with white. Had there ever been this much snow so soon? Behind her the long tail of headlights, like a wake of yellow phosphorus, slowly dwindled down to one lone pair. Not long before she turned onto the last and most minor of the roads that led to Brenda's, it, too, disappeared.

111

Is something wrong?

Just can you make it.

Francie came to Brenda's gate — and found it wide open. Had she left it unlocked last night in her distress? What other explanation was there? She looked once more in her rearview mirror, saw nothing but bright moonlight shining on a black-and-white wilderness: deep, crisp, even, but ahead of its time. She drove through.

Ned's car, an all-wheel sedan, had cut two well-defined tracks in the snow. Francie followed them down to the jetty, found the car. But Ned wasn't in it, and the inside of the windshield was already frosting over with the freezing breath he had left behind. In the moonlight — the dazzling moonlight of a full moon in a clear sky over clean snow — she saw footprints leading across the white river. She followed them.

Reasoning that where he had gone, she was safe to go, that the river had had one more day to freeze, that she had to see him, Francie walked across the river and didn't think once of the night before. She reached the other side, still in Ned's footprints, their inch-deep walls black-shaded in the moonlight, took the path under the elms to the dark cottage — at least she hadn't left it open, too — and climbed the stairs to the porch.

Ned stepped out of the shadows. She jumped. "What the hell were you thinking?" he said.

Francie put her hand to her breast. "The call?"

"Yes, of course, the call." He came closer, his face strange in the stark light: much older, its future lines blackened by the night. "How could you do something so — so flippant?"

"It was meant to be funny."

"Funny?"

"And a private message as well."

Ned's voice rose, lost its beautiful timbre. "Message? What message?"

"Ned — I'm sorry."

"Me, too, believe me, since I'm the one at risk. But what was this message that was so important? Tell me now. You have my full attention."

He was even closer now, in her space, as if they hadn't been lovers, and a droplet of his spit — tiny, insignificant, barely felt — landed on her cheek. Unintentional, he wasn't even aware it had happened, but all at once Francie remembered the deal she'd made under the ice with the god she didn't believe in, and she felt her whole body stiffening, and words came out of her mouth unedited, unconsidered, but from deep within: "Maybe we'd better call this off."

"What did you say?" He stepped back, as though struck by a sudden gust.

Francie didn't repeat it; she just watched his eyes, dark and still.

Ned spoke again, his voice nearer its usual range. "I didn't mean to get into something unpleasant, Francie. I just wanted an explanation."

She shook her head. "I'm starting to see what I should have seen already. This is too much for you, Ned — it's making you unhappy."

He stared at her. His eyes changed, grew

damp, reflected the moonlight. "What are you saying?"

"You don't need this."

"You're telling me my needs?"

"I think I know you, Ned."

"Do you?" The dampness spilled over his lower eyelids, onto his face. She had never seen Ned cry, had never seen any man cry, except at funerals and in the movies. "You can be god-damn arrogant sometimes," he said, his voice quiet and thick. "You think I don't know what you're really saying?"

"What am I really saying?"

"And now you're going to toy with me, too. You're really saying this is making *you* unhappy, *you* don't need *me*."

"Please, Ned. No psych one-oh-one."

His face crumpled. "When did you stop loving me?" Ned pushed past her, hurried down the stairs, down the path toward the river. Some-where behind the house a clump of snow fell from a tree and landed with a thump. Ned stum-bled on snow-covered rock, kept going. Francie went after him.

He didn't walk back across the river to the jetty but straight out into midstream, in the di-rection he'd come paddling from in his kayak the very first time. Francie caught up to him out in the middle of the river, in the middle of all that whiteness, as bright as day on some planet where the skies were always black.

She touched his shoulder. He stopped at once.

114

"It's dangerous," she said. "Come back."

He turned, stood before her, hands at his sides, moonlit tears streaming down his face. "When? Just tell me that. When did you stop?"

"Never," Francie replied, and put her arms around him.

"Oh, Francie," he said, taking a deep breath, letting it out slowly, a white cloud — the only one — rising in the night. He nuzzled against her, leaned on her — she felt his weight. "Do you know how rare this is?" he said. "Wouldn't there be something wrong with two people who could just throw it away? We'd be . . . diminished."

Francie held him tight. Ice cracked, but far away.

"You do love me?" he said.

"Yes." He was right: she'd never felt this for any human being, knew she never would again. Now she was crying, too.

They walked back to the island. Francie unlocked the cottage. They went upstairs to the little bedroom, to the world under the down comforter. They lay still for a long time, holding each other. A long, healing time to get back to their places in the relationship; Francie, at least, couldn't find her old place, but the new one was not far from it, and maybe better. The lying-still phase came to an end.

After, Francie said, "There will have to be some changes."

"I know."

"I have to be able to call you. Somewhere, sometime."

"All right. I'll figure something out."

"And there's someone I have to tell. I won't say it's you, if you don't want, but I have to tell."

"Who?"

"My best friend. She already knows, anyway."

Ned's body tensed beside her. "How does she know?"

"Nora knows me. She hasn't said anything, but she knows."

"Nora?"

"You'd like her."

Pause. When it came, his response was a surprise. "Maybe I'll meet her someday. After . . . after Em's grown up."

He had never before held out the promise of a better future. Francie lay beside him, savoring the implication of his words. "I'm going to get a divorce," she said.

Another silence, longer than the last. "Maybe not right away, Francie," he said.

"Why not? It's no pressure on you."

"I know that. But aren't there ever times you feel you're in a very delicate situation, where everything is poised just so?"

"I'm not sure," Francie said, and it occurred to her that in some ways he had more feminine intuition than she had. If there was an emotional IQ test, Ned would probably come out on top, the same way Roger did intellectually.

"You must have felt that sometime in your

life," Ned said. "When the slightest disturbance, even of something that doesn't seem related at first, upsets everything."

Francie immediately pictured deformed sperm under a microscope. "I won't do anything right away."

"Or without telling me?"

"Or without telling you."

He kissed her. "Now you're thinking."

She laughed. He did, too. "You're a bastard," she said. "You know that?"

"All men are bastards," he said.

"Some more than others."

"Then there's hope for me?"

"Yes," she told him.

He switched on the bedside lamp, checked his watch. "Oh my God," he said. "The sitter." He started to get up, turned to her. In the yellow light of the lamp, his face was its youthful self again. "Maybe I can get out here on non-Thursdays once in a while," he said.

"That would be nice."

"And it might help if I had a key. It's cold out there."

"I'll get you one," Francie said. "Wimp." She smacked his bare butt as he got out of bed.

There was a toolshed behind the cottage. Roger had found an ax inside. He held it now in his gloved hands, staring up at the light in the window, through which had come sounds Francie had never made for him. It was easy to muse on perfect crimes and abstract killers when evidence was circumstantial. It wasn't easy now when evidence was hard. Why not simply crash his way inside, charge up to that lighted room, start swing swing swinging this goddamned ax? His blood rushed through his body at the thought, his muscles tensed, his teeth ground together. He took a step toward the door, and a few more. A bird — owl — glided down from the sky and settled on the roof. Great horned, *Bubo virginianus*. Roger halted.

Why not? Because of after. Would the ax-swinging feel good enough to render him content to spend the rest of his life in jail? For that would surely happen, given the shambles there would be inside the cottage, the pools of DNA, the two cars parked by the jetty, the obvious suspect with no alibi.

Roger returned the ax to the shed, crossed the river a few hundred yards upstream, retracing the route that kept his footprints out of sight, made his way to the wrought-iron gate where he had left his car. From there, he could just make out the upstairs light in the cottage, dim and partially blocked by trees. He was glad of the sight: a guarantee that he had imagined nothing. The light went out as he watched.

10

Think.

A penny drops from the Empire State Building. Someone in China pushes a button.

Think.

Think, Roger told himself, sitting in his basement office, of murder most antiseptic. He went over his list, now committed to memory. *Accidents — mechanical, household, while on vacation; poison; contract killer; arson; disease; bombing.* All wrong, for one reason or another. *Think.* All thinking boiled down to two procedures, rearranging the pieces on the board and inventing new ones. What were the pieces? Motive, means, opportunity; evidence, suspects, alibis. A complexity of permutation and combination, orbiting this central problem: if a wife is murdered, the husband is the first suspect and remains so until ruled out with certainty. That was what made murder disguised as something else — accident or disease, for example — so attractive. The murderer would be left with nothing to do but mourn, and he could do so without anxiety, no crime being suspected.

To mourn: Roger knew exactly what suit he would wear to the funeral, a black wool-and-cashmere blend from Brooks Brothers, bought years before. Did it still fit? He went to the closet, tried it on, checked himself in the mirror. Perfect. Still wearing the suit, he returned to the computer. Roger entered none of his thoughts on it, just felt better being near it when there was thinking to do.

A penny. A Chinese penny. Rearrange the pieces: husband, wife, lover, cottage, painting. Was he missing something? Yes: killer. Husband, wife, lover, cottage, painting, killer. Six pieces, four human, two objects. Deep in his brain, Roger felt a slight tectonic shift. These were promising numbers, might be made to work, and this was in all likelihood a fundamentally mathematical problem, as most problems were.

Item six: killer. Almost from the beginning, he had rejected the idea of a contract killer, automatically forcing item six, killer, into congruence with item one, husband. Had he been too hasty? At first he couldn't see why. A contract killer had power over the contractor. Before-the-fact power: what if the contract killer was also an informer, for example, or decided to become one in order to extricate himself from some past or pending legal difficulty the contractor knew nothing about? The contractor thus sets up himself. And after-the-fact power: supposing everything follows plan but sometime in the future the contract killer decides he wants more money or is arrested on some other charge, say another murder, and starts casting about desperately for a deal? The contractor is thus dealt.

But was this flaw so basic that the contract killer idea must be abandoned? The flaw, thought Roger, start by isolating the flaw. Trust, it was a matter of trust. The contract killer could not be trusted. But trust was a factor only in honest relationships. *Rearrange the pieces.* In a dishonest relationship, dishonest now from the contractor's point of view as well as the subcontractor's — yes, that was the proper term, subcontractor; getting the terms right was half the battle — trust was irrelevant. Deep in his brain, he felt a further shift.

What followed from that? His fingers shifted to the keyboard. The urge to make a list was overwhelming. Roger gave in to it, but with great care. No computer, of course, with its memories so hard to erase completely, possessed, like humans, of a kind of subconscious, but pencil and a single sheet of paper, torn from the pad so no impression could be left on the page beneath. Under the heading *Dealing with subcontractor,* he wrote:

1. The contractor is Mr. X. In this scenario, the subcontractor does not know the contractor. Either he is (a) working for a middleman, (b) thinks he is working for someone else, or (c) does not know whom he is working for.

A was out. It merely transferred the flaw of the subcontracting method to someone else. *B* was intriguing. Who could this someone else be? Supposing, as one had to, that the crime was "solved"; then the subcontractor would be arrested, and would eventually lead the police to the person he thought he was working for. This person, this false contractor, would therefore be required to have a plausible motive of his own, or the police would keep looking. *Rearrange the pieces.* Some artist, perhaps, some disappointed artist, one of those scruffy, half-mad types she so often dealt with, is finally rejected once too often? Why not? Roger foresaw procedural difficulties but couldn't see a mistake in the theory, so didn't rule out the artist at once.

Who else would have a motive? The lover's wife, if indeed he had one. Roger toyed with a wild idea of finding this wife, seducing her. What triumph that would be! But not to the purpose. The wife had a motive — enough. He disciplined his mind, running a line through *A,* circling *B,* and ran his eyes down to *C.*

C: does not know whom he is working for. That would mean the subcontractor never meets, talks to, or has written communication with the contractor; ideally does not even suspect the existence of the contractor. The implication: he believes that the crime originates in his own mind!

Oh, this was wonderful, to work so hard, to drive his mind through all these difficulties like an icebreaker. Ice. Roger thought at once of Brenda's cottage, and then of cubes floating in a tumbler of Scotch. Perhaps one little snort would help him think even better. He went upstairs to the kitchen, saw through the barred oval window on the landing that it was day.

And there at the table sipping coffee with a faraway look in her eye sat Francie, wearing a robe. Roger composed his face into friendly upturned patterns — that was essential from now on — and said, "Morning, Francie. Not working today? I thought you were feeling better."

"It's Saturday, Roger."

"So it is." He checked the clock: 9:45, perhaps too early for a drink. He poured himself a cup of coffee instead.

"But you look like you're going somewhere," Francie said.

"I do?"

"Somewhere dressy," she said. "Or a funeral."

Roger glanced down, saw with dismay that he was still wearing his black Brooks Brothers suit. And just as sloppily, he'd left his list on the desk in the basement office. Suppose she'd been in the laundry room, not the kitchen, and wandered in while he was upstairs? "The fact is," said Roger, "I was going to ask you out to lunch."

"With the godfather?"

He made himself laugh, that strange barking sound. But how could it be a normal laugh when he had no desire to take her to lunch at all? And to think how recently he had tried to get into her bed! It suddenly hit him, after the fact, and perhaps harder for that reason, what her state of mind must have been that night. He laughed again, needing some outlet for the hot surge inside him, and said, "That's a good one, Francie — your reference being to the suit again, I take it."

Francie gave him an odd look. *Well, it might be odd, you slut, you whore.* He kept his eyes from veering toward the block of knives on the counter.

"Did you say something?" he said, vaguely aware that she had.

"I said I won't be able to make lunch today, but thanks."

"Otherwise engaged?"

"The tournament," Francie said. "Second round."

He had forgotten that she had indeed been at the tennis club last night, had not lied about that; he sensed gaps in his knowledge, gaps that might undermine his thinking, thinking being no substitute for research. "You won?"

Francie nodded.

"And celebrated long into the night?"

"If you call one whole beer a celebration," Francie said.

He could have killed her easily, right then. "Who's your partner?" he heard himself ask.

"You wouldn't know her."

He busied himself with cream and sugar, mastered his emotions. "Don't be so sure. I've traveled widely in tennis circles, in case you've forgotten."

"Her name's Anne Franklin."

"I knew Bud Franklin — played for Dartmouth. Is she married to Bud?"

"I haven't met her husband."

"Is he in real estate? Bud went into real estate."

"I don't remember what he does. But it wasn't real estate."

C. Back downstairs, Roger had trouble bringing his mind to bear on the problem. How he regretted that night in her bedroom. How hobbled he was by his breeding, education, background. Any bricklayer or welder would have punched wifey in the mouth and raped her on the spot, restoring order. On the other hand, he suddenly thought, what if she was now the carrier of some disease? Maybe he'd been lucky after all.

C. He began to focus. *C: does not know whom he is working for.* Ah, yes. This concerned the subcontractor never communicating with the contractor, ideally not even suspecting his existence. The subcontractor believes the crime originates in his own mind. An elegant concept, but did it have any practical application?

How could there be no communication between contractor and subcontractor? Even a map sent in the mail, or an anonymous call from a phone booth, constituted communication and therefore carried risk. Roger spent an hour on this problem, by the clock, dwelling on hypnosis, confessionals, memory-altering drugs, and other fancies, without finding a viable way of hiding the contractor from the sub. Therefore he must abandon *C* or approach it from a different angle.

A different angle. What was the essence of the idea? Was it the noncommunication of contractor and sub? No. Another tectonic shift, this time a big one. No. The essence of the idea was the subcontractor's belief that the crime originated in his own mind.

Yes.

Roger gazed into the computer, seeing not what was on its screen, the Puzzle Club, but an image of Francie lying dead, the sub standing over her, the police bursting in. Caught in the act and with a guilty mind: nice.

Nice, but in the next instant, Roger had an idea so brilliant, so glittering that it took his breath away. Indeed, for a few moments he couldn't breathe, put his hand to his chest, felt his heart racing, thought he was about to die right there and then, at the worst possible moment, as if Columbus's heart had burst at the first sight of land.

Roger's heart did not burst. Its beat slowed, not quite to normal, but out of the danger zone, and he recovered his breath. Then, too excited to sit, he rose and paced back and forth in the basement office, contemplating his revelation. Francie lies dead, the sub standing over her, yes, but is it the police who come bursting in? No. It is the husband.

The husband: with no record of violence in his past, no criminal record of any kind. But even if he had such a record, would any prosecutor try him for what would happen next, any jury convict? No. The husband, in his rage, in his grief, in a red blackout, could take his vengeance with impunity. He would be a hero. And therefore, to bring C to its conclusion, whatever thoughts the subcontractor had about the arrangement did not matter in the end because he would not live to reveal them.

IQ 181, and possibly that had been an off day. Roger laughed at this joke, not a bark but long, gut-busting hilarity, tears rolling down his face.

The door opened: Francie, folded warm-up suit and other tennis clothes in her hands. He froze.

"Are you all right, Roger?" she said.

"Fine, fine," he said, animating his body. "Just . . . something funny on the Internet."

"Like what?" Francie said, turning to the computer. Roger stepped between them — his list lay by the keyboard — but casually, he made sure of that.

"Oh, it's gone now, gone into space."

"What was it?"

"A . . . a play on words. About ataxia. The more ataxic the state the higher the taxes. That kind of thing."

"I don't get it. What's ataxia?"

"Just a word, Francie, just a word." He rocked back and forth, beaming down at her. "Maybe not that funny after all. Maybe I'm simply in a good mood."

She took another look at the computer, another at him, left the room. Soon after he heard the garage door open and close.

Theoretical phase complete. Now to find the sub. Roger thought right away of the man whose name had come up during the Puzzle Club discussion on capital punishment. He didn't remember all the details of the crime, and the story, related by Rimsky, the prison guard, had been garbled in the telling, interrupted by on-line idiots, and would now indeed have disappeared into space, but the name came to him at once. Perhaps it had lain deep in his mind the whole time, steadying his thoughts like a keel.

All problems were fundamentally mathematical, their solutions wonderfully satisfying: an incoherent sea of data reduced to a simple equation.

Chinese penny = Whitey Truax.

Roger held a match to his list and dropped the flaming paper in the wastebasket.

11

"Got some pornos," said Rey, Whitey Truax's roommate at the New Horizons halfway house. He popped one into the VCR. They watched.

"Turn up the sound," said Whitey.

"The sound? Who gives a fuck about the sound?"

Whitey gave Rey a look. He didn't like Rey. He didn't much like Hispanics anyway, not the ones he'd met inside, and on top of that, what was Rey? A nobody: drunk driver, deadbeat dad, some punk thing like that. Inside, he wouldn't even have dared talk to Whitey. Here he had opinions.

But Rey turned up the sound without another word. They watched some more. "You think those women are real?" Whitey said.

"Real as it gets, Whitey," Rey said. "They're amateurs."

"What's that supposed to mean?"

"Says so right on the box — 'Amateur House-wives, volume fifty-four.' " He flipped Whitey the box.

Real housewives having real sex, Whitey read. *You might see your neighbor.* He watched two amateur housewives entertaining some men by a swimming pool. "They've got tattoos on their tits," he said.

"So?"

"So since when do real housewives have tattoos on their tits?"

"Jesus, Whitey, where have *you* been?"

Of course that pissed Whitey off. He threw the first thing that came to hand — a Pepsi can, full — at Rey. Not playfully, like some frat boy: Whitey didn't have that gear. The Pepsi hit Rey in the face, bounced on the floor, sprayed all over. The door opened and the social worker looked in.

"Boys, what's going on?"

"Little spill," said Rey, dabbing blood on his sleeve. "I'll clean it up."

The social worker's gaze went to the TV. "Adult videos? 'Fraid not, boys — against regulations."

"Innocent mistake," said Whitey. "But seeing as you're here, maybe you could settle something for us."

"What's that?" said the social worker, his eyes on the screen.

"Rey claims those women are real. I say they're not."

"Real, Whitey?"

"He don't believe they're amateurs," said Rey, "even though it says right on the fucking box."

"Is it anything to be angry about, Rey? But I agree with you, there's no reason they couldn't be amateurs — think of how many home video cameras there are in this country."

Whitey was impressed. "Hadn't thought of

that," he said. "Where would you run into one of these amateur housewives?"

"At home, of course," said the social worker with a laugh. Rey laughed, too, and finally Whitey as well.

But because of the memories the joke stirred up in Whitey, there was nothing funny about it. They kept him awake that night, those memories of cottage country.

Whitey and his ma lived in a trailer close to Little Joe Lake, although not close enough for a water view. Little Joe wasn't a big lake — Whitey first swam across at the age of nine — but there were about two hundred cottages, most of them owned by city people who didn't seem to care that it was too small for speedboats and contained no fish worth the trouble. It was a good place to grow up: that's what the locals said. In summer Ma was busy cleaning the cottages. In winter they had the welfare checks. Ma watched TV and drank; Whitey went to school, played on the hockey team, but mostly skated by himself on the frozen lake, sometimes long into the night.

Despite a personal visit by his coach — Whitey had made third team, all-state as a sophomore — he dropped out of school the next autumn. Algebra, history, biology: he was almost nineteen and he'd had enough. That winter he skated on the lake, shot a few birds, got bored. One day, he broke into a cottage, not to take anything but just to see how the city people lived. He liked the way they lived; even more, he liked being inside their cottage — quiet, secret, powerful. He got the feeling that the cottage somehow knew he was there but of course couldn't do a damn thing about it.

Whitey broke into another cottage the next week. This time he took an electric guitar. He tried to teach himself how to play, but that didn't work, so he hocked it for forty bucks in a pawnshop across the Massachusetts line, where no one knew him. He bought a jug of wine, borrowed Ma's heap, took one of the cheerleaders to a spot he knew. But she had signed some nondrinking pledge at her church and wanted to do nothing but talk about the high school kids and the teams and all that shit he'd left behind. Just to snap her out of it, he almost brought her to one of the cottages with the idea of breaking in together, like Bonnie and Clyde. But he didn't — that would have destroyed the secret part; he tried to feel her up instead. She pushed him away; he pushed back, pushing her right out of the car, and drove off.

Whitey broke into cottages, two, three times a week. He was tidy: used a glass cutter to take out a windowpane, puttied it back in place when he was through. No one passing by — a state trooper patrolled once a month or so — would have suspected a thing. You had to go inside to see what was missing: TVs, microwaves, toasters, fireplace screens, golf clubs, cutlery, sleeping bags, tents, record players, scuba gear, crystal glasses, china figurines, rugs, paintings, barbecue grills, canoes, stone carvings, stuffed animals, chess sets, booze. No one knew. The city people didn't come to open up until Memorial Day weekend, at the earliest. With the profits, Whitey bought himself a used pickup, a gold chain, a leather jacket.

Long before Memorial Day — he still had plenty of time to make plans for when the city people did return — Whitey broke into a cottage he had previously ignored. A little cabin, old and run-down, alone on a tiny island at the far end of the lake, connected to the shore by a footbridge.

Snow was falling as Whitey walked across the footbridge, cold, hard flakes blown sideways by the wind; they stung his face in a way he didn't mind at all. Whitey circled the cabin, found a rickety door at the back, took out his glass cutter. But when he pressed it to the pane, the door swung open on its own — not the first unlocked cottage he'd found.

Whitey went inside. He still got that rush, right away, of being inside a living thing that knew but couldn't do shit about it. Besides, it was nice and warm in the cabin, and even quieter than usual, probably because of all the muffling snow.

Whitey moved into the kitchen. Not much there: toaster oven, coffeemaker, china bowl on the table, unopened bottle of gin on the counter. He checked the fridge, as he always did. Usually they were shut off and empty except for baking soda or moldy lemons, but sitting on the top shelf of this one was a cake. A chocolate cake with pink icing flowers, *Happy Anniversary Sue,* and a big pink *One.* He plucked a pink flower, popped it in his mouth, washed it down with a hit of gin. He liked gin.

Whitey went into the living room. Not much there either: brass fireplace set, framed Sacred Heart of Jesus on the mantel, cases full of books, useless to him. He mounted worn stairs to the floor above, looked in on a bedroom: a bed, unmade, more books. Nothing. Not even a TV. He was about to turn and go back down when a door opened inside the bedroom, a cloud of steam floated out, and then a woman — naked, except for the towel wrapped around her head. Her eyes opened wide, her hands went to her mouth, then her breasts. How satisfying was that? And there he was, in the leather jacket, with the gold chain around his neck and the glass cutter in his hand. Whitey knew right then that this was what the rush was all about; this was what he'd been waiting for.

"Hi, Sue," Whitey said. Christ, he was quick, putting it all together like that. He heard a sound like buzzing in his head.

"Truax," called a voice. "Phone."

Whitey sat up in bed. Sunlight in the room, Rey already gone. Morning, but he hadn't slept at all, and nothing but a doctor's note could get

134

him off work — one of the parole conditions. He rose, went to the front hall, picked up the phone.

"Donald?"

"Ma."

"You're in the new place?"

"Yeah."

"How is it?"

"How is it?"

"Nice?"

"Yeah, Ma, nice."

"Well, it has to be a sight better than that other . . ."

In the pause that followed, Whitey heard a clicking sound that might have been her dentures. "Got to get to work, Ma."

"You got yourself a job?"

"Yeah."

"What kind of job?"

"For the municipality."

"My God, Donald. For the municipality?"

"Got to go, Ma."

"But, Donald — when are you coming home?"

"Home?"

"Course, I'm in a different place now. Had to, 'cause of . . . all the fuss."

"I know that."

"But there's plenty of room, for a visit, I'm talking about. And they say there's ice on the river already — I'm on the river, did I tell you? Knowing how much you like the skating — and besides, you haven't met Harry."

"Who's he?"

"My cat. He's the funniest little cat, Donald. Why, the other day —"

"Bye, Ma."

"Good to talk to —"

Whitey speared trash on the median, speared it angrily when he bothered to spear it at all. He was exhausted, robbed of a night's sleep by that dickhead Rey and that asshole social worker. And the fucking sun was hotter than ever. He'd been in Florida for three years now — cheaper for New Hampshire to farm him out for the last part of his sentence — but he hadn't got used to the heat. He saw another bullfrog and didn't even bother; he might have if it had tried something or even looked up at him, but the frog sat there doing nothing. Then a scrap of newspaper drifted by and came to rest against the steel tip of his pole. Glancing down, Whitey saw a baldness ad and above it a short article headlined HOTEL CLERK REMAINS IN COMA. Next to the article was one of those police artist sketches of a man: an ugly son of a bitch who didn't look like him at all, except for the hair. He stabbed the paper and buried it deep in his bright orange trash bag.

12

Wearing his black suit from Brooks Brothers, Roger took a little business trip to Lawton Center, New Hampshire, an old mill town where the mills were all boarded up and the river, a tributary of the Merrimack, flowed through unimpeded, clean and useless, as it had in the past. The river was frozen now. A vacant-eyed boy in a Bruins sweater rattled slapshots off the bridge support as Roger drove across. An ugly town — he didn't care for the countryside either, preferred the south of France to anywhere in New England, anywhere in the United States for that matter. Why not live there? Why not buy a *mas* in the Vaucluse or the Alpilles? No reason at all . . . after. He parked in front of the public library and went inside.

The library had microfilm volumes of the *Merrimack Eagle* and *Gazette* going back to 1817. Roger found the year he was looking for, spooled the roll onto the machine, slowly scrolled his way through the arrest, trial, and sentencing of Whitey Truax.

The first thing he liked was the photograph of Whitey, age nineteen. He had crudely cut hair, very pale, eyebrows paler still, eyelashes invisible, but dark, prominent eyes; and a strong chin, slightly too long. He looked confident, crafty, and stupid: a combination Roger couldn't have improved on if he'd invented the character.

But even better, almost startling, was the photograph of the victim, Sue Savard, accompanying her obituary. She looked like a cheap version of Francie. The resemblance amazed Roger. Staring closely at the woman's image, he could blend it into Francie's in his mind, the way the director in some art film Francie had dragged him to long ago had blended the faces of two actresses. At that moment, Roger realized that writing Francie's obituary would be his responsibility. He quickly sketched it out in his mind, doing a conscientious job, dwelling on her love of art, her contributions to the artistic community, mentioning her tennis in passing. Probably wise to read Nora the rough draft when the time came, in case she had any suggestions. And Brenda, too — no doubt Brenda had a soft spot for him after that business with the lilies.

Photographs: good and better, but best of all were the details of Whitey's crime. Rimsky's Puzzle Club account of the crime on Little Joe Lake, a few miles to the west, had been promising; the *Eagle* and *Gazette* delivered. Whitey had been arrested at his mother's place near the lake within an hour of the event. Sue's husband — and there was a sidebar about him that Roger scanned quickly: a rookie cop in Lawton, apparently, and he'd caused what the paper called a disturbance when they finally brought Whitey to the station in Nashua; but not material, and Roger factored it out — the husband, driving to his cottage to celebrate their anniversary that evening, and thus discoverer of the crime, had passed Whitey's pickup on the way out, and was able to give the police a good description. Whitey's first story was that he'd been passing by the cottage, seen an open door, and gone to investigate, like a good neighbor, so finding the body. When the police asked him why the Savards' toaster oven was in the bed of his pickup, Whitey admitted that he'd gone there to steal but had found the body, already dead. The police then turned to the cuts and scratches on Whitey's hands and face. Whitey should have asked for a lawyer at that point, or long before, but instead again changed his story, now claiming that the woman had attacked him in the course of the robbery, and he had struck out in fear, killing her unintentionally in self-defense. The medical examiner arrived soon after that with his preliminary report that there was evidence of rape, and other outrages not spelled out in the small-town paper. Mrs. Dorothy Truax — the whole discussion had taken place in her trailer — jumped up and shouted that Sue Savard was a well-known whore. Prompted by that cue in a direction his mother hadn't intended, Whitey then said that the woman shouldn't have been wandering around naked in the first place — he wasn't made of stone, after all. If only she hadn't threatened to sic the cops on him, no real harm would have been done. He signed a statement to that effect.

Faced with this confession, Whitey's public defender sent him to a psychiatrist in hope of manufacturing some sort of insanity defense. The psychiatrist did his best, testifying that Whitey's compulsive housebreaking was rooted in a desire to avenge himself for early childhood abuse by his mother, to recover the parts of his personality that had been lost, the form of the residential dwelling, with its narrow doorway leading to a mysterious interior, being essentially female. Further, when an actual female suddenly appeared, the modus of symbolic compensation was instantly destroyed, and Whitey, decompensating rapidly, descended into madness, the rape and murder being the result of an insanity that was necessarily temporary due to the uniqueness of the circumstances.

Whitey's peers on the jury were not persuaded. After a two-hour deliberation, they found him guilty of murder in the first degree as charged. The judge, taking into account Whitey's age, handed out fifteen to thirty years, instead of a life sentence. There was a final photograph of Whitey climbing into a police van, a silly half smile on his face, as though he'd thought of something funny.

Roger switched off the machine, rewound the spool. It was a shabby little library, with no one inside but himself and the librarian at her desk.

She was looking at him now and her lips were moving.

"I said, is there anything I can help you with, sir?"

"Perhaps the local phone book," Roger said.

She brought it to him: a smooth-skinned but gray-haired woman with fingerprint smudges on her glasses. "Looks like quite the winter we've got coming," she said.

"Does it?" said Roger. He glanced out the window, saw hard little snowflakes blowing by. The librarian withdrew.

The uniqueness of the circumstances. What were the circumstances? Cottage, break-in, unexpected presence of a woman. If Whitey's psychiatrist was right, that combination, given his background, had guaranteed the result. Roger inferred that if such a combination were to occur again, and Whitey were introduced into it, he would replay his role, unless he had changed in some fundamental way. And if the psychiatrist's explanation was wrong, Whitey still might come through, for other reasons that might yet be fashioned, especially with that amazing resemblance.

No use speculating. Roger opened the phone book to the Ts, found one Truax: Dot, 97 Carp Road, Lawton Ferry. He found Lawton Ferry on a map, seven or eight miles to the east, on the Merrimack — not far downstream from Brenda's cottage. The details were still unclear, but somehow geography, too, was on his side.

141

Lawton Ferry wasn't one of those picturesque New England towns city people liked to visit; now, mostly hidden under the falling snow, it looked its best. Carp Road ran along a bluff on the west side of the river but took no pleasure in the view, the houses, small and worn, all lining the wrong side of the street. Number 97 was the last house, the smallest and most worn, a peeling box with a single duct-taped window facing the street. Roger drove slowly by, came to a chain-link fence at the end of the road, turned around. A dented minibus with writing on it — LITTLE WHITE CHURCH OF THE REDEEMER — came up the street and parked in front of 97.

The driver climbed out, slid open the passenger door, helped a thin old woman step down. She wore enormous square-shaped sunglasses, carried a white cane. The driver took her arm, led her around the minibus to the recently shoveled walk. There she shook herself free of him and tap-tapped to the front door by herself. The driver, annoyed, got back in the minibus, closed the door hard, made a three-point turn, and drove off while the woman still fumbled with keys.

She opened the door. A cat darted out. The woman disappeared inside.

Roger stayed where he was, parked by the chain-link fence, running the engine to keep warm. After a while, the door to 97 opened slightly and the woman, no longer wearing her sunglasses, stuck her head out. Roger switched off the engine. "Harry," called the woman, "Harry."

Roger could see the cat, foraging in an overturned trash can in her driveway, in plain view from the house. The cat stopped, swiveled its head toward her.

"Harry," she called again, "where are you, you naughty boy?" The cat didn't move. The woman closed the door. The cat crept back into the trash can.

Roger got out of his car, approached the old woman's house, stopped before the trash can, conscious of arriving at the border between theory and practice, between thought and action: his Rubicon. He crossed it without hesitation, saying, "Here, kitty." A fine beginning. The cat emerged at once, tail up. Roger bent down, held out his hand. The cat brushed its whiskers against his skin, laid back its ear. Roger picked it up and carried it, purring, to the house. Cats had always liked him.

He knocked at the door.

"Who is it?" called the woman.

"Missing a cat?" Roger called back.

The door opened. The woman peered out; that is, held her head in the attitude of peering. Her eyes, pale blue irises encircling glazed pupils, seemed to stare over his shoulder. "You've got Harry?" she said.

"If that's the little fellow's name," said Roger.

She put on her sunglasses. "Reason I have to

ask, I can't see, not down the center. Just at the edges a little, if I turn my head like this." She turned her head. Roger covered his face, as though rubbing his brow. "And even then it's no good, all flickering, like when the picture tube is on the fritz. Come to Ma, you bad boy."

Roger put the cat in her arms; it resisted for a moment, digging its claws into the sleeve of his funeral jacket before letting go.

"Naughty boy," she said, stroking it. "God bless you, mister."

"Bless you, too, ma'am." And then his memory reached back to chapel at Exeter for something if not exactly apposite, then at least suggestive: "Better a neighbor that is near than a brother far off."

The woman went still, her head tilted up at him as though searching his face. "You're a Christian?" she said.

"Certainly," Roger said, "although I wouldn't impose my belief on anyone."

"No danger of that here," said the woman. "Jesus is my life."

"Mine as well."

She reached out with her free hand, touched his arm. "Maybe you'd like a cup of tea?"

"No need to go to any trouble," said Roger, looking beyond her to a photograph on the television: Whitey in hockey uniform. "Although I wouldn't mind a chance to wash my hands — Harry gave me a little inadvertent scratch."

"Oh, the bad, bad boy. Come right in. My

144

name's Dorothy, by the way, Dorothy Truax. But you can call me Dot."

"Nice to meet you," said Roger, stepping inside but leaving his own name unspoken. He looked around the tiny room: couch, TV, icebox, hot plate, card table, two folding chairs, sink.

"Bathroom's just down the back," said the woman.

Roger took two steps down a dark corridor and into a bathroom full of unclean smells. He ran the water for a few moments and returned to what the woman no doubt called the parlor. She had plugged in a kettle, was hanging tea bags over the sides of two stained cups, moving with the confidence of a sighted person in her own home.

Water boiled. They sat — Roger at the table, Dot on the couch — drinking tea. Not drinking, in Roger's case. "This hits the spot," he said, reaching his cup toward the sink without rising and pouring the tea slowly and silently down the drain. "Who's the fine-looking hockey player?"

Dot rested her cup on the saucer in her lap. "That would be my son Donald. But everyone called him Whitey practically from day one, no matter what I did."

"Who does he play for?"

"Oh, Donald doesn't play anymore. How could he? That picture's from before all the trouble."

"Trouble?"

"Which was really what drove me into the arms of Jesus, since it was all my fault, according to that wicked doctor. And he must of been right since I've gone blind, too, for my punishment."

"What wicked doctor was this?"

"The psychiatrist at Donald's trial. He said the most disgusting things. What he couldn't understand was that a boy needs discipline, firm discipline, especially after his father run off, and at such an early age."

"Discipline's essential when it comes to children."

"You're so right. You have kids yourself, Mr. — ?"

"A houseful."

She raised her chin, an aggressive chin slightly too long, like her son's. "Then you know they sometimes need the buckle end of a belt to keep them in line, especially suggestible ones like Donald."

"Suggestible?"

"Easily led astray."

"For example?"

"For example? There are examples aplenty. Why else would he have served such a horrible long sentence?"

"You're saying he was manipulated?"

"By everyone, his whole life. Nothing easier than manipulating Donald — on account of he's basically a good person."

Roger, on the verge of asking again for an example of his straying, decided not to push it too hard. Easily led: that was good enough. "He's free now, I take it?" he said.

"If on parole is free. They've got him at the New Horizons House."

"Is that nearby?"

"Of course not. It's in Delray Beach. Just to make things worse they made him finish his time in the stinking heat down in Florida." Her hands squared off into bony little fists.

"What are his plans?" Roger said.

"Do you think he tells me? He never calls, and when I call him he's short with me, so short. Since he heard what that doctor said, things haven't been the same between us." Tears rolled down from under her sunglasses, glistened on her wrinkled face: an unpleasant sight. "Mr. — sir, being as how you're a good Christian, maybe you could see your way clear to helping me now."

"How?"

"Just by praying with me — saying a little prayer for Donald."

Without further warning, the woman fell to her knees on the dusty, threadbare carpet, held out her hands. Roger knelt in front of her, took her hands, ice-cold hands that seized his in a death grip.

"Dear Lord," said Roger, "please hear this prayer for our beloved Whitey —"

"Donald, if you don't mind," the woman interrupted.

"— for our beloved Donald, and help guide

him in useful ways. Amen."

Dot toppled forward on him, sobbing. "Sweet, sweet Jesus, what a beautiful prayer." Her tears wet the side of Roger's face, ran down his neck; he cringed. "So perfect," said Dot, her mouth moving against his shoulder. " 'Guide him in useful ways.' That's all Donald needs, all he's needed his whole goddamn life." She clung to Roger. "You're a preacher, you must be. Praise the Lord." She raised her hands, felt his face with her fingertips. Roger flashed forward to a little scene of Dot Truax doing it again, only this time with him seated in a witness box and a jury watching. He glanced at her scrawny neck, doubtless easy to snap, but that wasn't him, wasn't smart.

"A preacher," the old woman breathed, fingertips still on his face. At the same time, Harry rubbed up against the side of his leg. Roger's skin crawled.

13

Francie, in her office, checked out slides of rain paintings submitted by a new artist. Not paintings of rain but paintings made by rain falling on fast-drying color fields of thick pigment. A gimmick perhaps, and making a statement that had been made many times, but the paintings themselves were strangely beautiful, especially the two deep, roiling blues, *Madagascar* and *Untitled 4*; they reminded her of the primeval soup that all earthly life was supposed to have come from. She was reaching for her loupe to take a better look when her phone rang.

"Hi." It was Ned. "What are you doing this second?"

"Looking at rain paintings." Her heart beat faster right away.

"I thought it would be something like that," he said. There was a silence. "I really just wanted to hear your voice."

The rain paintings, her office, her job, all shrank to insignificance.

"I'm at the studio, but I can't work at all today," Ned said. "Does that ever happen where you are?"

"Yes."

Another silence, thick with tension like that of desire, at least in her mind, and then: "I keep thinking about you — something you did once, in particular."

"What?"

He lowered his voice. "Something you did to me. We did together. At the cottage."

In his mind, too. Francie's heart beat faster still. "What was it?"

"You don't remember?"

"Stop teasing me."

He laughed. "Say you love me. Then I'll tell."

"You know I do."

"But say it."

"I love you," Francie said.

The door opened and Roger walked in. Francie felt the blood draining from her face as though a plug had popped out the bottom of her heart. Had he heard? For a moment, he stood very still at the door, his eyes on her — a very brief moment. Then he was raising his hand and fluttering his fingers in a delicate little greeting that wasn't him at all. At the same time, Ned was saying, "I dream about it sometimes. Don't you remember the first time you ever —"

"I'll have to get back to you on that," Francie said.

"Someone's there?" said Ned.

"As soon as I see the report," Francie said. Roger was walking around the office, examining things with interest. "Talk to you then."

"I hope they didn't —"

She hung up.

"Some big mover and shaker?" said Roger, sitting in one of the chairs opposite her desk.

"What?"

He nodded to the phone. "In the art world."

"No," said Francie. "What brings you here?"

"Can't hubby pay a visit to wifey's work-place?"

But why now? It had never happened before. She looked at him closely, trying and failing to penetrate the facetiousness, the big smile, to discover if he had indeed heard anything as he came in the door. All at once the lying, the subterfuge, and maybe most of all her talent for it, made her sick. She rose, almost stumbling, mumbled something about the bathroom, hurried out.

In the cubicle, Francie stood over the toilet for a few moments. Her nausea ebbed. She went to the sink, splashed cold water on her face. A pale face, she saw in the mirror, and the eyes troubled. Yes, she hated the lying, but she wanted love — was that too much to ask? And even if she didn't, it was too late. She was in love, close to the kind of love the poets wrote of, love that took away hunger, that focused the mind, waking and sleeping, on the loved one; a kind of love that turned out to be not just a literary conceit but real, after all.

Francie returned to her office. Roger was standing by the desk, talking on the phone. "Oh, here she is," he said. "Nice talking to you, too. I'm sure we will." He handed Francie the phone.

"Hello?" she said.

"Francie? Anne here. They want to reschedule

our match for tomorrow, same time."

"No problem."

"Great," said Anne. "I think I just met your husband."

"You did."

"I didn't catch his name."

"Roger," said Francie, looking at him. He smiled.

"He sounds so nice."

"Remember Bob Fielding?" asked Roger, gazing out the window of Francie's office. "And you've got a view."

"No," said Francie.

"Sure you do. Used to be with Means, Odden. Now he's running his own place in Fort Lauderdale."

Francie had a vague memory of whiskey breath and air kisses that always managed to land. "Maybe I do."

"You must. Can't forget a character like Bob Fielding. The fact is, he's doing very well. And there just might be something appropriate for me down there."

"Have you talked to him?"

"I'm way ahead of you," Roger said. "My flight leaves in a couple hours, if you don't mind giving me a ride to the airport."

Francie drove him to the airport. He seemed happier these days, indeed almost happy; it had been years. She caught a glimpse of a civilized end: Roger working in Fort Lauderdale; she, in

Boston — he would never expect her to leave her job; Em reaching the age where Ned would consider divorce.

Francie dropped Roger in front of the terminal. "Good luck," she called through the open window as he walked away, garment bag over his shoulder, briefcase in hand. An affecting figure, she thought at that moment, even brave, and she felt a sick little stab beneath her heart.

Roger turned. "Luck is not a factor," he said. A gust of wind caught the skirts of his open trench coat and raised them behind him like wings.

Roger's first flight — discounting babe-in-arms vacations to the Caribbean, London, Paris — his first conscious flight had been from Logan to Palm Beach at the age of six. Some of the excitement of that day, long worn away by the tedium and annoyance of countless flights since, returned to him now as he sat in a window seat and watched the earth recede. He ordered a Scotch, but just one, and came very close to talking to his neighbor.

A smooth beginning: landing on time in Miami, renting a car, meeting Bob Fielding in his dismal office. Bob hadn't heard Roger was no longer with Thorvald and asked *him* for a job, but no matter: this was all a play, a fiction designed for the day, if it ever came, when he could swear under oath and prove beyond a reasonable doubt that, yes, he had flown to Miami but, no, not for any illegal, to say nothing of deadly, purposes — only to feel out a former colleague about the possibility of a job, as Bob Fielding would attest. Bob Fielding: long forgotten, but still, a piece on the board, to be rearranged. IQ 181 — on a bad day. Roger hurried down to his car and drove north to Delray Beach.

Fucking mosquitoes. They'd moved the highway crew west, onto 441, practically in the Everglades. Clouds of mosquitoes rose up whenever Whitey jabbed at the grass with his steel-tipped pole, whining around his head, tormenting him. Plus the heat and the humidity were too fucking much. He was tired of sweating that clammy sweat every time he moved, of the sun burning down on the back of his neck. And then there was the threat of AIDS. Rey said you couldn't get AIDS from a mosquito, but why not? Would you bite someone that had AIDS? No. Getting bit by a mosquito that had bitten an AIDS victim was the same thing. Ever seen the blood when you squish a mosquito? he'd asked Rey. Could be anybody's blood, the blood of some ninety-pound faggot junkie on his deathbed. Whitey swatted at one now, just after it got him right on the face, and examined the palm of his hand: crushed mosquito parts in a red smear. "Fuck," he called out aloud. "Fuck, fuck, fuck." There was no one to hear, the traffic being light, car windows all rolled up against the heat.

A Lexus went by, then a Benz and a Porsche. Whitey stabbed a scrap of aluminum foil, dropped it in the bright orange plastic bag. "Done much thinking about your future?" the social worker had asked the day before.

"Fuck," said Whitey. "Fuck, fuck, fuck." He was too busy spearing trash, swatting mosquitoes, and being angry about the future to notice the car pulling to the side of the road behind him. The opening and closing of the door didn't really register either — what was he trained to do? fuck all; society had completely failed him — and it was only when a voice, a male voice, educated and polite, said, "Excuse me, sir," that Whitey turned.

Sir? Whitey couldn't remember ever being called sir before, certainly not by anyone like this: a tall man, almost as tall as Whitey, with dark hair cut in a distinguished way like that black-and-white actor, the name didn't come to him, smooth skin, an expensive black suit. "Me?" said Whitey.

The man smiled. "Maybe you can help me," he said, producing a map. "I'm a little lost."

"Where you headed?" said Whitey as the man came closer, donning rimless glasses, unfolding the map. A banknote fell out, fluttered to the ground, where a sudden breeze caught it, rolled it over, threatened to carry it away. Without thinking, Whitey speared the bill, raised it up on the steel tip. "Dropped something," he said, and saw what it was: a one-hundred-dollar bill.

The man plucked it off the steel tip with thumb and index finger, said: "How the heck did that get there?"

Whitey thought, *Plenty more where that came from.* Sharp thinking, because the next second the man was returning the bill to his money clip — a money clip, not a mere wallet, and gold besides — and Whitey saw them, thick and green. Whitey took all that in from the corner of his eye, crafty, unnoticed.

"Thanks," said the man, tucking the money clip into his right front pocket; Whitey made sure to note the exact location, although he had no idea what he was going to do with the information. "Now, what I'm looking for," said the man, frowning at the map, "is Abner and Sallie's Alligator Farm. It's supposed to be around the junction of . . ." His voice trailed off.

A rich guy, maybe, but not very bright. Whitey could see the back of the sign for the turnoff to the alligator farm about two hundred yards away; the man had driven right past it. "The alligator farm?" said Whitey. "That's a bit tricky."

"I was afraid it would be," said the man.

Whitey paused, quickly scanning the man's face again, confirming his first impression: an innocent. "Tell you what," he said. "How about I just hop in with you, make it easy, like."

"I couldn't really ask that," said the man.

Whitey wasn't sure what that sentence meant. "Meaning I'll guide you there," he said.

The man laughed, a strange barking laugh that

Whitey didn't get and forgot about almost at once. "That's very good of you," the man said, "but I couldn't take you away from your work."

"Not a problem," said Whitey, "long as I'm back at five."

The man checked his watch, a Rolex — Whitey had seen them in *Playboy* — and said, "I guarantee it. And I'll pay you for your time . . ."

"Yeah?"

". . . Mr. . . ."

"Whitey" — Christ, maybe having his real name out there wasn't such a good idea, especially if this guy ended up getting rolled, or something — "Reynoso." Rey's last name.

The man held out his hand. "Pleased to meet you, Mr. Reynoso. Everyone calls me Roger."

They shook hands, got in the car. A brown leather jacket, soft and luxurious, lay on the front seat. Whitey lifted it carefully and thought of the leather jacket he'd had long ago, leatherette, actually. "Here's your jacket."

"Not mine," said Roger, starting the car. "Belonged to my assistant — former assistant. Just toss it in the back."

Whitey tossed it in the back and said, "That way," and Roger drove back up the highway. A nice car, with sunroof, CD player, cell phone. "Hang a right," said Whitey, and Roger — a cautious driver, Whitey saw, both hands on the wheel, back straight, eyes on the road — swung onto the turnoff. The road narrowed from two-lane blacktop to one, the blacktop turned to dirt, huge ferns and other growths Whitey didn't have names for closed in from above, and then they were at a barbed-wire gate on which hung a sign: WELCOME TO ABNER AND SALLIE'S ALLIGATOR FARM. OBSERVE ALL RULES.

"You certainly know your way around," said Roger. "Are you from this area, Mr. Reynoso?"

"Hey, call me Whitey," said Whitey. And: "No." Giving him that much, but not actually divulging where he was from, playing it close to the vest.

"Where are you from, if you don't mind my asking?"

"New . . ." Whitey was going to say New Mexico, then remembered something about the best lie being close to the truth, and thinking what the hell, said, "Hampshire. New Hampshire."

"No kidding," said Roger.

"You're from New Hampshire, too?"

"I have interests there," said Roger.

Interests — Whitey liked the sound of that, wanted to know more. "Interests?" he said.

But maybe that was too subtle, because Roger said, "And what brought you down here?"

"Well, Florida, you know," said Whitey.

"The climate?"

"Yeah, the climate," said Whitey, although he hated it. "And the mosquitoes," he added, a remark that just popped out.

Roger laughed his strange laugh. "You've got a sense of humor, unlike . . ." He didn't finish the sentence, but somehow Whitey knew he was talking about the former assistant. The jacket must have been almost new: Whitey could smell the leather. "I like a sense of humor," Roger said.

"Me, too," said Whitey. He tried to remember a joke he'd heard about a rabbi, a dildo, and a parrot, but before he had it clear in his mind, an enormous woman with thighlike upper arms poking out of her tent dress came to the other side of the gate. Roger slid down the window.

"You all for the gator show?" she said.

"Yes," said Roger. Whitey thought for a moment about his job, but as long as he was at his post for the five o'clock pickup he was fine, and it was only three-thirty; besides, he'd never seen a gator show.

"Four bucks apiece, 'stead of five. On account of no rasslin' today."

"I beg your pardon?" said Roger.

"No gator rasslin'. My husband's the rassler, and he's with the lawyer right now." She leaned on the car; it rocked under her weight. "The environmentalists, they got a court order to stop the rasslin'. For 'protecting the health and safety' of the gators. Of the gators! Ever rassled a gator, mister?"

"No," said Roger, handing her money, his nose narrowing as though he were trying to cut off the sense of smell.

"Well, I sure as hell have — where you think I got this scar? — and I can tell you it ain't the gators need protectin'. Park it in the lot and stay on the people side of the fence."

She opened the gate. Roger drove into a dusty little yard, parked beside the only other car, a rusted-out Chevy on blocks. A few feet beyond it stood four or five rusted rows of bleacher seats, and beyond that lay a ditch, filled with algae-crusted water and lily pads, and fenced in with ten-foot-high chain-link. Six alligators, five of them between eight and twelve feet long, the sixth a baby, lay motionless on the far bank.

Roger and Whitey sat in the bleachers, read the rules — *Positively No Feeding, Do Not Stick Fingers Thru Fence, No Teasing* — watched the gators. The sun was hot, the air full of small, sharp-edged flying things, the gators still. After only a minute or two, Whitey's shirt was sticking to his back; he noticed that Roger, in his black suit, didn't seem to be feeling the heat at all.

For no reason that Whitey could see, the baby gator suddenly rose up and made his way to the ditch. It stood at the edge, seemed to be looking at Whitey and Roger, the only spectators across the way, then slid into the water and disappeared.

"Cute little bugger," said Whitey.

Silence. Roger was staring at the water. Whitey was just about to say "cute little bugger" again when Roger turned to him. Whitey realized for the first time that there was something about Roger's gaze that made him reluctant to meet it; in fact, he couldn't. "You seem like a bright guy," Roger said. Whitey looked modest. "So let me ask your advice on something."

"Like what?"

"Maybe it's even happened to you."

"What has?" said Whitey, starting to lose the thread. A frog croaked nearby; Whitey spotted it, a big bullfrog, even bigger than the one he'd speared on I-95, sitting on a lily pad.

"Reducing it to the simplest possible terms," said Roger, "did anyone ever take something valuable from you?"

"Not that I can remember." But then Whitey thought of his freedom, and wasn't sure.

"You're a lucky man," said Roger. "But suppose someone did. What would you do?"

"Like what kind of thing?"

"Call it a work of art."

"Get it back, of course," said Whitey. "I'd go after the fucker and get it back."

"And which is more important?"

"Huh?"

"Of the two. Revenge or recovery of the object?"

Whitey felt Roger's gaze on his face, suddenly knew the word for what this was — networking, or maybe mentoring. In any case, he knew this was an important question. Revenge or recovery of the object: he tried to sort out the terms. The right answer, from his point of view, was to go after the fucker. Who gave a shit about art? On the other hand, maybe Roger was the type who

161

did give a shit about art.

"That's a tough one," Whitey said, searching Roger's face for some clue. Their eyes met, and Whitey turned away, again unsettled by looking into Roger's eyes, and as he turned, he saw the baby gator surfacing in a patch of lily pads, weeds trailing off its snout. Eeny meeny minie moe, said Whitey to himself, eeny being revenge and meeny recovery. Recovery won.

"The art," said Whitey, and could see from Roger's nod, a satisfied nod, as though he'd expected Whitey to do well all along, that he'd guessed right. "Recovery of the art," Whitey said, "every goddamn time."

"My former assistant thought otherwise," Roger said.

"He did, huh?" said Whitey, shaking his head.

The baby gator glided over to the bullfrog's lily pad. A green blur, some splashing, and then the bullfrog's legs were dangling from the baby gator's mouth. The baby gator submerged.

"He is a cute little bugger," Roger said. "Awakens old, old memories."

"Oh yeah? Like what?"

"I wouldn't want to bore you," Roger said.

"Hey, you're not boring me, Rog, I swear."

Roger's face tightened, for no reason Whitey could see, as though he'd felt a sudden pain. He glanced at Whitey — again Whitey looked away — and went on. "I brought one like him home the first time I ever went to Florida, with my aunt. I was six years old."

"So you're not from here?" But Whitey knew that already from the way Roger said "not," just like he did.

"Can you guess what happened?" Roger said, maybe not hearing the question.

"It escaped?"

"A good guess, Whitey, a very good guess. But no. My parents didn't let me keep it. They made me give it to the zoo."

"I know just how you feel," Whitey said. "Same thing happened to me with a weasel. Only it wasn't the zoo. My ma just made me let it go, back in the woods."

"Did she?"

"You don't know my ma — that's her through and through."

"This was in New Hampshire?"

Whitey saw no other course but to admit it. He nodded.

"You know your way around the woods up there?"

"Shit yeah, Rog. I grew up like that goddamn what's-his-name."

"Natty Bumppo?"

"Never heard of him. It'll come to me."

But nothing came. The baby gator appeared on the far side of the ditch, climbed out, lay with his elders in the sun; no sign of the bullfrog. Roger said, "My former assistant didn't."

"Didn't what?" said Whitey, who was thinking of his own bullfrog, and the crown-shaped ring of blood on its bumpy green head.

163

"Didn't know his way around the woods."

"No, huh?" Whitey conceived a brilliant question: "What were his qualifications, anyway?"

"Not the right ones, evidently. Do you know that saying about law and sausages, Whitey?"

"Law and sausages?"

"You don't want to look too closely at how either of them is made. My work's a bit like that."

Law and sausages. Whitey didn't get it. Was Roger trying to tell him he was a tough guy or something — dangerous? Whitey couldn't see it. He, Whitey, was tough and dangerous — he thought of that stupid whore and her pimp with the baseball bat, and what had happened to them. Or was Roger trying to tell him that the assistant had to be tough and dangerous? Or maybe —

Roger checked his watch, his Rolex, stood up. "Better get you back to your post," he said. "Wouldn't want to put your job in jeopardy, would we?"

"Well, the thing is —" said Whitey, but Roger was already walking away and didn't seem to hear.

Roger pulled over at the side of 441. He turned to Whitey, who'd been smelling the leather coat in the backseat, again gave him that look that seemed to see deep inside. "I said I'd pay you for your time." And there was a one-hundred-dollar bill — not the same one, because there was no hole — held out for him. He

164

was thinking all kinds of things to say, like it's too much, and I didn't really earn it, but while he was in the middle of thinking them, he grabbed it.

Roger smiled.

Whitey opened the door, started to get out. But how could he let this go without at least trying? What was there to lose? "This assistant thing," he said, "are you looking for a replacement?"

Roger raised his eyebrows in surprise. "I hadn't really thought about it yet." He seemed to be thinking about it now, staring into the distance. "I'd need someone more discreet this time," he said. "Discretion is the sine qua non in this business."

That threw Whitey, and he licked his lips a couple of times before saying, "You never said what the business is exactly."

"I thought I had," said Roger, sounding disappointed in him for the first time. "It's the recovery of valuable objects."

"Such as what?"

"Paintings, shall we say."

"Like that someone's stolen?"

"Precisely like that."

The DPW truck came into view, shimmering on the horizon.

Now or never. "I want the job," Whitey said.

"Do you —"

"Swear to God."

"— know the meaning of discretion, Whitey?"

"It means no questions and keep your fuckin' mouth shut."

Roger nodded. He scribbled a number on his alligator farm ticket stub. "Call me tomorrow. We'll set up an interview."

Whitey stuffed the ticket stub and the money in his pocket, got out of the car. A job interview: he'd never had one. This was the big time.

The DPW truck dropped Whitey at the depot. He caught the number 62 bus, reached the stop a block from New Horizons at five to six. He was almost out the rear door, had one foot on the pavement, when he saw the cop car parked up the street. Did that mean anything? No. But he said, "Oops," like he'd almost gotten off at the wrong stop, and stepped back on the bus. The driver, watching in his mirror, muttered something Whitey couldn't hear.

The bus drove on, picked up speed, approached New Horizons. Whitey saw a cop on the sidewalk, talking to the social worker. As the bus drew closer, Whitey saw that the cop was showing something to the social worker, a piece of paper. And as the bus went right by, within a few feet of them, Whitey saw what it was: the artist's composite, with nothing right except the fucking hair. Whitey stayed on the bus.

Roger was sleeping the deepest sleep he'd had in a long time when the phone rang. He fumbled for it in the darkness of the strange room, answered.

"Rog? It's me, Whitey Tru— Whitey Reynoso. I'm calling like you said."

"But it's four in the morning."

"Kind of anxious to get started, is all."

Was he drunk? Stoned? Planning some scheme of his own? Was this not going to work, after all?

"Rog? You still there?"

"Yes."

"So maybe you could come and pick me up."

"Where are you?"

"On 441, of course. Where you picked me up before."

Was he armed? Alone? His voice was full of impending surprise. "Very well," said Roger.

His motel room had a kitchenette. Roger took the biggest knife from the drawer, hid it under the seat of his rented car, drove out to 441. Could he kill Whitey? Certainly. There was a deep, violent well of hatred in him, as he was sure there was in most people; he'd known it since boyhood. It made war possible, and perhaps all human civilization. The only problem was scheduling: Whitey wasn't supposed to die yet.

Roger came to the spot where he'd found Whitey, saw a lone man in the headlights, slowed down, slow enough to bring any overeager accomplices out of the bushes, slow enough to see that Whitey was holding some sort of bundle, slow enough to hear him cry, "Hey, it's me," as Roger went by.

A few hundred yards beyond, Roger made a U-turn and drove back. He stopped the car, one hand on the knife. Whitey came out of the shadows, opened the passenger door, got in. His eyes were bright. "Hi, Rog. Had me concerned there for a minute. Here. I brought you something."

Roger inched the knife out from under the seat. Whitey laid the bundle between them: something wrapped in a denim jacket. "Open it, why don't you?"

With his free hand, Roger opened the jacket — and there was the baby gator, its mouth fastened shut with packing tape. Roger felt Whitey's gaze on him, waiting for his reaction.

"You've done well, Whitey, very well."

Whitey laughed with delight. "Feisty little bugger, that gator, let me tell you."

"Not an alligator, actually," Roger said. "It's a crocodile — you can tell from the angulation of the jaw."

"Whatever. Tore my jacket to shreds. My only jacket."

Roger silently counted three and said, "You can have the one in back."

"Cool," said Whitey, donning the leather jacket right away. It felt great. The gator watched with its slitty yellow eyes.

14

"Any hints?" asked Anne, eyeing their opponents across the net as the players took their serves before the top-bracket semifinal of the club championships.

Francie checked them out: two wiry women wearing elbow braces and knee pads. She thought she recognized the taller one from her college days; she'd played for Brown, or possibly UConn — a distant memory, no more than a fragment, but unpleasant.

"How was your overhead in the warm-up?"

"I didn't make a single one," said Anne with alarm. "You think they're going to lob us?"

"To death," said Francie.

Francie was right. The wiry women, tireless, unsmiling, grim, fed them — Anne particularly, as they saw her game begin to fall apart — junk, chips, dinks, lobs; they served conventional, Australian, from the I, even both back for a point or two; and they called the lines very close. First set: 6–2, the 2 coming on Francie's serve.

On the changeover, while the wiry women iced their elbows and knees, Anne turned her flushed face to Francie and said in a low voice, "I'm so sorry. They're hitting every ball to me and I'm playing like shit."

Francie put her hand on Anne's knee, felt it

trembling. "First of all," she said, "it's only tennis. Second, it's not over." She leaned forward, spoke in Anne's ear. "This set we're going to do a little lobbing of our own."

"Will that work?" Anne asked. Francie saw the blue disk of her eye in profile, inches away: still, waiting for the response.

"At least those fucking knees of theirs are going to ache tonight," she said. The blue disk brightened, bulged slightly; Anne laughed.

She laughed, but her game did not come back, at least not right away. Her lobs were short, and the wiry women proved adept at putting them away, one of them grunting an annoying little "Ho!" on every overhead. Francie and Anne fell behind 1–3, 1–4.

Anne's serve. "This isn't working," she said as Francie handed her the balls.

"Any other ideas?" said Francie.

"No," Anne replied, her face pinker than ever. Francie watched a vein throbbing in her forehead. She wanted to say *forget whatever's fucking up your mind and just play*. Instead she glanced across the net, saw the opposition waiting restlessly on the other side, eager to get on with the demolition.

"Go with your second serve," she told Anne.

"What good will that do? They're clobbering my first."

"Probably none, but try it."

Anne tried it. The wiry women, fooled by the change of pace, netted the first two returns. On the next two, they were ready and hit aggressive crosscourt shots, but Francie poached on both and put them away, the second drilling a padded knee and drawing an angry glare — unintentional, on Francie's part, but somewhere in her heart, she said *yes*. 2–4.

Anne's lobs grew stronger and deeper in the next game, forcing the wiry women to scramble in the backcourt for the first time in the match. Now Francie and Anne were making the easy putaways. 3–4. Francie's serve. Four all. Francie and Anne then broke serve again, but Anne, serving for the set, double-faulted twice. Both sides held after that and they went to a tiebreak.

A long tiebreak, full of jittery errors on both sides, kept alive by an outrageous out call on the far baseline that brought a surprisingly furious look to Anne's face. 7–7. "Can you believe that call? It was in by a foot."

"Anne?"

"Yes?"

"Just win this point."

Their eyes met. Francie thought she saw through the doubtful outer person to a stronger one inside. Anne nodded.

Next serve to Francie, a spinner into the body. She hit a weak return, picked off at the net, angled at Anne's feet. But Anne made one of her miraculously quick reflexive shots, catching the ball on her racket, deflecting a soft lob, her best of the match, over outstretched racquets on the other side, landing indisputably within the lines for a winner.

"Beautiful," said Francie, suddenly filled with the feeling — rare for her, but the greatest pleasure the game had to give — that she could do anything she liked with the ball.

She took two of them from Anne, put one in her pocket, bounced the other a few times, tossed it up, bent her knees. The ball reached the top of its arc and seemed to pause. With all the time in the world, Francie hit it in the bottom right quadrant as hard as she could: an ace down the middle.

"Oh, yes, Francie."

Match tied at one set apiece.

But it was really over, probably decided somewhere in the middle of the second set, perhaps at the moment Francie volleyed the ball off that padded knee. Francie and Anne began playing better and better; the wiry women, their soft game beaten, had no fallback. In what seemed like a few minutes, Francie and Anne went up 5–0, 40–15 in the third set.

Anne serving at match point. To the backhand. One last lob, a good one, over Francie's head. She went back to take it, calling, "Got it."

Anne came across behind her: "Mine."

"Got it."

"Mine."

They were both in midswing when Francie ran her over. A cry of pain from Anne; their racquets collided — but somehow struck the ball, which arced toward the net, ticked off the tape, and dropped untouched on the other side. Game, set, match.

Anne lay on the court, face ashen, lips blue. She sat up, tried to rise, could not. Francie knelt beside her. "What hurts?"

"Ankle. What if I can't go on?"

"Don't have to. We won."

"That went over?"

"Yup."

Anne made a fist, almost pumped it.

Francie sat on the court, gently removed Anne's shoe, rolled off her sock, and supporting the weight of Anne's leg in her lap, examined the ankle.

Shadows loomed over them. "Did you hear a cracking sound?" said one of the wiry women, not quite hiding her satisfaction.

"More like a little rip," Anne said.

Francie looked at the wiry women pursing their lips. "Nice match," she said, reached up to shake hands, and asked them to send someone from the desk. They went away. Anne was gazing up at her. "You'll be okay by Saturday," Francie said.

"You think?"

"I've done that ripping number a hundred times. We're going to win this goddamn tournament."

Color began returning to Anne's face.

But it was her right ankle, and she couldn't

drive. Francie and the desk attendant helped her out to the parking lot, and Francie drove her home in Anne's car.

"I hate to inconvenience you like this," Anne said. "My husband will drive you back the minute he gets home."

"No trouble," Francie said. "Got anything to drink? Beating a pair like that's worth a celebration."

"I never thought we could. You were so cool out there, Francie."

"I like to compete," Francie said. True, but not the kind of remark she'd normally make, possible now only with the endorphins flowing through her brain.

"And you were serving so hard — just like Nora."

"That turns out not to be a compliment," Francie said. She explained Nora's Newtonian theory of big hips and hard hitting.

Anne laughed and said, "You know you've got a great body."

"I most certainly do not."

"Come on — men on the other courts are always looking at you. That's never happened to me in my whole life."

Anne lived in Dedham, a small Federal house with a big lawn, not far from the green. Leaning on Francie, she limped up the shoveled walk, unlocked the door. They moved into a little hall, with cut flowers — irises — in a vase beside the mail and a stack of audiotapes. "I'll get ice," Francie said, seeing the kitchen straight ahead.

A bright kitchen, with three places set on the table and a note stuck to the fridge: *Anne — I'll handle dance pickup. Back at 8.* A note probably written early that morning; Anne's husband would be tired, in no mood for more driving. Francie checked her watch: twenty minutes to. She opened the freezer, found an ice pack under a container of rocky road ice cream, took it to the living room.

Anne sat in a corduroy-covered chair, her leg up on a footstool. The ankle was more swollen now, but Francie had seen worse. She laid the ice pack on it.

"You're an angel," said Anne.

"Does it hurt?"

"No. There's some wine in the cabinet over the sink, but I don't think it's very good."

"Let's save it for Saturday night," said Francie, picking up the phone.

"What are you doing?"

"Calling a cab."

"Please don't," said Anne, glancing out into the darkness. "They'll be home any minute."

Francie started dialing.

"Please. I feel guilty enough already."

Francie paused for a moment, then gave in. She hung up the phone, poured Romanian wine for both of them, sat on the couch.

"To victory," said Anne.

They drank a toast to victory.

Paintings hung on Anne's walls, all but one framed reproductions, of no interest to Francie. The one original, partly obscured by a desk lamp, was a still life of a bowl of grapes. She thought at once of *oh garden, my garden.* This painting had none of its resonance, but the technical skill of the artist was as high, perhaps higher: the grapes glistened, as though they'd just been washed.

"I like that painting," Francie said.

"You do?"

"Who's the artist?"

"Well," said Anne, "the fact is, me. Although I wouldn't say artist."

Francie rose, took a closer look at the painting, liked it even more. *A.F.* was painted in a bottom corner, almost too small to read. "Tell me more," she said.

"Like what?"

"Where you learned to paint. What other stuff you've done. Et cetera."

"I can't say I ever really learned. And I haven't done anything in years, Francie."

"How come?"

Anne shrugged. "Family life." Her gaze turned inward. "And I guess I got discouraged." She brightened. "But are you really telling me you like it?"

"I am."

"That means a lot. The truth is I'm so jealous of you. I'd kill for a job like yours, Francie."

"I'm not an artist," Francie said.

"Neither am I."

"Don't be so sure. I'd like to see more."

Anne thought. "They're all packed away in the basement," she said. "Except one I did of my husband, just after we got married. My last real effort, now that I think of it."

"Where is it?"

"In the bedroom. You can go up. First door on your right."

Francie went into the hall, climbed the stairs, entered the first room on the right. A bedroom, with a king-size bed, and over it, in oil, the head of a dark-eyed young man, all greens and browns, edged in white. Not as good as the grapes in technique, but it resonated more — whether because of Anne's artistry or the subject's resemblance to Ned, Francie didn't know. An astounding likeness, not photographic, but in affect, and perhaps all the more powerful for that reason. It froze Francie on the spot, there at the foot of Anne's bed. She stared at the painting, unaware of time, unaware of anything until a car door slammed, close by.

Francie hurried downstairs, through the hall, into the living room. Anne looked up with a smile. "Find it okay?"

"Yes. Anne —"

"And what did you think? I've never been that happy with it, but it's Em's favorite for some reason."

"Em?"

"Emilia. My husband started calling her Em, and it stuck."

Francie heard the front door open.

"Speak of the devil," Anne said.

15

A nightmare that began with cute domestic touches.

"Honey, I'm home," called Ned in a parody of a sitcom-daddy voice. Not someone who sounded like him, but Ned: beyond doubt.

And a girlish voice responded, "Dad. Don't be such a dork."

Francie, motionless in Anne's living room, her motionlessness that of the dreamer desperate to flee the nightmare but suddenly paralyzed in every muscle, heard the words, heard Ned's voice, and Emilia's, Em's — Em, Em, Em, a warning often sounded, completely missed — heard their voices strangely distorted, as though all sounds but the highest treble and deepest bass had been eliminated. Visual distortion came, too. Colors — the walls, the rug, Anne's face — veered toward yellow.

"In here," Anne called back, her eyes brightening. She glanced at Francie with the expectant look of someone about to introduce people certain to like each other, about to bring two positive components of her life together. Francie felt blood rushing to her throat, her cheeks; she blushed like the kind of schoolgirl she'd never been.

Footsteps in the hall. All her senses, all her

thoughts in turmoil, Francie glimpsed her face in the mirror over the fireplace. She looked normal, even composed. No trace of a blush, no discomfort, completely cool. How was that possible? She should have beheld an image of terror and shame. Then Ned walked into the room, his daughter, Emilia, Em — with his dark eyes, his erect posture — at his side. He saw Francie, stopped dead, went white: horrified. Horrified for all to see.

Anne saw. "It's not as bad as it looks, Ned," she said. "Just a sprain. Please don't worry. And the great thing, the important thing, is we won the match."

"The match?" Ned said.

"We're in the finals! Ned, this is Francie, my new tennis partner. Francie, my husband, Ned."

Their eyes met. Ned tried to hide what was going on within, but he couldn't do that from Francie. She saw horror — his first thought must have been that Anne knew all, the second perhaps that Francie had had some kind of breakdown and come to confess — give way to confusion. Neither moved to close the space between them, to shake hands. Francie spoke first. "Hello," she said, not coming near the right note, unable to remember how to say hello to someone for the first time.

"Nice to meet you," he said, also hitting it wrong, and adding a faltering little smile that was off target as well.

Francie, aware of Anne's glowing face, almost a caricature of enthusiasm, tried to think of something to say. She met people all the time, always knew what came after *hello* and *nice to meet you*. But this time nothing did. There was no light remark, no easy meaningless flow. The room and everyone in it grew yellower and yellower, and the urge to bolt from it grew as well, almost overwhelming her. At the same time an inane phrase — *nice to meet you, too* — readied itself in her mind. But *nice to meet you, too* was playacting, a lie. She didn't want to say it, not unless she absolutely had to, didn't want to smile and be a villain; she just wanted to get out. The silence went on and on. Surely Anne, so sensitive to atmosphere, would notice, would feel the awkwardness.

"Well, then," Ned said. "I guess congratulations are in order. As long as you're not really hurt. Sweetheart."

"I'm fine," Anne said, somehow missing not only the silence, the awkwardness, but also the fact that while Ned was speaking to her, while he was saying *sweetheart,* his eyes were still on Francie. "Never better, in fact. Winning a match like that — and it was all thanks to Francie — is just so . . ." Words failed her. "How would you put it, Francie?"

All eyes moved to her. Her tennis self took over, rescuing her. "We haven't won anything yet," she said automatically.

"You see, Ned?" said Anne with delight.

"That's my partner, right there. Just like Vince Lombardi."

"Thanks," Francie said, and Anne started laughing at the way she said it, but she was the only one.

"Who's Vince Lombardi?" Em said.

The question was directed at Ned. He licked his lips and quoted: " 'Winning isn't everything, it's the only thing.' "

"Puke," said Em, glancing at Francie to see if she really thought like that. Francie caught the glance — this was a child she could like; at the same time, she was aware of the proud paternal smile that flickered briefly on Ned's face, despite everything. *Em came first.* Again Francie glimpsed herself in the mirror and was stunned to find a smile on her face, too.

"Not that I'm suggesting she resembles Vince Lombardi in any other way," Anne was saying. "Quite the opposite, as you can plainly see. In fact, the men on the other courts are always —"

"I've really got to get going, Anne," Francie interrupted, her voice much too loud, or so she thought.

"But Ned just arrived," Anne replied. "You've hardly had a chance to meet. At least finish your drink first. And why don't you have one, too, Ned? Even if it is that Romanian stuff."

"I'm not really —"

"Come on, Ned. You wouldn't want Francie to think you're a wine snob."

Ned's mouth opened. Francie knew what was

on his mind: *Francie knows better.* He said nothing, went into the kitchen. Em moved closer to her mother, gazed down at her ankle. Francie had already seen the Ned in Em; now she saw Anne in Em's graceful stance. "How did you win playing on that?" Em said.

"Your mom's tough." The words popped out of Francie's mouth unbidden. Now her subconscious was defending Anne, shoring her up. Not hard to understand why, like the guilty parent who buys her child an ice cream cone an hour after the spanking. Her next thought was conscious, and she kept it to herself: *she'd better be.*

Em was looking at her in surprise.

"She knows that's not true," Anne said.

Ned returned with an empty glass. "What's not true?" he said, an overflow of anxiety in every syllable. Surely Anne heard it, too.

But she did not. "That I'm tough," she explained, handing the bottle to Francie. "Mind filling Ned's glass?"

That forced them into proximity. Ned held out his glass. Their eyes met briefly; his filled with pain, then went blank. Francie poured. Their hands, so familiar with each other, almost touched and even at that moment seemed right together, like perfect lovers in miniature, at least to Francie. The two hands right, and everything else wrong.

"Thank you," he said. And: "Cheers." He wasn't good at this, but she was worse.

"Cheers." She made herself say it, too.

They drank. Francie tasted nothing, wasn't even conscious of the wetness.

"It happened on the last point," Anne was telling Em. "Two–six, seven–six, six–love."

"So you didn't choke?" Em said.

"Em!" said Ned.

"But Mom always chokes in the big matches. She says so herself."

"Couldn't this time," Anne said. "Francie doesn't know the meaning of the word."

"Oh, but I do."

"Don't listen to her, Ned. She's very modest. Why, I didn't even know about her job till just the other day, a job I'd die for."

Another silence.

"Oh?" said Ned at last.

"Tell Ned about your job, Francie."

"It's nothing, really."

"Nothing! Francie buys all the art for the Lothian Foundation."

"Oh?" said Ned.

"Is that all?" said Anne. " 'Oh?' Men, every time — right, Francie?"

"It's not a big deal," Francie said. "In fact, there's a committee, and —"

"Mom's an artist," said Em.

"I know," Francie said. They all turned to the still life behind the desk lamp. Grapes. And here was the girl, in the room, as though she'd stepped out of *oh garden, my garden*: a wild card.

"You should see the one she did of Dad — it's

much better. I'll get it."

"I —"

But it was too late. Em was flying up the stairs. They watched the long Day-Glo laces of her sneakers flap out of sight.

"She can be a bit wild sometimes," Anne said.

"She seems like a great kid," said Francie.

"She is," said Ned, his voice suddenly thick. Anne shot him a glance. He cleared his throat, drank from his glass, perhaps a bigger drink than he'd planned, because a red trickle escaped from one corner of his mouth, ran diagonally down his chin. He didn't notice, but Anne did. "Ned," she said in a half whisper, and mimed a cleaning-up motion, another domestic detail — a wifely detail — that made Francie writhe inside.

"Excuse me," Ned said, wiping his chin.

And then Em was back with the portrait.

"Really, Em," said Anne, "I don't think Francie —"

"It's all right," said Francie. She gazed at the painting. So did Ned and Anne, while Em gazed at them. Francie's eye couldn't help seeing things. Ned's sensuality, for example, one of his most obvious characteristics, was completely missing. And perhaps because of the immobility of the pose, and the way his body almost filled the canvas, like Henry VIII in Holbein's portrait, Anne's Ned appeared more powerful than in life, even dangerous. She'd missed him, not entirely, but by a lot, yet somehow the resemblance was still astounding.

"Well?" said Em.

"I like it very much," Francie said.

"Think it's worth anything?"

"Em!" This time they said it together, husband and wife.

"Is it for sale?" Francie said.

"Of course not," Ned said. Too quick, too emphatic — and Francie knew at once that he was afraid she might do something crazy, like make an offer, the way she'd called *Intimately Yours*. Anne noticed: Francie caught her giving Ned a look; he caught it, too. "I wouldn't want to part with it, is all," Ned said. "But it's not my call."

Anne smiled at him. He smiled back, another faltering smile, even more false than the first, but Anne appeared to miss that.

"You like it 'cause it makes you look cool, right, Dad?" said Em.

"Right. Cool, that's me." He tousled her hair. She made a face. Anne laughed.

Francie set her glass down on an end table, not softly.

"Yikes," said Anne. "We're keeping you."

"Not at all," said Francie. Em was staring at her.

"Mind giving Francie a lift, Ned?"

"A lift?"

"To the tennis club — her car's there."

"Not necessary," Francie said. "A cab will be fine."

"I wouldn't hear of it," Anne said.

"No, really," Francie said, and reached for the phone. Anne covered the receiver with her hand. Their fingers touched.

"You know where it is, Ned?" Anne said. He nodded. "And we're out of milk, if you get a chance."

"Thanks for the drink," Francie said, moving toward the door.

"Thank you," said Anne. "For driving me home, for being so kind, for everything." She started to get up.

"Don't," Francie said.

But Anne did, hardly wincing at all. "See? It feels better already." She leaned forward, kissed Francie on the cheek. "We're going to win this thing."

Em gave her mother another surprised look. Ned held the door. Francie walked out: a cold night, cold everywhere, except the spot that Anne's lips had touched. That burned.

"And to celebrate we'll get together for dinner," Anne called after her. "The four of us."

They drove in silence, down the block, around the corner, both staring straight ahead.

"The four of us?" Ned said, speaking quietly, as though there were still some risk of being overheard.

"You and her," said Francie. "Me and Roger."

"God."

Francie sat up straight, hands folded in her

lap. What was there to say? She felt Ned's eyes on her.

"It's so incredible," he said. "It almost makes you believe there's some God. Or anti-God."

Francie said nothing.

They rounded another corner. Farther now from home, Ned's voice rose to conversational level. "I thought I was going to have a heart attack," he said.

"It was horrible." Francie knew that the full horror of it wouldn't be apparent for a long time: a series of little revelatory bombshells awaited her.

Ned licked his lips. "I know. But . . ."

"But what?"

"But looking at it rationally, what does it change, really?"

She gazed at him. "I beg your pardon?"

He shrugged. "This just adds the visual component to what you already knew. I have a wife. That wasn't a secret. Now you've seen her. It could be worse."

"How?"

"Suppose she'd been your sister, for example."

Her stomach turned.

"Things like that happen, Francie."

"Not to me."

Ned's hand left the wheel, perhaps on its way to touching her, paused, and went back. "We fell in love," he said. "That's a fact, and nothing changes it."

"You're wrong."

Ned pulled into the parking lot at the tennis club. Lights glowed in the windows of nearby houses, sparks flew from a chimney and vanished in the night sky. He faced her. "Are you saying you don't love me anymore?"

Francie didn't speak.

"Because if that's the case, I want to hear it."

She remained silent. She thought she saw tears in his eyes, but then a cloud covered the moon and they were gone. "I love you," he said. "More than ever."

"What do you mean, more than ever?"

"The way you were tonight. With Em. With Anne, even. You bring out the best in her."

"Stop it."

"And in me. It's true. You were the only adult in the room. I adore you. I'll do anything you want, leave Anne, anything."

"Don't you see that's impossible now?"

"Why? Why is it impossible?"

There were two reasons. First, what would be left of him, after? Second, she couldn't allow it, not now, not knowing Anne — and the girl. Francie gave Ned the second reason.

She watched him absorb it, saw his pain, also saw how young he looked, and more beautiful than ever. Yes, there was no question: he was beautiful. Beauty in pain was something to which she reacted strongly, especially when it was visible to the eye. "Then that leaves us right where we are, doesn't it?" he said. "Why can't

189

we just go on like this?"

Francie laid her hand on his knee. "You're a sweet man," she said. "But . . ." For a moment, there was a lump in her throat and she couldn't get the sentence out. But only for a moment. ". . . where we are is intolerable now," Francie said.

"What are you saying?"

"It's over, Ned."

"You don't mean that."

"I do."

His lip quivered. Then he mastered himself and said, "Tell me you don't love me."

She said nothing.

He covered her hand, still on his knee, with his: two hands that still went together perfectly. "Until you can say that, nothing's over."

"Then —" began Francie when the car phone buzzed.

"Shit," said Ned.

It buzzed again. "Answer it," said Francie, thinking that Anne might have fallen, might have reinjured her ankle.

Ned put the phone to his ear, said, "Hello?"

But it was on speaker, and the car filled with a woman's voice, not Anne's. "Ned? Hi. Kira."

"Kira?"

"The same."

"I'm very sorry," Ned said. "I don't have those figures yet. I'll call you in the morning."

Pause. "Okeydoke." Click.

Ned put the phone down. "Syndication," he said, rubbing his forehead as though struck with a sudden ache. "Go on, Francie."

She withdrew her hand and said, "Let's just leave it like this: we can't see each other anymore."

"You know that won't work."

"It has to."

"Please, Francie." He leaned toward her, put his arms around her, brought his face to hers. She leaned back, forced herself to lean back, because it was unnatural, like rejecting herself.

"It won't work — you already know that in your heart," Ned said. "How could someone like you ever throw this away?"

"How couldn't —"

Someone tapped at her window. Francie pushed Ned away, hard enough so his back hit the door, then twisted around, saw Nora peering through the fogged glass, racquet bag over her shoulder, steam rising off her hair, still wet from the shower.

"To be continued," Ned said softly.

16

"I heard all about it," Nora said as the windows of Ned's car slid down. "Way to fire, kiddo. How's Anne?"

"It's just a sprain," Francie said.

"She going to be ready to play for the hardware?"

"She says so." Francie opened the door. She turned to Ned, found she couldn't quite look at him. "Thanks for the lift," she said, again attempting to find the tone she'd use with a new acquaintance, again getting it wrong.

"The pleasure was mine," he said, not even trying: more than that, making a deliberately careless reply, one she didn't like at all. And then, could that possibly have been his hand she felt, brushing the back of her thigh as she got out of the car?

Francie glanced at Nora — what had she seen? what had she heard? — but Nora's eyes weren't on her. "Hi, Ned," she was saying. "How's it going?"

He peered at her. "Nora, right?"

"Got it in one. Legal Seafood, at Chestnut Hill — you and Anne were ahead of us in line."

"I remember."

"Finally caught your show the other day," Nora continued, talking past Francie, turning on the charm, in fact. With her profile view of Nora's face, Francie could see her doing it. "Blended families, I think it was," Nora said. "Are those callers for real?"

"Paid-up members of Equity, each and every one," Ned replied. Nora laughed, was still laughing when Ned said, "Good night, ladies." His eyes lingered for a moment on Francie, then turned orange under the sodium arc lights as he drove out of the parking lot. They watched him swing into traffic and accelerate away, tires spinning on a patch of ice.

"What do you think of pretty boy?" Nora said.

"Pretty boy?"

"Come on. He's gorgeous. Gorgeous, smart, sexy — and funny, too."

"Grow up," Francie said.

"Testosterone versus estrogen — what could be more grown-up than that? No holds barred. On the other hand, he's married, and I soon will be. Bernie wants me in white — can you believe it?"

"Why not?"

"Why not?" Nora said, and gave Francie a look at a bad moment, the very moment the first of those bombshells she'd anticipated was going off in Francie's brain: *Someone like Anne, that's different — modest sex drive at best.* What were the implications of that now?

Nora's eyes narrowed; then she went on: "Maybe you're right. Some marriages — I'll take that a little farther — most marriages baffle me.

Why should mine be any different?"

Francie hadn't followed, was aware that a question had been asked, no more. She nodded.

"What does that mean?"

Francie didn't answer. She had meant to tell Nora about Ned, the constant omission of this fact of her life putting too great a strain on their friendship, but how was that possible now? Nora knew Anne — and more, much more, had speculated about Anne's sex drive, found Ned attractive: how horribly tangled every little aspect of this was — and would thus be put in the intolerable situation of having to lie for Francie, an adulteress once removed. Impossible. Impossible and unnecessary, since it was over. She had just seen Ned for the last time. That was that. The resolved and the unresolved, all in a box. It just had to be closed and put away: a tidy, persuasive image, like slicing through the Gordian knot. But the back of her thigh still tingled in the place he'd touched it, if in fact he'd touched it at all.

"Are you saying that Anne and Ned make sense to you, for example?" Nora asked. "As a couple, I mean."

Francie whipped around to face her. "Who the fuck does?" she said.

Nora stared at her. "What's wrong?"

"Nothing."

"Bullshit. You're a thousand miles away, and when you're not, you're mean as a snake. And you look like you've seen a ghost. I'll take that farther, too — you look like shit, if you want the truth, which isn't your style at all. Something's wrong, very wrong. Fess up."

Francie took a deep breath. At that moment, she remembered the conversation on the ice: *There's someone I have to tell. I won't say it's you, if you don't want, but I have to tell.* Had she mentioned Nora's name? Yes. Had Ned therefore assumed that Nora already knew? How else to explain his reply when she'd thanked him for the ride? *The pleasure was mine.* Was it a sort of inside joke, inviting Nora in on the secret? If so, why now, when he'd always been so careful? Did the burden of the secret sometimes grow so intolerable that the truth had to burst out, even be flaunted? That could be dangerous — could have been, Francie corrected herself, because it was all going in a box, resolved and unresolved.

"Go on," Nora said. "Spill it."

"There's nothing to say."

Nora nodded. "Okay, pal." She swung away and walked off toward her car. Francie wanted to call out to her, *Nora, Nora,* and just let whatever happened after that happen. But she didn't. She hadn't done any damage yet, not to Anne or Em, and that was the way it had to be.

Francie went home. The answering machine was beeping in the living room. She switched on lights, listened to the message. "This is Roger," said Roger. He hated speaking to machines — she heard it in his voice. "Things are . . . promising. Vis-à-vis Bob Fielding. I'll be here for another day or two. No need to pick me up." Long pause. "And good luck. I'm referring to the tournament. If you're still alive." Another pause. "In it, that is. Good-bye."

Francie saw the future: Roger in some condo in Fort Lauderdale, she staying here. Just a few hours ago that would have seemed if not ideal then much better than what she had. But now there would be no Ned to complete the imperfect picture. Even if he did leave Anne, no Ned. She told herself that a few times, then went upstairs, stripped off her warm-ups and her tennis clothes, lowered herself into a hot bath. No Ned. But what if he did leave Anne, and then some time went by — how long? six months? a year? more? — and after that he called her? Was that okay? No. Why not? She was trying to answer that question when the phone rang. Francie picked it up, expecting Roger.

"How's Saturday night?" Not Roger, but Anne.

"Saturday night?"

"After the match. For our little foursome. I thought we could try Huîtres — am I saying it right? Ned loves seafood."

"Are you sure you're going to be able to play?"

"I'm on my feet right now! No pain. Maybe it's all mental, like they say. Your confidence is rubbing off on me. That's what Ned thinks."

"He said that?" Francie said, wishing she could have phrased it as "Does he?" or just

196

kept her mouth shut.

"No, but it's what he thinks. I can tell. So how about it?"

Never. "Roger's out of town right now. I'll have to get back to you."

"Okay. But I'll go ahead and make the reservations. I hear it's a pretty hot place."

It had been hot, as Francie recalled, the year before; then cursed herself for the thought. "Sounds nice," she said. "Take care of that ankle."

"I told you. No pain. We could go out there and whip 'em right now, you and me."

Call waiting sounded. "I've got another call," Francie said.

"Then bye. And thanks again."

Francie pressed the button. "Think if this were France," said Ned. "Or Scandinavia."

Her mouth went dry. "Where are you?" she said, thinking Anne might walk in on him any second.

"Back in the car," Ned said. "I forgot the goddamn milk. Serendipitous because it gives me a chance to call you."

But he'd never called her at home before. "What are you doing, Ned?"

"What I should have been doing from the start. As I would have done, I hope, in France or Scandinavia."

"What are you talking about?"

"You've been there. You know, better than I, how the Europeans handle this kind of . . . situation. There's no either/or. We could be open, semiopen at least, like Mitterrand, and no one would think twice. And above all, no guilt. That's the part I'm cutting out — the horrible guilt, the headaches. Is love something to feel guilty about, Francie? They understand these things in Europe."

"Would Anne?"

"Why not, under those circumstances?"

"Here in America, Ned. Would Anne?"

Silence.

"Would Em?"

Silence.

Would Roger? she asked herself, the most worldly of the three, certainly the one with the most experience of Europe. *Possibly,* she told herself. But they weren't Europeans; they lived not in a land of complaisance but of either/or. "Then that answers that," Francie said, "doesn't it?"

"You're letting guilt run your life," Ned said. "And there's nothing to feel guilty about — you've got to see that."

"I don't. There is — and there could be a lot more. That's what we've got to prevent."

"Then just tell me you don't love me."

She couldn't.

"And even if you did" — his voice broke — "even if you did say it, even if you meant it, I wouldn't give up. I'd make you love me again."

Francie covered the mouthpiece with her hand. She didn't want him to hear her crying.

"Francie? Are you still there? Francie?"

"Yes."

"I thought you'd hung up. Don't hang up."

"I'm not."

"I should have called you at home long before this. I can't tell you how many times I've wanted to — I memorized your number, even though I never used it. I've been so fucking careful, I almost forgot what this is all about."

Francie covered the mouthpiece again.

"Francie? Are you still there?"

She mastered herself. "I've got to go."

"Why? Is he there?"

"No."

Pause. "Where is he?"

"Out of town."

"Then why do you have to go?"

"I just do. And Ned?"

"What is it, angel?"

His first term of endearment. "Don't call me that. And don't call here anymore. Not here, not at the office, nowhere."

"You don't mean that, Francie. You couldn't. I'm not some stranger. I know you."

She hung up. It rang again, almost immediately. Had he not only memorized her number but entered it in his speed dialer? How did that reconcile with his spycraft? Suddenly she saw him in a new light, knew what must have been happening inside his head for months, months of struggling against his own spycraft, fighting the urge to call, the urge to see her, the urge to live with her. Francie saw him in a new light, but she let it ring.

After it stopped, she got out of the bath, dried herself. There she was in the mirror again: nothing normal or composed about her now.

She put on her nightie, went down to the kitchen, brewed tea. Found herself brewing tea, more accurately, although she seldom drank it, didn't like it. Brewing tea and thinking of Mackie, a Scottish baby-sitter hired by her parents when she'd been small. Mackie drank tea from morning to night, following a strict ritual, a ritual Francie followed now. Mackie: her red arthritic fingers wrapped around a china cup, her pale eyes squinting through the steam, her opinions. Mackie had many opinions — about Catholics: hypocrites; dogs: diseased; men: nasty — opinions that had given Francie nightmares and gotten Mackie fired. But the warm cup felt good now in Francie's hand, and so did the hot tea inside her. *Men are nasty, dear; don't you ever be trusting them. But Mackie, what about Daddy? Now that's a sharp question, isn't it, dear? Some, not I, don't you know, but some, might even say the kind of question a Jewish lawyer would be asking, not a sweet-tempered lass such as yourself.*

There was a knock at the front door, perhaps one in a series only half heard. Roger? Home on some earlier flight, with sudden news, good or bad? Francie went to the door, put her eye to the peephole. Not Roger, but Ned. Ned with flowers in his hand, irises, fucking irises of course. She

200

leaned her head against the door. He knocked again.

Francie opened up.

He smiled. "I like your nightie," he said. "It's so chaste."

Francie, forcing herself not to glance furtively past him at the neighbors' windows like some cartoonish sloven that Grosz might have painted, said, "What do you want, Ned?"

"Aren't you going to invite me in?"

"Go deliver the milk." Francie closed the door in his face.

But she didn't go away, just stood there. He knocked again. Francie didn't move. He spoke, quietly, but she heard. "That wasn't nice, about the milk," he said.

Francie just stood there, just stood there for as long as she could, and then opened the door. Ned walked in.

He closed the door behind him. "Brought you some flowers," he said, holding them out.

"I don't like irises."

"You don't?"

"Not particularly."

It wasn't so much the crestfallen look on his face per se, but that of all possible emotional reactions to the situation they were in, it had dominated, that did something to Francie. He was mortified that he'd been giving her irises all this time and hadn't known. There, standing in her front hall, the flowers now dangling uselessly at his side, he looked . . . adorable: a horrible girlish adjective, a horrible girlish trap, but there was no other way to put it.

She took him in her arms, could not stop herself.

"That feels good," he said in her ear. "I was afraid it might never happen again."

"This is the last time," Francie said, but she didn't let go.

"Don't say that." The tip of his tongue stroked her earlobe. The feeling triggered some force in her body, in her mind, irresistible. "Let's go upstairs," he said.

"No," she said, pushing him away, or trying to, or at least sending her hands a message that he should be pushed away. But he stayed where he was, his breath in her ear, his arms around her, their bodies close, feeling together the presence of another world, not far away. "We can't," she said. "Anne."

"There's no help for that."

"Don't be stupid."

"No, Francie. This happened. It's happening. You might as well try to . . . to . . ." He couldn't think of an analogy. "We're not machines," he said, finding another image, "with an off switch."

"But Anne," Francie said.

"I'll get a divorce."

"No."

"Then she can't know, that's all. She can never know."

"No."

"That's the best we can do. No one gets hurt."

No one gets hurt. Was it possible? Francie didn't know. But how could it go on, now that she knew Anne, played tennis with her, had started to become a friend, knew her daughter? It couldn't. There was no future for her and Ned. But tonight? Just one night? No one would get hurt tonight.

She turned toward the stairs. He followed her up, his hand trailing down her back like a charging device.

Having caught an afternoon flight from Lauderdale, having found Francie not at home, and having left a clever little bit of misdirection on the answering machine just because it felt like the kind of nifty move he would be making from here on in, Roger lay dozing on the couch in his basement room. The phone woke him. He ignored it, preferring to let his mind return to what it had been dwelling on during the plane ride, the details of the post-Francie stage of his life. At first, he'd imagined living alone, staying in the house, soldiering on. But why rule out female companionship? He thought of Brenda, Francie's friend in Rome, thought of how she'd sounded on the phone. He remembered how attractive she was — rich, too, which was important because even with the insurance settlement he would never be able to see to the needs of a woman even more high-maintenance than Francie. Brenda: wasn't there some story of a party she'd once been at where Pavarotti and Sutherland had sung Beatles songs around an upright piano? He could see himself building a life out of things like that. What was the name of that tailor's shop near the Trevi fountain where he'd had that gray suit made, the one with the subtle navy flecks? He could picture the facade perfectly, but the name eluded him, was still eluding him when he thought he heard a voice upstairs — not a voice, but two voices, female and male.

Roger removed his shoes, left his basement room, crept up the stairs in stocking feet. The door to the kitchen hung open a few inches, admitting a yellow wedge of light. He hovered in the darkness, listening. He heard a man say something about divorce. A man with the sickening voice of a pleaser: radio boy. Then Francie said something he didn't catch. And Roger wanted to hear, wanted to hear everything. He stuck his head in the kitchen, saw no one, nipped around the corner into the unlit back hall, and from there along the corridor, also unlit, that led to the front of the house. He hung in the shadows beside the stairs leading to the second floor. And there they were, in a foul embrace.

Whitey, I need you now.

Francie said, "No."

Radio boy said, "That's the best we can do. No one gets hurt."

They were still for a few moments; then Francie turned, turned so that she was looking right at Roger, right at him, and he thought, *Now you're dead*. But her eyes were wet and he was in the darkness, and she didn't see him. Up the stairs she went — what had she meant by *no?* — and radio boy followed, up and out of sight, but not before Roger got his first good look at him, the image predictable. Roger listened to their withdrawing footsteps with all the concentration at his command, but it wasn't necessary. He knew where they were going: into her bedroom, their bedroom, in fact, their marital bedroom. After a few minutes, he went up, too, silent as a big cat in his stocking feet.

The marital door was closed and no light leaked out from under. But Roger didn't have to see; he heard the sounds of their lust, those cries of Francie's that she'd never made for him, and the passionate noise of radio boy, and bullshit words of love. Simple death was too good for her. But if he was honest with himself, Roger had known as soon as he had researched the Sue Savard case that there was nothing simple about the kind of death that Whitey handed out, hadn't been anything simple then, and after all those cooped-up years would be even less simple now. Fair enough. After tonight, he wouldn't feel bad about it anymore, would cast off any future guilt. She was violating him in every way; it was a form of rape. This was a rape crisis and there was nothing to feel guilty about. His conscience was clear.

And what of radio boy? He was in the marital

bed, raping him, too. Roger thought again of searching out some weapon, knife or poker, then bursting in to bludgeon and stab. Again he asked himself, would any jury convict him? And again the answer: in this rotting, leveled-out, lazy-minded country, yes, any jury could. No matter. He had Whitey. How complicated would it be to troll radio boy in Whitey's path? Complicated, perhaps, he conceded when no immediate solution presented itself, but he'd been born to solve puzzles. This was his métier. The stakes were higher, that was all. He was coming into his own.

On the other side of the door, Francie made some vulgar sound of culmination. *Come, bitch.* Roger imagined her in an open coffin at the funeral home, her face expressionless.

17

"Where were you?" Anne said.

She was sitting at the kitchen table, foot resting on a chair, ice pack on her ankle. Ned set the milk down in front of her, a half gallon of nonfat and a pint of 2 percent for her coffee, the cartons still cold although they'd been sitting in the car for almost two hours; it was a cold night. "I had a flat," he said. But two hours!

"A flat?"

"A flat tire."

"But you know how to change a flat, Ned."

"The spare was flat, too. And all the gas stations around were those self-service-only kind. I had to walk for miles."

"Oh, I'm sorry."

"Don't be. Just one of those things."

"I was starting to worry."

"About what?"

"That you'd had an accident or something."

"I'm fine."

Anne took off the ice pack, set it on the table. As she leaned forward, an idea came to her; he saw it coming in her eyes. "Why didn't you call AAA?" she asked.

The unexpected. "Are we still members?"

"I think so. Doesn't the fee show up on the Visa?"

"Damn. I forgot all about it."

"Or I could have come and got you."

"Not with that ankle." *Wasn't that the whole point of all this, that you couldn't drive, for Christ's sake?*

"You're sweet," Anne said. She held out her hand. He helped her up. "It's late," she said. "Let's go to bed." She led him from the room. They were in the doorway, almost out, when she stopped and said, "The milk." Ned turned back, picked up the cartons, took them to the fridge. Em had posted a new watercolor on the door: two big women, almost filling the frame, holding up a golden trophy. It gleamed. The quivering Keith Haring lines radiating from it showed that. At the bottom was written, *Go for it, Mom and Francie!*

Anne saw him looking at it. "Isn't she great?"

"She's got real talent, in my opinion."

Anne looked puzzled. "What do you mean?"

"I've always loved her art. You know that."

Anne laughed. "I meant Francie," she explained.

"Oh."

"What did you think of her?"

He shrugged, and thought at once of Judas. "She seemed nice enough," he said.

"She's more than that. She's so . . . together. They live on Beacon Hill."

How disappointing she could be. He nodded.

"I haven't met her husband yet, but we will after the match. We're going out to dinner, the four of us."

That had slipped his mind. Unable to counteract it, he said nothing.

"That's all right, isn't it?"

"Oh, sure."

They went upstairs. Anne used the bathroom first, went to bed, kissing her fingers and pressing them to his lips as they passed in the doorway, blushing only a little. Ned showered, flossed and brushed his teeth, stimulated his gums with the rubber-tipped brass stick, sprayed deodorant under his arms, took as much time as he could, then followed. The bedside light was off. He quietly got in at his side, lay down near the edge, his back to her, hoping she was asleep by now.

But she was not. He knew that, knew her, knew even before her hand lightly stroked the side of his ass, moved around to his stomach, down. At the same time, he felt her nipples pressing into his back, importunate.

Her nipples were hard, but he was not. It took an uncharacteristic amount of effort to make him so; finally she did it with her mouth. That was unusual, too. Then she slid on top of him, cocked her hips over him, settled down with him inside her.

"Your ankle," he said.

"Hush."

Anne started moving. Did uncharacteristic events come in threes, like plane crashes? This time they did. He began to go softer, softer and softer by stages — like a goddamned flat tire — with each grinding of her hips. Not a development that lent itself to secrecy, and Anne soon felt the change. She arched back, fondled his balls, and when that didn't work reached farther, got a fingertip between his buttocks: an insinuating first. What had she been reading? But it did no good. Nothing did, nothing could, not with the image of Em's triumphant trophy-raising painting so fresh in his mind. Anne and Francie, going for it. His penis slipped out of her and nestled down at its base. DNF, wasn't that what they said in horse racing? Did not finish.

"Sorry," he said.

"It's all right."

But it had never happened before. If there was a God, one of the old-fashioned, narrow-minded, judgmental sort, he would now of course be in the process of sabotaging his erectile capacity for life. But Ned didn't believe in any god like that and, worse, was also psychologist enough to know that such sabotage could be easily accomplished by, and against, the self.

Anne rolled off him, lay on her back. He knew those sensitive eyes of hers were open, staring into the darkness. Had she been close to an orgasm? Yes, of course, and what modern husband could leave her there? Not him. Ned crept down in the bed, began running his tongue down her stomach, lightly and teasingly, he hoped.

"Don't," she said, and turned away from him, drawing her knees toward her chest.

Lightly, teasingly: all wrong. This wasn't about seducing her, for Christ's sake; the job was to make her come. He should have been direct: licked her like it was the last night on earth, the way he'd just been doing to Francie. He'd been false, pro forma, more like a bad date than a husband, and Anne didn't miss things like that.

Time passed. Ned heard a siren far away, the furnace firing up in the basement, Anne's breathing, growing steady and even. He closed his eyes, but sleep wouldn't be fooled that easily.

Another siren; the furnace switched off; and Anne spoke. Startling him: so sure he'd been that she was asleep.

"Did Kira Chang get hold of you?"

"What?"

"You know. Kira Chang. From syndication, or whatever it is. She called while you were taking Francie back to the tennis club. I gave her the cell phone number."

"Thanks. She did." Silence, the kind that had to be filled. "Some minor screwup — I'll take care of it in the morning."

The furnace switched back on, ran for a while, went silent. Anne was silent, too. The headache started behind Ned's right eye, where it always did, but this time spread deeper than ever before. Deeper and sharper. *What the fuck am I doing?* he thought. *What the fuck am I doing?*

"Ned?" Anne said quietly, and then a little louder, "Ned?"

He was asleep.

Anne slipped out of bed. Having gone to bed naked in preparation for sex with Ned, she put on the long sweatshirt she usually slept in and went downstairs. She didn't turn on any lights, didn't need them, knew her own house. Through the kitchen, through the door that led to the garage, a single-car garage where Ned's car, the later model, had precedence over hers. Anne switched on the garage light, and there was his car. She walked around it, saw just that: his car. All the tires seemed the same, none noticeably flat. What was she looking for? She didn't know.

Anne opened the driver's-side door, popped the trunk, where the spare was. She looked inside, saw his roof rack, kayak paddle, a bag of rock salt, a bouquet of flowers — irises, still fresh. The spare lay under the floor mat. She unsnapped the snaps, rolled it back. On top lay the tools — jack, crank, lug wrench — all still sealed in factory plastic. Beneath the tools she found the instructions, also sealed in plastic, and under them was the spare. It had never touched pavement: the manufacturer's label was still stuck to the treads. That didn't mean it wasn't flat, or hadn't been flat earlier that night. Anne moved to lift it off but couldn't. It was bolted in place. The bolt had to be loosened first, and the wrench had never been used. So no one had ever removed the tire to try it out.

Anne ran her hand over the spare, prodded it,

punched it softly with her fist. It seemed as rounded and firm as the others, but she really couldn't tell. She stood over the trunk, gazing down inside, gazing at the roof rack, the kayak paddle, the rock salt, the irises, the tools, the spare. Anne had never been good at solving puzzles, had hated math, didn't like crosswords, was always nervous when people started playing games like Botticelli. She knew what she was seeing had to add up to something, but she couldn't make it happen. Then she noticed a road map wedged between the spare tire and the wheel well. She tugged it out.

A road map of New Hampshire. So? She unfolded it. Just a New Hampshire road map, territory very familiar to her. She ran her eye over some of the spots — Tuckerman's Ravine, Franconia Notch, Wildcat, Waterville Valley, Lake Winnipesaukee. Some time passed before she spotted the little red X on a tiny island in the middle of the Merrimack River.

A red X. Meaning? Anne had no idea. But her next thought gave it some: Kira Chang. She closed the trunk, leaving the irises to die.

18

A pretty girl got on the bus in Bridgeport, just after dawn. The only empty seat was on the aisle beside Whitey, so she took that, might have taken it anyway, he thought, catching the way she checked out his leather jacket from the corner of her eye. It was a cool jacket, no doubt about that, the coolest article of clothing he'd ever owned. He'd also bought himself a pair of cowboy boots from his first week's salary, made in Korea, but very cool as well, black with silver stitching and thick heels that must have made him at least six-four. And he still had two hundred dollars and change left over, plus what remained of his gate money. *Yeah, babe,* he thought, giving her another look, *check me out.*

A pretty girl, but kind of cheap-looking: spiky hair, lots of earrings, and — as she shrugged herself out of her coat — a little snake tattoo coiling up from her cleavage. Whitey got hard right away. There was a bathroom at the back of the bus. Was it possible to get her behind that door and fuck her brains out? Things like that happened. He remembered that exact scene from one of Rey's videos, except it took place on a plane, not a bus. The girl on the plane had made the first move, dangling her long red fingernails in the guy's lap.

This girl didn't do that. Neither did she have long red fingernails; hers were unpainted and bitten to the quick. Whitey made himself interesting by staring out the window for a while, like a guy having deep thoughts, then sat back and glanced at her as if noticing her for the first time, and if she happened to glance back and see how built he was under the leather jacket or even better the bulge in his pants, they'd be on their way. But she didn't.

"Where you headed?" he said at last.

"Providence."

He nodded. "Rhode Island," he said. Nothing else came to mind. A few miles went by. "Just passing through?" he said.

"I'm sorry?"

"Providence. Just passing through?"

"I go to Brown."

Brown — what the hell was that? He thought back, all the way back to his high school days on the ice.

"The college?" he said.

"I'm sorry?"

"Brown. The college."

"Yes."

Now they were getting somewhere. He noticed that her neck wasn't completely clean. Necks — where had he heard that if you squeezed a woman's neck while she was coming she had a better orgasm? Why not just say to her: Hey, ever hear about this neck thing? And then they'd be in the bathroom at the back of the bus,

215

trying it out. He licked his lips a couple of times, getting ready to say it.

The girl took out a book, some kind of art book. She opened it to a picture, one of those pictures any kid could do, just a bunch of rectangles, and stared at it. He squinted at the title, *Entrance to Green*. There wasn't even any green in it, for Christ's sake. She took out a pencil and wrote in the margin, *Anuszkiewicz: geometric recession counterbalanced by tonal shift — cool* → *warm*. His hard-on went away.

She studied the art book the rest of the way, gazing at one bullshit picture after another. Whitey stole sidelong peeks at the coiled snake rising and falling in its soft, springy lair as she breathed. Only as the bus was pulling into Providence station did Whitey get an idea. *It's the recovery of stolen objects. Paintings, for example.* Why hadn't he thought of that earlier? The girl gathered her things and started up the aisle. "I'm in the art business myself," he called after her. She didn't seem to hear. He thought of the steel-tipped pole he'd left behind, and that snake, rising and falling on her breast.

Whitey got off the bus in Boston. He'd been there once before to play in a tournament at the Garden, but all he remembered was eating oysters, the first and only time he'd ever tasted them, horrible slimy things that were supposed to make you horny but hadn't; he'd puked in the locker room that evening, and they'd lost to one of the big Catholic schools, the way they always did. So he had to ask some loser on the street, "Hey. Where's the Garden?"

"Ain't no more Garden, pal. Where you been? It's the Fleet."

"Huh?"

"Fleet Center, now. But the same location. What you do, you —"

"The Public Garden," said Whitey, realizing his mistake. The man looked at him funny but gave him the directions. The Garden, gone. For a few blocks that pissed Whitey off, more than pissed him off, reminding him of the big percentage they'd cut out of his life. But after a while he began to see the bright side. If Gardens could come and go, then anything was possible, and that included a big score.

Whitey followed the directions, soon found himself walking on a street lined with fancy shops, their windows full of Christmas displays. He saw a leather jacket, a lot like his, went closer: identical to his, right down to those little V-shaped upturns on the chest seams. He checked the name of the shop — Newbury Leather — then took off his own jacket to examine the label. It had been cut out. He stood there wondering about that until he felt the cold, noticed that snow was falling. He hadn't seen snow since they'd sent him down south. Whitey gazed straight up into the sky. From that angle the snowflakes were black against the cloud cover. He'd grown up in snow and never seen that effect before. Change was possible. He was changing, getting smarter. Black snow was an interesting idea, for example, the kind of interesting idea someone in the art business might have, someone like him. *Someone like me, you bitch,* he thought to himself, meaning the girl on the bus. He crossed a street and entered the Public Garden.

Roger was waiting under the statue of George Washington, just as he'd said he'd be. Snow clung to the brim of George Washington's bronze hat, and to Roger's hat, too, a black fedora, or some other hat with a name. Roger even looked a little like Washington, except he was smiling. He held out his hand, gloved in black suede. Whitey shook it, squeezing harder than normal because his own hand was bare, *so it was a bit of an insult,* like Roger was a prince and he was a peon or something.

"Ever play any tennis, Whitey?"

"Tennis?"

"You'd have been good."

Whitey wasn't sure how to take that: tennis was for fags. "Well, here I am," he said.

"I never doubted you." Roger handed him an envelope. "A week's salary, plus an advance I hope you'll find suitable."

Whitey took it. Was he supposed to open the envelope and count the money? Only an asshole would take money without counting it. But the envelope stopped him, although he didn't know why. Whitey stuck it unopened in his pocket.

"Familiar with the city, Whitey?"

"Yeah."

"Then why don't you take the day to get situated? Saturdays are difficult for me, this one especially."

"Okay," said Whitey, who would have bet anything it was Friday.

"Come here tomorrow, same time. If it's convenient. I may have something for you by then."

Something? Convenient? Whitey was a little lost, but he said, "Sure, I can make it."

Roger's smile faded. "Tomorrow, then," he said, and walked away.

Whitey watched him go. Roger followed the path around a frozen pond and headed across the park. He wore a long black coat that matched his hat and gloves, looked rich, untouchable; and was almost out of sight, obscured by distant trees and thickening snowfall, when Whitey's mind finally processed what his eyes had seen at once: Roger had been wearing slippers, plaid ones lined with sheepskin. What did that mean? That Roger couldn't be trusted? Whitey ripped open the envelope, found ten fifties. What had Roger called it? An advance? What did that mean? Five Cs for something he didn't even understand: that bought a lot of trust. But slippers? Whitey tapped the bills against his palm: slippers. And then he thought of the cut-out label from the leather jacket and realized this had to be Roger's neighborhood — he was close to home. And where would that be, exactly?

Whitey went after him.

Roger came to a street that bordered the park, crossed it. Whitey closed the distance between them until he could distinguish the red of Roger's slippers. Too close, probably. If Roger glanced back he would certainly recognize him. But Roger didn't glance back. Whitey knew why: because he was a prince and Whitey was who he was. Roger kept to a steady pace, up a hill lined with big brick houses, all with fancy grillwork, fancy doors, fancy knockers. He turned left on a street that mounted still higher, stopped at a door, took out his keys, opened it, and went inside. Whitey walked past, noted the number and street name, kept going.

He'd accomplished something; what, he wasn't sure, but it gave him a good feeling. He walked to the top of the hill, down the other side — stepping carefully, because his cowboy boots were slippery on the snowy bricks — found a bar at the bottom. Money in his pocket and a day to kill. Whitey went inside and ordered breakfast: a draft and a large fries. Same again. Then another draft. He was free, and feeling good.

The bar began to fill up. Someone next to him ordered oysters. Whitey eyed them, glistening on crushed ice, felt a little funny. He started thinking about Sue Savard. Strange, how the mind worked: he hadn't thought about her in years, would have supposed he'd completely forgotten what she looked like, but now that he was back up north, back up north and free, he could picture her, especially her eyes the moment he'd gotten himself inside her. The truth was that he'd never had sex like the sex he'd had with Sue Savard. And he hadn't meant to hurt her at all — that business with the glass cutter had been mostly just to tickle her, give her a little added pleasure. Women had an enormous capacity for pleasure, according to Rey, and his amateur housewife videos proved it; real housewives, even the social worker said so, real housewives with video cameras. Someone — a mustached man with thick lips — slurped down one of those oysters. Whitey paid his bill and left.

Money in his pocket. A day to kill. Whitey returned to the bus station, got on the bus to Nashua, took a taxi to Lawton Ferry, 97 Carp Road.

A dump, as he knew it would be. He knocked on the door five or six times, called, "Ma," then walked around the side, peering in the windows. He saw dirty dishes, dirty clothes, pictures of Jesus, but no one was home. Fine. He didn't really want to see her anyway. What he wanted was the pickup.

He found it in the rotting barn behind the house. His old pickup, but painted white now, with LITTLE WHITE CHURCH OF THE RE-DEEMER stenciled on the side. That, and the fact she'd never mentioned it, pissed him off, so much that he started kicking with his new cowboy boot, kicking a hole right through the wall of the barn. What gave her the right to do that? He calmed down when he realized that if the pickup hadn't been used he'd never have gotten it started after all these years. Besides, he'd soon be able to afford something much better. Whitey opened the door, saw a cat curled up inside. He yanked it out, found the keys under the seat, fired up his old car.

Whitey drove east to Little Joe Lake, took the rutted road that led to the far end. Nothing had changed, or if it had, the snow was hiding all the signs, but everything seemed strange. He had changed: he was bigger, stronger, smarter, and that made all the difference.

Whitey parked by the footbridge to the little cabin on the island. He sat there for a long time. Square one, and he was back. If only Sue Savard was inside now, everything would be different. This bigger, stronger, smarter him would make sure of that, would know how to stop the screaming in some harmless way.

Not that it had been his fault, all that screaming. Why hadn't she realized what it would lead to? Why hadn't she been able to stop it herself, to keep her own goddamn mouth shut and not force him to do it for her? Her fault, but still Whitey was filled with regret — he'd blown his chance with Sue Savard, the sexiest woman he'd ever known. What would Sue Savard have been like now?

19

"Hello. Is Francie there?"

"No."

"Well . . . I . . . This is Anne Franklin. Her tennis partner? We spoke once before."

"Yes."

"We — did Francie mention the dinner plans?"

"Dinner plans?"

"We were thinking of going out to dinner after the match."

Silence.

"The finals, tonight. Didn't Francie mention it?"

"I've been out of town."

"Oh. I was just calling to confirm the time: seven-thirty at Huîtres. I booked a table for four in nonsmoking, if that's all right with you."

"Four?"

"Ned's coming, too."

"Ned?"

"My — my husband."

Silence.

"I'm not sure I caught his name."

"Ned. Ned Demarco. Francie's never mentioned him either?"

"Perhaps I've been inattentive."

Roger's mind ran through its gears, each one

more powerful than the last, spinning, whirring, so fast that he had to pace, the excess mental energy escaping into his body. *The lover's wife, if she existed:* at one stage, a hypothetical and false contractor in a superseded plan for Francie, but now that she did exist, he felt . . . confusion, so strange for him. Fact: Francie was sleeping with the husband of her tennis partner. He found that harder to believe than the adultery itself. It reduced her to the basest commonality, like one of those illiterates on a TV tell-all show, a walking mockery of his taste. Was it possible for him to have misread her so grossly? Or — or was this something different, something more sophisticated: could it be possible, for example, that this tennis partner, this Anne, knew of the affair and accepted it? Roger's mind was already at the next stop, waiting with a disgusting image of Francie in bed with the two of them, and before he could digest that, was preparing another, even worse, with four participants. He felt a responding pulse in his groin. No! Were they animals, beasts, mere rutting things? Not him. He stopped pacing, poured water; it trembled in the glass, like an earthquake warning. He drank, tried to calm himself. *It's all right,* Roger, he thought, quashing all images. *The lover's wife is just another piece on the board, part of the problem, and all problems are fundamentally mathematical. Permutations and combinations.*

The door opened and Francie walked in, snow in her hair, her appearance revealing nothing at all of what he now knew hid within. "Hello, Roger." She glanced around. "Were you on the phone?"

"No." But had he said *permutations and combinations* aloud? The air in the room felt disturbed, as though the last ripples of a sound wave hadn't quite flattened away.

She took off her coat, her old coat — *where's the new coat, Francie?* — and hung it over the back of a chair. "When did you get back?" she said.

"Moments ago."

"How was the trip?"

"Didn't you get my message?" Enjoyable, asking that. *Dance on my string, Francie.*

"Yes, but it didn't say much."

Enough to do the job. "Cautious optimism, then — how does that sound?"

"Fine." She was watching him, waiting for details, waiting for . . . for some suggestion that he might be moving to Fort Lauderdale, of course! What better moment to spring a surprise:

"Your tennis partner called. She's invited us to dinner tonight."

Oh, Francie was very good, showing almost no reaction at all. "Don't worry," she said. "I'll cancel."

"Why would you want to do that?"

"I know how you hate those things."

"Not at all. In fact, I've already accepted."

"You want to go?"

"Why not? She sounds . . . charming, and she

is your tennis partner. You must be a nice fit."

"A nice fit?"

"On the court. You're in the finals, after all."

"Anne's a good player."

He poured another glass of water, started for the door that led to his basement room, stopped with his hand on the knob. "Her husband's coming, too," he said. "I didn't quite catch his name." He paused, his back to her. "Fred, is it?"

"Ned."

That surprised him. He'd expected something craven: "I'm not sure" or "Ned, I believe." Surprised him and infuriated him. He went downstairs without another word.

Roger sat by the glassed-in window in the spectators' gallery off the bar, overlooking court one. On the court, the umpire was already in her chair, and the players were warming up their serves. He studied them one by one. First, the opposition: a stocky woman with an uncoordinated service motion, each component slightly mistimed, and a thinner one with better form but little power. Then he turned to Francie and her partner: Francie had improved her serve since he'd last seen her play, years before; she'd perfected her slide step, now got her legs nicely under the ball, hit it hard. And her partner, Anne: a delicate-looking woman, she reminded him of a Vassar girl he'd dated long ago, his only serious girlfriend before Francie. Anne had the best form of all, but she wasn't putting a single serve in the court. He leaned forward, trying to figure out why, at the same time hearing the gallery — there was room for fifteen or twenty people, no more — fill around him, hearing Francie's name mentioned more than once. He should have been prepared, but was not, for that smooth voice.

"This seat taken?"

He turned to face radio boy. "No."

"Thanks." Radio boy sat down beside him. He held up crossed fingers. "My wife's playing for all the marbles."

"So is mine," said Roger.

Radio boy looked down at the court. "Which one is she?"

Roger pointed her out.

"Oh, Francie," said radio boy. "I met her the other night — when Anne twisted her ankle." He held out his hand. "Ned Demarco."

Smooth, smoother even than Francie. Roger had no choice but to shake his hand, hand that had been all over his wife. "Roger Cullingwood."

"Nice to meet you, Roger. Let's hope we bring them a little luck."

Roger smiled, a smile that spread and spread, almost culminating in that laughing bark. But he held it in and said, "There's no luck in tennis."

"Heads," said Francie. The coin spun in the air, bounced on the court. The umpire bent over it.

"Tails," she said.

Francie and Anne touched racquets, moved back to return serve, Anne in the deuce court, Francie in the ad. "How's the ankle?" Francie said.

"I feel fine."

But she didn't look fine: her face was colorless, except for the mauve depressions under her eyes, and the eyes themselves couldn't meet Francie's gaze.

"Hungry?" said Francie.

"No."

"Me either," said Francie. She glanced up into the gallery, saw Roger and Ned side by side, talking. Even though she hadn't been able to derail Anne's dinner plans, had prepared herself for the possibility that they might sit together, she wasn't prepared. She swung her racquet a few times, tried to make her arm feel long. "Let's work up a fucking appetite," she said.

Anne smiled, a smile barely there, quickly gone. *Was she about to burst into tears? What the hell was going on? Tennis, Francie. Just watch the ball.*

The server tucked one ball under her skirt, held up the other — "Play well," Francie said — and served. Not a hard serve, not deep in the box, on Anne's forehand. By now Francie had seen Anne do many good things with a serve like that — the crosscourt chip, the lob into the corner, the down-the-line putaway. She had never seen her jerk it ten feet wide, never seen her hit with such a tight, awkward motion. A little spot of color appeared on Anne's cheek.

"Sorry," she said, not for the last time.

"Not a problem," Francie said, also not for the last time.

When the match ended an hour and fifteen minutes later, the red spot had spread all over Anne's face, down her neck, vanishing beneath her collar. But Francie had stopped seeing that bright redness, stopped hearing the "sorry's," stopped saying encouraging little things, stopped noticing Anne's double faults, unforced errors, mishits, blocked all that right out. Blocked out everything in her life as well — Ned, Roger, the cottage. She just played, forgot her life and played as she had never played before: winning her serve at love in almost every game, hitting winners from all over the court, making shots she seldom even attempted, topspin lobs from both sides, inside-out forehands, backhand overheads. Everything went in. At the same time she learned that Vince Lombardi had been wrong, that winning wasn't the only thing, or everything — it was nothing. All that mattered was hitting that ball on the goddamn nose, again and again and again; pounding, booming shots that never came back. The sound of the ball off her racquet was frightening. They lost 4–6, 4–6.

The umpire handed out trophies, big ones for the winners, little ones for Francie and Anne. The winners stayed on the court to have their pictures taken. Anne, her face now draining of blood and as blank as a shell-shocked soldier's, went into the locker room, Francie behind her.

A fancy locker room, with whirlpool, sauna, steam, all deserted on a Saturday night. Francie started to lay her hand on Anne's shoulder, held back. What to say? All she could think of was "Jacuzzi?"

"In a minute," said Anne, not looking back at her. Anne turned down the row that led to her locker; Francie moved on to hers.

She sat on a stool without stirring for a minute or two, the muscles in her legs tingling, a human version of the hum of idling machines. She felt great. What other potentials were locked up in her? The potential for love had already been freed by Ned, and others still inside probably had to do with the children she'd never had and never would. She felt less great.

Francie stripped off her clothes, opened her locker, put on the faded maillot hanging inside. The whirlpool was at the back of the locker room, near the showers. She switched on the timer, got in, closed her eyes, and had a crazy idea almost at once: Why not just take off for somewhere far away, by herself? The Atlas Mountains, Prague, Mombasa. She'd driven through the Atlas Mountains years ago with Brenda, stoned on kif — that many years ago — remembered robed Berber children holding up chunks of amethyst by the roadside, stunted magicians performing their purple tricks. Why couldn't —

Francie opened her eyes. Had she heard something over the sound of the bubbles? She twisted the timer down to zero, listened, heard it again, then got out of the whirlpool and followed the sounds to Anne's locker.

Anne was sitting on a stool, her back to Francie. She was wrapped in a towel, her head in her hands, her shoulders shaking.

"Anne?"

No reply, just her sobbing, full-throated and ragged. Francie moved around in front of her. "Anne. Please. It's only tennis."

Anne looked up, tears streaming down her splotchy face, snot, too: misery undisguised. "It's not the tennis, Francie. I —" The sobbing took over. Her towel slipped, exposing her breasts, but she didn't notice. Francie couldn't help noticing, even at that moment couldn't help comparing them to her own: the two pairs of breasts in Ned's life.

"Please, Anne." Francie touched her shoulder. "Everything's all right."

At her touch, Anne fell forward, grabbed Francie around the waist, clung to her, her wet face against Francie's wet bathing suit. "Help me, Francie."

"With what? What's wrong?"

And then Anne's face was tilted up at her, imploring, and Anne, fighting the sobbing demon inside her for control of her own voice, got the words out. "It's N— it's Ned. I . . . I think he's having an a-a-affair."

Francie, stroking the back of Anne's head, went still. The towel had fallen to the floor, and Anne, naked, was holding on to Francie harder than ever, her crying eyes locked on Francie's, desperate, pleading. "Oh, God," Francie said, doing all she could not to cry herself. "I'm so sorry."

At that moment, with them in each other's arms, Francie saw Nora standing wide-eyed at the end of the row of lockers. Francie shifted her own eyes once in the direction she wanted Nora to go. Nora went.

Anne made a sound, partly smothered by Francie's breast, somewhere between laughing and crying. "Don't you be upset, Francie. It's not your fault. You're the best thing that's happened to me in a long time. She's" — the laughing component vanished — "she's just so much prettier than me, and so much smarter. I guess he couldn't resist."

Francie stepped back, freeing herself from Anne's grasp. "Who are you talking about?"

Something — the new distance between them, the change in Francie's tone — made Anne grow aware of her nakedness. She reached for the towel, rewrapped herself, rose unsteadily to her feet. "No one you know, Francie. It's terrible of me to inflict this on you, especially after that exhibition out there."

"Fuck that," Francie said. "Who?"

"Her name's Kira Chang. She's high up in some big media outfit in L.A. She even had dinner in my house. Can you believe it?"

"Are you sure?"

"Sure?"

"That it's happening. That he's . . . doing this."

"I haven't walked in on them or anything, if that's what you mean."

"Then how do you know?"

"I just do." She shivered like a baby after a long cry.

"But based on what?"

"Little things, but a wife always knows deep down, doesn't she?"

"What little things?"

"Like the other night, the night he drove you back here. He didn't come home for hours and he had some feeble story about a flat tire. I know he was with her."

"How?"

"She called him. It must have been about the arrangements. She's that brazen."

Brazen. Francie flinched at the word; did Anne not see? "But how can you be sure?" Francie said. "What's your evidence?"

Anne stopped mopping her face with a corner of the towel, stared at Francie. "You think I'm stupid."

"You know better. Why do you even say things like that?"

"It's your tone. I haven't heard you like this

before, so impatient."

Francie took a deep breath. Anne had the right story but the wrong name; that meant she really knew nothing, not with certainty, and it had to stay that way. What Francie was seeing now wouldn't compare with what would happen to Anne if she ever learned the truth. "I just don't want you jumping to any false conclusions," Francie said. "How do you know he didn't have a flat tire, for example?"

"I checked the spare. He said he hadn't been able to use it because it was flat, too, but in fact he hadn't even unbolted it to look."

"Does he have a pressure gauge?"

"Pressure gauge?"

"One of those little sticks to put on the valve. That's all you need to check pressure — the tire can stay where it is."

"I don't know."

"That's what I mean about jumping to conclusions."

"Do you think I should ask him?"

"Why not?"

"I'm not good at that kind of thing."

"Then — then just look in his car."

"That's a good idea. You're so smart, Francie." She stared at her feet. "God — what I've put you through tonight."

"It's still early."

Anne looked up, started laughing, laughter that threatened several times to turn to tears, but did not. "You're the best, Francie," she said, and embraced her again, kissing her on the cheek. "Don't be mad at me."

"Let's just hope he has that pressure gauge," Francie said, hating herself for it, but it was just the kind of pragmatic remark she would have made if Kira Chang really were a suspect, and she had to stay in character, Anne's tennis partner and newfound friend.

"Oh, Francie. Do you think he does? I love him so much." Her eyes filled with tears, but not tears of misery this time; she had hope, was starting to believe in her marriage again. "I even have these fantasies of us getting old together, going for long walks in the woods, that kind of thing. Do you?"

"Do I what?"

"Have fantasies like that."

"Everybody has fantasies."

Anne bit her lip. "Francie?"

"Yes?"

"If you had to bet on the pressure gauge?"

"It'll be there," Francie said.

Quick, Francie. Shower, dress, dirty things in the gym bag, out, out ahead of Anne. Francie hurried up to the bar. A few people actually applauded as she came in. Francie hardly heard. She scanned the room for Ned, found him — drinking Scotch with Roger. She went to their table. They both rose, something she couldn't recall either of them doing separately, ever.

"Very well played, Francie," Roger said.

"Just incredible," Ned said. "If only —"

"Thanks," said Francie, interrupting whatever was coming after that. "I'm thirsty."

They sat down. The waiter appeared. Francie ordered water and a beer. Anne would be there any moment. She had to get Ned alone, but how? Both men were looking at her, both a little flushed, both on the point of making some remark as soon as the waiter left. "Damn it," she said, kicking Ned under the table, "I forgot something. Excuse me." She got up, left the bar, went down to the lobby, borrowed a pen and a piece of paper at the desk, drank from the fountain, did this and that, looked busy. Where was Ned? Didn't he get it?

Ned walked into the lobby, saw her. By now she was at the bulletin board, pretending to scan it. He stood beside her. "You didn't have to kick me so hard," he said, eyes on the bulletin board.

"Is there a pressure gauge in your car?"

A pause, but very brief. Francie was sure she felt him reeling inside. "What does she know?" he said, almost too low to hear.

"She doesn't *know* anything. She thinks you're having an affair with Kira Chang."

Francie glanced at him. His eyes were closed and there was a V-shaped groove on the right side of his brow. He opened his eyes, turned to her. "What are we going to do?"

Get on the next plane to Marrakech, she thought, *you and me*. She said, "Do you have a pressure gauge, yes or no?"

"No."

"Give me your keys."

He glanced around, handed her the keys.

"What did you tell him?" Francie said.

"That I was going to the bathroom."

"Then go."

Ned headed for the locker room. Francie hurried back upstairs to the bar, thinking fast. She had come in Roger's car, Anne in Ned's. Roger would have a pressure gauge; she seldom went in his car, had never actually seen his pressure gauge, but she knew him.

Roger was writing something on a napkin as she approached the table. He smiled. "I was getting lonely all by myself." He folded the napkin, pocketed it.

"I can't find my hairbrush," Francie said, the kind of female inanity he wouldn't question. "I must have left it in your car, if you'll give me the keys."

"Your hair looks fine to me."

"Thanks," she said, holding out her hand. He gave her the keys.

Downstairs, across the lobby, out. The two cars were parked side by side under the full glow of a sodium arc light. Francie unlocked Roger's, flipped open the glove box, riffled through the contents: manual, warranty, maps, calculator, touch-up paint; pressure gauge. She grabbed it, locked the car, unlocked Ned's car, opened his glove box. The contents burst out, cascaded to the floor: CDs, tapes, floppy disks, bills, letters, receipts, crayon drawings, crayons, elastics, tokens, and M&M's, which in turn came spilling out of their box in a second flood. Francie scooped everything up, crammed it all back in the glove box, jammed in the pressure gauge, and was just about to lock up when she noticed the front door of the club starting to open. She tossed Ned's keys on the seat, banged the door shut with her foot, leaned against Roger's car.

They came across the lot, Anne in the middle, Roger and Ned on either side, their faces orange under the light. She handed Roger his keys. "Find that hairbrush?" he said.

"No."

"I think I've got one," Anne said, waiting for Ned to unlock his car.

"It's open," Ned said, getting in.

"You're a trusting soul," said Roger, unlocking his car.

Anne got in, opened the glove box. Everything exploded back out again, into her lap. "Yikes," she said, starting to sort through it. "I thought I had a hair —" Francie saw Anne's hand closing on something, saw her raise it up into the light for a better look: the pressure gauge. She gave Francie a quick smile, private and conspiratorial, through the window.

20

"I hope this doesn't offend anyone," said Ned, dispensing with his elegant little fork and slurping the oyster right off the shell. "The only way to eat them," he said, patting his mouth with a napkin. He'd ordered a dozen, the others — Francie, Anne, Roger — half a dozen each.

"Not at all," said Roger. "Boldness is all when it comes to certain of the appetites."

"I'm sorry?" said Ned, pausing, the next oyster halfway to his mouth.

"You know that old saw," Roger said, tasting the Montrachet he'd ordered and nodding to the waiter. " 'He was a bold man that first eat an oyster.' "

Francie could see from the look on his face that Ned didn't know. "Swift, isn't it?" she said. "And since the bold man probably wasn't bold enough to venture into the kitchen, his wife must have tried it first."

Laughter. Roger raised his glass to her. Ned's eyes lingered on her face; didn't he realize those eyes were too obviously appreciative, even loving, if you knew them? Next his foot would be touching hers under the table; she drew her feet under the chair and said, "The bread, please." Ned passed it to her, his hand moving a little quicker than Roger's.

The waiter filled their glasses. Anne drank half of hers in one gulp. "Swift," she said. "Do you know the *Marriage Service from His Chamber Window*?"

No one did.

She drank some more. " 'Under this window in stormy weather / I marry this man and woman together; / Let none but Him who rules the thunder / Put this man and woman asunder.' "

Silence.

"How times change," Roger said.

Anne looked across the table at him. "Beautiful, isn't it? I wanted it read at our wedding."

Roger refilled her glass.

"This is wonderful wine, Roger," Anne said. She glanced at Ned. "I'll know something to order from now on."

"If we win the lottery," Ned said. Roger's eyes swept over him; Francie thought Ned's dark face darkened some more.

Roger turned to Anne. "But?" he said.

She put down her glass. "But?"

Roger smiled. "But Swift didn't make the grade?"

Anne glanced again at Ned.

"It wasn't raining on our wedding day, for one thing," Ned said. "And we were indoors."

Roger topped off Ned's glass. "Where was this?"

"Our wedding? In Cleveland."

"Ah," said Roger.

"We're both from Cleveland," Anne said.

"I've never actually been there," Roger said, sipping his wine. "Have you, Francie?"

"Yes," she said, stupidly adding, "it's very nice."

"I'm sure it is," Roger said. "And what brought the two of you here?"

"Ned did postdoc work at B.U. We liked it so much, we stayed."

"Your field, Ned, if it's not rude to ask?"

"Psychology."

"You teach at B.U.?"

"I have. Now I'm in private practice."

"Don't be so modest, Ned," Anne said. "He's also on the radio five days a week."

"Really?" said Roger. "In what capacity?"

"Ned has his own show."

"Psychology instruction?"

"More like advice," Anne said. "It's called *Intimately Yours*. *Boston Magazine*'s doing a piece next month."

"Dear Abby of the air?" said Roger.

"I wouldn't put it that way," Ned said.

"My apologies."

"None necessary. I just try to help the callers think things through on their own."

"From what perspective?"

"I'm not sure I follow."

Roger shrugged. "The usual suspects. Freud? Jung? Adler? Frankl?"

"All and none. I take what I need from what's out there. I've found that sticking to dogma usually makes things worse."

Roger looked thoughtful. "Taking what you need," he said. "Sounds interesting. I'll be sure to listen in."

"WBRU," said Anne. "Ninety-two point nine."

The waiter returned and started clearing the first course. "And what do you do, Roger?" Ned asked.

"Nothing as sexy as that," he said. "I raise private investment capital. Very drab."

"What's the name of your company?"

"That," said Roger, "I'm not at liberty to say at this moment." Then he winked at Ned; Francie had never seen him wink before, would almost have thought him incapable of it.

"Finished, sir?" the waiter asked Ned, seeing he'd left three oysters uneaten.

"Yes."

"Can't let those go to waste," said Roger, lifting one off Ned's plate. "Mind if I emulate you?" he asked, and ate it off the shell; his lips glistened. "You're so right," he said. "There's no other way."

"Excuse me," Francie said, and went to the bathroom.

Her face in the mirror: still looking normal. How was it possible, with Roger at his very worst? With what she was doing to Anne? And Ned — why was he asking questions he knew the answers to? Yet there was her face. Normal. Why wasn't it an ultrasound of what was happening inside, like Anne's? She splashed cold water on it anyway.

Anne came in, talked to her in the mirror. "Isn't this fun?" she said. "You never told me Roger was so smart."

Anne went into the single cubicle, and then came the tinkling sound of her urine flowing into the bowl. "And so distinguished-looking," she continued unselfconsciously, as though they were sisters. "Can I ask you something personal?"

"Sure," Francie said, and in the mirror her expression changed. It was the eyes: they grew alert, like an animal's, even those of a dangerous one.

"Why didn't you and Roger have children?"

Finally, something that made her face change. It crumpled.

"Francie? Have I said something wrong?"

"No." Face still crumpled, but voice even. "We wanted them but it was a physical impossibility."

"I'm sorry."

"Nothing to be sorry about. It happens all the time. We got over it."

Francie heard her tear off a strip of toilet paper. "Em was so impressed with you."

"It was mutual," Francie said. Her face began to smooth itself out.

"Really? You liked her?"

"Who wouldn't?"

Anne came out of the cubicle. "What nice

soaps," she said, and washed her hands. Their gazes met in the mirror. "Do you have any sisters, Francie?"

"No."

"Neither do I. I always wanted one."

Francie handed her one of the plush little towels folded on the granite sink top.

"Are you mad at me?" Anne said.

"Why would I be mad at you?"

"The way I played. Will you ever forgive me?"

"I don't think like that."

"Oh, I know you don't, Francie. You're like a lion — that's how *I* think of *you* — strong, proud, loyal."

"Stop it."

"If only you'd told me about that" — Anne lowered her voice — "pressure gauge" — and raised it — "earlier, we would have won that goddamn match."

"Next year," Francie said, although she knew she couldn't bear a whole year of dinners like this, ski weekends, double-dating, conspiracy.

Anne grinned. "Is that a promise?"

"Francie's promised we're going to try again next year," Anne said.

"I'll put it on my calendar," Roger said before calling for another bottle of Montrachet.

He went to the bathroom between the entrée and dessert, as Francie knew he would. She'd been his wife for a long time, was familiar with

244

his bladder capacity.

"How awful would it be if I stole one of those soaps?" Anne said.

"Which one?" Francie asked.

"Guess."

"The oatmeal."

"She knows me so well, Ned." And to Francie: "Do you think it would be all right?"

"I'm sure they budget for it," Francie said.

So Anne went, too. And then they were alone. Their eyes met. "You never told me what a shit he is," Ned said.

"Didn't I?"

"No. Why the hell did you marry him? Or is that out of bounds?"

"You can ask me anything," Francie said. "He was different then."

"No one changes that much."

"And maybe I misjudged him. He seemed so . . . original to me then."

"Original? He's a throwback, Francie."

"It's not that simple," she said. She didn't like the way Ned was looking at her, as though her stock had fallen in his eyes because of the company she kept. "And please, don't bring out your tool bag. It's been a long, slow decline, maybe worse since he lost his job, which you knew about, if I'm not mistaken."

"I was just making conversation."

"Were you?"

"No." He smiled, a rueful, boyish smile, and looked . . . adorable, even at a time like that.

Francie reached out with her foot, felt for his, found it.

"A long, slow decline," she said. "I didn't realize the extent of it, until . . ."

"Until what?"

"Till you came in your kayak."

Ned's eyes changed. She knew what he was going to say before he said it, was already thinking the same thing. "I want you," he said.

They looked at each other in a way they shouldn't have, not in a public place.

"Monday night," he said. "At the cottage."

"Monday?"

"There's no show — they're broadcasting the Pops Christmas concert."

Francie thought, *We can't*. But she didn't say it.

"Six-thirty?" he said.

Francie thought, *No*. Ned's foot pressed against hers; that little touch, through shoe leather and so far from erogenous zones, nevertheless sent a wave of sensation through her so powerful, it almost made her gasp. She couldn't get that *no* out, began having counterthoughts like *how can one more time hurt?* and *if I'm saying good-bye it should be in person,* and then Roger was back, and Ned's foot was gone.

"So," said Roger, picking his napkin off the chair and replacing it in his lap as he sat down, "what's the plan?"

"The plan?" said Francie.

"Just coffee? Or perhaps something sweet."

Francie had coffee, Roger and Ned cognac, Anne a cake called death by chocolate.

"This is incredible," Anne said, "but I can't possibly finish it. Anybody want some?"

No one did.

The bill came. Roger took it from the waiter's hand.

"Wait a minute," Ned said. "Let's split it, at least."

"Sharesies?" said Roger. "After you win that lottery. No, this is my treat. Mine and Francie's, that is. It's been a pleasure."

"But Roger, it was my idea," said Anne.

"And a very good one. We'll do it again soon."

Outside a cold wind was blowing. Anne and Francie stood hunched inside their coats while the men went to the parking garage across the street.

"Do you think it's true what they say about oysters, Francie?"

"No."

Anne was quiet for a moment. "Then maybe it's the wine."

"What is?"

"If it's not the oysters."

Francie was silent.

"Having an effect on me. If you know what I mean." Anne looked at Francie sideways. "Can I ask you something?"

"I'm going to kill you," Francie said.

Anne laughed. "Sorry. And sorry for saying

sorry. But it's kind of . . . intimate."

"Ask away."

"In a marriage," Anne said, "after you've been together for some time, if you see what I'm getting at. What do you do to keep him — to keep things stimulating?"

Francie felt sick.

"I don't mean you personally. What does one do? I read in *Cosmo* — on *Cosmo*, actually — that some men like dirty talk. In bed, I mean, during . . ."

"I don't think it's a matter of tricks," Francie said, realizing the truth of it as she spoke.

"Then what is it?"

"Enthusiasm." That had been missing from her bed — hers and Roger's in the days they shared it — if not from the start, then certainly since their procreative fiasco.

Anne nodded; Francie could see she was making a mental note.

The two cars drove out of the parking garage, stopped in front of Huîtres. "Good night," Francie said. And she thought, *Good-bye. Have the fucking strength to make it good-bye, good-bye to you both.*

"Night, Francie," said Anne, getting into Ned's car. She smiled over the top of the door. "Enthusiasm — I should have known."

Francie went to bed alone. She lay awake for a long time, staring at the ceiling. Then she got up, found sleeping pills in the back of the medicine cabinet, left over from the bouts of sleeplessness that followed the last artificial insemination. She took two, returned to bed, waited for them to act, which at last they did.

Anne went to bed with Ned. They lay in the darkness.

"How were your oysters?" she asked.

"Fine."

"Mine, too. Better than that."

"That's good."

"I've decided I love oysters." She moved closer to him, not quite touching. Enthusiasm, but perhaps *Cosmo* was right, too. Why not come out with all guns blasting, as Francie would? She put her mouth to his ear, breathed into it. His whole body tensed gratifyingly, giving her the courage to go on. In a low voice she said, "I love your cock, Ned. I want to . . . do things to it." She reached down his body.

He stopped her hand. "I'm sorry, Anne. I have a splitting headache."

She froze. "That's supposed to be my line," she said, the kind of witty remark Francie might make. But she couldn't keep it up; all the air went out of her, and then her mind started dragging her down a long spiral, down and down while Ned fell asleep.

A long spiral, all the way back to the pressure gauge. Anne got out of bed, left the bedroom, walked down the hall. She heard Em make a noise in her sleep, paused outside her door. Em rolled over in her bed, then lay quiet. Anne moved on, downstairs, through the door that led from the kitchen to the garage. Yes, he had a pressure gauge, but did that mean he had used it? No. But perhaps she would be able to tell whether that little rubber thing, the protector, the guard, whatever they called it, had ever been unscrewed from the valve. Might there not be greasy fingerprints on it, or stripped threads inside? She opened Ned's trunk, examined the rubber valve guard on the spare. No fingerprints. She unscrewed it. It stuck just a little before giving way, as though this were the first turning, but she didn't know enough about the subject to make that judgment. She peered inside, could see nothing wrong with the threads. Proving? Nothing. He did have that pressure gauge, he did get headaches sometimes, and over the years she had been less and less sexual with him: it was probably her own fault. Why had she been like that? She didn't know. Perhaps she would work up the nerve to discuss it with Francie.

Anne was about to close the trunk, to go back to bed, to try the enthusiasm gambit again, perhaps the next morning or tomorrow night, when she noticed that the map that had been jammed into the wheel well against the spare was no longer there; and the irises: gone, too. Anne searched the trunk, the glove box, under the seats, behind the visors, but she didn't find them.

She stood in the garage, thinking, getting nowhere, and her gaze fell on the trash barrels, lined up along the wall. She began with the nearest one. It held two green plastic bags. She took out the first, unknotted the red ties, dug through, found nothing but recent garbage. Then she removed the second bag, was starting to open it as well, when she noticed the irises, crushed at the bottom of the barrel. The map of New Hampshire with the red X in the middle of the Merrimack River lay under them.

Picking his napkin off the chair and replacing it in his lap as he sat down! Roger lay on the couch in his basement HQ, his mind racing much too fast for sleep. Weren't they aware that the proper place to leave a napkin while away from the table was to the left of the forks, folded in half, and that only a boor would leave it on his chair? Evidently not: it was symptomatic, emblematic, of the contrast between them and him. Picking the napkin off the chair, replacing it carefully on his lap, because why? Because under it was this little digital recorder, not much bigger than a credit card — birthday gift from Francie, he recalled, so he could record business ideas while in the car — spinning silently away. He rewound it and listened again, editing out background noise — laughter, cutlery clattering on china, chair legs scraping the floor — transcribing it black-and-white in his mind.

N: *You never told me what a shit he is.*

F: *Didn't I?*

N: *No. Why the hell did you marry him? Or is that out of bounds?*

F: *You can ask me anything. He was different then.*

N: *No one changes that much.*

F: *And maybe I misjudged him. He seemed so . . . original to me then.*

N: *Original? He's a throwback, Francie.*

F: *It's not that simple. And please, don't bring out your tool bag. It's been a long, slow decline, maybe worse since he lost his job, which you knew about, if I'm not mistaken.*

N: *I was just making conversation.*

F: *Were you?*

N: *No.*

F: *A long, slow decline. I didn't realize the extent of it, until . . .*

N: *Until what?*

F: *Till you came in your kayak.*

N: *I want you.*

PAUSE: laughter, cutlery on china, scraping chairs.

N (cont'd): *Monday night. At the cottage.*

F: *Monday?*

N: *There's no show — they're broadcasting the Pops Christmas concert. Six-thirty?*

LONG PAUSE: more laughter, cutlery, scraping.

R: *So. What's the plan?*

21

Late Saturday afternoon, the sky glowing orange through the grillwork of bare black trees — oak, maple, poplar — around Little Joe Lake. Riding in his own car, a ten-year-old Bronco with 124,000 miles on the odometer — many of the taxpayers knew Saturday was his day off, and wouldn't care to see him swanning around at their expense in the cruiser with CHIEF on the side — Joe Savard followed the lane that ran up the east side of the lake. With snow on the ground he preferred the Bronco anyway, at least until the town came through with new tires for the cruiser. His request had been tabled till the April meeting, along with the school textbooks, the cable TV contract, and the landfill amendment. And of course the streetlight question, he added to himself, nosing over to the side to let a white pickup go by; the streetlight question, a hopeless perennial, like mud in the spring. The driver raised his hand in thanks, perhaps flashing the peace sign, although with the pickup's windows so dirty, Savard couldn't be sure. The body, too, although not so dirty he couldn't read the words on the side panel: LITTLE WHITE CHURCH OF THE RE-DEEMER. Savard pulled back into the lane and kept going.

At one time, there'd been many Savards in the

area and they'd owned the whole lake. It was probably named after a Savard: in a box somewhere lay a family Bible signed by generations of them, and they seemed to have restricted themselves to three male names, Joseph, Lucien, and Hiram; so he could have done worse. Now he was the last one, and all he owned was the single cabin built on what wasn't much more than a big rock a few yards from shore at the north end, reached by the lopsided little footbridge that might not last another winter. That rock being the last of the land, him being the last of the people: probably the reason he hadn't sold the cabin back when he should have, after Sue.

Not that he'd done much reasoning during that period. He'd just left the cabin unattended for a few years, unwilling to see it or even think about it. But after his second marriage, he'd started renting the cabin out in summer, hoping to raise extra cash for some of the little things his second wife seemed to like. Later came the divorce, another good time for selling out. But it was around that time that he'd discovered his hobby, and now he drove out to the cabin almost every day off.

Savard parked at the end of the turnout that led from the lake road to the footbridge. Lifting his chain saw off the passenger seat, he stepped down and noticed that someone else had parked there, not long before. He could tell from the way the tires had pressed four deep prints in the snow after tracking in from the south, as he had

— old tires with hardly any tread left at all. He followed their route with his eyes, backing out, returning to the south, through the long shadows of the trees on the snow, snow turning red-black in the dying light.

The footbridge creaked once or twice as Savard walked across. He wasn't especially tall — six feet if he stood his straightest — but he had the broad and powerful family build. Many Savards had anchored the Dartmouth line, going back to the early years of football, although not him — he'd gone to Vietnam instead. Not by choice; he just hadn't been able to get the kind of math scores Dartmouth required. Algebra 1, geometry, algebra 2: a maze he'd wandered through in high school without finding his way, despite never missing class, sitting in the front row, staying after for extra help, puzzling over the homework problems every night, but too often failing to solve for x. SAT math score: 470. He still remembered that goddamned number, probably the only number that had ever been solid in his mind. Four seventy led to war; war led to law enforcement, which became a profession after Sue. End of story. The truth, which had come to him years later the way truths did in his case, if at all, was that he hadn't liked school anyway, except for sports, and would probably have disliked Dartmouth, too.

Savard opened the cabin door, went inside. It was no longer the kind of cabin anyone would want to rent. Savard had gutted it, sledgehammering all the partitions on both floors — some emotions had got loose that day, the room where it had happened, all the rooms, were now gone — ripping out the second floor itself as well, down to the structural beams. He'd left one toilet, one sink, both unusable now with the water turned off and the pipes drained for winter. The rest was space, high and open, mostly shadows at this hour, except for the red glare on the lakeside windows, a color reflected dully on the unpolished surfaces of the bears.

Savard still thought of them as bears because that was what he'd been after at the start, life-size bears carved — if cutting with a chain saw could be called carving — from the biggest cedar trunks he could find, dead standing and naturally dried when he could get it. After the divorce, those days off had gotten a little too long, and he'd gone to work once a week for a woodlot across the Maine line, not far from Kezar Falls. The work was hard; he'd been handy with a chain saw since boyhood; he got to wander around in the woods; they paid him: a good job. One evening, while he was walking back toward the logging road and his ride out, a big bear had reared up at him through the trees. He did what you were supposed to do, which was nothing. He wasn't afraid, not with that chain saw in his hands — the noise alone would do the trick. The bear didn't move either, as if following the same guidelines, and after watching for a minute or so, Savard realized it wasn't a bear, but a tall tree stump that looked like a bear.

Savard went closer, circled the stump, then without thinking, pulled the cord and raised his saw — a heavy Black & Decker four-footer — and gave it a little more definition between the head and shoulder. Almost too much: he went at the snout with more finesse, narrowing it, then rounded off that big muscle pad behind the neck. He stepped back for a better look — terrible.

But he'd gotten the bug, and the next Saturday he drove home with ten foot of cedar, most of it sticking out the back of the Bronco. White cedar, specifically: he'd always liked the soft, sunny glow hiding under its sappy skin. Savard had floated his log across the water to the cabin, dragged it up to the door with the ATV he'd had then — one of those little things he'd thought would please his second wife; she'd ridden it once — and humped it through the door.

The carving had taken a year. By the end of that time he'd settled on the right tool — an electric Stihl 14, only four pounds or so, delicate enough for eyes, claws, nostrils — and had learned the most important lesson: to let the wood guide the saw. His first bear was man-size and stood by itself on its hind legs, but he didn't fool himself into thinking it was anything but crude. There was just one good thing about bear number one: it had that poker face that makes bears so dangerous. Savard brought back a new tree trunk the next week to see if the poker face had been an accident.

Savard didn't finish bear number two, if finishing meant carving a complete bear down to the ground; in fact, he never attempted another complete bear. He'd gotten the second bear's poker face almost right away — this one was even more ambiguous, if that was the word — and was sawing his slow way down to the chest when he lost focus. As he worked, he began to find himself watching not the side of the chain where the bear was emerging, but the other side, the tree side. For no reason, he decided to make bear number two half-bear, half-tree. There was a . . . relationship between the bear and the tree, a complicated one, not especially pleasing to either of them, if that made any sense. It took Savard four months to reach that point with the second bear. Bear three began the next Saturday.

By now Savard had lost track of the number of bears he'd carved with his chain saw. Many had ended up in the woodstove, making floor space for new bears. Not that anyone looking at the recent ones would have identified them as bears. Savard was interested in only two things now: the struggle, if you could call it that, between the bear and the tree, and the pokeriness, if that was a word, of the face, even though there no longer was anything resembling a face. Struggle and pokeriness, his terminology for what he was doing with the bears. It didn't have to make sense because he never discussed it with anyone. No one else ever came inside the cabin; no one else had ever seen them.

Savard lit the woodstove, dragged the floor lamp — the only piece of furniture in the place — into position, switched it on. He surveyed his latest bear, a big one because the trunk was big: old, slow-growth cedar, with thin-spaced rings and a grain that felt like satin. His latest bear — a massive, twisting shape, almost too massive to be able to twist, but it did — locked in combat with some force in the wood. He knew the force was real, having felt it through the saw. Strapping on his Kevlar-lined chaps — he'd had over thirty stitches in his legs by now, didn't want more — he filed the teeth and rakers in the chain as sharp as he could get them, put on his headphones. In the beginning he'd kept his ears uncovered, lost in the sound — much quieter than a gas-powered saw, but still whining and buzzing nastily as metal turned wood to dust. Later, noticing that his hearing wasn't as sharp as it had been, he'd worn protection. Now he preferred music, Django Reinhardt specifically. That was the way he worked: Paris singing in his ears — he'd never been to Paris, never been anywhere, really, except Vietnam, but Paris must have been something like Django's music, if it wasn't still — Paris singing in his ears, the saw throbbing in his hands, sawdust shooting through the yellow pool of lamplight, swirling past the blazing windows that faced the setting sun.

Joe Savard worked all night. When dawn came, and the east side windows lit up, first milky, then butter-colored, he saw what he had seen so many times before, that he'd only made things worse. Still, as in all those other times, he felt good just the same. Hard to explain. A feeling kids get when they stand in a doorway pressing their arms against the jambs, then quickly step free, arms levitating by themselves, as though weightless; a feeling like that, but all over.

A good feeling, followed by ravenous hunger. Savard closed up and drove to Lavinia's, a diner he liked a few miles up 101. Black coffee, bacon and scrambled eggs, side of hash browns. While he waited for his order he asked for a phone book. He found a listing for the Little White Church of the Redeemer in Lawton Ferry, on the eastern border of his territory.

Food came. He ate it all, almost ordered the same again; would have, even a year or two ago. But he was up to 220, and that was the limit.

"How about a blueberry muffin, Joe?" asked Lavinia. "Baked personally in the oven of yours truly."

No refusal possible. He ate the muffin, but without honey, even though he was very fond of honey.

"I like appetite in a man," Lavinia said, clearing his plate, refilling his cup.

"Sure you do," Savard said. "You own a restaurant."

She gave him a look, a complicated one that he didn't meet for more than a second. He had no desire to get closer to Lavinia. Not true: he had a strong desire to get closer to Lavinia, but only once or twice, and that wasn't for him.

Savard drank up, paid his bill, leaving a bigger tip than usual, and was halfway out the door when he paused, then went back inside and picked up the pay phone. He dialed the Little White Church of the Redeemer.

"You have reached the house of God. No one is here to take your call right now."

Savard left a message after the tone.

22

"Ah, right on the dot," said Roger, standing beneath the statue of George Washington, Sunday at ten. "Punctuality is the courtesy of kings."

"It is?" said Whitey, red-eyed, yellow-faced, blue-lipped, rumpled, as though he'd spent the night drinking and then slept, or passed out, in his car. But he didn't have a car, and where had he slept, come to think of it? An unknown factor, quite certainly inconsequent; still, it was a relief to remember that Whitey wouldn't be around much longer.

"Just an expression," Roger explained, at the same time calculating with some precision the time remaining to Whitey — thirty-three hours, at most, thirty-two and a half, at least. A romantic concept, in a way: hadn't innumerable potboilers been based on the conceit of a character given only a short, fixed time to live? Although not, Roger thought, a character like this. He found himself smiling at Whitey.

"Never heard of it," Whitey said. Not a conventionally likable character, but a character nonetheless, in his silly leather jacket and pointy cowboy boots, beyond vulgar.

"No matter. How about some coffee?"

"Now you're talkin'," said Whitey.

They walked out of the Public Garden, waited

for the light to change. Just as it did, Roger caught sight of a large, well-dressed family coming out of the Ritz across the street: an unmatronly mother with upswept blond hair, two tall young adults, some teenagers, one smaller child, and then the father. Something familiar about the father, and in that instant, Roger said, "Go."

"Huh?" said Whitey.

There were people in front of them, blocking at least their lower selves from view. Roger ground his heel on the toe of Whitey's cowboy boot. "Fast. Be back in one hour."

"What the fuck?"

But then the light changed and Roger had no choice but to step off the curb and start across the street, couldn't look back to see whether Whitey was following instructions, or tagging after him and thus aborting his plans, possibly forever. Roger's path intersected that of the monstrously teeming haut-bourgeois family, and in its rear guard the father — Sandy Cronin — spotted him and said, "Hello, Roger."

But therefore, if spotting now, hadn't spotted him earlier, as he waited for the light. "Sandy. Well, well. And all the little ducklings. Merry Christmas."

"And to you, Roger. You and Francie both."

"Thank you, Sandy. I'll make a note to pass it on."

Roger walked on, across the street, along the sidewalk, to the awning of the Ritz, and there, passing behind a top-hatted doorman, he glanced back. The Cronins were well inside the park now; the little one had tossed a chunk of ice at one of the bigger ones, and they all seemed to be laughing. Sandy himself, in his camel-hair coat, was patting a snowball into shape. What kind of justice was this, that a mediocrity like Sandy could so prolifically pass on his mediocre genes, while he, Roger, had been denied? Beyond justice, for justice was merely a human construct, after all, what kind of science was it? How could nature select Cronins over Cullingwoods, unless the degradation of the species was the goal? In his mind's eye he saw again that ineradicable microscopic image of deformed sperm — his — twitching spastically in the petri dish. Ineradicable, yes, but also ineradicable was his suspicion that somehow, in some way yet unknown, it was Francie's fault: Francie, with her babbling of adoption, missing the whole point.

Roger noticed that the Cronins were gone. Noticed, too, that there was no sign of Whitey. The Cronins hadn't seen Whitey — more important, had not seen the two of them together. The plan remained viable, but it had been a near thing. Roger recalled chaos theory, how a butterfly fluttering its wings in the wrong patch of sky could destroy the world. No amount of planning could permanently overcome the inexorability of the natural forces. But all he required was thirty-three hours, to keep those butterflies at bay for thirty-three hours.

Whitey wandered around for a while, at one point sensing he was close to the old Garden, but failing to see any sign of it or its replacement. He did find a bar in the shadow of an overpass and, gloveless, hatless, feeling the cold through his leather jacket — not as warm as he'd expected — went inside. Had a beer. Two. Three. And a shot. He didn't like being stepped on. What was the word? Literally. He'd been stepped on, literally. Why did he have to put up with that shit? He was a free man.

Whitey, pissed, looked around the bar, hoping for some customer who might rub him the wrong way. But he was almost alone, the only other drinkers being a few old drunks with disgusting faces. Stepped on, literally. He knew why, too, had figured it out immediately: Roger hadn't wanted to be seen with him, not by his buddy in the camel-hair coat. A buddy of some kind, no question: screened by the statue of George Washington, Whitey had watched them gabbing in the middle of the street. Roger couldn't have been ashamed to be seen with him, or why would he have offered the assistant's job in the first place? A legitimate assistant, and therefore someone who should be introduced to camel-hair-coated buddies crossing the street. Instead he'd been stepped on. Why? Whitey couldn't figure that out.

He checked his watch, had one more shot to

ward off the cold, laid a fifty on the bar. A fifty: that made him think. Just days back in the world, not the halfway house world but the real one, and already making good money. And it wasn't like Roger was some kind of dangerous dude — he was in the art business, for Christ's sake — while Whitey had known many genuinely dangerous dudes, had spent almost half his life with them. Roger: not dangerous, a well-paying employer — but maybe not to be trusted either, not completely. That was all, Whitey told himself. Just be smart. He left the bar feeling much better.

"You're a bit late, Whitey."

Back under George Washington, temperature falling, refreezing the snow below snowball-making range, condensing the breath that rose from Roger's mouth with his words.

"Got a little lost," Whitey said, playing it smart.

Roger looked at him for a moment, thinking. For the first time it occurred to Whitey that his boss might not be the brightest. Talked fancy sometimes, but that didn't make him bright.

"Thought that was your point," Whitey went on, "for me to get a little lost." That was pretty funny, and he laughed at his own joke.

Roger did not laugh, clearly didn't get it; for sure, not the brightest. He licked his lips, his tongue bright red in contrast to the cold chalk color of his face and lips. "Remember how we spoke of discretion, Whitey? How important it is in this business?"

"Yeah."

"And I'm sure you realize that competition is a factor in all businesses."

"Like McDonald's and Burger King."

"So you won't be taken aback to learn that I have competitors, too."

"In the art recovery business?" Whitey said. Just to nail it down, that that was the business.

Roger smiled. "Sharp today, Whitey, are you not?"

At least Roger had the brains to see that. Whitey shrugged. "No more than usual." Roger's smile broadened. Whitey wondered whether this was too soon to ask for a raise.

"That's why I hired you," Roger said. "But wouldn't it be foolish to show every card to the competition?"

"That guy on the street's a competitor?"

"He thinks so."

"And I'm one of the cards?"

Roger put his gloved hand on Whitey's shoulder. "You're my ace in the hole."

Roger's car was parked nearby.

"What tunes have you got?" said Whitey as they drove along the expressway in light traffic.

"None."

"With a CD player like that?"

Roger said nothing. Whitey flipped on the radio.

"— Ned Demarco, reminding you we won't be in our usual time slot tomorrow, but please tune in for the annual Christmas —"

Roger jabbed at the control buttons. Metallica came on, "The Shortest Straw," one of Whitey's favorites. "That's more like it," he said, glancing at Roger with surprise; he wouldn't have taken him for a metal fan. Roger stared straight ahead.

They got on 93, followed it northwest through the suburbs, toward New Hampshire. After a while Roger turned down the radio and said, "Can you take care of yourself, Whitey?"

"Take care of myself?"

"This business has rough edges sometimes."

"The art business?"

"Any business where big money's involved."

"Big money?"

Roger glanced at him. "I may have an assignment for you, Whitey. Its successful execution would most probably lead to a substantial escalation in your salary."

Execution? Escalation? Whitey kept mum, playing it safe.

After a period of silence, except for the radio — White Zombie doing "Warp Asylum," another favorite — Roger said, "A raise, Whitey. Of sizable proportions."

"Big, you mean?"

"I do."

How big was big? Whatever it was, he deserved it, was worth every penny. Watching the scenery go by, very cool, very something else he

268

couldn't remember the word for, started with "non," Whitey said, "What's this, like, assignment?"

"We'll get to that, but first — are you hungry?"

"Nope."

"Thirsty?"

"No."

"Need to use the bathroom?"

"Soon."

Roger nodded. "After that we'll talk."

Pit stop. Roger gassed up, Whitey took a long piss, picked up some Reese's on the way out, a little hungry after all. Back on the highway, Roger switched off the radio.

"Listening, Whitey?"

"Why wouldn't I be?"

"I'm going to describe a painting to you."

"Shoot."

"It's called *oh garden, my garden*."

"About hockey?"

Roger's eyes shifted toward him. "Why would you think that?"

"No reason." Except for Boston Garden, now gone. It made a kind of sense, didn't it? But maybe not the kind he could get across to Roger. They'd faced Xaverian the only time he'd skated on Garden ice, and Whitey had scored their only goal, before being ejected in the third period for spearing.

". . . grapes," Roger was saying, "and in the background, or more accurately the middle

269

ground, a girl on a skateboard. Can you visualize it so far?"

What was this? Grapes? Skateboard? Girl? "What's she wearing?" Whitey said.

Roger paused, and again Whitey reflected that he might be a little slow. What the girl wore would have been the first thing he himself would have noticed. "I'm not certain," Roger said. "Perhaps a tunic of some sort."

Tunic? What the hell was he talking about? At that moment it was clear to Whitey that Roger was a little out of touch, and he made a decision, then and there: he was working for Roger, yes, would follow orders, but — would use his own . . . discretion! Discretion. Wasn't that what Roger was always going on about, the importance of discretion in this business? Everything was coming together.

"Tunic," Whitey said. "Gotcha. Anything else?"

Another pause to think. Jesus, discretion and plenty of it. "You're sure you've got it so far?" Roger asked.

"Yeah. I mean, what's to get?"

"The name of the painting, for example."

"*My garden.*"

"*Oh garden, my garden,*" Roger corrected.

"Whatever."

Silence descended for some miles. The Merrimack appeared, frozen but snowless, the color of the low clouds overhead. Whitey occupied his mind with the lyrics of Metallica's "Harvester of Sorrow," those he could remember. He ate the last of the Reese's. No Reese's on the inside, for some reason; he realized how much he'd missed them.

They crossed to the west bank of the river, left it behind. Roger spoke at last. "Do you know the word *provenance*, Whitey?"

"Providence?" said Whitey, thinking of the girl on the bus, the snake between her breasts, her breasts themselves.

"Provenance," Roger said, a little slower.

"Sort of."

"No matter," said Roger. "It's a technical term, specific to our business. The reference is to the chain of ownership of a given work, establishing authenticity, you see. In the case of *oh garden, my garden*, the chain has been broken."

"Yeah?" said Whitey. He pictured a thick gold chain, the kind pimps wore. A diner came into view. It had a red neon sign — Lavinia's — and an old Bronco parked out front. "Still haven't had that coffee," Whitey said.

"Perhaps on the way back," Roger said. "I'd like to beat the weather."

Whitey glanced up at the sky. "No snow till tomorrow," he said.

But it made no difference. Roger passed the diner by, took a back road, then another, came to a gate in the middle of nowhere. He got out, unlocked the gate, then drove on, crunching snow on a track thawed and refrozen, up a long hill. He stopped at the crest. Below lay the river, frozen but snow-blown clear by the wind, with an island in the middle and a single cottage on it, sheltered by trees. A stone jetty jutted from the near bank, two dinghies tethered to it, caught in the ice. Roger sat there in silence, waiting for — what? Whitey didn't know.

At last Roger made a sound, a kind of laugh, maybe. "Ever been married, Whitey?"

"Nope."

"Not unwise, in the final end. But without marriage, we'd be out of business."

"We would?"

"The dissolution of marriage leads to conflict when it comes to the ownership of material objects. Take our little painting, for example. Its rightful owner is our client, a woman who lives in Rome." Roger nodded toward the island in the river. "Whereas this little retreat now belongs to her former husband. Not enough for him, apparently — he made off with the painting, too, sometime in the past, oh, few weeks, say. According to information we've developed, he intends to secrete it away in the cottage. Do you see where this is headed?"

"Sure," Whitey said, opening the door. "Won't take five minutes."

Roger grabbed Whitey's arm, held on to it hard; Whitey didn't like that at all. "Intends, Whitey. I said intends."

"What the fuck does that mean?" Whitey said, shaking free of Roger's grip.

For one moment, Whitey saw a strange look in

Roger's eyes, as though he was about to take a shot at him or something. Cold wind blew in the open door. Roger covered his eyes with his hand, rubbed them hard, and the look was gone. "My apologies, Whitey. This business can be . . . intense at times. Perhaps it's led me to be unclear somehow. What I'm saying is that the painting in question is not at present in the cottage. Not now, at this moment."

"No?"

"No."

Whitey closed the door.

"But it will be there tomorrow," Roger continued, "if we can rely on our information."

"Coming from where?"

"I beg your pardon?"

"This information," Whitey said, "where's it coming from?"

Roger stared at him for a moment, then smiled and answered, "Rome."

"Good enough," Whitey said. "Then tomorrow I go in and get it."

"You're way ahead of me, aren't you?"

"Well . . ."

"Yes, you go in, but not until night, at six-fifteen precisely."

" 'Cause of the darkness, right?"

"Partly. And partly because that's the earliest the painting will be there in an unguarded state."

"It's coming in a Brinks truck?" Whitey asked. Yes, he was sharp, couldn't remember ever being sharper.

"Nothing like that — this is just a domestic dispute. But why court acrimony?"

That made sense — Whitey wanted nothing to do with guards or courts. "You're telling me," he said.

"We're agreed, then. You go in at six-fifteen, not a moment before, not a moment after. And this is very important, Whitey: you arrive by taxi."

"Taxi?"

"Available at the bus station in Nashua. Have the driver drop you at the gate — and get a receipt."

"What for?"

"Reimbursement, of course."

Meaning? Whitey wasn't quite sure. "But what about the driver?" he asked.

"What about him?"

"Making me in a lineup or something."

"Lineup! What an imagination you've got, Whitey. This can never become a legal matter. The painting belongs to the woman in Rome. The ex-husband has no standing to pursue it. Any law enforcement agency would laugh him off, I assure you."

Silence.

"Understood?" Roger said.

Was it? A lot of blah-blah but basically it came down to six-fifteen, taxi, painting. "It's not complicated," Whitey said.

"You may have a real future in this business," Roger told him.

Whitey grunted.

"Once beyond the gate," Roger went on, "you cross the river and enter the cottage." He handed Whitey a key. "Don't turn on any lights. You'll need a flash. Save the receipt. Upstairs are two bedrooms. The one on the right is not made up. The painting will be hidden somewhere inside it. I'll be told the location at exactly six-thirty. There's a phone on the bedside table and I'll call from the car and tell you where it is. Then you simply collect it, recross the river, and return here, where we are now. I'll be waiting. Any questions?"

It was a snap; Whitey grasped the whole scenario, even the parts he hadn't been told. "The woman — she's going to call you from Rome, right?"

"No putting anything past you."

"And the place used to belong to her — that's how come you have the key."

"Another bull's-eye." Roger punched him softly on the shoulder. "And one more thing."

"What's that?"

"She doesn't want the frame."

"How come?"

"How come?" Roger drew a deep breath. "I believe it was chosen by the mother-in-law."

"I get it."

"And since she doesn't want the frame," Roger continued, "you'll have to cut the painting out."

"With what?"

"Something sharp," Roger said.

Whitey knew what was coming, beat Roger to the punch. "Save the receipt?" he said.

Roger shook his head in admiration.

23

"Sleep well?" Roger said.

Monday morning. Francie, who hadn't slept at all, came downstairs to the kitchen and found Roger standing at the stove, glancing up from a cookbook to smile at her over his reading glasses, doing something with eggs.

"Yes, thanks," Francie said, trying and failing to recall any previous time he'd done something with eggs.

"Good," said Roger, "good, good. Take a pew — chow'll be down in a jiff."

Take a pew? Chow? Jiff? Francie took another look at him, saw exhilaration in the flush on his face, in the sprightliness of his movements. "More news about the job?" Francie said.

He paused, steel whisk poised above the blue gas flames. "Job?" he said.

"In Fort Lauderdale."

"Oh, that. Promising, as I believe I mentioned. More and more promising all the time."

There was one place set at the table. He gestured to it with the whisk.

"Aren't you eating?" Francie said.

"I already have. Up betimes."

Francie sat down, although she wasn't hungry at all. Roger bustled over with a plate of eggs and toast. He watched her, beaming, as she tasted the eggs.

"Delicious," she said. They were. Why was this talent emerging now, after so many years spent anywhere but the kitchen? "You can cook, Roger."

"Much like a chemistry experiment," he said. "And you never know when it might prove useful."

Lauderdale: that was his way of telling her it was going to happen, that he'd soon be cooking for himself in some one-bedroom condo on a waterway, that what was left of their marriage would fade to a civilized end. But it was too late for her and Ned. She had proved to herself that she could cheat — the word people used, as Nora said, no point avoiding it — proved she could make a mockery of Swift's *Marriage Service from His Chamber Window*, but she couldn't do it with Anne's husband. A long, confused night of thought and counterthought had boiled down to that: not with Anne's husband. She was surer of that than anything she'd been sure of in her life. All that remained was telling him so in person, at the cottage in — she checked her watch — a little more than ten hours.

Roger went to the cupboard, returned with a jar of Dundee's. "Last of the marmalade," he said, spooning some — too much — onto the edge of her plate. "You might as well finish it off." Then he poured coffee for both of them and sat across the table. Francie managed two forkfuls of eggs and half a slice of toast; her body had its priorities, wanted no food until she had done the right thing.

"Ever been to the Empire State Building, Francie?" Roger asked.

"With my father, when I was ten. Why?"

"Or China?"

"You know I have — on the NEA trip. What are you getting at?"

"Getting at? Nothing, really. Maybe we should do more traveling, that's all. Think of all there is to do and see, had we but world enough and time, et cetera."

Francie sipped her coffee. It, too, was excellent, better than hers.

"Possibly with another couple," Roger went on.

She put down her cup.

"Anne and Ned, for example," he continued. "A pleasant evening, didn't you think? Although I can't say much for the restaurant."

Francie said nothing.

Roger tilted his cup to his face, revealing those white nose hairs — it hadn't been her imagination — then set the cup carefully down in the saucer, as though the object were to make no clinking of porcelain on porcelain. "Does he play tennis?"

"Who?"

"Who? Ned, of course. Ned Demarco." He watched her. "You're not ill, are you?"

"I don't know if he plays."

"No? I thought Anne might have mentioned it."

"Not to my knowledge."

"Because if he does, I might pick up the old racquet again myself. How does a week of mixed doubles in the Algarve sound? Or possibly Sardinia."

"I didn't think we were in the financial position for that sort of thing."

Roger's eyes left hers. He picked up the empty marmalade jar. "Perhaps not at this moment," he said, carrying it to the sink.

Francie rose. "I'd better get going." She paused at the door that led down to the garage. "I may be late tonight."

Roger opened the cabinet under the sink. "As you wish," he said, and dropped the jar in the trash.

A dark day, the clouds so low and thick that the streetlamps of the city remained lit for the morning commute, and headlights glowed from every car. Dark, too, in Francie's office, where the phone was ringing as she came in the door. She picked it up.

"Francie?"

"Nora."

"Thought you might call yesterday," Nora said. "Maybe to explain that teary little scene in the locker room."

"Anne was upset, that's all. About losing."

"And what about you, babycakes?"

"Me?"

"Were you upset about losing, too?"

"I don't like to lose. You know that."

"But I've never seen you look like that about it," Nora said. "I've never seen you look like that about anything."

The words marshaled themselves in Francie's mind: *I've got something to tell you, Nora.* But she didn't voice them, couldn't, not without making Nora her accomplice, or risking the loss of Nora's friendship, or damaging Anne. Those were the three possibilities, none acceptable, the worst being damaging Anne, and therefore Em as well. Francie hadn't done any damage yet, had to keep things that way for only a matter of hours more, had to put everything, resolved and unresolved, in a box and close it forever. So instead of *I've got something to tell you, Nora,* she replied, "There's always a first time."

"And you do what you have to do, what goes around comes around, you get what you pay for. Are we going to talk in clichés from now on?"

"You and I?" Francie said. But she saw it was possible, a possibility her mind squirmed from.

"You and I. Something's wrong, very wrong, and you're not telling me."

"Nothing's wrong."

"Bullshit," Nora said. "Bullshit, bullshit, bullshit. Not only is something wrong, but it's something you can't handle by yourself."

Francie didn't dare speak, knowing that nothing she said could be right.

"Tell you what," said Nora, sounding a little

281

more gentle, as gentle as Francie had ever heard her, in fact, although most people would have called her tone crisp, "I'll meet you somewhere after work. How's five-thirty?"

"I can't."

"Why? It's not Thursday."

"What do you mean, not Thursday?"

"For months now you haven't been available on Thursdays. I'm clumsy and slow, Francie, but I get there."

Francie almost spilled everything on the spot. What was left to spill? But she thought, *No damage yet,* and found a way out. "Now who's the bullshitter, Nora? There's nothing slow and clumsy about you, as you know. And this Thursday's fine. I'll meet you then."

A long pause, followed by: "You're too smart for me. See you then, babycakes."

"Bye."

"B— oh my God, I've got it. Anne's sick, isn't she?"

Francie held on to the phone.

"Or — or you are." Francie heard a strange new note in Nora's voice, almost frantic. "Is that what those Thursdays are about, Francie, some kind of treatment?"

"I'm not sick," Francie said, but thought, *Is there something wrong with me, after all?*

"It's Anne, then."

"No."

"You don't have cancer?"

"No."

"Neither does she?"

"No."

Nora laughed with relief. "So it can't be that bad, can it? Whatever it is."

Francie was silent.

"See you on Thursday, then," Nora said. "How about Huîtres?"

"Somewhere else," Francie said. "I'll call you."

Francie left the lights off in her office. The world outside the windows grew darker. She did no work, just thought about what was to come. She would get to the cottage first, of course, as she always did, but would leave the woodstove unlit, wait for him in the kitchen with her coat on. Then, when he came in, she would stand and say, *It's over, Ned. Because of Anne it's over.* After that, whatever he said or tried to do, she would stick to that point: because of Anne. That was what couldn't be rationalized, argued away, compromised. *Just stick to it,* Francie told herself, *and stay out of the square little bedroom upstairs, whatever happens.*

But the thought of that little bedroom . . . her mind returned to it over and over — the brass bed, the comforter, what happened beneath. By three-thirty Francie had had enough: enough waiting, thinking, sitting still. She left the office, got her car from the parking garage, headed for New Hampshire.

The first snowflakes fell as Francie crossed the

state line, tiny ones, laceless and hard. She barely noticed them, was too busy trying to cap all the memories her mind boiled with — black kayaks, those dark eyes, his skin; too busy clinging to her mantra: *It's over, because of Anne it's over.* She was going to be early, earlier than she had ever been. Perhaps she would light the woodstove after all, wait for him beside it. Nothing wrong with lighting the woodstove, was there? It wasn't necessary to sit in the cold, to fabricate symbolic expressions of her coming internal state. Everything could be normal tonight and she could still do her duty, as long as she didn't go up to the little bedroom. Then, out of nowhere, her mind offered up an image that would keep her out of that bedroom. The image: Anne's face, but the giant face of a two-stories-tall Anne, like a character in a children's book, watching through the bedroom window from the outside. There was nothing scary about Anne's face, but this image scared Francie just the same. She tried to blot it out and found it wouldn't go away.

Snow fell harder as Francie drove north, isolating her in a twilit cocoon, a strange cocoon that felt not the least protective. She was too preoccupied to notice the snow much, but she was very aware of the unprotected part.

24

At six-fifteen, precisely. Roger had been clear about the timing, clear about everything, going over and over the details until Whitey tuned out completely. He already had it all down pat in his mind anyway: the taxi, the receipts, the call from Rome, the hidden painting, the necessity for a cutting tool, a sharp one. Piece of cake. The only problem was Roger. Two things. First, it was now evident to Whitey that he was smarter than Roger. Second, after that toe-stepping bullshit, Roger couldn't be trusted, not completely. Whitey kept juggling those two things in his mind. Not too bright, not too reliable. Not too bright, so maybe his plan could be improved. Not too reliable, so Whitey would have to make any improvements on his own. He didn't grasp all that at once, but by the time his eyes opened Monday morning — Whitey waking slumped in the cab of his pickup in the parking lot of some suburban mall where he'd spent the night, running the engine for five or ten minutes every hour or so to keep warm — he had most of it.

Whitey checked his watch: not even six, still dark, just over twelve hours to go. He climbed down out of the pickup, pissed against somebody's tire, considered Roger's plan. For one thing, he didn't like the taxi part. He'd ridden taxis three or four times in his life and hadn't been comfortable, not with that meter ticking away. And, despite Roger's reassurance, why drag a witness into the picture, especially when he had the pickup? Funny, too, the pickup with redeemer now written on the side. Didn't people redeem things from pawnshops, things like paintings? Whitey tried to tie it together into some sort of joke, and almost did. All that thinking before he even finished his piss! His mind was sharp today, speeding as fast as it ever had, maybe faster. He had barely zipped up and returned to the cab before he had another thought, connected to the pawnshop idea — and Christ! to get this picture of how his own mind was working, making connections, redeemer and pawnshop — how amazing was that?

The pawnshop connection was this: How much was the garden painting worth? *My garden*, or *oh my garden*, or whatever the hell it was. Roger had never said anything about its value, just that it was part of a divorce dispute. But would anyone fight over something worthless? No. So the question was: How much? Whitey turned the key and goosed the engine a couple times, *vroom-vroom*. How much? A word almost came to mind, a word they used in war movies when some guy, usually the toughest, was sent ahead to check things out. The toughest guy, who just nodded and did whatever it took. Whitey put the pickup in gear and drove out of the mall parking lot.

He made a few stops along the way. First, a pizza place for breakfast: deep dish with everything and an extra-large Pepsi. Second, and by now he was almost in New Hampshire, a hardware store for his supplies: a flashlight, batteries, and something sharp. He was still searching for the right sort of sharp something when a clerk approached.

"What are you lookin' to cut?" asked the clerk.

Canvas. Painting canvas. But what was painting canvas, exactly? Whitey wasn't sure. "Like cardboard," he said. "Heavy-duty cardboard."

"Heavy-duty cardboard," said the clerk, moving toward a bin. "This here should do you."

"What is it?"

"Box cutter."

"Does it come any bigger?"

"There's this one."

"I'll take it. And I need the receipt."

Third, a stripper's bar for lunch. Whitey sat by himself at the back, had a beer, a Polish sausage, another beer. That Polish sausage was something, squirting in his mouth with all those spices. They didn't serve food like that inside. The reminder of what he'd missed out on pissed him off a little and he ordered another beer — just the one, since he was on the job — plus a shot of bar whiskey, even though he could now afford better.

The place was packed: smoke, noise, suits and

ties, hairy hands stuffing money into garter belts. Red garter belts, because it was Christmas, and some of the girls wore Santa Claus hats as well, but that was all. He watched them jiggle around, rub themselves against brass poles, bend over. He got a hard-on, all right, but it didn't last. The problem — and he could figure it out easily the way his mind was working today — was he could see right through everything. It was all a fake: those huge, hard tits, the way their hands went down and almost started going to work on themselves, but not quite, how they opened those lipstick mouths as though feeling pleasure while their eyes flickered here and there. They were pros and what he wanted were amateurs — amateur housewives, like the women in Rey's video. He wanted to show one of those amateur housewives what he could do, to make her make those sounds for real. Women, amateur women, were helpless when they were making those sounds, and the dick was the tool that did it. Sue Savard should have given him the chance. There was a body, a real amateur body. Whitey got hard again recalling it, ordered another beer — and a shot. This really was the last; when the glasses were empty and the hard-on was gone, he paid his bill and went outside.

Snow falling, just as he'd told Roger it would, falling hard, cleaning everything up, whitening the world. He'd always liked snow, now wondered for the first time — what a day he was having, mentally, and it had barely begun! —

whether it had anything to do with his name. They'd called him Whitey because of his hair, of course, not because he liked snow, but maybe he liked the snow so much because of the name; identified with it, he thought, remembering a word the prison shrink used all the time. And right after remembering that word, he remembered another: *reconnoiter,* what the toughest guy did in the war movies. He wiped his windshield clear with the sleeve of his leather jacket, got in the pickup, drove on. Time to reconnoiter.

Whitey came in sight of the Merrimack a couple hours ahead of schedule. That was one variation from the plan. No taxi was a second. And now came a third: Whitey didn't cross the river, over to the side with the gate, the lane through the sloping meadow, the jetty, those frozen-in dinghies. He had his reasons. What sense did that six-fifteen precisely shit make when it would be dark long before then — soon, in fact? And what had Roger said about a Brinks truck? Wouldn't be too smooth to run into that on the way in, would it? But the biggest reason was that Roger had stepped on his toe. No excuse for that, no forgiveness. He was a free man now, and much more, an administrative assistant, a professional. He had rights. And what he had in mind wouldn't be difficult. He knew his way around these woods. Whitey recalled that Roger had asked him about that at the gator farm, almost in those same words: *Know your way around the woods up there?* Probably figured

Whitey for this job at that very moment; maybe Roger was a little smarter than he'd thought. But not in Whitey's league, especially not on a day like today. Following back roads on the east side of the river, Whitey sped north, fishtailing around the curves. He knew the woods, and he was one hell of a driver.

Snow fell harder. The plows gave up on the back roads and the traffic dwindled to nothing, except for Whitey in his pickup. When the time came, he didn't even pull to the side to put on the chains, just stopped in the middle of the road and got them out of the truck bed. So quiet with the snow all around like cotton, he could hear his own pulse. He climbed back in the cab, switched on the radio, but couldn't find the metal station they'd picked up in Roger's car. The station had been playing Metallica, but not "Master of Puppets," his all-time favorite Metallica song. He felt like hearing it now: *Master of puppets I'm pulling your strings, twisting your mind and smashing your dreams.* Pure poetry, but Whitey couldn't find the station and kept going in silence.

He spotted the island from the top of a rise. It looked different from this side of the river, wilder because the cottage was almost hidden from sight by those big trees and everything whiter even than yesterday, snow coating not just the branches and the roof but the trunks themselves, and the sides of the cottage. Whitey found a lookout two or three hundred yards farther on, drove to the end of it, his chains crunching on the unpacked snow. From this angle, on the edge of a steep incline leading down to the river, he had a view of the upstream end of the island, and beyond it the long sloping meadow on the other side. He saw no sign of a Brinks truck, or anything else; nothing moved except the snow, angling down now as the wind began to rise. Whitey turned up the heat.

He watched the island, the unlit windows of the cottage, the smokeless air above the chimney. What were the details of the garden painting? Nothing to do with hockey, he recalled, but something about a girl in a miniskirt. Eating grapes, was that it? Sounded kind of interesting, just on its own, but the question, the big question, as Whitey saw it now, remained: How much?

Snow. Supposing, Whitey thought, you were a Brinks truck driver, and you knew snow was on the way. Wouldn't you try to beat the weather, make your delivery earlier, in the morning, say? Sure as shit you would. Meaning the painting was already there, and any tracks left on the lane through the meadow were wiped out, as was the lane itself. Whitey checked his watch: 4:15, precisely. Precisely, you fucker. Roger would be waiting for him at the gate in a little more than two hours. Meanwhile snow was falling harder and harder, and now darkness was falling, too. Someone planning to cross the river would be smart to do it soon, while he could still see where he was going. There was no one around to see *him* in this storm, so the argument about waiting for darkness didn't stand up anymore. Brinks truck, cover of darkness — no longer factors. Was there another reason for him not to go now? Whitey couldn't think of one; at the same time, he could feel the key Roger had given him, an ordinary brass key, inside his pocket, waiting there against his thigh, pressing on his skin. Paintings could be worth millions. Millions: wouldn't that be something? A garage full of cars — Benz, Porsche, the biggest goddamn pickup on the market — plus any woman he wanted. He could advertise for them, for Christ's sake, and they'd come running with their tongues hanging out.

Whitey clipped the flashlight to his belt and opened the door. All these reasons, all this back-and-forth, all this thinking, but it came down to one thing: he couldn't wait to get inside. Back in action. Yes! He climbed out of the pickup, locked the door — no one around, but you never knew — and looked around for the easiest route down to the river, the easiest route down, but more important, the easiest route back up. Roger could sit by the gate on the other side all night if he wanted. Meanwhile, he'd be on his way to — to somewhere — with a million-dollar painting in his truck. The idea of it made Whitey laugh to himself a couple of times. He stopped laughing when he realized he'd almost forgotten the box cutter. Whitey unlocked the door and took it off the seat.

Whitey started down, slipping and sliding on the snowy bank in his cowboy boots, grabbing at branches for support with one hand, holding the box cutter in the other, but never in danger of falling. He did know his way around the woods, and he'd always had great balance, had been up on skates at the age of two. As he walked across the river, plodded, really, sinking to the knees with every step, snow getting inside his boots but not bothering him at all, he felt for the first time the full force of his freedom. He was a giant, could do anything — reach the island in a single bound, rip one of those trees right out of the earth, smash the cottage to bits with it. The song came to him again and he sang it as he went, the wind driving thick snowflakes right into his mouth. *Master of puppets I'm pulling your strings, twisting your mind and smashing your dreams.*

Whitey walked onto the island. Moving under the shelter of those big trees, he heard a sharp hooting high above, glanced up, saw an owl making shivering motions, shaking the snow off its feathers. It stopped shivering as he watched, stared down at him with yellow eyes.

Whitey stepped up to the porch through smooth, untrodden snow. He brushed more of it off the little round window set in the front door, put his face to the glass: a shadowy kitchen, everything gray except the half-full bottle of red wine on the table. No sound, no movement, no armed guards. Whitey took out the brass key, tried to put it into the lock. It wouldn't go. He had a horrible moment, even began to hear that panicky buzz. Had Roger lied to him? But why? And worse, was it some kind of setup? He glanced around, saw no one, just snow swirling through the trees. Then, probably because his mind was working so well today, he solved the problem just like that, solved the problem by sticking the key in his mouth. Whitey gave it a good lick, tried again. The warm wet key slid right in. He turned it, opened the door, went inside. A little avalanche tumbled in after him; he closed the door as well as he could, without actually bothering to bend down and get rid of all the snow now packed in against the riser.

Whitey looked around: a pine-smelling cottage, all polished and clean, the kind that belonged to rich people from the city. He picked up the bottle of wine. Chateau something: French. What had he had a shot of at Sue Savard's? Gin. He pulled the cork with his teeth, took a hit. He'd only drunk wine once or twice, so long ago he didn't remember the taste, just that he hadn't liked it. He didn't like it now. Maybe he'd get used to it. Rich people, the kind who owned million-dollar paintings, drank wine. He moved through the dining room, more quiet and careful than in the old days, around the corner to the living room, found the stairs. They rose up into darkness. *Don't turn on any lights. You'll need a flash.* Whitey unclipped his flashlight, switched it on, started up. Outside the owl hooted. The sound sent a jolt through Whitey, but not a sharp one, not sharp enough to set off the panicky buzz, although he did tighten his grip on the box cutter.

Upstairs are two bedrooms. Whitey shone his light into each, one made up, one not. That was where things got a little complicated. The painting was hidden in one of them, but which? Roger hadn't made that clear, as usual. Whitey went into the made-up bedroom, facing the side of the river with the jetty and the dinghies, now completely buried under the snow, and the sloping meadow, featureless in the failing light. From this spot, he'd easily see any headlights, Roger's, for example. He checked his watch, found he couldn't read it without the flash. Four-fifty-one. Plenty of time.

But which room? Fucking Roger. Whitey went into the one that wasn't made up because searching it would be easier. He saw a closet, a chest of drawers, a bed. He opened the closet. There was a shelf at the top. He reached up, ran his hand along it, found nothing but dust. Empty wire hangers hung on the rail. On the floor lay a single pair of shoes: women's shoes. Whitey picked them up, soft leather shoes, deep red in color. He shone his light inside one, read *Fratelli Rossetti, Roma*. He held it to his nose, sniffed deeply, smelled several smells he couldn't identify, and knew he wanted a woman, bad. An amateur housewife woman, yes, but of the special kind who would wear shoes like this. Once he had the painting, he could have a woman like that, more than one. A woman with Sue Savard's body, but — what was the word? — a classier face. To get a blow job from a woman with a classy face: wouldn't that be something?

Where was he? Right. Looking for the painting, the garden painting with the girl in the miniskirt, sucking on grapes. Not in the closet. He tried the chest of drawers, opening the bottom one first because he'd seen the technique used years before by burglars in an episode of *Miami Vice*; on the cell block, of course. There was nothing in the drawer but a magazine called *Bellissima*, with a beautiful woman on the cover. Whitey leafed through it and found nothing interesting; women, all right, but modeling clothes and makeup instead of fucking, sucking, and begging for it up the ass. Besides, the writing was in another language.

Whitey opened the next drawer, leaving the bottom one open as well. That was the point: you could work faster if you didn't have to take the time to close one drawer to get to the next one. On the other hand, leaving the drawers open meant that the break-in would be discovered by the first person who entered the house. Had Roger said anything about covering his traces? Whitey couldn't remember. But why not cover them? He closed the next drawer from the bottom, closed the bottom one, reopened the one above. There was nothing inside.

And nothing in any of the others. Whitey paused, drumming his fingers on the wood.

Where would he hide the painting? Under the chest? Down on his hands and knees he peered under the chest and, while he was there, turned and swept the beam of his flash under the bed. Nada. He got up, raised the bare mattress, saw nothing but bare springs. Quiet and careful, but not fun, like all those other break-ins long ago, grabbing all those toasters and TVs. This was a drag, and pissed him off. His gaze fell on the mattress. Was it in there? He slashed at the mattress with the box cutter. It sliced through the covering with surprising ease, exposing the stuffing. Whitey tore it out by the fistful until he was sure the painting wasn't inside. No painting, but a big fucking mess. That answered the question of whether he should cover his tracks. No way was he about to pack all that shit inside by flashlight and do whatever else — he couldn't begin to even imagine the steps involved — he'd have to do to make everything look normal.

So, no painting, and it was 5:13. What next? He remembered the other bedroom.

Whitey crossed the hall and entered it. His light glinted on the window, a mirror, a vase full of dead flowers. Same kind of room as the other one, but all made up, meaning more work. Work made him thirsty, and maybe that wine hadn't been as bad as he'd first thought. Whitey went downstairs and downed the bottle.

Back in the made-up bedroom, feeling better, Whitey got busy. By now he had a system — systems were the sign of an administrative assistant, a professional man, an operative like him. He began with the closet. Two life jackets hung on the rail, and a terry-cloth robe. Whitey sniffed the robe and smelled something faint, faint but nice. Then he pointed the beam along the shelf, a high shelf, higher than the one in the other room. Something at the back caught his eye. A box, round and silvery. Jewelry? Whitey stuck the box cutter between his teeth and reached up for it. A slippery box: as he drew it toward the front of the shelf, it slipped from his grasp, started to fall. He grabbed at it, missed, and the box fell to the floor, bouncing off his head on the way down. The next thing Whitey knew there was powder all over the place and he was sneezing — perfumed powder on his jacket, up his nose, sticking to his face. He patted his hair, checked his hand under the light: sticky pink powder, now on his palm and fingers, too.

What the fuck? Whitey thought. He found the silvery box in a corner of the room, examined it under the light: Lancôme, he read, and more writing in another language. He threw the box at the wall, hard. On the follow-through, the flash in his other hand shone up in his face and he saw himself in the mirror, the box cutter between his teeth and his hair, pink. He snatched the box cutter from his mouth, said, "What the fuck?" aloud.

Whitey went to the mirror, brushed at his hair, couldn't get rid of the powder, stinking faggot powder all over himself. He checked his watch

— pink powder on it, too: 5:22. He had time. Time for what? Face it. There was no fucking painting. The storm had kept the Brinks truck away, would keep Roger away, too. Nothing left to do but haul his ass out of there, back across the river, back to the pickup. But first a shower. He wasn't going anywhere covered in pink.

Whitey went into the hall between the bedrooms, left into the bathroom, jabbed his beam here and there: toilet, sink with a toothbrush and toothpaste in a wall cup, towel on a hook, shower. He turned on the hot tap, not expecting hot, since the tank would be switched off for the winter. Whitey didn't care, since cold didn't bother him, but it was nice when hot started flowing anyway; if not hot, at least warm. He laid the box cutter and his watch on the rim of the sink, positioned the flashlight on the toilet tank so it pointed at the shower, then stripped off his clothes and stepped under the water.

"Ah." It felt good. Whitey realized he had a little alcohol hum going in his body, the way you sometimes realize that in showers. He wasn't drunk or hammered or anything, just humming. *Master of puppets I'm pulling your strings, twisting your mind and smashing your dreams.*

Shampoo, there on the little tile shelf. He held it to the light: Principessa, and more foreign writing. Christ, it was like he'd left the country or something, gone far away. He squeezed a big dollop on his palm, started scrubbing his hair. Scrub, scrub. He worked his way down, reached his dick, first just cleaning it, then thinking, what the hell, he had time, when the water went cold, just like that. Whitey turned off the tap and got out of the shower, the flash spotlighting his neglected dick, already down to semihard. He reached for the towel, hanging on the hook, and went still.

A footstep. He'd heard a footstep, downstairs. Whitey had a funny thought, a thought that scared him, awoke the panicky buzz: the last time Sue Savard had been in the shower and this time it was him. So what Whitey-thing was down below?

25

The box cutter lay on the rim of the sink. In the spreading cone of light from the flash, Whitey could see the blade glinting there in easy reach, but could he pick the thing up cleanly, without first knocking it into the basin or on the floor, or making some other noise? He wrapped the towel around himself, extended his right hand toward the sink, saw how it shook; that had to be the booze, couldn't be fear — he was as tough as they come. Whitey took a few deep, silent breaths to sober up. He heard the wind outside — it had risen to a howl while he was in the shower — but he didn't hear another footstep. Maybe he'd imagined it, maybe it was nothing but the old roof beams creaking in the storm. Yeah, the beams for sure, or possibly —

He heard another footstep, a footstep beyond any doubt, and snatched up the box cutter without making a sound, quick as a snake. The next moment, not even aware of having done it, Whitey had the flash in his other hand, switched off. Total darkness, black as black could be, his friend. He waited, motionless, listening for more footsteps, hearing none. An idea came to him: maybe the Brinks truck had turned up after all, not early, but late, because of the snow. Made more sense. If so, they would be coming up the stairs any second to hide the painting in one of the bedrooms. All he had to do was stay where he was, silent and still — and hope that the Brinks men just did their job and hit the road, hope that none of them had to take a piss. Then, with any luck, he could still grab the painting and get out before Roger arrived. This was going to work!

It was all in the timing. What time was it? Where was his watch? He'd just seen it. He remembered: on the rim of the sink — a digital watch he'd stolen on the cell block, but a cheap one without a glow button. That meant he would have to switch on the flash to read it. Too risky. Thank Christ his mind was working so well today. Whitey stepped back into the shower. He set the flashlight carefully down, freeing his hand to silently draw the curtain, one of those curtains that was not quite transparent, not quite opaque. The air in the shower stall quickly lost its warmth, but Whitey didn't care — he'd never minded the cold, was sweating anyway.

The sound of the storm rose higher. Listening only for footsteps, Whitey was slow to hear the change in tone, a low rumble that mixed in like a bass line. Then the wind slackened for a moment, and he heard the new component clearly, felt it through the icy tiles of the shower: something motorized down below, electrical — a generator. Of course there'd be a generator out here on an island in the middle of the —

A thin strip of light shone through the crack

under the bathroom door. Fucking Jesus. They'd turned on the lights, and darkness was his friend. Brinks guards carried guns, didn't they? How many could he take out, how fast? Some, for sure: he could do things when that buzz was buzzing in his brain, and it was buzzing. Everything depended on how many there were — if they opened the door at all. He almost wanted them to now, to pay for making him sweat like this.

Footsteps on the stairs, slow, very slow, but coming up. Whitey heard some good news in those footsteps: First, there was only one set of them, only one person, although that didn't mean there weren't others waiting downstairs. And second, that one person had a light tread, so probably wasn't very big, certainly not as big as Whitey. He kept his eyes on the glowing crack under the door.

The footsteps, light, almost soundless, as though the guard was wearing tennis shoes, reached the landing and paused. Whitey could almost feel the guard going over his instructions. The footsteps receded into the bedroom that wasn't made up, and Whitey remembered the way he'd left it, mattress stuffing all over the floor. Before he had time to figure out what could come of that, there was a faint click — light switch going on — and another pause, longer than the first. Whitey waited for a call downstairs for help, a voice talking into a cell phone, a police whistle, something, but nothing happened. No movement at all, meaning the guard wasn't hiding the painting. Then the footsteps returned to the landing, paused again, continued into the other bedroom, where Whitey had had the powder accident.

Another click, another pause. Whitey heard a sniffing sound. Then came a few of those light footsteps, followed by another pause, and then a soft grunt, almost too soft to hear. A grunt: the kind you make when you're reaching for something, or — or bending down, like maybe to slide something under a bed! Whitey had astonished himself. His mind had never been like this, not even close. *All right,* he thought, *job done, split. Then my job: scoop up the painting, out the door, across the river, into a future full of money.* Whitey pictured his getaway clearly, at fast-forward speed.

But having hidden the painting, the guard didn't seem in a hurry to leave. Whitey heard the metallic clicking of wire hangers on the closet rail. Then came another one of those sniffing sounds. More footsteps. After that, a faint creaking, the kind bedsprings make. *For fuck sake,* Whitey thought, *don't take a goddamn nap.* But he knew he might do the same thing if he had a job like that. He was toying with the idea of silently slipping into the bedroom while the guard slept and whipping the painting right out from under him, when the bedsprings creaked again; another sniff, like the guy was smelling something — oh, Christ, that goddamn powder —

and then more footsteps. Footsteps getting louder, coming closer. *Don't you start with me,* Whitey thought. Buzz buzz. *Get out of my fucking life.*

But that didn't happen. There was another pause. Whitey saw two black breaks in the lit crack under the bathroom door, breaks that would be made by two feet standing just outside. An armed guard on the other side of the door, and all Whitey had was a stupid little warehouse tool. His hand tightened around it.

Whitey heard another metallic sound: the doorknob turning. He retreated to the back of the shower; from there he couldn't see the crack under the door, hoped that meant the guard couldn't see him either. He heard the door open, heard the click of the switch, and the bathroom filled with light, blinding him. Even as it did, even as he blinked furiously and shaded his eyes, he remembered his clothes, all over the floor.

Sniff, sniff. Whitey, his eyes adjusting to the light, heard that sniffing, didn't move. A footstep, another, and another. Whitey clung to the box cutter: he wasn't going back to prison, no matter what. One more footstep, and then the guard was right in front of him, but turned toward the sink, his image blurred by the shower curtain. Not a big guard at all, holding something in his hand. A gun? No. More like — dead flowers, the dead flowers from the vase in the made-up bedroom.

No gun at all, as far as Whitey could see. In

305

fact, the guard didn't seem to be wearing a uniform, but a long coat instead. The guard's other hand moved, picked up something from the sink — Whitey's watch. Slowly the guard's head came up, from the watch to the mirror over the sink. And in that mirror, through the translucent shower curtain but clear enough, Whitey got his first look at the face of the guard: not a guard, certainly not a Whitey-thing, not even a man. A woman. The relief was indescribable. He flung the curtain aside.

The woman spun around, dropping the watch, dropping the flowers, putting her hands to her mouth, making a lovely frightened little noise in her throat.

Whitey smiled. "Nothing to apologize about," he said, holding up his hand, the empty one. Totally in control, master of the situation. Master reminded him of masturbate — was there a connection between the two words? — and of what he'd been about to do before the water turned cold. No longer necessary. "Nothing at all," he said. "I know you've got a job to do."

She backed up as far as she could before the sink stopped her. "Job?" she said. Whitey liked her voice, an educated voice, classy. He saw that the woman was just that: classy. This was no pocket-change whore like that pockmarked hag in Florida. This woman had snow melting in her hair, soft skin, innocent eyes. She was pure, amateur, perfect. She was the one. The buzzing rose and rose inside him.

"The painting, and whatnot," Whitey explained, not sure his voice was at the right volume, with the buzzing so loud.

Painting — the word got her attention; he could see that in her eyes, and what eyes, unlike any female eyes that had ever looked at him. And she was looking at him, no doubt about it.

Looking right at him, so why pussyfoot? Why beat around the bush? Whitey almost laughed aloud at his own wit. Almost, but he had to be cool. Cool as he could be, he hit her with his best shot: "How about us two we go back into that bedroom and see what we can see?"

The woman's eyes, still on him, shifted a little, gazed down, came to the glass cutter in his hand. He had forgotten to hide it behind his back, and anyway it was a box cutter. Glass cutter was the last time, not that it —

And then she was gone, just like that. Whitey had never seen a woman move so fast. He moved, too, out of the shower, out of the bathroom, onto the landing in time to see something he hardly believed, the woman leaping right from the top, taking the entire staircase in the air, hitting the ground floor with a loud squeak of her tennis shoes, her body contracting into a ball to absorb the force of the fall, staying on her feet. By that time, Whitey was halfway down himself, saw her darting off toward the living room, following the L to the dining room, kitchen, the door. He chased her, making stormlike howls of his own as he remembered his mother chasing him around the yard, her belt buckle whistling past his ear, beside himself with the tremendous charge of it all. But the woman — what a body she must have under that coat! — was fast, really fast, almost as fast as he was. He didn't catch her until she reached the door, forced to slow down to jerk it open. She actually had it halfway open, was on the point of disappearing into the storm on those quick feet, when Whitey sprang right over the kitchen table, flew across the room, and caught her a good one with his shoulder.

A real good one. The woman bounced off the doorjamb, back into the room, sprawled facedown on the floor. Whitey caught his breath, picked himself up, walked over to her. She was already up on her hands and knees. He bent over, got one hand in her hair — beautiful hair, so soft and clean, he'd never felt anything like it — raised her head, held the box cutter to her throat.

"This is going to be something else," he told her.

But then somehow she was rolling out of his grasp, leaving him with a handful of hair and a sharp pain, high up the inside of his leg: the bitch had tried to kick him in the balls. He tripped her up; she fell again, knocking the table over; he leaped on top of her — leaped right into the path of the wine bottle, already in her hand, arcing at his head. The bottle caught him right in the face, smashing against his nose, broken glass digging deep long tracks down his cheeks. He saw nothing but red, but at least she was under him; he could feel her wriggling. Whitey got hold of her somewhere, he didn't even know where, but it didn't last: wriggle, wriggle and she was out from under, rolling again, getting away. He slashed out blindly with the cutter, a last, desperate try, and felt the blade slice home, dig deep in flesh. At the same moment, he heard a loud pop — her Achilles, you lucky bastard — and a cry of pain. Lucky, lucky bastard, because she was down again, crawling toward the door, yes, but her running days were over. Whitey crawled after her, through a red haze, jabbing with the cutter. The woman swung round, still had a piece of the bottle, got him again, got him in the face again! He was fighting a fucking woman for his life. Whitey went crazy. Slash slash slash with the cutter. And some more.

Silence.

Not quite silence, Whitey realized after a while. There was a dripping sound, drip drip. He got to his knees, found the towel he'd been wearing, wiped blood from his eyes, picked shards of glass from his face, wiped more blood. The woman lay still, what was left of her. He wanted to kill her even though she was dead.

Time passed. Drip drip. Whitey gripped some piece of overturned furniture, pulled himself to his feet. He gazed around, reeled a little, made his slow way back around the L, through the dining room, living room, then even more slowly up the stairs. He went into the bathroom, sat on the toilet, put on clothes, took a breather, put on the rest of them. His watch was frozen at 5:33. He dropped it in the wastebasket.

Whitey went into the made-up bedroom, lowered himself to the floor, hands on the bed to support his weight. He checked under the bed: no painting. *Garden,* or whatever it was. No painting at all. He knelt there breathing for a while, then got up, went downstairs, back along the L, past the woman, out the door.

Still snowing. Whitey felt cold at once, much colder than he'd ever been. He walked as far as he could, two hundred feet or so, and sat down to rest with his back against one of those big trees.

While he rested, Whitey noticed that he'd left the lights on in the cottage. Was that smart? He tried to think — painting, divorce, Brinks truck, *six-fifteen precisely* — and got nowhere. Nothing added up. Didn't matter anyway: maybe he had the strength to get back across the river; he didn't have the strength to go back inside and close things down first. Where was that box cutter, by the way?

And other things. Whitey was trying so hard to think of other things he might have left behind that he almost didn't notice a flash of headlights on the east side of the river, where the pickup was. A flash in a snow-filled sky, and then gone: his imagination again? What was this imagination all of a sudden? Then the pain started: no imagining that.

Whitey thought about getting up, almost did once or twice. That woman: he didn't understand her at all, had never dreamed there could be a woman like that. She'd ruined him. *Master of puppets I'm pulling your strings, twisting your mind and smashing your dreams.* Whitey didn't sing the words aloud, just mouthed them. That was a good thing because sometime later a figure came out of the shadows behind the house.

A tall figure, certainly a man this time, almost as tall as Whitey. He carried something in his hand and bent low as he went by the dining-room windows so he wouldn't be seen from inside. A cunning kind of guy — Whitey could tell right away. The cunning guy crept around to the door. The porch light gleamed on what he had in his hand: an ax. The cunning guy slowly straightened, peeped quickly in through the round window. The next moment he whirled around and scanned the darkness. The porch light shone clear on his face: Roger. He was looking in Whitey's direction but would never see him, not through all that falling snow, not in that darkness. Darkness was Whitey's friend.

Raising the ax, Roger pushed the door open and went inside. Whitey forgot about his weakness and pain, stood up at once. He headed for home. High above, the owl hooted, or it might have been something new in the storm.

26

Snow, handled by Roger's car with ease, but as he drove up the eastern side of the river — despite and because of what he'd told Whitey, Roger had no intention of crossing to the gate side until it was all over and time to call in the local constabulary — he began to think he'd had enough of northern winters, perhaps enough of America itself. Rome: mild in winter, homogeneous in culture, and how long would it take to learn the language? Two or three months? An expensive city, of course, but with the insurance settlement, plus whatever he retained from the sale of the house — and the market was improving at last — supplemented by his pension and Francie's, there would be enough to meet his modest needs. *Roma aeterna, Roma invicta*. Latin had been one of his strongest subjects; therefore, he could assume that the vocabulary was already in place. Call it six weeks to moderate fluency, two months at most.

A necessary result of the execution of his plan, of course, would be some sort of contact with Brenda. She would probably attend the funeral; indeed, it would be his obligation to inform her of it. No doubt she would feel some sort of misplaced responsibility, given the involvement of her cottage. A drama easily foreseen: hand-wringing, if onlys, et cetera. He would absolve her. Thus they would have roles to play with each other, right from the start, his infinitely sympathetic. Simpatico.

Roger came to the lookout he had chosen, a treeless ledge on a rise almost opposite Brenda's island, but on the east side of the river. It wasn't a question of distrusting Whitey, but more that concepts like trust couldn't fairly be applied to someone like him. Whitey responded to stimuli, a frog in a laboratory, and although Roger had done all that could be done to predetermine the stimuli Whitey was about to encounter, he could not, because of randomness, unpredictability, chaos theory, account for them all. Better, then, if the frog expects the scientist to approach from the left, to approach from the right.

Roger checked the time — 5:40. On schedule, despite the snow, everything still according to plan. He used the singular for convenience, but to be accurate there were three plans: the plan as it was understood by Whitey, the plan as it would be executed by the participants, the master plan laid out in Roger's mind like lines of programming language or a sequence of DNA. DNA, that was it — and Whitey not a frog, but a gene of the most mutable type, capable of warping whole chromosomes, of growing into a monster. A monster under Roger's command: deployed in the unused bedroom, searching for a painting that wasn't there — although it existed, would be disposed of in the denouement, when Roger resigned from the tennis club and cleaned out his locker, perfect reason to be there with a plastic garbage bag. Funny — creative, really — this use he'd made of the painting, like Picasso making a bull from bicycle parts. But a minor detail. Major detail: the monster trapped as Francie and her oyster boy came up the stairs. Would it happen right then, Whitey making some little mistake that gave away his presence, leading to panic, his and theirs? Or would they get safely to their little nest, begin doing the things they did, with Francie crying out her petty pleasures, and Whitey listening and listening until he could hear no more, bear no more; he would want some, too, lots and lots.

And all the time, Roger would be waiting in the woodshed at the back, arriving not after Whitey but before; not waiting at the gate, as Whitey expected, but coming inside, to react with horror.

"Whitey, what have you done?"

And Whitey makes his stupid reply.

And Roger, saving the day, commands, "We've got to get this cleaned up. Come quick."

They run together, a team, to the woodshed, where the props stand ready.

"Hand me that mop, Whitey, in there." Prop one.

Whitey reaches down, baring his neck for the ax. Prop two.

Lines of programming language.

How quiet it would be after that, a tranquil interlude for arranging bodies, adjusting evidence, driving over the river bridge, around to the gate, parking his car beside the others, dialing 911, waiting to tell his story. A story slightly different from the one he'd first outlined, changes necessitated by the addition of the lover — horrible oleaginous word, quite appropriate in this case — to the dramatis personae. A story that now went like this: *A Christmas Eve surprise party, Officer, for Ned's wife — she was so upset over that tennis match. The three of us were meeting here tonight to put up the decorations, with the idea of having everything ready when we brought her here on the twenty-fourth. A surprise, you see, to show how we all care, to cheer her up. But when I arrived, a little late, what with the snow and all, I found . . . [breaks down, composes self] And he saw me, Officer, and I — I panicked. I ran and ran. He chased me, caught me by the woodshed. We struggled, I remember falling, grabbing the ax; it's all a jumble after that.*

All a jumble, but beautifully organized, planned like a mini-Creation: Roger even had a bag of red decorations in the car. *Merry Christmas, Noel, Joy to the World.* Prop three.

Roger pulled off the road, parked in the lookout — and saw another car parked nearby. A pickup truck, actually, but so covered by the blown snow, it was hard to tell. Abandoned, perhaps, possibly for the duration of the storm, possibly forever. Putting on his hat and gloves, zipping up his parka, taking the decorations and his twelve-inch, heavy-duty flashlight from L.L. Bean, Roger got out of the car, locked it, started down toward the river, hunched against the wind. In its perfect, triple-helix form, the plan wound so beautifully in his mind that he almost didn't notice, almost didn't process an obvious sight in the middle of the river: lights shining on Brenda's island.

Lights? Lights on the island? Hadn't he been clear about the flash? Should he have supplied Whitey with one? No. He wanted Whitey to buy it himself, wanted the receipts for everything — taxi, flash, weapon — found on Whitey's body: the master plan. Roger tore off a glove, read his watch: 5:49. Lights at 5:49? There were to be no lights at any time, and Whitey wasn't to be inside until 6:15. Six-fifteen precisely, with Francie and lover arriving at 6:30. It was a two-bladed plan, timing and psychology snipping together like scissors. Timing had been the easy part. So why lights? Why lights at 5:49?

Roger hurried across the river, or tried to, but the snow was deep and light, and he sank to his waterproof, insulated-to-minus-forty-degree boot tops with every step. By the time he reached the island — lights glowing in every window of the cottage — he was breathing heavily.

Roger's mind fired possible explanations at him: Francie and lover had arrived early, or one or the other; Whitey had arrived early, gone inside because of the storm, forgotten about the lights; someone else — repairman, tramp,

Brenda! — was inside; a surge in the wires had activated some automatic timer. And other explanations waited like bullets in an ammunition belt, but by now he was at the woodshed, reaching in, grabbing the ax, moving swiftly toward the cottage.

Swiftly, but not without thought. Smarter than ever in a crisis, or potential crisis, as he corrected himself, Roger remembered to crouch low as he went by the windows, staying out of sight from within. He heard nothing from inside: no voices, no music, no movement. The electric surge–automatic timer explanation rose higher on the list. A simple matter to switch it off, restore darkness, hide as planned by the woodshed, continue as before, everything on schedule. He climbed onto the porch — and saw that the door wasn't quite closed.

Almost, but not quite: snow packed in against the riser. Therefore? Roger straightened out of his crouch, peered through the window. And saw disorder, all a jumble, all a scramble, red, red, red, but —

The deed was done.

Deed done, deed done, deed done; there she was, laid out facedown beside the overturned table, in tennis shoes, one white, one red, and her hair a new color, red, red, red. From idea to reality, from conception to birth: his plan had borne fruit. But —

No Whitey. No Whitey to close the circle with, to write the last line of code, to make it perfect.

Roger whirled around, whirling with his body as his mind was already whirling inside, stared into the night, into the storm, saw nothing but night and storm. Red, so much red: she'd struggled, fought, perhaps hurt Whitey — even, oh what luck that would be! — killed him. Was it possible? Could he still be inside, dead or dying? What a simple revision that would be; in a second or two an amended plan took shape in Roger's mind, complete. He shouldered the door open and went in, the ax in his hands.

Silence. Red in streaks, in drips, in pools; the cottage a shambles, the overused word never more fitting. Roger found a roll of paper towels on the counter, dried off the soles of his boots, mopped the damp tracks he'd already made, stuffed the paper towel in his pocket for later disposal — *flake of dandruff falls off your head, you fry* — and followed the red trail.

Dining room, living room: no Whitey. On the staircase: no Whitey. In the unused bedroom: cupboard drawers pulled out, mattress stuffing all over the floor, no Whitey in the closet, no Whitey under the bed. In the love-nest bedroom: red handprints on the duvet, a red row of penny-sized drops, almost perfectly straight, on the floor by the side of the bed, pink dust or powder here and there, perfumed air, no Whitey in the closet, no Whitey under the bed.

Roger tried the bathroom last: no Whitey curled up dying on the floor; a flashlight, not a body, in the shower. But someone had taken a shower — condensation still clung to the margins of the mirror. What else? More red: the tiles, the toilet, the sink; more perfumed powder — he realized the whole cottage was redolent of feminine scent; and a watch, Whitey's watch — Roger recognized it — in the wastebasket. He picked it out with his gloved hand. It had stopped at 5:33. He checked his own watch: 6:15. *Six-fifteen precisely*. What had happened? Theories readied themselves in his mind, but what good were they? The deed was only half done and Whitey was on the loose. Roger saw himself in the mirror, eyes enormous, deep V-shaped notch between them, ax in one hand, Whitey's watch in the other. He dropped the watch back in the wastebasket, started downstairs.

Down the stairs, through the living room, dining room, careful to avoid contamination with the red, mind working, working. Suppose — suppose the lover was on his way even now, due in twelve minutes? Suppose Whitey was lying out in the snow somewhere? Crawling toward the gate, perhaps, in hope of finding Roger. Ergo, what? Roger had no idea. No idea. That scared him. It wasn't a matter of cognition, knowing that he was in a dangerous situation. It was a matter of feeling fear. Had he ever felt fear before? Not like this.

Roger went into the kitchen, his body trembling now. He stared out the window, holding tight to the ax handle. Never this afraid, but never had he failed to sort his way through suppositions, premises major and minor; never had he failed to think. What had gone wrong? Francie and Whitey had both arrived early, but why? Who had been first? And then? And then? His mind, powered by those 181 IQ points, came up with nothing but question marks. All problems were fundamentally mathematical, yes, but in this case there were too many unknowns. The chaos butterfly had fluttered its wings. Clutching the ax in both hands, Roger plummeted down and down into depths of fear he hadn't imagined.

But that was nothing. Nothing, because the next moment, something caught his eye — a movement reflected in the glass. He whirled around, whirled again as he had whirled at the front door, again with his brain whirling inside: whirled around in time to see her raise her bloody head off the floor, see her turn toward him, see her look him right in the eye.

But not Francie. It was Anne.

27

Paralysis.

Roger knew paralysis for the first time in his life. He couldn't move, couldn't speak, couldn't even think: paralysis physical and mental, paralysis complete. All he could do was accept sensory input — not process it, not analyze, syllogize, parse, deconstruct, induce, deduce, subdivide, ramify — merely accept. The worst part was that during this period of paralysis, however long it lasted, and of that he wasn't sure, his eyes were locked on Anne's, the whole long time.

And hers on him.

As he watched, the intensity of light in Anne's eyes slowly changed, as though someone were adjusting the dimmer, turning it down. But not all the way. At one point, the dimming halted, and Anne opened her mouth and formed a word. No sound came out, but the word was clear: *Help*.

Roger didn't move. He had his reasons, knew them without thinking, since he couldn't think, a priori. First, this inexplicable paralysis. Second, he had no qualifications to provide help of the kind required. Third, he doubted it was in his interest. Of that he couldn't be sure, not with so much data missing, but if forced to make an unsupported mental leap, he would have had to conclude that the survival of Anne would be of no help to him. So: help, no. He just couldn't.

Roger didn't tell her that, didn't say *no*, because he couldn't speak, but perhaps she understood anyway. The dimming control inside her began to turn again, down, down, down to nothing this time. Her head dropped to the floor — no, not dropped, she lowered it delicately, or since she couldn't have had the strength for that, it was lowered delicately, as though by some unseen, protective force. Impossible, of course, the existence of such a force, for reasons too manifold to list.

With that, with her eyes no longer locked on his, her eyes still open, eyes in every manner but the essential, and therefore no longer eyes at all, Roger's paralysis lifted. His mind cried out at once for data, starved for it, writhing around inside him for the lack of it. Whitey and Anne: it made no sense. How would Anne ever have known about this place? Why would she have come here? Was it conceivable that she'd been conducting an investigation much like his, but from the other side? Roger didn't know. He needed data. Still, he couldn't quite ignore a feeling, not of satisfaction, because of the miscarriage of his plan, but of a related wistfulness, bittersweet, based on the realization that he had come so close. So close: some bug in the programming had upset the timing; some other factor, probably uncontrollable, was responsible for the presence of the wrong woman.

Enough. A digression, although at the speed his mind worked it probably lasted less than a second, and therefore cost him nothing. Data. Start with the time: 6:30. Six-thirty! Was it possible that Francie and her boy were still on their way, might walk in at any moment? Roger hurried to the door, stuck his head out, saw nothing but snow, falling straighter now, and less heavily; heard nothing but the wind in the trees, lower in tone. But, yes, it was possible. Roger glanced around the kitchen. Could he somehow clean up, hide the body, hide every trace? Probably not. Was it in his interest? Why would it be? It wasn't even in his interest to turn off the lights, in case the following question lay waiting for him in the future, in a courtroom, for example: *Who turned out the lights?* No. Simply get out and get out fast. And if they were coming? Roger didn't know. Then he thought: what if Whitey was even at this moment crawling to the gate? Simultaneously — it could still happen! Not as planned, but in essence. If only he could be lucky just once in this goddamned life. Roger took the ax and went outside.

He made his way across the river to the western bank, toiled up the snowed-in lane through the meadow. Snow fell, but lighter now, and the wind was dying. Wouldn't Whitey's tracks still be visible if he'd gone this way? Roger shone his light back and forth across the meadow, saw snow unmarred all around.

He reached the gate: locked. Beyond it sat one car, covered in snow but a minivan from the shape — not Francie's car, as he would have known at a glance had he come from this side, but Anne's. Could Whitey be curled up behind it, or possibly inside? Roger unlocked the gate, walked around the car. No Whitey. But inside? More than unlikely, almost impossible. But if Whitey was inside, then at least he could control the damage by simply finishing him off right there. It meant leaving evidence because he would first have to brush snow off the window. Decision: Roger stood by Anne's minivan, following long and complex ramifications through his mind. Then he brushed a swath of snow from the windshield and shone his light inside. No Whitey: just an open road map on the front passenger seat and a shopping bag from F.A.O. Schwarz in back. Were children involved? Roger didn't recall. He scooped up some snow, tossed it on the bare glass. It wouldn't cling for some reason, though he tried and tried. No matter. The falling snow would do the work, as it would cover his own tracks, tracks he saw clearly in the beam of his flash. He relocked the gate and started back to the island, failing to notice until he was almost there that the snowfall had stopped.

No snow, therefore tracks, L.L. Bean tracks, therefore — what? Process, process, process, Roger instructed his mind. But instead of processing, his mind writhed. "How much fucking data do you need?" he said aloud, perhaps shouted. Nothing came, not a wisp of an idea. This had never happened before. His mind had always risen eagerly to any challenge. Now challenge had become torment. No Whitey, no more snow, Anne dead, the cottage all red inside. Therefore? Nothing. No response. "Think," he said, and smacked his forehead with the palm of his hand, hard.

Nothing.

Roger walked back across the river and onto the island, avoiding the circle of light around the cottage. He leaned against a tree in the shadows, waiting for an answer. Perhaps a mind as powerful as his had powers that couldn't be completely understood and so couldn't be completely commanded, like some supercomputer approaching the realm of artificial intelligence. A calming thought. Roger relaxed slightly, shone the light on his watch: 7:00. Would they be coming now? No. They had a hot thing going, but not so hot they'd venture out on a night like this, with the prospect of so many clement nights lying ahead. Therefore — and just as Roger felt his mind come to life at last, felt it really readying itself to think — he realized he had seen not only his watch in the flashlight's beam but something else as well. He switched it back on, swept it across the snow, saw dark stains on white.

Little stains, like ink drops on blotting paper, but these, he saw as he knelt in the snow, were red, not blue. They'd melted down into shallow pits, the red congealing now, still slightly wet. He took off his glove to make sure of that, touched the red with a fingertip, felt the wetness. After that he plunged his hand into clean snow, rubbed, rubbed, rubbed it off. At the same time his mind was spooling out lines of programming.

Subject: damage control. Datum: Whitey bleeding, perhaps to death. Task: to make sure he did so. Then came a mental leap, too swift to follow exactly, although he half caught images flying by: pattern of blood drops, unmarred snow by the gate, the snow-covered pickup parked at the lookout. Knowledge.

The next moment, Roger was on his way back across to the east side of the river, ax in hand, properly gripped near the head, blade down. Yes: Whitey curled up dying in a parked car; Roger had picked the wrong vehicle, that was all. He reached the east bank, scrambled up the ridge, grasping at tree branches, up over the top, onto the lookout. The pickup was gone.

And the hood of his own car had been brushed off, to identify it, of course. Therefore: Whitey and he weren't . . . a team anymore. Roger darted around the car, checking the tires — unslashed. The only sign of Whitey's mental state was the smashed-in rear window. Not good enough, Whitey. Roger unlocked the car, got in. Where would a Whitey-type go in these circumstances? The answer came at once: home to Mama. Not good enough either, Whitey. Roger started his car, backed out of the lookout. In the headlights, snow was falling again, falling hard. His tracks, the brushed windshield of Anne's car, any other evidence left behind — all would be gone forever in a matter of minutes. This was a tidying-up operation, and nature was helping. The murder of Anne would be a perfect crime, just not the perfect crime he'd had in mind. Roger considered Columbus, bold discoverer of what he hadn't been looking for. That was one similarity they shared. But Columbus's greatest accomplishment had been in crossing that un-crossed ocean for the first time. After that the voyage was easy. The lesson: as long as he emerged tonight immaculate, he could deal with Francie at his convenience, like Columbus on a later trip, or Cortés, Pizarro, Balboa. At the same time, he felt an inner stirring, deep in his brain, in the heart of its very core, that some route toward his original goal still existed, a route involving Whitey. If he could make contact with it, draw it to the surface, examine for feasi-bility and refine for deployment, all before finding Whitey, then he might have to prolong Whitey's life, or prolong it even more, to be ac-curate, since Whitey had already exceeded his allotment by almost an hour. Otherwise he would merely tidy up, as planned. This was more like it: he was doing what he did best, what he'd perhaps been born to do — ordering dis-order. As he turned south on the lane, Whitey's treadmarks not quite filled in with snow, Roger caught a glimpse in his rearview mirror of the cottage glowing on Brenda's island. He prepared his reaction to news of the tragedy.

Drip drip. Lawton Ferry, 97 Carp Road. A dump. Whitey knocked on the door. Why would he ever think this was home? He'd never even been inside. He knocked again. *Come on, you stupid bitch.*

"Who is it?" A high, shaky voice, but hers: Whitey knew that at once from the way it grated on him.

"Open the fuckin' door."

Pause. "Oh my God."

Click. The door opened. A thin old woman, bent and ugly, stood there gazing up in his direction, the centers of her eyes milky where they should have been black. "Oh, Donald," she said. "You've come home at last." She held out her arms.

"Are you nuts?" Whitey pushed past her, went inside, glanced around. A dump, and a stinking one.

She closed the door, followed him, sliding along crabwise, her head at a funny angle.

"What the hell are you doing?" he said.

"This is only how I can see just a teeny little. Around the edges like. Don't work for TV at all, but I can't say I miss it. Have you any idea the kind of filth —" She stopped, her face averted, but maybe seeing him semiclear from that angle. "Oh, Donald, has something happened?"

"Why would you say a stupid thing like that?"

"But you're bleeding. Aren't you? Aren't you bleeding, Donald?"

"That matters to you? Acting like you never seen blood before?"

"What do you mean?" she said. He started down the hall to the back of the house. She twisted her head frantically, trying to get him in her field of vision. "It's all the fault of that ungodly psychiatrist. I hope he burns in Hell for a thousand years."

"Shut up, Ma," Whitey said. "Where's the sewing stuff?"

She started to cry: same old cry, like fucked-up crows. He went back into the front room.

"What the hell's the matter with you?"

She wiped her eyes, her snotty face, on the back of her hand. "You said *Ma,* Donald."

"So?"

"It's been a long time."

"You're out of your mind, you know that? Now, where's the sewing stuff?"

"Sewing stuff?"

"I don't have time for this. The sewing stuff, in that basket thing."

"My sewing basket? The wicker one handed down from Granny Nesbit?"

"Just tell me where."

"But, Donald, I don't sew anymore. Haven't for years. I can't see the TV, never mind for sewing. I'm having eye difficulties, or haven't you been listening?"

Whitey wanted to smack her, smack and smack and smack, but he was too weak, hurt too much, and it wouldn't get him the sewing stuff any quicker, if at all. So he just took her by the wrist, and squeezed a little, family style. "I don't want you to sew. I'll sew. Just get me the basket."

"But what's torn, Donald? I knew you were hurt, just knew it."

"No one's hurt. A little fender bender is all."

"A fender bender? Cross your heart?"

"Every time."

She disappeared in her bedroom, returned with the sewing basket. "What's there to drink?" said Whitey, taking it.

"Tea, of course," she said, "and some Pepsi."

"I mean a drink."

"Like alcohol?"

"Yeah. Alcohol."

"But you always liked Pepsi."

"I want a fucking drink, for Christ sake."

"None of that here, Donald, not since I joined up with the Redeemer Church. Have I mentioned them? And I really wish you could see fit not to take the Lord's name in vain."

He was already in the bathroom at the end of the hall, closing and locking the door. A stinking little bathroom. He turned on the light, looked at himself in the mirror. Blood, and plenty of it. *Someone was going to pay.*

Whitey found gauze and a roll of tape in the cabinet, also a bottle labeled Vicodin. Wasn't that one of Rey's favorites? He swallowed the three or four remaining tablets, took off his jacket and shirt, began to bandage himself. A long slash across his gut, a puncture in his chest that he picked a sliver of long green glass from — and that reddened the bandages almost right away — others. But they'd heal, no problem. The worst was under his chin, where a big flap hung down like a goddamn bullfrog tongue, dripping red in fat round plops: no bandaging that.

As Whitey opened the sewing basket, he remembered the bullfrog he'd speared through the head down on the I-95 median. Now, what the hell was that supposed to mean? Like God was watching from up in the clouds or something? He'd done nothing wrong on the median — thought it was a snake, remember? He'd killed the wrong thing, was all. And out on the river just now, he'd been put in an impossible situation, done what he'd had to. When the going gets tough, the tough get going —

"What's that, Donald?"

"Get the fuck away." He listened for her retreating footsteps, heard them.

— and he was as tough as they come. He found a satin thing, cushion or whatever it was, full of needles, selected the thinnest, threaded it with beige thread, to blend with his skin, tied a knot in the end, got to work. Whitey had seen it done before, between periods in his last season. A skate blade had sliced his forearm, right above the glove, and the beery-breathed doc who came to all the games had sewn him up in the dressing room. Whitey stitched the chin flap back into place, hissing from time to time, but getting it done, making himself whole again; he was no fucking bullfrog.

He put his shirt and jacket back on, went into the kitchen. She was standing in the middle of the room, squeezing her hands together.

"Where's that Pepsi?" he said.

"In the fridge, Donald. Are you all right?"

Whitey popped the can open, sat at the rickety table, drank. It hit the spot. He liked Pepsi.

She came closer, hovered. "A bit to eat, maybe?"

He wouldn't have minded, except for the smell. "What stinks in here?" he said.

She sniffed. "I don't smell anything."

"What's the matter with you? It's like a god-damn shithouse."

She sniffed again. "Maybe it's the Kitty Litter. I'm not strong enough to carry it out anymore. And Donald? You know the awful part? Harry's gone."

"Who's he?"

"The cat."

Gone as far as the barn. Maybe he'd tell her, maybe not.

"I must have mentioned our marvelous cat," she was saying. "On the phone, wasn't it, at that New Horizons place? And now you won't be meeting him. Isn't that the way? He disappeared

332

the day that man came to visit. Vanished."

"What man?"

"A sort of preacher man, but not with the Redeemers. He said a prayer for you."

"Huh?"

"A beautiful prayer — *please hear this prayer for our beloved Donald* — I made him change it from Whitey, such a silly nickname — *and help guide him in useful ways.*"

"Are you making this up?"

"No, Donald, that's what he said. The most beautiful prayer I've heard in my entire life. How could I forget?"

"Guide him in useful ways — is that what he said?"

"Don't shout, Donald. My hearing's perfectly fine. It's the vision that —"

"When did this happen?"

"Oh, some time ago."

Smack, smack, smack, but only in his mind, even though he was feeling a little better now, what with Vicodin and Pepsi. No smacking Ma. "Where was I?" he said.

"Where were you?"

"Yeah. When this visit happened."

"Why, down there at the New Horizons establishment, naturally. And I wanted so much for you to meet Harry. He was the smartest little —"

"What did he look like?"

"Gingerbread, I guess you'd say, although —"

"The man, asshole — what did he look like?"

Her forehead got all cross, the way it used to:

kind of funny now, with her eyes like that, and no belt buckles possible. "Look like?" she said. "I'm afflicted with vision problems, or can't you get it through your thick skull?"

Not that funny. Smack. He did it then, but who wouldn't have? And it felt good; why hadn't he done it long ago? He picked her up off the floor, sat her at the table. "What I'm trying to find out, Ma — I know you like when I call you Ma — is would you know him if you heard him again?"

Ma repositioned her dentures, gave him one of her hateful looks, but not so hateful now with no eye power behind it, and said, "Honor thy father and mother."

"Accidents happen. Would you know him if you heard him again, yes or no?"

"You could try saying please."

"If I do you won't like it."

One of the best things he ever said. It silenced her. At last she hung her head — oh, why hadn't he done it long, long ago? — and said, "I'd know him."

" 'Cause why?"

"He talked fancy." She sniffled.

"Fancy?"

"You know."

"I don't."

"Fancy. Like with Harry. Harry has these long claws. The gentlest possible cat, but long claws. And this preacher man said they gave him an *inadvertent scratch. Inadvertent,* Donald. Now, who

334

on God's earth talks like that?"

Whitey knew the answer to that; he didn't know what or why, but he knew who. He was nobody's fucking bullfrog, nobody's . . . puppet. Did Roger really think of himself as the master? Whitey would see about that.

First things first. It took him no time to find his mother's purse, pocket what was in it, walk out the door without another word, a six-pack of Pepsi in his hand.

Lawton Ferry, 97 Carp Road. No pickup: an unpromising deficiency, but not definitive, and because not definitive, Roger took the ax with him when he left his car and went to the door.

He knocked.

"Donald? Is that you?"

"A friend of his."

Pause. "I know your voice."

"I'm your friend, too."

Pause. How slow people were. "But how could you be Donald's friend? You don't know him."

Slow, and they didn't even get there. "I prayed for him. Doesn't that make me his friend?"

"I don't know." Pause. "Harry disappeared the day you came."

"But he's right here, by the trash can."

"You don't mean it."

"As I live and breathe."

Pause. "Are you sure it's him?"

Roger described the animal as he remembered it.

"Merciful God — it's Harry!"

"Why don't I bring him in?"

"I'd be obliged."

"Here, kitty," said Roger into the night. "Kitty, kitty, kitty."

The door opened. The woman had a split lip, far too insignificant to account for all the blood Roger saw — on the kitchen table, the counter, the refrigerator, down the hall to the back.

"Have you got him?" said the woman, her sightless eyes gazing up at him. He didn't like seeing sightless eyes again so soon, therefore was a little gruff perhaps when he said, "He's absconded once more."

"I don't understand," the woman said. "Harry," she called, leaning outside, "Harry."

Roger went past her into the house. He followed blood down to the bathroom; formed meaning from gauze, tape, needle, thread; returned to the kitchen; saw the open purse, a hideous object made of shiny green plastic; made meaning of it, too.

"Harry, Harry."

"It's useless," he said. "Close the door. Snow's coming in."

"But he'll freeze."

"Harry? He's a survivor."

"Do you really think so?"

"Without question. Nine lives, and all that related folklore."

She closed the door, came inside. "You're right. Harry's a survivor."

"Then shall we agree not to worry about him? The pertinent question is — what are we going to do about Whitey?"

"Donald."

"Donald."

"Good question." She moved to the table, sat down, closed her eyes. A tear or two escaped her almost lashless slits. "He wasn't the nicest boy to his mother, not tonight, not anytime. And after all the sacrifices I made." She gazed up at Roger, unseeing. "Do you know what I've done for him?"

"What you could, I'm sure. Now our job is to help him, don't you agree?"

"But how?"

"You must think."

"Should we say another prayer?"

"In a minute. But first, we should establish where he's gone."

"He didn't tell me."

Roger laid the ax silently on the table. "Perhaps he let slip some clue."

"Clue? You talk like a cop." She turned her head sideways, trying to catch a glimpse of him. "What's your name, anyway?"

"Harry."

"But that's the cat's name."

"No matter. What matters is where your son has gone."

"No need to raise your voice. That's the same

thing I said to him. Now I suppose you'll smack me, too."

"What a suggestion. All I'm saying is that surely even someone of your — surely you can appreciate that in order to help him, I have to know where he is."

"He didn't say. Maybe back to New Horizons."

"It's a thought."

"You know about New Horizons?"

Her face tilted up in inquiry. This, as Roger had suspected for some time, was an impossible situation. Simply put, oversimply perhaps, this woman was negative. She knew all of the bad and none of the good: a potential witness of the most damaging kind.

"Useless now, dangerous in future."

"What's that?"

"Did I say something?" Roger rose.

"It sounded like a prayer, the beginning of prayer. Like the next line is *oh Lord, hear my humble call.*"

"Yes," he said. "Why not?"

"We're going to pray for Donald?"

"Let us kneel."

They knelt.

"Maybe that's a good omen," she said, "you having the same name as Harry."

"There are no omens," said Roger.

Still, how odd, his idle thought at their previous encounter of the ease of snapping her neck. And now here they were. Data: her

338

memory of his voice, the timing of his visits, her knowledge of his awareness of New Horizons — those were his rationale; her split lip, Whitey's bloodstains, the psychiatrist's testimony establishing motive — those were his protection. Anything else? Oh, yes, the gloves, still on his hands, rendering him immaculate. His gloved hands: he raised them.

She lifted her head in unseeing synchrony, waiting for his prayerful words, exposing her scrawny neck. Roger performed the logical act, but it wasn't as easy as he'd anticipated, in the doing

28

Francie tucked her car in behind a plow and stayed there, creeping along through the rolling country on the west side of the river at twenty miles an hour. In the darkness of late afternoon, she could see nothing but the back of the plow, lit in a way not at all comforting, more like an alien spaceship with monstrous creatures hidden inside. An alien spaceship leading her on to her wretched task: Francie tried rehearsing the little speech for Ned in her mind. It sounded pitiful; aloud, would be even worse.

At the intersection of the lane that led to Brenda's gate, the plow continued north and Francie turned east, out of its shelter. Any local could earn extra money by clearing the roads, and someone had done a quick job on the lane, perhaps an hour or two before. Blowing wind and fresh snow were undoing it almost as quickly, but the lane was still drivable, and Francie was halfway to the gate when her car phone buzzed.

"Hello?"

"Francie?" It was Ned.

"Yes."

"Are you on the way already?"

"I am."

"I hope you haven't gone too far."

"I just left," she said, lying because she sensed what was coming, didn't want to waste emotion, his or hers, on what would now be a side issue.

"Still in the city?"

"Yes."

"That's a relief," Ned said. "Because I'm not going to be able to make it. Something's come up, and I just can't."

"Something about Anne?"

"No, no. Nothing like that. Work related. I'll explain later."

"It doesn't matter," Francie began, and prepared to blurt out the whole thing, get it over with. Why had she cared about the *setting* in the first place? Why had she wanted to pretty it up? Doing it, getting it done, was all that counted. "It doesn't matter, Ned," she repeated, "because —"

"You're too good to me," Ned interrupted, then lowered his voice, as though there was a risk of being overheard. "But it does matter. It matters to me. I'm really sorry, Francie. And I wish I could say it won't happen again, but you know I can't even promise that. Oh, how I wish —" His voice caught, the way it did sometimes, a hint of the emotions underneath that always stopped her in her tracks but that she couldn't allow to stop her now. "I can promise I'll make it up to you somehow," he went on.

"No, Ned, it doesn't —"

"But right now I've really got to go — I'm al-

341

ready running late. Call you tomorrow. I'm sorry, Francie."

"Just —"

Click.

Why go on? That was the first thought to rise out of Francie's confusion. She had no desire to be in the cottage alone and stepped on the brake, too abruptly. Her car fishtailed in momentum-gathering swings, then whipped around and glided backward, weightless and out of control, but slower and slower, straight up the lane toward Brenda's gate. Francie did nothing to stop it, felt no fear, just waited for the out-of-control period to end. It was easy to see this spinout, this loss of control, as a metaphor, and Francie did, even as it happened: a metaphor of her and Ned in toto, and even of their coming denouement as well, now slipping away from her. She had to tell him, had to tell him now, would have no peace until she did.

Gravity reasserted itself; the car came to a soft padded halt halfway up the hill. Francie still had the phone in her hand. But where was he? Not at work, because *Intimately Yours* had been bumped by the Pops Christmas concert. And calling him at home was out, because Anne might answer, and saving her from all this was the whole point. Anne, that two-stories-tall Anne of the fairy tale, was the only one who mattered now, had become the master, in some funny way. Francie's car was pointed back toward home, the engine still running. She gave it gas, rolled down Brenda's lane, and realized at that moment that she would never see the cottage again.

A self-pitying thought she attacked immediately: too fucking bad. Was there a right to be happy, if that insipid word was the word? She'd been happy with Ned, happier than ever in her adult life, but she'd been sucking the happiness out of someone else's universe. There was no right to that. A clear decision, and once made the hard part was done: in her mind if not yet in life, she and Ned were over, finished. Telling him was all that remained. Anne would never know. Period. No harm done, and nothing to cry about.

Francie reminded herself of that last part several times as she turned left on the highway, headed home, was so deep in her own thoughts that she didn't notice she'd drifted across the center line until the headlights of an oncoming car were almost upon her. Francie swerved, once more losing her grip on the road; the other driver, also across the center line, swerved, too. They missed each other by inches, Francie continuing south, the other car — a minivan — going north, much too fast. As her wheels gained traction, Francie had a crazy thought: what if they'd collided, what if she'd been killed at that moment, with Ned still untold? A tidy ending for everyone, all loose ends forever unknown. She slowed to thirty miles an hour and kept the speedometer there until she reached the interstate. Anna Karenina, Emma Bovary — exemplars from a superseded age, a darker one for women, and not for her.

"Chief Savard?"

"Speaking."

"John More, returning your call."

Savard, just back in the office after clearing a pileup out at the Route 139 three-way stop — invariable pileup site whenever it snowed — thought he recognized the voice but couldn't recall the name. His caller sensed that before he had to admit it out loud.

"Reverend More, of the Little White Church of the Redeemer."

The pickup. A minor matter, especially on a night like this, but he had the reverend on the phone. "It's about your pickup."

"My pickup?"

"The church's, I guess it is. I happened to see it over near my place on Little Joe Lake and . . ." And he'd been curious, as he would have been about any vehicle parked there. Curiosity gave him no legal right to ask any questions, so he didn't.

"Is this about the taillight on the minibus? It's going into the shop on Friday. I really hope you're not planning to issue a ticket. They were booked solid."

"This isn't about the minibus, Reverend. It's about the pickup."

"We don't own a pickup."

"A white one, with the name of the church on the side panel."

"Oh," said the reverend. "That doesn't belong to us in an official sense. It's registered to a parishioner. We do use it from time to time, for dump runs and such."

"The dump's closed on Sunday."

"As well it should be." There was a silence. "Was there some question you had, sir?"

"That's when I saw your pickup," Savard said. "Yesterday. Sunday."

"Impossible. We only use it in the summer, and never on Sundays, of course. It isn't even insured right now — we renew the policy in May."

"I thought you said it belonged to a parishioner."

"And so it does. But since she can't drive it herself and has been generous enough to provide it, we handle the insurance and registration."

"Why can't she drive it herself?"

"The poor woman's legally blind."

"Well, someone was driving it."

"I don't see how that could be. It's shut up in the barn behind her house." The reverend paused. "Oh my goodness — you're not suggesting that someone stole it?"

"I'm not suggesting anything."

"Would it be asking too much for you to drive out and have a look?"

"Can't do it tonight, Reverend, not with the storm. But give me the address."

"Ninety-seven Carp Road, Lawton Ferry."

"And the name of this woman?"

"Perhaps you should mention me first when you call on her. Not that she's in any way lacking as a citizen. She's quite an independent sort, that's all — lives alone with her cat, remarkably self-reliant."

"I'll do that," Savard said, opening his notebook, taking out his pen. "What's her name?"

"Truax," said the reverend. He spelled it.

Savard didn't write; his pen was still, poised above the unblemished page.

"Mrs. Dorothy Truax," the reverend continued, "but everyone calls her Dot. God bless."

The snow had stopped by the time Savard parked in front of 97 Carp Road, and the air had stilled, but the temperature was falling fast, as it often did after a storm. The moisture in his nostrils froze before he reached the front door.

Savard knocked. No answer. The house was dark, but why would a blind woman and a cat need lights? He kept knocking, kept getting no answer. "Mrs. Truax," he called, loudly in case her hearing was going, too. "Mrs. Truax." Speaking the name did something to him, something unpleasant. That made him knock harder, but it didn't bring a response.

Savard went back to the cruiser for his lantern, shone it on the barn. The doors were unlocked but closed, and would be kept that way for a while by a snowdrift two or three feet high. Savard walked around the barn, found a hole in the wood, down at kicking level. He knelt, shone light through it, saw lots of rusted junk in the barn, but no pickup. Savard was just starting to rise when something twitched in the darkness. He reached for his gun — a first in his career, despite many provocations much stronger than a stirring in a shadowy barn — and a cat leaped out of the hole in the wall, flowed out of it, really, and landed soundlessly at his feet. The cat faced him, registered his presence, ran across the snow to the house, scratched at the front door.

Savard waited by the barn. He remembered the woman from the trial, everything about her, could picture her perfectly as she was then; remembered, too, the psychiatrist's testimony. Nothing would have surprised him less than seeing the door open, glimpsing a bony hand usher in the cat. But that didn't happen. The door remained closed, with the cat outside.

Savard arced his beam over the house, noticed the peeling paint, the duct tape on the lone front window. He considered peering through it, had taken a first step in that direction, when his radiophone buzzed.

He took it out of his pocket. "Savard."

"Hi, Chief." Carbonneau — all the others called him Joe. "Got a call from a snowmobiler, out on the river." Savard heard shuffling paper, waited for whatever it was Carbonneau had misplaced. He was long past the stage of being amazed that snowmobilers would be out on a night like this, prepared to hear that one or more had fallen through, even though the ice was six or seven inches thick by now. No matter how cold it was, there were always soft spots in the river, as one or two snowmobilers learned every year. "Had the name somewhere here, Chief," Carbonneau said.

"Are we going to need Rescue?" Savard said. "Dive team?"

"Oh, it's nothing like that," Carbonneau said. "I don't think. This guy was on the river, out by Pinney Point."

"The lookout?"

"Yeah. Not our side . . . but now that you mention it, Chief, what about that island?"

"With the cottage?" Savard said. He hadn't mentioned anything, only thought it; Carbonneau was far from perfect, but there were advantages in having worked together for a long time.

"Yeah. Whose side is that on?"

"I don't know," Savard said. "What's up?"

"This guy — I'll have the name in a minute — saw lights on in the cottage. All lit up like a Christmas tree."

"So?"

"That's what I said. It's Christmas, right? The thing is, this guy goes out on the river every winter, year after year, like. And he's never seen lights on in there, not once."

"Sounds like kids." Cottage break-ins weren't common on Savard's side of the river, at least not ones committed by local boys; local boys knew that Savard was strict about cottage break-ins — he'd dealt summarily with one or two cases in his early years, and that had been enough.

"That's what I thought," said Carbonneau. "Maybe still out there, Chief."

"Send Berry," Savard said.

"Berry's back down at the three-way. More bumper cars. And Lisa called in sick."

So it was him. Savard turned from the darkened house, walked down to the street. As he got in the cruiser, the cat made a screeching sound that ended on a high, keening note. A cold night, but cats could take care of themselves; this one would find its way back to the barn, wait for Dot Truax there. Savard put the cruiser in gear and headed for the river.

Francie slept a troubled sleep, caught in one of those partially controllable dreams where the real and the fantastic were all mixed up. Outside, the city was quiet, except for the rumble of the plows she half heard, muted by sleep, muffled by snow. In her dream, she wrestled with a problem: *oh garden, my garden* was back under her bed, the bed she was sleeping in, and she had to get rid of it at once, but what explanation would she give to Anne, two-stories-tall Anne, watching through the window? She had to come up with some scheme to make Anne go away, but what?

The phone started ringing. Maybe that would

work, maybe Anne would answer it, giving her time to grab the painting and run from the room. But Anne couldn't be distracted that easily; the phone rang and rang until finally Francie reached out of her dream and answered it.

"Francie?"

"Brenda?" The glowing red numbers on the bedside alarm read 4:37. Perhaps Brenda had made some mistake with the time difference.

"Oh, Francie, thank God you're there."

"What's wrong?"

"Thank God it's you. I was going out of my mind. Something awful's happened. At the cottage."

"At the cottage?"

"There's been a murder, a horrible killing, Francie. Some policeman, the chief, I think, just called me — my number's on the tax roll, of course. And I thought it might be you. An unidentified woman, he said. They must have assumed it was me, I guess. A local-type policeman, he wasn't very clear. Are you sure you're all right, Francie?"

"Yes. You're positive he —"

"Wait — I've got another call."

Francie, on her feet beside the bed, phone clutched in both hands, waited. *You're positive he said a woman?* That was the question she'd begun. What if Ned had gone to the cottage anyway, had changed his mind, changed his schedule because he hadn't believed she was still in the city, had felt guilty in consequence, or had simply worried about her out there in the storm? What if it was Ned?

"Francie? Sorry. It was —"

"Are they sure it was a woman, Brenda?"

"Yes. That was the policeman again. They've made an identification. It's some poor woman from Dedham."

"Dedham?"

"Yes. I have no idea what she was doing there — her name wasn't familiar to me at all. Franklin, I think he said. Anne Franklin."

On the edge of frenzy, mental and physical, she tried the number, Anne and Ned's number, in Dedham, almost incapable of hitting the right buttons. Busy. She tried again and again and again. Busy, busy, busy. She snapped on lights, ran down to the kitchen, threw open the door to the basement — more light, more light — ran down those stairs, too, burst into Roger's room.

Roger: not sleeping on his couch but sitting in front of the computer, face silvery in its light, bent over a sheet of paper covered with a pattern of connected boxes, pen moving rapidly. He swung around, startled, as she came in.

"Oh, Roger, something terrible's happened."

"What would that be?" he said, rising, pocketing the sheet of paper.

"Anne. She's been killed, Roger. Murdered."

Francie went to him, almost staggering, clung to him, began to shake. She buried her face in his chest. He patted her back.

29

In the kitchen, Francie tried the Dedham number, over and over, getting a busy signal every time. Murdered. In the cottage? Had there been an arrest? How? When? Why? Brenda had told her almost nothing. She called Rome, heard Brenda in Italian: *"Questa è la segretària telefònica di . . ."* She left a message, ran upstairs, threw on some clothes. When she came back down, Roger was waiting in his crimson robe with a package wrapped in foil.

"What's this?" she said.

"I made tuna sandwiches. Isn't it customary to bring food?"

"Are you coming?" she said.

He spread his arms, like great red wings. "It wouldn't be right," he said. "My relationship was peripheral."

But he walked her down to the garage. Their cars sat side by side, both in pools of wintertime snowmelt. Francie saw that his rear window was shattered.

"Oh, that," said Roger, although she hadn't said anything. "Some smash-and-grabber, it would seem, but nothing was taken. The alarm must have scared him off." He handed her the sandwiches. "Don't forget to offer my condolences."

Francie drove west on Storrow. Not yet dawn, but incoming commuters were already on the road, a yellow stream of headlights paralleling the dark one of the Charles. Their world was no longer hers. Murder: all those questions and many others roiled in her mind, including the one she most wanted to avoid — what had Anne been doing at the cottage in the first place? Wasn't there only one thing she could have been doing? And didn't that mean she must have found out about what went on in that cottage? But how? Had Ned confessed? *Something's come up,* he'd said. She'd asked, *Something about Anne?* And he'd said, *Nothing like that. Work related.* Therefore? Francie had no idea. And murder? Francie was lost.

She parked in front of the house in Dedham. The downstairs lights were on, silhouetting the stocky form of a snowman in the front lawn, a ski pole over one shoulder like a sentry's rifle. Francie walked up the path, unshoveled but packed down by many footsteps going in both directions. Worse than lost, Francie, because at that moment, standing at the door with its Christmas wreath, she had the most unworthy thought of her whole life: Perhaps there would now be some future for her and Ned after all. Even with Anne's wreath hanging there, Francie had that thought. What was she made of? She knocked on the door.

"Who is it?" said a woman almost at once, as

though she'd been waiting by the door. Francie didn't recognize her voice.

"Francie Cullingwood," she said, and added, "a friend of the family."

The door opened. A gray-haired woman in a quilted housecoat stared out at Francie with big dark eyes: Ned's eyes. The woman didn't have to tell Francie who she was.

"I'm Ned's mother. You've heard?"

"Yes."

The dark eyes gazed past her, into the sky, graying in the east. She shivered. "Come in."

Francie went into the little hall. Everything looked the same: a stack of mail on the table, a few audiotapes, irises in a vase. Francie glanced sideways into the living room, ahead into the kitchen.

"Ned's gone," the woman said, as though reading her mind, and Francie thought, *Does she know?* Francie saw no sign of any such knowledge in the woman's face, and besides, she hadn't seemed to recognize her name. "The police came down from New Hampshire," Ned's mother went on, "and took him to do . . . what needed to be done."

They went into the kitchen. "Tea?" said Ned's mother. "Or maybe coffee? I suppose you'd call it morning."

"Nothing for me."

"I'll have tea," the woman said, going to the stove. "Keep moving." She had trouble with the switches. "Why anyone would need such an elaborate oven I have no idea." Gas ignited with a pop, settled down to a steady blue flame.

Francie tried to remember what Ned had said about his mother, recalled nothing. He almost never spoke of family life; she thought of the Chinese walls dividing different departments of Wall Street law firms in the interest of preserving the appearance of something or other. But didn't his mother live in Cleveland? Weren't they all from Cleveland?

"How did you get here so fast?" Francie said.

The woman paused, tea bag dangling in her hand. "I don't follow you."

"I thought you lived in Cleveland."

"True. I flew in yesterday, to spend the holidays."

He hadn't mentioned that either.

"Holidays," Ned's mother said, coming to the table, cup clattering on the saucer. "Can you imagine?" Their eyes met and Francie sensed that this was the moment for tears, but none came. Big dark eyes, just like Ned's on the surface, but much drier underneath.

"It's a good thing you're here, Mrs. Demarco," Francie said.

The woman shrugged that aside. "There's nothing good," she said. "And it's Mrs. Blanchard, actually. I remarried." She sat down, sipped her tea; Francie remained standing. "What was your connection again?" said Mrs. Blanchard. "To the family, I mean."

Francie hadn't said. "Anne and I . . . ." Tears

were on the way now, but hers; she stopped them, cut them off completely and at once, went on. "We were tennis partners."

"Oh, yes, the tennis," said Mrs. Blanchard. Tea slopped out of her cup, splashed on the table, dripped off the edge, stained her house-coat. She didn't appear to notice. "As a friend of hers," she said, "can you give me any idea what in God's name she was doing —"

The phone rang. Mrs. Blanchard crossed the room and grabbed it off the wall before it could ring again.

"Yes? Are you all right, dear? What's hap— no, nothing." Her eyes shifted to Francie, sponging up the spilled tea. "There's a visitor, that's all." She covered the mouthpiece, spoke to Francie. "What was your name again?"

Francie repeated it. The woman talked into the phone, raised her eyebrows, held it out for Francie. "It's Ned," she said. "He wants to speak with you."

Francie took the phone. "Ned. Ned. I —" Mrs. Blanchard sat at the table, back to Francie, head still, still and alert. "I don't know what to say."

"Don't say anything, Francie," he said.

"Oh, but Ned, it's so —"

"Don't say anything to anybody," he went on, and she realized she'd misinterpreted him; he hadn't been referring to the uselessness of words at a time like this. "And don't say *Ned*

356

like that, not to anybody," he continued. "You sometimes look in at the cottage as a favor to your friend, that's an unavoidable fact, no hiding it, but nothing more, nothing about me, nothing about you and me." Francie had never heard his voice like this, low and pressing, the words coming fast. "Do you understand?" he said.

"Not really." She turned her back, hunched over, spoke softly and right into the phone so Mrs. Blanchard couldn't hear. "I don't see how it makes —"

"Is my mother there? Nearby, I mean?"

"Yes."

"Then shut up, for Christ's sake. She misses nothing." Francie heard a coin dropping into a pay phone. "But you're wrong about what you were going to say, Francie. It does make a difference. Just think about it."

"How?"

"Goddamn it. Why are you doing this? Don't you care about me at all, Francie?"

She did, much more and without a doubt, but the thought of replying to the question at that moment sickened her. And she still didn't understand what difference it made now if their relationship was known; also knew that she wasn't going to find out, not with Ned's mother in the room. She changed her tone for him, tried to approximate the tone she'd have used if she really had been nothing more than Anne's tennis friend, but had no idea what that would sound like either. "Do they — do they know what happened?"

A pause, a long one. Then came a sob, thick and ragged. "She was slaughtered, Francie. Slaughtered. That's what happened."

Click.

Francie put down the phone. Mrs. Blanchard was on her feet. "He didn't want to speak to me?"

"He had to go."

Ned's mother gave her a close look. She might have been about to say something, but at that moment Em walked into the room in her pajamas.

"Morning, Grandma," she said, and then noticed Francie. "Oh, hi."

"Hi," said Francie.

Em brushed her hair out of her eyes. "Getting ready for another tournament?"

"No."

The girl hit the button on the countertop TV, reached up in the cupboard for cereal and a bowl, put them on the table. On the screen, a commercial for pain relievers ended and two newscasters appeared at a desk. Francie was right beside the TV; she switched it off. Em and her grandmother both turned to her, understanding registering on the woman's face, surprise on Em's. Francie, unable to invent any explanation for her conduct, said nothing. She went to the fridge, opened it, said, "Two percent or nonfat, Em?"

"Two percent," said Em, glancing at the dark screen of the TV.

Francie poured milk in her bowl. "How about some strawberries on top?" She'd seen them in the fridge.

"Sure."

Francie took a handful of strawberries from their carton, washed them in the sink. Not a good idea, strawberries, because a strawberry couldn't remain a simple strawberry, of course, but had to be red, ripe and full of life. Francie put them on a plate, set it before Em.

"Thanks," said the girl, popping one in her mouth and placing the others one at a time among the cornflakes in a star-shaped pattern. She raised her head. "Mom up yet?"

Francie and Ned's mother looked at each other; neither answered.

"Hey," said Em. "What's up, Grandma?"

"Maybe you'd better go," Ned's mother said to Francie.

"I'd like to help."

"That won't be necessary," said Ned's mother. "Most considerate of you, but it's a family matter."

Francie turned to Em, but what could she say? Em's mouth opened, strawberry-red inside.

Francie didn't put up a fight; she left, now a coward on top of everything. She was outside on the walk, almost to her car, when she heard Em's wail: piercing, unmitigated, unbearable — catastrophe beyond repair.

And she'd forgotten to leave the sandwiches, somehow still in her hand. She realized she'd loved Anne. It wasn't too strong a word.

30

Back in her own house, Francie found a stranger talking to Roger in the living room. "Here she is now," said Roger as Francie came in. The stranger rose, a big, broadly built man with a broad face; he reminded her of the blacksmith in the background of a Dutch genre painting she could picture but not identify at that moment.

"Francie, this is Mr. Savage, chief of police in Lawton Center," said Roger. "Mr. Savage, my wife."

"Pleased to meet you," said the chief, speaking to Roger although his eyes were on Francie. "And it's Savard. Joe Savard."

"My apologies," said Roger. "Will you be needing me any longer?"

"No," said Savard. "Thanks for your help."

"Think nothing of it," said Roger. He came to Francie, took both her hands in his, said, "Oh, Francie. It's dreadful, just dreadful." Then he left, pausing to pick a few dead leaves from the base of a plant as he went out.

"Please sit down," Francie said. Savard sat on the window seat, back to the morning outside, darkened by thick, low clouds; Francie couldn't sit, but leaned on the arm of a chair by the fireplace, about three steps away. "What happened to Anne?"

"She was murdered sometime last night, Mrs. Cullingwood, in the cottage owned by your friend —" He leafed through his notebook.

"Brenda."

He found the page. "It says here Countess Vasari."

"She's not a real countess," Francie said, an unconsidered remark that made her sound like a pompous fool, exactly the opposite of her intent.

Savard looked up from his notebook. "What's the difference?"

A good question. What had she meant? That Brenda was back to being plain Brenda Kelly again; that she didn't want this man to form a false impression of her, Francie, because of some improbably and temporarily titled friend. "Nothing. I didn't mean to interrupt."

"There's not much to interrupt at this stage. The lab guys are still at the scene and we haven't got a suspect." Savard closed the notebook, laid it on his knee. His hand was big, thickened by some sort of hard work, but not ugly. "I'm hoping for some help from you," he said.

"Anything," Francie said.

He nodded. "Your friend says she hasn't been to her place for two or three years — she couldn't remember exactly — and that you kept an eye on it for her."

"That's true."

"How often did you go up there?"

"A few times a month in summer. Sometimes more."

"And in winter?"

"Almost never."

"When was the last time?"

A Friday. The day after she'd fallen through the ice. Ned had called her for the first time on her car phone, had been waiting there, surprising her on the darkened porch with his fury over her call to the radio show. She made the calculations in her head — it took longer than it should have because she kept remembering him out on the river: *wouldn't there be something wrong with two people who could just throw it away?* — and gave Savard the date.

He wrote it down. "Did you notice anything unusual when you were there?"

"No."

"No sign of a break-in, or an attempted one?"

"No."

"Nothing missing or out of place?"

"No."

"Anything spilled, knocked over, broken?"

"No."

There was a pause. Francie had a cast stone figure by Jean Arp on the bookcase Roger's wedding present to her, not a big or important one, but Arp nevertheless — and the policeman's eyes were on it: whether taking it in or thinking about something else, she couldn't tell.

His gaze swung back to her. "I assume you have a key to the cottage?"

"Two," Francie said. "One for the gate, one for the door."

"Have you ever lost them?"

"No."

"Given them to someone else?"

"No."

"Had copies made?"

"No." Although Ned had asked for one, she now recalled: *Might help if I had a key. It's cold out there.* But she'd never gotten around to doing it: everything had fallen apart first.

"You know of no other person with access to the cottage, then?"

"No."

"Would you mind showing them to me?"

"Showing what to you?"

"The keys, Mrs. Cullingwood."

They were in her car in the garage, hanging from the ignition. When she came back with them, Savard was standing by the bookcase, bent over the Arp, his hands behind his back. Francie almost said, *You can touch it if you want.*

But did not. Instead she said, "Here they are," and handed him the keys.

Savard glanced at them, handed them back. Standing next to him by the bookcase, Francie sensed his physical strength. Not that he made himself look big or puffed out his chest — he slouched a little, if anything. Neither was he dressed in clothes designed to show off his physique — he wore a baggy gray suit, a little shiny at the elbows. But she sensed it, all the same.

"So Anne Franklin didn't have keys to the cottage."

"No."

"Did she know your friend Brenda?"

"No."

He nodded to himself. It suddenly hit Francie that this man, or an assistant, had probably asked Ned these same questions already, hours before, that he might be searching for discrepancies as well as facts. She was considering the implications of that, and how they fit with Ned's instructions — *nothing about you and me* — when Savard said, "How long has she known about it, then?"

Francie felt a strange rush of blood to her face and neck, as though she were going scarlet; couldn't have been, of course, not with her complexion. "It?" she said.

"The cottage."

"I don't understand."

"Its existence and location," Savard said. "When did you first tell her about it?"

Discrepancies: awareness that he might be searching for them was no help without knowing what he'd heard already from Ned. She stuck to the truth. "I never did."

"So she made no mention to you of going up there?"

"We never discussed the cottage."

Savard opened his notebook, read to himself. Francie, reading upside down, saw lines of neat handwriting too small to make out, culminating in a circled notation writ larger at the bottom of the page: *FC — nexus?* That scared her for many reasons, not the least of which was the presence of a word like that in the notebook of a man who looked like this. She realized she had no idea what was coming next.

"I wonder, then," he said, closing the notebook, "how she found out about the cottage."

"So do I," Francie said.

"And what she was doing up there."

Francie said nothing, was sure she knew the horrible answer to that question, lacked only the steps in between. Was silence the same as a lie? In some cases, like this one, yes.

"When was the last time you saw her?"

"Saturday night. We went to dinner, the four of us, after tennis."

"How was she?"

"In what way?"

"Her mood."

Francie thought of the scene in the locker room. "A little upset, at first."

"Any idea why?"

"We'd just lost the match." Was a partial truth the same as a lie? Ditto.

"Is that enough to upset a grown woman?"

"Ever play competitive sports, Mr. Savard? It was the club championship."

Savard gave her a quick look; for a moment she thought he was about to smile, but he didn't. "Who else knows about the cottage?"

"You mean that Brenda has it? Lots of people."

"And were any of them acquainted with Anne, to your knowledge?"

Besides Ned, there was only Nora. Francie gave Savard her name and number. Why not? Nora knew Brenda, so he would have found her eventually.

Savard wrote Nora's name and number in his notebook and said, "Then there's your husband."

"What about him?"

"I assume he knew about the cottage as well."

Had Roger known? Francie had never told him: at first, for no particular reason other than the kind of marriage it had become — he wouldn't even have expected to hear a detail like that — and later because of Ned. She gave Savard a careful answer: "Roger didn't know Anne — they met for the first time on Saturday night."

His eyes went to the sculpture, were still on it when he said, "What was Anne like, Mrs. Cullingwood?"

"She . . ." Francie got a grip on her emotions; if she was going to get through this, whatever *this* was and whatever *getting through it* meant, she would have to keep that well capped. "She was wonderful, Mr. Savard."

He gave her a sharp glance. "Do you want to sit down?" he said. "A glass of water?"

"I'm fine. Anne was . . . good. There was no

meanness in her, if you're thinking about ene-
mies, or something like that. She was good."
Francie, realizing she had raised her voice, lowered it, went on: "She was talented, she was
loving."

"In what way talented?"

"She was a fine tennis player, for one thing.
And a very good painter."

"Painter?" he said.

"Yes."

"Do you mean an artist? The kind you evaluate in your job?"

How did he know about her job? Roger, of
course. "I didn't evaluate Anne. She was my
friend."

"I'm just making sure I understood what you
meant by painting, that's all," Savard said. "The
fact that she painted could be important."

"Why?"

"Let's sit down."

"I told you I'm fine."

"Whatever you say," Savard said, but he returned to the window seat. Francie followed,
leaned again on the armchair, feeling manipulated in some way. "It doesn't surprise me to
learn she was an athlete, Mrs. Cullingwood."

"Why not?"

"There's evidence of a tremendous struggle
last night."

Francie felt faint, might have fallen had it not
been for the chair; had he foreseen that? Savard's
image began to dissolve, almost did, then slowly

returned to normal, as though some director had changed his mind about ending a scene. Savard was watching her closely.

"Go on," she said, her fingers digging into the fabric of the chair.

He folded his massive hands in his lap, a gesture that seemed ceremonial to her, even religious. "Before she died, she managed to write a word on the floor. Very small. She must have changed her position slightly after that, because it was covered by her arm and we didn't see it at first. The word she wrote was *painting*."

"Painting?"

"Yes. Do you have any idea what she could have meant by that?"

"No."

"But you must know something about her work — in order to have made the judgment that she was good."

"I've seen some of her paintings."

"Do any stand out in your mind?"

That was easy: the portrait of Ned. But *nothing about you and me.* "No one more than another," Francie said.

"Do you know of any painting she might have been working on recently?"

"No."

"Or something she wanted to try in the future?"

"No," Francie said. "Do you think she meant to . . . to tell us who killed her?"

"Perhaps not the actual attacker."

"The actual attacker? I don't understand."

Savard unfolded his hands, rubbed them together slowly. "How would you characterize her marriage, Mrs. Cullingwood?"

"In what way?"

"Were they happy together?"

"I rarely saw them together."

"Meaning you saw them separately?"

He was so quick; didn't look like he would be, but was. "Meaning I didn't see them together enough to form an opinion about something like that," Francie said as calmly as she could.

"Did Anne ever say anything that led you to believe they had problems?"

Yes, in the locker room. "No," Francie said. A lie: total, direct, inescapable.

"How would you describe her self-confidence?"

"That's a strange question."

"There's not much to go on, Mrs. Cullingwood, as I mentioned. Getting a picture of her in my head will help."

"Self-confidence. It's not easy to know something like that about a person."

"I disagree," Savard said. "In my experience, it's one of the first things you notice."

They looked at each other. He was right, of course. Quick, and there was more to him than that. "Not as high as it should have been," Francie said.

"On a scale of ten," Savard said.

"Isn't that a rather brutal method for measuring something as abstract as self-confidence?" Francie said.

"No," Savard replied. "Brutal was what happened to her in your friend's cottage."

It finally hit her. "What did she use to write with — the word *painting?*"

"I think you've figured that out."

Francie didn't speak; for a moment she couldn't even breathe.

Savard rose, came closer. "I need your help," he said. "And so does she, if you accept that rationale."

"Three," Francie told him. "The answer to your question is three."

"Any reason a woman of such qualities would have a self-confidence level like that?"

"I don't know."

"You must have thought about it."

"Why do you say that?"

He opened his mouth, said, "You're," then stopped. "I'll withdraw the question." A beeper went off. Savard took it from his pocket, read something on its screen, put it and his notebook away. He moved toward the door, then stopped and turned. "Sometimes women unhappy in their marriages have affairs," he said.

Francie again felt the upsurge of blood in her neck and face.

"If she was," Savard continued, "what's to be gained by hiding that now?"

"What are you saying?"

"When a wife is murdered, we always check

the husband first, Mrs. Cullingwood."

"I thought you said there was no suspect."

"I misspoke. We have no evidence pointing to a specific suspect. But Mr. Demarco has no alibi for last night."

"No alibi?"

"No convincing explanation of his whereabouts during the period when his wife was killed." He handed her a card. "Call if you can help."

He went into the hall; Francie followed. "But there was a struggle, you said."

"I did."

"Then wouldn't there be signs of that on the attacker?"

"There would. On the actual attacker."

Savard opened the door. Roger was outside, sprinkling a handful of salt crystals on the walk. He looked up. "Safety first, Chief," he said.

"You're so right," Savard said. "I meant to ask if you've ever been to Brenda's cottage, Mr. Cullingwood."

"Never. The fact is, I'd forgotten all about it, if I ever knew in the first place. Did you ever mention it, Francie?"

"I don't think so."

Roger spread his hands. "It was Francie's baby, Chief."

Savard glanced back at Francie, then got in his car, not an official police cruiser but an old Bronco, and drove away. Francie and Roger looked at each other. "Close the door, Francie," he said. "You're letting in all the cold."

Roger went inside a few minutes later. He didn't see Francie in the kitchen, the hall, the living room. He walked over to the plant in the corner, a dieffenbachia. *Pausing to pick a few dead leaves from the base of it as he went out!* Who could compete with brilliance of that magnitude? He plucked the digital recorder that Francie had given him from behind the stem and dropped it in his pocket.

31

Francie had no distance from what she was doing, no inner watchfulness, no control. This, life after Anne, or at least in the first few hours after Anne, had all the intensity of loving Ned, an inverse intensity that now served to heighten pain, not pleasure. From her bedroom, Francie dialed Ned's number, heard his mother's voice on the machine: "You have reached the Demarco residence. Please leave a message at the tone."

She had to see him. Francie hung up, realizing as she did that he might not be home yet — might still be in New Hampshire, or on his way back. Had to see him. On his way back: she was thinking car keys, coat, Dedham, was turning from the phone — had to see him — when it rang. She snatched it up.

"Francie, is it true?" Nora, not Ned.

"About Anne, you mean?"

"What else would I mean?"

"It's true."

"Oh, God. What happened?"

"They don't know."

"But she was murdered?"

"Yes."

"At Brenda's place?"

"Yes."

"What was she doing up there?"

"They don't know."

Pause. "I'm coming over."

"Not now, Nora. I'm on my way out."

"Where?"

"Please." Had to see him. "There are things I have to do."

"Like what, Francie? What's going on?"

"I'll call you later."

"But —"

Francie hung up.

She drove back to Dedham under a sky that was one low sagging cloud from horizon to horizon. Ned's garage door was open, no cars inside. Francie parked on the street and waited.

The house was quiet, the curtains drawn. Francie stared at it for a while, then at the snowman with the ski pole over one shoulder. She noticed that he wore a name tag, frozen into his chest, with writing on it too distant to see. After a minute or two, she had to get out of the car, walk up the path, read it: *Mr. Snowman, VP Xmas Productions.* Anne humor. Francie dug the tag free with her fingernails, put it in her pocket, went back to the car. She had pulled it out three times for another look when Ned drove up at last. He wheeled into the driveway, braked in front of the garage, hurried toward his front door. Had he not noticed her?

Francie jumped out of the car. "Ned."

His head snapped around. He saw her, began to speak, stopped himself, glanced back at the house, then came toward her, cutting directly through the knee-deep snow in the yard, ice balls clinging to the tassels on his loafers.

Then he was on the sidewalk, and she got a good look at his face. Had to see him. But what had become of her beautiful man? This blue-lipped gray face, red around the eyes, had all his features but was not him, and the eyes themselves, fugitive, blinking, burrowing things, were not him either. Francie wanted to wrap him in her arms, somehow make him better, settled for holding out her hand.

After a moment or two, he took it and then held on tight. "Oh, Francie, it hurts so much."

Francie, determined not to cry, to hold it all in, almost did.

"I'll never ever be the same," he said. His voice had changed, too, lost its richness and musicality, now did no more than deliver the words. "And what about Em? Tell me that? What about Em? I'm going to have to go in there now and tell her . . . tell her."

"She knows."

"She knows?"

"Your mother told her."

He dug a knuckle into his forehead above the right eye, hard. "Are you sure?"

"I was here."

"You were?"

"Don't you remember? We talked on the phone."

He squeezed his eyes shut, opened them.

"What is happening to me?"

She stroked his hand. He withdrew it, looked back at his house. "But you can't come here, Francie. People will suspect."

"Suspect what?"

"About us, of course."

"What difference does it make now?" Francie said. Over his shoulder she saw a curtain part, Ned's mother peer out. Their eyes met. The curtain closed.

"How can you say that? It makes all the difference. I don't want Em to ever know, ever to think that everything wasn't . . . wasn't just the way it seemed."

That made no sense to Francie, not anymore, but the intensity of her reaction surprised her. "Is that what your life's going to be from now on?" she said. "Preserving some past that never was?"

Ned's arm twitched. For a moment Francie almost imagined he was going to hit her. An unworthy thought, beneath them both, contemptible — until she happened to glance down and catch his hand uncurling from a fist. But a fist could mean tension, not violence, and she knew there was no violence in Ned, had never seen the slightest sign, so he couldn't possibly have been involved in Anne's death, no matter what this man Savard suspected. Francie could barely allow her mind to articulate the thought. Could she have known him that little? No. Savard was far off course. She didn't believe it, not for a second.

Ned took a deep breath. "You're tough, Francie. That's one of the things that . . . attracted me to you. But your timing's not always on."

"What do you mean?"

He came a little closer, lowered his voice. "What do I mean? What's the matter with you? How can you say what you just said about my marriage? My wife is dead. Where are your feelings?"

"Where are my feelings?" Francie, who had never struck a human being in her life, did it now. Her scarlet handprint took shape on his washed-out face. She walked away.

He followed. "Wait, Francie. I take that back. I'm not myself. Please."

He touched her shoulder; she halted. Even at a moment like this, his touch sent that familiar, irresistible feeling down her back. The man for her; it was inescapable. She swung around and asked him, "Where were you last night?"

He seemed to jerk back, almost as if she'd hit him again. "What kind of question is that?"

"Savard's question."

"You've talked to him?"

"He came to the house."

"What did he want?"

"To know what I thought of your marriage."

"My God. What did you tell him?"

The mark she'd made on him was already fading, but it sickened her to see it. "Don't worry about me, Ned."

"I don't understand."

"I won't let you down."

Ned's eyes met hers at last. "Oh, I know that, Francie. I wish I could hold you now, so much."

"So do I." She wanted to kiss that redness on his cheek, dared not. Was there somewhere they could go? Was that an evil thought? What was she made of?

"But it doesn't really answer my question," Ned said. "What exactly did you tell him?"

"That I didn't know enough to comment on your marriage."

"And nothing about us?" he said.

"Nothing."

"Perfect," he said. "Perfect as always. I'm sure that'll take care of it."

"It won't, Ned, because Savard thinks she was the one having an affair."

"That Anne was?"

Francie nodded.

"And I followed her out there?"

"Or paid someone to do it."

He laughed, a strange, barking laugh, almost like Roger's but lower in tone. "That's idiotic."

"Then why not tell him where you were last night?"

"Please, Francie, not the third degree."

"You think this is the third degree? Why can't you tell him? You said on the phone that it was work related. Is there a patient confidentiality issue, or something like that?"

"Something like that. Please don't ask me more."

"I won't," Francie said. "But he will."

"He's just a small-town cop, nothing to be concerned about."

"You think so?"

"Yes."

"He's trying to find out how she — how Anne knew about the cottage."

"I have no idea."

"Maybe not how. But we can both guess why she went out there."

"She didn't know anything. There has to be some other explanation."

"Like what?"

He had no answer.

"It must have come from you, Ned."

"Impossible. You know how careful I've been."

Had he? Careful maybe about the cottage, but not careful the one night at her house, the night of the milk run and the invented flat tire, the night he discovered she didn't like irises. Francie, remembering the pressure gauge, turned to Ned's car in the driveway.

"What are you looking at?" Ned said.

"Maybe she found something in your trunk."

"Like what?" But he was already moving toward the car. Francie went with him. He opened the trunk: roof rack, rock salt, kayak paddle; and under the floor mat, tools and the spare. "What's there to find?" said Ned, just as an old

Bronco pulled into the driveway. Ned and Francie wheeled around, backs to the open trunk.

Savard got out of the Bronco, carrying a shiny metal box. He nodded to Francie, spoke to Ned. "I'd like to see your wife's paintings, if you don't mind."

"Her paintings?"

"Mrs. Cullingwood hasn't explained?"

"No," said Francie. "I have not."

"It's kind of pressing," Savard said to Ned, "or I wouldn't bc bothering you like this. We found something after you and I talked last night." He told Ned what Anne had written on the floor of Brenda's cottage.

He didn't seem to understand, his eyes, those new eyes, going to Francie, back to Savard. "I haven't even seen my daughter yet," he said.

"I won't come inside," Savard said. "You could bring them out here, if there aren't too many."

"Her paintings?"

"I'll help, if you want," Francie said.

"I'll do it myself." Ned went into the house.

Savard gazed into the open trunk, then at Francie. "Did Anne ever ask you to buy one of her paintings for your foundation?"

"Why do you ask?"

"Just wondering whether you ever turned her down."

"The answer is no to both."

"You must do that a lot — turn people down."

"It's part of the job."

"Do you tell them the truth?"

She met his gaze: surprising eyes, almost unguarded, almost as though interested in the answer for its own sake. "Enough of it, Mr. Savard," Francie said.

Ned came into the garage from the house with some paintings, went back for more, leaving the door open. Francie heard Em crying in another room, heard him talking to her, his voice closer to normal, comforting, sweet; Francie knew the effort that must have taken. He came back with more paintings, arranged them all in a row of seven leaning against the wall.

Anne's paintings: the still life with grapes, another still life with fish and wine, two seascapes, a desert landscape, an abstract with deep blue spirals, a self-portrait. Francie wanted them to be great, was already toying with a fantasy of Anne's posthumous fame, and her its engineer. But they were not great; the still life with grapes was the best, and even it was not as good as she'd first thought, flawed in ways she hadn't seen before; she argued with herself that the fault lay with the harsh strip lighting in the garage, and lost.

"That them all?" Savard said.

"Yes," said Ned.

But Francie knew it wasn't. Where was his own portrait, the one that hung over the bed in the master bedroom? Francie didn't look at Ned, or at Savard, kept her eyes on a slightly fussy cactus in the desert landscape. How could he have missed his own portrait? She thought of Dorian Gray.

Savard examined the paintings one by one, spending ten or fifteen seconds on each. Francie had watched many people look at paintings, their levels of concentration ranging from superficial to profound. Savard's was of the latter, but she had no idea what he was seeing. "Are there any works in progress?" he said.

"No."

"Did she have a studio somewhere?"

"No."

"So this is it?"

"Yes."

Savard studied the self-portrait: a younger Anne in a black turtleneck, holding a paintbrush, a dull gold band almost invisible on her ring finger.

"Will you be needing me any longer?" Ned said.

Savard took his eyes off the self-portrait. "Just one more thing," he said, and opened the little metal box, an evidence kit, Francie realized — she'd seen them on TV. At the bottom lay a road map of New Hampshire, folded open to a panel of the southern part of the state. She saw a small red X on the Merrimack River. "Have you seen this before?" Savard said.

Ned shrugged. "A road map. Is it important?"

"That remains to be seen."

Ned reached for the map. Savard jerked the

box out of his reach. "Haven't dusted it yet." He checked to see if they understood. "For finger- prints," he explained. "We'll also check for fi- bers — try to match car interiors, floor mats, that kind of thing. But does it look familiar, Mr. Demarco, at first blush?"

Ned gazed down into the box. Savard turned to Francie, seemed suddenly to notice her pres- ence. "I'm sorry, Mrs. Cullingwood. Didn't mean to keep you so long."

A dismissal. Polite, almost deferential, but a dismissal. Why? And why now and not before? Francie had no choice. She tried to establish the proper distance in her tone. "If there's anything I can do, Ned."

"Thanks, Francie." He did it better.

Francie got in her car and drove away. In her rearview mirror, she saw Ned and Savard talking in the driveway, or more accurately, Ned talking and Savard listening, very still.

Roger took his car to an auto glass shop and had a new window installed. On the way home, he stopped at the newsstand of the Ritz, found mention of Anne, but none of Mrs. Truax, none of Whitey. He parked in his garage, closed the door, carried the ax inside, and tucked it behind the woodpile in the storage room off his base- ment HQ, woodpile left over from the evenings when they'd had fires. Then he went upstairs and poured himself a Scotch, drank it looking down on the street from the living room window.

Whitey was (*A*) dead in the woods, perhaps not to be found until spring, or (*B*) alive and somewhere out there. *A* would be lovely, but he had to plan for *B*. Roger tried to quantify the threat represented by Whitey, in the event he fell into the hands of the police. Not, based on the evidence on his digital recorder, that the police were much to worry about: a dumb cop confused in predictable ways. Roger had already dealt quickly with the puzzle of lover boy's reluctance to explain his whereabouts. The answer was obvious: he and Francie had met somewhere else. Perhaps determining where might be useful.

But not exigent. Exigent was identifying the points of vulnerability represented by Whitey. A leather jacket with no label. A small sum of money in untraceable bills. A story of alligators and a disputed painting. A name: Roger. Not much, but neither was it nothing, especially the name. Roger sensed a complex equation that could only be balanced by the death of Whitey. But the problem was deeper than that, much deeper, because the perfect solution, perfect in that it rendered him blameless, even sympathetic in some eyes, had involved tying two deaths together in an invulnerable little package, and how could he do that now? That meant — my God! — that in order to be rid of Whitey, to be rid of him and blameless of that ridding, he would have to design another, completely separate, perfect crime! Roger foresaw a horrifying string of perfectly unincriminating homicides stretching on and on into a never-ending future, horrifying in the vastness of its numerology, in the demonic intertwining of its permutations and combinations. What kind of a life was that? He had a dreadful premonition — no, not premonition, no such thing — that the truly perfect part of a perfect crime might be the inevitable, wired-in-from-the-inception, inclusion of its own punishment: the perpetrator being the true target from the start. But, no, that was sophistry of the most unscientific and moralistic kind, and in this case outrageous — he was not the one in the wrong. But what a thought, Whiteys row on row, all in need of being put down with all their fingers pointing elsewhere. Chaos. Chaos leading to madness, even in a being possessed of a thousand brains like his. Oh, *A* would be lovely.

"Please, *A,*" he said aloud, as Francie came walking up the street. In a well-ordered world, in a world that meant something, Whitey would be lying frozen solid under a dark tree, but since this was what Roger had been given for a world, he had to plan for *B*.

And there was Francie, so alive, alive at least in the sense a cow lives, unaware of the concept of slaughterhouse. So lucky, and she didn't even know it! But what was this? As she came closer, Roger saw that she was crying; not making a sound or anything like that — her mouth was closed — but tears were streaming down her face. Why?

And then facets rotated slightly in his mind, and he thought, *Of course! She blames herself, the whore.* He took a little satisfaction from that, but there was more — he could feel it coming, coming: a tremendous improvisation. Nothing mystical about improvisation, nothing more than normal, logical thought process, simply speeded-up exponentially, like subatomic particles in an accelerator. His brain had an accelerator mode, and now it offered up an improvisation based on the theme of Francie's despondency and guilt over — could he push it that far? yes! — over engineering the murder of her tennis pal, an improvisation that would end on the final triumphant note of her suicide.

There was even a coda, written for a potential reappearance by Whitey: a few simple notes that tied Whitey, the instrument, to Francie, the mastermind. What credibility would a convicted killer like Whitey have, faced with the awesome probative impact of her suicide? And how tidy. The name Roger, for example? Why wouldn't Whitey have heard the name of the mastermind's husband, poor cuckold?

Maybe there was a God, after all.

Francie came up the brick walkway. Roger stepped back from the window. What kind of suicide would she choose, what method would be character-appropriate? An important question. Were there any asps in the house? Roger laughed aloud. What a brilliant joke! Francie would have loved it.

32

Savard walked into the station just before three that afternoon. "He cracked."

"Yeah?" said Carbonneau, looking up from his chair at the duty desk.

Something was wrong; Savard knew that right away, but not what. "Cracked in the sense that he coughed up his alibi, anyway. And it checks out."

The next question should have been: *What's his alibi?* Instead, Carbonneau said, "Well, uh, maybe not surprising."

Savard didn't get that at all. Something was wrong: too crowded, for starters — Berry, Lisa, Ducharme, Morris, Feeney, more. The whole department in the room, every shift.

"This a mutiny?" Savard said.

"Oh, no, Chief," said Carbonneau, but he didn't seem to want to go on.

"Then what?" said Savard, starting to smile; a birthday or something like that he was supposed to remember but hadn't.

"Those prints," said Carbonneau, and glanced around for help that didn't come. "Prints we lifted off that bedspread."

"Duvet," said Lisa. "Goose-down duvet."

Carbonneau gave her a look; that wasn't the kind of help he'd had in mind. "The lab got a match." He bit the inside of his lip. Berry was doing it, too, biting the inside of *his* goddamn lip.

"And what?" said Savard. "They were mine? What's going on?"

Their heads all swung around to Lisa, sitting at her desk with the coffee cup full of candy canes. She looked at Savard, almost in the eye. "They were Whitey Truax's," she said.

The name did something physical to him, sent a cold wave down his shoulders and back, heated up his face at the same time. He sat down in someone's chair, heard a voice saying, "You all right, Joe?"

"Yeah." Then, still in the grip of these weird physical sensations, he realized the mistake he'd made; the realization sent a pulse of adrenaline through him, made him normal again. He got up fast. "Let's go."

"Where?" someone said, but not Lisa; the best shot in the department, she was already unlocking the gun rack, taking her .303 off the wall.

They drove to Lawton Ferry in three cars, eighty miles an hour, lights flashing, sirens wailing, the whole performance. For once, all that sound and fury suited Savard's mood, calmed him down, if anything. Beside him, Lisa buckled on her vest.

"I called down to Florida," she said. "You knew he was part of that rent-a-con thing?"

"Yeah."

"He got parole early November, went missing from the halfway house after Thanksgiving. The asshole couldn't even give me the exact date. But he's wanted down there on an assault charge that could go up to something else if the victim succumbs. That's what he said. The asshole, I'm talking about. Succumbs. A social worker."

"They never sent us anything?"

"Nope."

He'd always known Whitey would be free someday, had even wondered at one time what he'd do if he saw him on the street. But as the years went by, he'd thought less and less about Whitey, and after hearing of the transfer to Florida, almost nothing. Hadn't forgotten him, more a case of reclassifying him as one of those bad accidents that can happen to people. Now, with Anne Franklin at the medical examiner's, it was all fresh again, and personal.

They pulled up at 97 Carp Road, jumped out, took aim, summoned Whitey on the bullhorn. Nothing, of course. Savard walked up to the duct-taped front window and did what he'd been about to do the night before: looked through.

"Goddamn it," he said. No one's stupidity bothered him like his own. He strode to the front door and broke it down. They went into the lousy little place and stood around the body of Mrs. Truax. The cat came in the open doorway and rubbed itself against Lisa's leg.

Whitey drank the last can of Pepsi, tossed it out the window. Late afternoon, deep in the woods on an old lumber road, maybe into Maine, running the engine from time to time to keep warm. The cold had never bothered him before, but it did now. Last can of Pepsi, and the gas — down to what? A quarter of a tank, although he could see space between the quarter line and the needle, a hair below. But call it a quarter. And on the radio, zip. Nothing but static — proving how deep in the woods he was.

What else? He felt like shit, hurt all over, chest and face especially. And that face in the mirror: nasty. Hungry, too, and nothing to eat. He counted his money: $542. Not bad — had he ever had more in his pocket? — but he couldn't figure out how to make it help him.

Whitey saw his breath, smelled it, too. When was the last time he'd had pickles? He thought of the stripper bar where he'd had lunch before . . . whatever had gone down went down. Those silicone tits or whatever they were — was that the same stuff they made computer brains out of? — seemed a lot more appealing now, out here in the cold. Too fucking cold. He switched on the engine again, cranked the heat up full blast, lay down on the bench seat. From there he could gaze up at the trees, all bare and spiky, pressing down from high above. He didn't like that at all, and closed his eyes.

When Whitey woke up, it was dark and the needle on the lit-up dash was down, way down, almost on empty, dropping closer and closer as he watched. Not that empty meant empty — he knew his car. Then the warning light went on. He switched off the engine. Metal popped for a minute or two, and by then it was getting cold again, much too cold already. A man, even a man like him, could freeze solid in the woods on this sort of night. Without gas in the tank, he would die. He turned on the light, counted his money again. Five forty-two: piss. Seventeen years and that was what he had to show for it. Made him mad.

And millions, or at least a million, had been in reach. He remembered how it felt to be a giant, capable of ripping trees out of the ground. He didn't feel like that now. *Master of puppets I'm pulling your strings.* Those words meant something, contained some message for his ears alone, but he didn't know what. And then there was the girl in the miniskirt, sucking on grapes. Sounded good. Worth a million or more, meaning it was painted by a famous artist, such as Picasso, or others, who didn't come to mind at that moment. Had Roger ever mentioned the name of the artist? No. Just one more of his fuckups. Whitey went over the fuckups — no Brinks truck, no painting, no mention of a woman who would try to kill him. No mention either that Roger would park on the wrong side of the river, would be lurking around the cottage with an ax. What had Roger been planning to do with that ax? Whitey knew the answer to that, had seen it on Roger's face under the porch light, had smashed in the window of Roger's car because of it, but still it made no sense. Did Roger blame him in some way for the fuck-ups? Whitey wasn't able to think his way through that one. Could have been killed, twice, and didn't even know why. Someone owed him an explanation. And what about benefits, like his medical expenses, and danger pay? He realized that everything had changed the moment Roger stepped on his toe. Why hadn't he done something then and there? He dwelled for a while on the memory of what had happened to an inmate down in Florida who'd just brushed against him in the chow line, spilling Whitey's pudding. This was a democracy. No special treatment for anyone. So what did Roger deserve now?

But he was cold, hungry, weak, deep in the woods: all on the bad side. Was there anything on the good side, anything going for him? Only the fact that he knew where Roger lived. And the night. Night was his friend. Whitey fired up his truck.

He nosed his way back out of the deep woods, out of the darkness, silence, long shadows, the chains taking him safely to the first plowed country road. A plowed road, but no sign of life, nothing but whiteness outside and the red of the warning light in the cab. By the time he saw the glow of the first crummy village, the needle had sunk far below the empty mark, almost the width of his baby finger. The engine stuttered once, twice, and died — just as he rolled up to a one-pump station at the crossroads. He got the feeling it was meant to be.

A kid appeared.

"Fill it," Whitey said.

The kid didn't move for a moment, staring at Whitey's face in the glare of the pump lights.

"Hockey game," Whitey said.

The kid nodded. "Sell Band-Aids inside."

Whitey went in, bought Band-Aids, sandwiches, candy bars, a shake, said, "Hockey game," to the woman at the cash before she could even ask; he was coming back.

"You guys," she said.

He was in Maine, all right, could tell by the way they talked. He got back in the pickup, stuck the Band-Aids over his stitches, tried a chicken sandwich. That hurt too much to eat, so he just downed the shake — had to keep his strength up for what lay ahead — and headed south.

Night is my friend. Sounded like a line from a song, a good one, a Metallica song. Whitey tried to think of what could come next. *End* rhymed with *friend,* but what went in between? He couldn't get from *friend* to *end,* soon gave up, tried the radio instead. Now a few stations came in, but unsteady and playing shit. He switched it off.

Whitey stopped in the last town before the turnpike, filled up again, bought two quarts of chocolate milk, drank them in the 7-Eleven parking lot, felt better right away. He worked his way through a candy bar, taking little bites, chewing carefully, then started on the chicken sandwich: yes, getting stronger — he was something else. A bus pulled in, BOSTON in the destination box, and a woman stepped down, followed by the driver. The driver went into the store; the woman got into a waiting pickup, almost as old as Whitey's, put her arms around the man behind the wheel, and gave him a big kiss. Then she saw Whitey watching and sat back in her seat; they drove away.

Whitey hit the radio button again. Plenty of stations now. He turned the dial, heard bits of this and that: oldies, folk, jazz, commercials, "—nald 'Whitey' Truax," "down to minus twent—"

His name? Had he heard his name on the radio? He twisted his way back up the dial, failed to find the station, or if he did, it was playing music now. His name on the radio? He thought ahead to the turnpike with its tollbooths, its speed traps; and his truck, all white with that RE-DEEMER shit on the side.

And got out fast. He walked across the parking lot to the bus, waited outside the closed door. After a minute or two, the driver came out of the 7-Eleven, scratching at instant tickets. "One," Whitey said to him, getting out his money.

"All the way?"

"Huh?"

The driver gave him a look, took in the Band-Aids and his fucking hair. "Boston," he said. "End of the line."

"Yeah," said Whitey.

Whitey sat at the back, the only passenger at first, one of only a few by the end. It was warm on the bus, and with the winter night gliding by outside and what he'd been through, Whitey should have fallen asleep right away. But he couldn't sleep, not with the flashing blue lights he saw from time to time, not with his name out there on the radio, not with things so uneven between him and Roger. He was back on a bus, didn't even have his truck — would never have it again. Would never have it again: he stopped thinking about the future right there, at least of any future beyond evening things up with Roger. What did he have? The night, and knowing where Roger lived. What did he need? A hat for one thing, to hide the hair he saw glowing back at him from his window at the back of the bus.

He bought one at the pushcart stand in South Station, red wool with *Holy Cross* written on the front. In the bathroom, he pulled it low over his ears and forehead, turned up the collar of his leather jacket, hunched down inside. He checked himself in the mirror: could have been anybody. Anybody nasty. Whitey walked out into the city.

And lost the night right away. The sky seemed to brighten almost at once, as though everything was speeding up, black rushing to turn blue, a cloudless icy blue with a cold wind whipping through the downtown streets and pain on the faces of all the well-dressed people walking fast to wherever. No one looked at anybody. Whitey walked fast, too, tall in his cowboy boots, trim in his leather jacket, anonymous in his wool hat. Daytime, but safe for now.

He was hungry, craved doughnuts, soft and sweet, hot chocolate, coffee with lots of sugar, but passed by every restaurant; couldn't go in, not with his name out there on the radio. He came to the statue of George Washington; an icicle hung from the end of his saber. A saber would make a decent weapon, much better than what he had, which was nothing.

Whitey went through the Public Garden, following the path around the frozen pond. He crossed a street, climbed the hill past all the big brick houses with their fancy grillwork, doors, knockers, turned left on another street, climbed higher. And there he was, standing outside Roger's door, a tall and massive door, black with gold numbers and fixtures. He noticed that Christmas wreaths hung from the doors of the neighboring houses but not from Roger's. That didn't help him with the next step. What was it? Whitey didn't know.

The mailman was coming up the street, red envelopes in his hand. No way he could just stay there, waiting outside the door. Whitey kept going, rounded the next corner, came to an alley. An alley, he realized, that backed against Roger's house, where Roger might keep his car, for example. Whitey walked down the alley.

He didn't see Roger's car in the alley, no cars at all, just garage doors lining both sides. No numbers on them either: how was he supposed to know which garage was Roger's? He thought for a while, wondered about going back around to the street, counting the houses on the block, or maybe trying to identify them by their rooftops, then coming back and —

A garage door slid up, three or four garages down the alley from where he stood, on the right. A car backed out. The rear wheels hadn't even appeared before Whitey recognized Roger's four-by-four, the window replaced already. All neat and tidy. Whitey ducked behind a trash barrel.

Over the top of the barrel, he watched the car emerge, caught the profile of a woman in the passenger seat, and Roger beyond her at the wheel, checking his mirrors. The front wheels angled out, the car backed toward him a few feet, then straightened and drove forward, off down the alley.

Safe.

But the woman! Had he ever seen a woman like that? Yes, as a matter of fact, but he couldn't think who at the moment. Could she possibly be Roger's? What a thought. Then it hit him: she was a grown-up version of Sue Savard, but oh so much better. A perfect Sue Savard, the way Sue Savard would have looked with an actress playing her. Whitey was so knocked out, so distracted by these unusual thoughts, that he almost didn't notice the garage door sliding back down, almost didn't realize that Roger had triggered some sort of remote control from his car, almost didn't grasp the significance of it all. He charged out from behind the trash can, flew toward that closing door, skidded the last few yards across icy bricks, jammed the toe of his cowboy boot — fucking toe stepped on by Roger — under it just in time. Yes: he was in; and got that old, old feeling.

33

"Not a cloud in the sky," said Roger, driving west on Storrow, hands at the proper ten-minutes-to-two position on the wheel. "My suit satisfactory?"

Had he ever asked her opinion of what he wore? Not that Francie remembered. She glanced at the suit: black wool, perhaps blended with cashmere, probably from Brooks Brothers. "It's fine," she said, recalling that they'd discussed this particular suit once before, her mind about to zero in on the occasion when he did it for her.

"Doesn't make me resemble a luncheon companion of the godfather?"

"What are you getting at?"

"Why, nothing. Quite a funny joke you made about this suit, that's all. Perhaps I'm just fully appreciating it now." He smiled at her. "You always had that sense of humor, Francie, come what may."

His teeth shone, his shave was close, skin smooth, color high. He might have just returned from a spa weekend. She decided to leave him.

Decided at that moment, regardless of Roger's situation, of whether the Lauderdale job came through, or whether the timing suited Ned. She would start searching for an apartment to-morrow — perhaps moving into a hotel for now. Why spend another night in the house? He could have the house, keep whatever he wanted; there'd be no trouble from her.

A decision that had nothing to do with Ned. But what about him? She had planned to end their relationship the night Anne died. Would she have been able to do it? Had it ended anyway? If so, if Anne's death should have ended it, her own will having failed, what was the reason? Was there a reason, precise and defin-able, more than lace-curtain niceties? Yes. She felt that reason in her throat, a hard lump of guilt that wouldn't go away. To put it as baldly as she could, to lacerate herself with it, she had been fucking Ned and it had killed his wife. But even punishment like that didn't make the guilt go away. And worse, that new apartment of hers — she could already picture Ned knocking on the door. What was wrong with her?

"Something troubling you, Francie?" They'd stopped at a traffic light and Roger's eyes were on her. "You seem preoccupied."

"We're on our way to a funeral, Roger."

"Yes," he said, as the light turned green, "it's emotional, I know."

They parked outside the church, five or six spaces behind a hearse and a black limo. The wind blew out of the west, driving snow off the ground, spinning it in various shapes. "I thought you had a warmer coat," Roger said, taking Francie's arm as they walked down the sidewalk, the wind in their faces.

"I'm not cold," she said, and was starting to pull her arm away when a car door opened in front of them and Savard got out. He hadn't shaved closely, hadn't shaved at all, and his color was bad.

"A quick word with you, Mrs. Cullingwood?" he said. "If you'll step into the car for a moment."

Francie saw Nora climbing the steps of the church. "About what?" she said.

"The investigation."

"Will you be needing me, too?" said Roger.

Savard shook his head. "This is only for those with some connection to the cottage."

"Of course," Roger said. "I'll save you a place, Francie."

Francie sat in the back of Savard's car, not the old Bronco this time but a police cruiser; a worn heel from someone's shoe lay upside down on the floor mat, rusted cobbler's nails showing. Savard got in beside her, opened a manila envelope, took out some photographs. "Have you ever seen this man?"

She examined a police photograph, full face and profile, with numbers at the bottom. "No," Francie said.

"Take your time."

She did, and gave him the same answer.

"Have you ever heard the name Whitey

Truax? Or Donald Truax?"

"No."

"Anne never mentioned that name?"

"No. Is that him?"

"Yes."

"What's his connection to Anne?"

"Probably none," Savard said. "I'm almost certain they met for the first time late Monday afternoon."

"I don't understand."

"He broke into your friend's cottage. Your other friend was there. He killed her. He's done it before — is on parole at this moment, in fact."

"For killing someone?"

"Yes."

"A woman?"

"Yes."

"Did she have some connection to Anne?"

"No." Savard was staring at the photograph. There was a silence, a strange one; she had the crazy notion that he was about to start crying. He did not, of course, but looked up at her with dry eyes and said, "There's no connection at all."

"How do you know it was him this time?"

"Normally I ask the questions." Their eyes met. Did he expect her to apologize for asking questions? She remained silent. "But yours are good," he said at last. "The answer is he left his prints all over the place. He also killed his mother a little while later, down in Lawton Ferry."

"Why? I don't understand any of this."

Savard put the photographs back in the envelope. "I'll fax you the testimony of the psychiatrist from his trial, if you're interested. Thanks for your time, Mrs. Cullingwood."

Francie reached for the door handle, understanding one little part. "This means that all those questions you asked me before . . ."

"What questions?"

"The ones that seemed to be leading to . . ."

"The husband?"

"Yes."

"Are irrelevant now," Savard said. "They were before we had the prints, actually." Pause. "It turned out that Mr. Demarco — or is it doctor —"

"I'm not sure which he prefers."

Another pause. "— had an explanation for his whereabouts."

"I'm not surprised," Francie said, a loyal remark, almost wifely.

"Why is that?"

"He has a private practice, as well as the radio show."

"So?"

"It must raise issues of patient confidentiality."

"Not this alibi," Savard said.

"Not this alibi?" Francie said. "What do you mean?"

Someone rapped at the window of the car. A man in a clerical collar stood outside. Francie opened the door so he could talk to Savard, but it wasn't Savard he wanted.

"Francie Cullingwood?"

"Yes?"

"I wonder if you could help us this morning."

"How?"

"The deceased had a longtime tennis partner from Cleveland." He frowned at a sheet of paper. "I'm not sure which one of these it is. In any case, it was thought that representatives of various aspects of her life might speak briefly at the ceremony. Tennis being one, you see. The problem is that the woman, the tennis partner, is snowed-in in Cleveland. It's been suggested that you might be able to find a few words."

"Ask Nora."

"Ms. Levin? She was the one who gave me your name."

Impossible, out of the question, never. Francie, searching for some polite way to tell the reverend, felt Savard's eyes on her back, on the back of her head, specifically. Impossible, out of the question, never — but how could she say no?

"I'll do it," Francie said, and got out of the car. Savard got out, too, opened the driver's-side door, gave her a little nod over the roof.

Francie sat beside Roger in a pew five or six rows from the front. Roger leaned into her ear. "What was your little colloquium about?"

"I'll tell you later."

Ned, Em, Ned's mother, and a gray-haired

man sat in the first row; all Francie could see were the backs of their heads and Ned's arm around Em's shoulder: the family. *Do you have any sisters, Francie? Neither do I. I always wanted one.* She saw Nora, across the aisle; a few tennis players she knew; forty or fifty other people she didn't know; the reverend, whom she stopped listening to as soon as she realized he'd never met Anne; and the coffin, a fine-grained blond wood coffin, not ornate. After a minute or two, she was looking at nothing, and withdrew into plans for her little speech.

Right away she thought of Swift's *Marriage Service from His Chamber Window: Let none but Him who rules the thunder.* She remembered exactly how Anne had looked reciting it at Huîtres, her face flushed from wine, tennis, emotion. *Wonderful wine, Roger. I'll know something to order from now on.* From Swift it was a quick jump to *Gulliver's Travels,* from there to the Brobdingnagians, and there she was, up against two-stories-tall Anne, watching through the windows.

Are you mad at me?

Why would I be mad at you?

The way I played. Will you ever forgive me?

And: *You're like a lion — strong, proud, loyal.* Francie sat in the pew, hearing nothing, but no longer seeing nothing; she was staring at the coffin, couldn't take her eyes off it. She almost didn't feel Roger poking her arm, then jerked her head up and saw the reverend beckoning her

406

from behind the lectern.

The next thing Francie knew she was the one standing behind it, overlooking the coffin, the eyes of the mourners all on her. *I have no right to be here, less right than anyone.* That was the truth, the honest beginning, but whom would it serve? Watching eyes and waiting faces. No impatience. They, all of them, had time in common. Faces: the gray-haired man's, same cheekbones, same chin, Anne's father; Em's, the face of the girl on the skateboard — and Francie suddenly understood what made *oh garden, my garden* work, the tension between the carefree girl and those tumescent grapes, just beginning to rot; Ned's, almost as white as the reverend's collar, except for two spots growing redder on his cheeks. And there was Savard standing at the back. She suddenly wanted to cry out: *Let none but Him who rules the thunder.* But did not, had nothing prepared; remembered Savard's little nod, started talking.

"I played the best tennis of my life with Anne. It's just a game, I know. But that's what Anne was like. She brought out the best in everyone. There was something about her, I don't know what it was, not to put in words. But I'm going to be thinking about it for a long time. About her. Even in death she'll still have that power, you see. To bring out the best, at least in me, I hope to God."

And what voice was this? Hers, of course, but strange in her ear — unmodulated, unmediated, undirected. Her inner voice. Had she ever heard it aloud before? Yes, once before: out on the ice with Ned, when she'd told him, "Maybe we'd better call this off."

Was there more to say? Just one thing, and Francie said it: "I'm going to miss her."

Then she was sitting beside Roger again, not knowing quite how she got there, left with three memories: Em crying; Nora squeezing her hand from her seat by the aisle; another little nod from Savard at the back, perhaps nodding to himself, not meant for her at all.

"Well done," said Roger.

At the graveyard: fewer people, a hole in the frozen ground, more talk. All familiar: she was in the art business, knew something of funerals. Coffin lowered, symbolic shovelful of dirt thrown in, ancient wordless method for getting the message across, and it did, sounding a wintry rattle on the coffin lid that made Francie flinch. She didn't believe in an afterlife, or God, although she'd just hoped to him in her little speech. And once before, made a deal with him, this time under the ice — a deal on which she'd reneged. Francie felt the cold then, through and through. The wind caught someone's hat, blew it between two gravestones and out of sight.

Ned, Em, and the two grandparents were standing at the gate as Francie and Roger went out. "Thank you both for coming," Ned said.

"So sorry," Roger said.

Anne's father stepped forward, took Francie's hand. "That was so beautiful, what you said. And true — everything about her, going back to when she was a little girl, came into focus for me when you spoke." His eyes filled with tears, but he blinked them away; Francie sensed some inner strength in him that hadn't been passed on. "Will you be coming to the house?"

"Grandpa and I are going to decorate the tree," Em said; she held tight to his hand. "It looks so bare." Or maybe it had been passed on after all, just skipping a generation.

"I . . ." Francie looked at Ned, saw that notch in his forehead above the right eye.

"Yes," he said. "Please do. Some people are stopping in." He turned to his mother. "You called the caterer, didn't you, Mom?"

She nodded. "But don't expect anything elaborate."

"Be that as it may," Roger said, "Francie and I wouldn't dream of intruding at a time like this."

"It wouldn't be an intrusion, would it, Ned?" said Anne's father.

"You could help with the tree," Em said.

Roger smiled down at her. "Perhaps some other —"

"I'd be honored," Francie said. "Why don't you take the car home, Roger? I'll be back later."

Their eyes met; his were cloudy, as though film were whizzing by at high speed, just beneath the surface. "As you wish," he said. "But don't be too too late."

The caterers had laid out a buffet in Ned's dining room: salads, cold cuts, a bar. There were people Francie didn't know, from the radio show, the B.U. psychology department, Cleveland. She poured herself a glass of red wine because she couldn't think of a convincing reason not to, and she needed it, and went into the living room.

The corduroy chair was gone, and in its place stood the tree, Anne's father looping a string of lights around it, Em cross-legged on the floor with a cardboard box of ornaments wrapped in tissue. Francie sat beside her.

"Mom," Em began, choked on the word, went on, "made most of these herself."

Francie wanted to comfort her in some way, to stroke her head, but it wasn't her place. She unwrapped an ornament. "She was a glassblower, too?"

"Oh, yes," said Anne's father. "She learned at summer camp. They said she had a knack for it."

Francie examined the decorations: delicate translucent balls, red, green, gold, and a few of all three colors at once, that changed from one to another as she turned them in her hand; tiny bells with tiny glass clappers that rang with tiny crystal peals; stained-glass saints with alien medieval faces but relaxed, modern poses; oddities, the opposites of gargoyles, she supposed — a dog with a pagoda-roof head, a bicycle with Marlon Brando faces for wheels, a smile made of

410

two glass snakes, one red, one green, and white Chiclets; and a Tower of Pisa, with a robed figure on top. Galileo, but studying him closely, Francie saw that he held not metal balls but a bottle of champagne and a stemmed glass, perfectly formed but no more than a quarter of an inch tall. "These are great," she said.

"Do you think so?" Em said, watching her carefully; so was Anne's father, from a footstool on the other side of the tree.

"Oh, yes." Better than her paintings, much, much better; of another order entirely. "Are there more?"

"Just the angel," Em said. "It lights up from inside."

But it wasn't in the box.

"Maybe it's still in the closet," Em said. "I couldn't reach the top shelf."

"I'll get it," Francie said, rising. "What closet?"

"Upstairs," said Em, "on the left." She gazed down at a glass elephant in her hand, playing its saxophone trunk.

Francie climbed the stairs, opened the first door on her left. Something wrapped in red tissue lay on the top shelf. She took it down, removed the tissue, saw a shining black angel with spun-glass wings and a face that reminded her of Miles Davis. Anne, in death, kept growing in her mind.

Turning to go downstairs, Francie saw the closed door of the master bedroom. Inside hung the portrait of Ned, unless he'd taken it down. She went closer. Why hadn't Ned shown his portrait to Savard? Perhaps he simply hadn't wanted to bother taking it off the wall, carrying it down. Francie knocked on the door. No response. She opened it slightly, looked in. The room was unoccupied and the portrait hung in its place. Francie went in.

Standing at the foot of the bed, she studied the painting, saw what she had seen before — the resemblance, unaccountable in strictly photographic terms, the powerful, dominating pose, the surprising absence of sensuality — but nothing more, nothing that would explain any reluctance to have it examined. Then it struck her that something might be written on the back, some title or dedication. She laid the glass angel on the covers, walked around the bed, leaned over, got her hands on the frame — and heard a moan.

Ned's moan. Francie whirled around, eyes on the closed bathroom door, heard him again. He was there, a few steps away, in quiet agony. Francie took those steps, not to say anything, not to put any pressure on him, just to hold him, to let him know she was there. She knocked quietly on the door.

Silence. Then he said, "Em? Is that you? I'll be down in a minute."

Francie heard agony in his tone, yes, but something else as well, something urgent and furtive that made her try the door. Locked. So she stooped, stooped to a lower level, to look through the keyhole in the old period door in Anne's old period house. Ned was there, but not alone, and she'd misinterpreted the sound she'd heard. Francie's eyes, expert eyes, trained for grasping detail and composition, took it all in, understood for her what her reeling mind could not: the half-clothed embrace, the glossy-haired woman, Chinese-American, leaning back on the sink, Ned curved over her, their faces turned toward the door in listening attitudes. Then Ned's gaze fell toward the keyhole, fastened on it, and slowly went through changes that ended in horror.

"Francie?" Ned said. "Francie?" Through the keyhole, she saw him push himself away from the woman. "Oh my God, Francie, no."

What happened next? Francie didn't know, only knew she was somehow bolting down the stairs, free-falling, not even in contact with them, the glass angel in her hand. There was Em, still on the floor, going through the ornaments.

"Here you are, sweetheart," Francie said, and gave her the angel. Then came a pause, in which neither of them seemed to breathe, and Francie took the liberty of touching Em's head; her hand did so, really, and she didn't stop it.

Then she was in the hall, getting her coat, walking out of the house, leaving. Walking fast, fast, fast. She could tell how cold it must have been from the hard bright snow on the ground and the icy sky and the whining wind, but she didn't feel it at all. She was burning up. Walking, walking, walking: Francie walked and walked, but couldn't escape the burning, and finally there was nowhere to go but home.

34

What a house Roger had! Whitey explored it from top to bottom. He'd been inside the cottages of the rich, the second homes, but never seen anything like this. The furniture, the rugs, the stuff! Even this sculpture or whatever it was on the bookcase in the living room, made of some material he'd never seen, maybe a rare stone or mineral, so smooth. What was it worth? Whitey picked up the sculpture — heavy, but not as heavy as it looked, maybe not so valuable after all — turned it in his hands: a strange, curved thing that reminded him of tits from one angle, ass from another. At that moment a phone rang, nearby and loud, startling him. He dropped the goddamn thing; it fell on the gleaming hardwood floor, just missing the edge of the thick carpet, and smashed in pieces. The noise was shattering; in the midst of it, he heard a voice, spun around, saw no one.

"Francie? Nora. I was going to swing by and ride out with you. Guess you've already left. See you there. God, I hate funerals, this one especially." Beep.

Beep. Just an answering machine. Whitey told himself to stay cool. He said it out loud. "Stay cool." Cool like ice, like snow. He glanced down at the remains of the sculpture. The cool thing, the smart thing, would be to leave no trace, right? In case some illegal act was going to happen, say. He went into the kitchen — what a kitchen! like there was a restaurant on the other side of the door — found broom and dustpan, swept up the mess, dumped it into a trash bin under the sink. Cool.

Beep. He jumped. The fucking thing had beeped again. Whitey returned to the living room, stared at the red light blinking on the phone. He wasn't sure which button turned it off; maybe better, cooler, to forget about it, leave no trace. But what about the jumpiness? He went to the cabinet beside the tall plant in the corner, a waist-high cabinet with a silver tray on top bearing bottles — Scotch, vodka, gin, all fancy brands. He tried the vodka, not that he liked vodka particularly, but because they said it had no smell: leave no trace. He was getting very smart, and it went down nice like that, surprisingly nice, warm from the bottle. Beep. He took another, just a tich, as Ma used to say back in her drinking days, before this religious shit. Didn't matter — he had no plans to see her again.

What were his plans, anyway? Exactly, like?

Mulling that question, Whitey opened the cabinet, just to have something to do while he thought. There were photograph albums inside. He leafed through one, saw Roger, a much younger Roger, in tennis whites, his arm around a beautiful woman, the woman he'd seen in his car, the super–Sue Savard. She wore a little tennis skirt. What a body! What was her name?

He'd just heard it on the answering machine. Francie. He searched the albums for more pictures of Francie, preferably nude, but there was nothing like that. Roger and Francie smiling on a chairlift, Roger saying something to Francie on a sailboat, Roger reading a menu at an outdoor café, Francie staring into the camera.

Beep.

Most of the pictures were dated underneath, none more recent than ten years ago. The last album, the most recent, petered out in the middle with two last pictures: Roger, Francie, and a big woman, standing on a tennis court, the two women laughing, Roger watching them; and Francie and another woman, both in bathing suits, sitting on a floating dock. They both had nice bodies, Francie's better — bigger tits, for starters — but the bathing suits weren't as revealing as some, and Whitey was about to close the book, when he realized there was something odd about that last picture. He studied it carefully, especially the wooden house behind the trees in the background, and then he recognized it — the cottage out on the island in the middle of the river. What did this mean? It had to mean something. Whitey didn't know. He peeled the photograph off the page and stuck it in his pocket.

Beep.

Whitey helped himself to another tich of vodka, more than a tich. It had to mean something. He went into the kitchen and opened the fridge, looking for chocolate milk. There was none, but he found a jar of peanut butter, scooped some out with his fingers, ate it. He wandered to the desk in the little alcove, glanced at the mail on top, opened a drawer, saw a twenty-dollar bill, pocketed that, too. Under it lay a newsletter from some tennis club. CULLINGWOOD-FRANKLIN TO VIE FOR DOUBLES CROWN, he read, a headline followed by a brief article summarizing tennis matches, and two photographs, one of Francie, the other of . . . could it be? Yes. How could he forget that face, face of the woman who'd tried to kill him? Meaning? Meaning that there were — what was the word? Connections. Had to mean something. What? Whitey couldn't take the next step, but the buzzing had already started, deep inside his head.

Beep.

Tich.

He didn't feel his strongest, because of what she'd done to him, and that might be bad. He ate more peanut butter from the jar to give him strength. What next? What next? There was still the basement. He found the stairs and went down.

Nice and dark, the only light coming from narrow windows at the top of the wall, at street level. He could see well enough, was in a laundry room: washer, dryer, clothes hanging on a line. Bra and panties, for instance, which he felt as he went by. He opened a door, entered a large room, darker than the first; here the street-level windows were covered with black paper, and the only light came from a glowing computer screen. Computer, printer, desk, file cabinets: an office, Roger's home office, where he worked late into the night, making all his money. Maybe he took little naps on that couch with the sleeping bag on top, or maybe that woman of his, Francie, sometimes came down for a quick one.

Beep. Very faint now, but he heard it; his senses were keen. That would explain in some way why darkness was his friend, but in what way, exactly, he didn't know.

Whitey sat at the desk, looked at the computer screen. On one side was a crossword puzzle. He checked two or three clues, had no idea. On the other side of the screen he saw a heading — Puzzletalk — and under it lines of print scrolled slowly by, a conversation of some sort. Was this one of those chat rooms, where, according to Rey, at least, you could pick up girls or download porn? He scanned it quickly, saw it had nothing to do with sex, but — what was this? *Rimsky?* His eyes flashed up to the top, catching a line as it disappeared from view.

criminals?

>BOOBOO: Oh, please, not capital punishment again!!!

>FLYBOY: Yeah, we know how you like to fry 'em up on a daily basis down there in Fla. but give it a REST.

>RIMSKY: This is why Rome fell. The barbarian's inside your walls and you don't even know it.

>BOOBOO: ???

>RIMSKY: Member that guy I was telling you about? Whitey Truax?

>BOOBOO: ???

>FLYBOY: Who gives a?

>MODERATOR: I remember.

>RIMSKY: First chance he got he jumped parole killed two more people, one of them his mother. Not a deterrent, kiddies?????

The buzzing grew louder. Whitey tried to read on, but the words had stopped scrolling; the response, if any, was off the screen, and he didn't know how to make it appear. *One of them his mother?* Impossible — he'd hardly even tapped her; picked her up, dusted her off. She'd been fine when he left. Rimsky had it wrong. And he could prove it, prove the asshole wrong, just by calling her on the phone.

Whitey picked up Roger's phone and dialed her number. It was answered on the first ring.

"Sergeant Berry," said a man.

Whitey snapped the phone back in its cradle. Beep.

Buzz, buzz. And Rimsky. What was he doing on Roger's computer? Whitey remembered Rimsky: a guard on his cell block, a shit disturber, which was what they called the ones who made a little extra effort during the cavity searches. And now here he was on Roger's computer. *Member that guy I was telling you about?* When? Telling who? Rimsky, on Roger's computer. Connections. Connections all over the place, past and present. Yes: past and present, an expression he'd heard before, and now understood a little better. One thing for sure, it was all about — yes! talk about connections — masters and puppets, and the goddamn thing was, the thing that made him want to puke up all that vodka and peanut butter — and he almost did — the goddamn thing was —

Whitey heard something over the buzzing, a mechanized, metallic rumble. The garage door. He rose, listening hard. A car door closed beyond the far wall. They were home, home from the . . . funeral. And he knew whose funeral it must have been. Connections. His mind was making them like never before. But what did it add up to? What was the complete picture? He needed time to think, but —

Footsteps: hard shoes on the cement floor of the laundry room, coming his way. He looked around wildly — no, not wildly, stay cool, stay cool — and saw another door, at the end of the row of filing cabinets. He hurried across the room, but quiet, quiet and cool, opened the door: a small room, cold and musty, with a single street-level window, not blacked-out but very dirty, and shadowy objects inside. Trunks, beach umbrellas, a woodpile. Beep. Whitey went in, closed the door silently, knelt behind the woodpile. An earthen floor: common in basements where he came from, but strange to find in a house like this. And there was something hard under his knee. He reached down, freed it, picked it up — an ax.

"Joe Savard of the Lawton police calling for Nora Levin. Missed you at Anne Franklin's funeral today, would like to talk. Please get back to me at one of the following numbers."

Roger entered HQ, glanced at the computer screen. *Times of London* puzzle up — one across, strengthening, eight letters: *roborant,* no doubt — saw some illiterate conversation taking place, switched off the machine. *Think,* he commanded, and the marvelous brain responded without hesitation.

Two problems: Francie and Whitey, once conjoined in an elegant solution, now separating fast like particles that had failed to collide. Of the two, Whitey presented by far the more unknowns, variables, intangibles, unless he was frozen solid in the woods, and that would be lucky, and he, Roger, had always had rotten luck.

So, Francie, less unknown, less variable, less intangible, first. Soon she would be home, despondent. Funeral day: the atmosphere would never be better for the ending he had improvised, but the details had to be right, had to be in character, had to be her. Would she leave a note?

No, not her style at all. No note. That made it easier. And what of the method itself? Suitable, fitting, Francie. Nothing messy, nothing violent, nothing brilliant. He heard a faraway beep. The answering machine. He ignored it: wouldn't be for him.

Where was he? Nothing messy, nothing violent, nothing brilliant — something feminine, something that would make her weeping friends agree, *Yes, that was Francie, all the way.*

The problem having been properly framed, the answer came at once: gas. Gas, of course. Gas was feminine. Gas was her.

What gas? CO.

CO. Roger pictured the molecule in his mind, a simple thing, not particularly attractive but sturdy, like a reliable peasant. CO — odorless, colorless, plentiful. And so simple, like one of those schoolboy science projects that never failed: insert subject in garage, close doors, run fossil-fuel-burning internal combustion engine, wait outside.

The details, the adjustments: his brain sketched those in without any active direction from him. Difficult to persuade or trick the subject into inserting herself into the garage for the requisite time, of course, but neither was it necessary, the only necessity being that her body be found there. Much easier to perform the operation elsewhere — her bedroom, say, while she slept — and then transfer the end result to the garage when convenient. After that, the performer of the operation had merely to open the bedroom windows for an hour or two, and then the garage doors as well, perhaps screaming a desperate plea into the alley — would a trashman come running? — those procedures to be followed by the frantic call to 911, punctuated with a cough or two. Perfect, perfect, perfect. Oh, to have a brain like this, to never know boredom.

Beep.

Gas, generated in garage, required in second-floor bedroom. How was gas transported? By pipeline, of course. At one stage of his life he'd done rather well in pipeline stocks; was it his fault that Thorvald had bungled the timing when he'd finally persuaded them to jump in with both feet? His mind stuck for a moment, stuttering on Thorvald, and he had to give it a little push, to remind it of the coming insurance settlement, sale of the house, the art — the Arp alone worth a tidy sum — and then Rome, or some other rosy future.

His mind got back to work. Pipeline. A garden hose was a pipeline, connectable to the gas outlet, in this case an automobile tailpipe, with tape, duct or electrical, both of which were available on the premises. How many feet of hose were required, from garage, upstairs to kitchen, around corner, up stairs, down hall, under bedroom door? One hundred? One hundred and twenty? Also available on the premises: several garden hoses, mutually attachable, were kept in the garage. Correction: not in the garage but closer at hand, in the storage room directly adjacent to HQ.

To begin: inspection of equipment. Roger opened the door to the storage room, went in, found three garden hoses coiled on one another in front of the woodpile. He paused for a moment, sniffed the musty air. What was that smell? Peanut butter? Impossible — no peanut butter in the storage room. He carried the hoses out and closed the door.

Roger inspected the hoses for punctures or tears, found none, screwed them together. Next? Fossil fuel supply. He went into the garage, checked the gauge on Francie's car — hers, not his; he would never make an error as fundamental as that — found it three-quarters full. Much more than enough. Next? Her bedroom windows. It was a cold night; they would be closed. Next? There was no next. That was it: a simple plan. The complicated part, the part that would ultimately be more persuasive than any forensics, was the psychology — in this case female psychology, believable in every detail. Despondency, despair, guilt, suicide: like train cars barreling down the track. No more thinking to be done. To pass the time, Roger sat at the computer and took a virtual tour of Rome, refreshing his memory.

35

Francie walked all the way home, the wind at her back most of the time, arriving just after four under a rapidly darkening sky. She was no longer burning up, was probably cold, although she didn't feel it, numb inside and out. She'd been through everything, now knew Ned's alibi and why he was reluctant to use it, knew all but the where of it; knew, too, something of how it felt to be in Anne's position, with another woman, unseen, exerting force on her life like some orbiting body composed of dark matter. A powerful force that shook, unsettled, reduced: could reduce her to the state of Anne sobbing on her stool in the locker room, fallen completely apart. But Francie hadn't earned the right to be in that state, was the other woman, not the wife — in this case not even that, but the other other woman — and so any falling apart would be ridiculous, absurd, pretentious. And shameful: a feeling with which she was filled to the brim already. So although her mind was ready to start writhing with the kinds of questions that must have tormented Anne — had he really been working on such-and-such a night? how had they met, how had it begun? what did he tell her in bed? what did they do? the same things? different things? the same things better? — she couldn't allow it. Among other reasons, she owed

Anne some dignity.

Francie went in the front door, stood in the hall. The house was dark, as always at this time of day in winter. She heard the refrigerator door close, heard the beep of the answering machine, crossed the shadowy living room to the flashing red light, pressed the button.

"Francie? Nora. I was going to swing by and ride out with you. Guess you've already left. See you there. God, I hate funerals, this one especially."

Francie reset the machine, stopped the beeping. She didn't call Nora, wasn't ready for that. What should she tell her? Everything? Why not? Was there any reason to go on keeping Ned's secrets? No. She thought of Savard — he had heard Ned's alibi, knew that secret, but hadn't told her. Ned's second secret: did its burden, too, sometimes grow intolerable, demand to be flaunted? Francie's memory readied the image seen through a keyhole. She closed her inner eye to it, or tried to, and returned to Savard. There was no reason he should have told her — he probably operated on a need-to-know basis, and in this case had decided she didn't fit the category. But then she remembered the little nod he'd given her, twice.

Francie went upstairs, through her bedroom, into the bathroom, drew a deep bath, stripped off her funeral clothes, lay in the tub. If there was no reason to keep Ned's secrets, there was no reason not to tell Nora. Oh, she didn't want to do that. How could she and Nora ever be the same? But were they the same now? Not really. It was a sham. So Nora had to be told. Tomorrow, not today: she needed breathing room.

There was a knock at the door.

"Francie? Is that you in there?"

"Who else would it be, Roger?"

"Of course, of course. Just being pleasant. There's dinner, whenever you're ready."

"I'm not hungry."

"One must eat, Francie dear."

Francie went downstairs in her robe.

"In here," Roger called from the dining room.

She entered the dining room. He'd set two places at one end of the table. Candles, the good silver, his grandmother's Sèvres. "Champagne, Roger?"

"Why not? Life does go on. Here we are, the proof." He filled two glasses, clinked them together in a toast, handed one to her. He drank, peered at her over his glass. "You look despondent, Francie."

"I'm all right."

"You'll feel much better after a little something." She sat down. "Isn't that what Winnie-the-Pooh used to say? A little something. Remember when the Latin translation came out? *Winnie-Ille-Pu*. Cute idea, wasn't it?"

"I don't remember, actually." But how she would have loved reading *Winnie-the-Pooh* to some child of her own. She took her first sip of the champagne, tasted nothing but the alcohol, downed half the glass in one swallow.

Roger raised the lid of a serving dish, revealing two plump and perfect omelettes. "An omelette sort of evening, don't you think?" he said, serving her.

Francie emptied her glass, refilled it. She began to feel, not better, simply less.

"*Bon appétit,*" said Roger, cutting a good-sized bite from his omelette. He looked up. "How do they say it in Italian?"

"The same. *Buon appetito.*"

"That's what I like about you, Francie. That flair." He chewed his omelette, patted the corners of his mouth with a napkin. "How do you like it?"

Francie tried some. "I can't believe how good you are at this."

"Pshaw," he said, waving off the compliment, an awkward gesture that overturned his glass, which knocked down hers as well. "Shit," he said, rising abruptly, sopping up champagne with his napkin. He took the glasses, both broken, to the kitchen, returned with sponges, new glasses, another bottle. "Oh, well," he said, filling the glasses from the first bottle, uncorking the second, "accidents happen, do they not?"

Francie drank, refilled her glass from what was left in the first bottle.

Roger returned to his omelette, wielding knife and fork, silver clinking on china. "How went the tree-trimming?"

"What you'd expect."

"And Ned? It is Ned, isn't it — name never anchored itself in my mind, for some reason. How is he taking it?"

Francie rose, too abruptly, and something silver clanged to the floor. "I'm sorry, Roger, I'm very tired. The dinner's very good, and it was . . . kind of you to prepare it, but I'm going to bed."

"I understand completely. Why don't you take the bottle with you?"

"Thanks. I think I will."

"Good night, then. Sleep well."

Francie went upstairs, taking the bottle and her glass, closed her door, got into bed, drank a glassful and then another. She put the glass on the bedside table and turned off the light.

Francie closed her eyes. *No tears, just sleep, go numb.* But first her mind tormented her with a parade of images: Ned in his kayak, Em on a skateboard, Anne at the net; Kira Chang. They faded when they'd had enough, and her last thoughts were of Roger: how nice he'd been, even considerate. She thought of going downstairs, inviting him up to lie with her. Would there be comfort in that, an omelette sort of thing? But no. And apartment hunting still began tomorrow.

"Mr. Savard? Nora Levin, returning your call."

"Thank you. I've got a few questions about the murder of Anne Franklin."

"I thought you had a suspect."

"We do. But I'm still puzzled about what she was doing at that cottage, and wondered if you had any ideas."

Pause. "No."

"Were you aware that she made an attempt to leave some clue about the murderer?"

"No."

"She wrote the word *painting* on the floor of the cottage. Does that mean anything to you?"

"I know she painted."

"I've checked all her paintings. I don't think that's what she meant. Is there some other painting she may have been referring to, a valuable one, perhaps?"

Silence.

"She wrote the word in her own blood, by the way," Savard added. *"Painting."*

He heard the woman inhale. "I have one thought," she said. "But I'm not even sure what I saw, let alone whether it's relevant."

Roger finished eating, left the rest of his champagne untouched, cleared the table. He scraped the leavings into the garbage disposal, loaded the dishwasher, except for the champagne flutes and the Sèvres, which he washed by hand, turned the machine on, using the energy-saver switch. He dried the glasses and the china, put them back in their cupboards, returned to the dining room and blew out the candles. Then he sat at the kitchen table and did nothing. The house was silent.

An hour later, by the clock, he rose, removed his shoes, went upstairs. He put his ear to Francie's door, listened, heard nothing. Francie had come through beautifully tonight, looking the part to perfection. *Despondent, officer, if I had to put it in a word. I tried to cheer her up, but . . .* Roger went into the guest bathroom at the end of the hall, returned with a towel, left it lying by the door. Then he started down to his basement HQ, where the pipeline project awaited.

First, like a surgeon, gloves. Then into the garage, the windowless garage, invisible. Roger stuck one end of the three linked garden hoses into the tailpipe of Francie's car. He secured the connection with duct tape, triple-wrapping the tape two or three feet along the hose, making it absolutely leakproof. He paused. Would used duct tape, found in the trash, say, constitute evidence, dangerous to him in any way? Probably not, but he made a note to ball up the remains afterward and melt them away on the stove, just to be safe. The hoses he would disconnect, recoil, put back in the storage room until spring. Anything else? No. He opened the door to Francie's car. Her key was in the ignition, where she always left it when parked in the garage, despite his every admonition. Taking hold of the key between gloved forefinger and thumb, Roger turned it, started the engine. He held the open end of the hose close to his face and felt a warm little breeze.

Then, out of the garage, up the stairs, uncoiling the hose, his mind making silent chortles as he went. First floor, through the kitchen, around into the first-floor hall, up the stairs, into the second-floor hall. He switched off the lights and walked softly to her door. About five or six feet of hose left: perfect.

Nora and Savard stood before the half-size wooden lockers in the corridor leading to the indoor courts at the tennis club.

"This one," Nora said.

"I'd need a warrant."

"And what if I did it?"

"That would be a crime."

"Arrest me," Nora said. She kicked in the locker.

Roger listened at the door again. Silence. *Are you sleeping, are you sleeping?* Of course she was. Lethe, refuge of the guilty feminine mind. Now came the tricky part, the only tricky part, really. With the end of the hose in his left hand, he took the doorknob in his right and turned it slowly, very slowly, very silently, as far as it would go. Then, holding it there, he knelt and pushed the door open an inch, very slowly, very silently. He laid the end of the hose on the rug inside the bedroom, closed the door back over it, flattening the plastic only negligibly. Then, door closed, the turning back of the knob, very slowly, very silently. Done. Still kneeling, Roger rolled the towel he'd left there — to be laundered later in the unlikely event it retained gas residue — into a long sausage and aligned it firmly in the strip under the door. Done and done! Roger knelt in front of Francie's door for five full minutes, by his watch, and heard not a sound, not a whisper of a sound, from the other side. He rose at the end of the fifth minute precisely. How did they say "the end" in Italy? Oh, Roger: perfect, perfect, perfect.

And then the light went on.

"I get it," Whitey said.

Roger spun around. Whitey! There was Whitey filling the hall, crude stitches in his face, an ax in his hands. Any other relevant details? *No.* How did he get into the house, for instance? Roger's brain turned on him: *not relevant, not relevant, not relevant. Let me think.*

"I get it now," Whitey said.

Think.

But how, with that look in Whitey's eyes?

Think.

"Get ready to have your dreams twisted," Whitey said.

Or some such gibberish. "You couldn't possibly 'get it,' Whitey."

"You must think I'm pretty dumb." Whitey took a step toward him.

"Not at all, not at all," Roger said, and what presence of mind, to keep his voice down like that. "You misunderstand me. The point, the salient point, Whitey, is that" — *Yes! Brilliant! Back in control!* — "we're both victims here."

"I'm nobody's victim," Whitey said, and took another step.

"Not victims in the sense you mean. I'm speaking metaphorically, if you will. The background is rather complex, but try to focus on the idea that everything can still work, surprisingly smoothly, even, if you — if we — keep our wits about us. The first step would be to switch that light back off."

Whitey did not. Neither did the look in his eyes disappear; in fact, it grew madder. "You set me up," he said.

"Oh, so that's it," said Roger. "Nothing could be further from the truth. But before I explain, I must ask you to keep your voice down."

Whitey did not. "There was no painting in the first place," he said.

"Certainly there was. I had it in my own hands at one stage in the proceedings." *Think. What is the goal? To get that ax, to drive it through Whitey's skull.* "What you must understand, what you've got to take on board, as it were, is that we've both been manipulated by a third party. Why don't we put down that implement, so out of place in a domestic setting like this, and go downstairs for a quiet discussion?" *Drive it through Whitey's skull, and then through Francie's, aborting the CO procedure.* An improvisation of an improvisation that could still work — his brain was already sketching in the adjustments.

Whitey's hands tightened on the handle; Roger saw the tendons pop out. "No one manipulates me," he said.

"Am I not aware of that?" *Adjust, adjust.* "And because of that attribute, so prominent in your character, this is going to be your lucky day."

"How's that?"

"Because the opportunity has arisen for taking revenge on your manipulator. Putative manipulator," Roger amended, to forestall another touchy reaction.

Whitey took another step, was now no more than six feet away. "You killed Ma," he said.

Perhaps *revenge* had been too potent a word, perhaps he'd introduced it too abruptly into the mix, too unadorned. But a daring counter presented itself; no time for even his brain to think it through to the end, but the feeling surrounding it was the feeling that always accompanied his best ideas. "I did it for you, Whitey."

Whitey, who appeared to be on the verge of taking another step, paused. "For me?"

Got him! "We're partners, Whitey. I'm on your side."

"What do you mean you did it for me?"

"I'm familiar with the psychiatrist's testimony, Whitey. I know she's responsible for the . . . perturbations in your past."

"Perturbations? Are you accusing me of fucking my own mother?"

"No, no, no. Perturbations, Whitey." How to explain it? *Think, think.* Whitey took another step. "Ups and downs," Roger said, perhaps too explosively, perhaps too loud. "Ups and downs."

Whitey halted. "You killed her because of that?"

"If I've gone too far, forgive me, Whitey. It was with the best intentions. And what kind of a life did she have, anyway? The crux of the matter is that we're partners. Share and share alike. If you've spent any time in this house, you know a certain amount of wealth is represented. Why, the Arp alone is worth its weight in gold."

"What's an arp?"

"What a character you are," Roger said. "He was a famous sculptor, and I've got a rare piece of his, down on the bookcase in the living room. For your next birthday, shall we say? Why don't we go down and take a peek at it?"

"Fuck that," Whitey said. And that look in his eye, the one Roger didn't like, which had faded a bit, intensified. Unaccountable.

"I hope I haven't offended you, Whitey. As your partner, the last thing I'd want to do is violate your amour propre in any way."

Whitey made a little flicking gesture with the blade of the ax, as though warding off insects, came closer, close enough for Roger to see the tiny drops of pus seeping through his stitches. "Killed her and set me up for that, too."

"No, no, no. Didn't you hear what I just said?" *Heard, but not understood. Yes, dumb, a dumb animal, almost preverbal. How to put it in his vernacular, to accord him the respect his like always craved? What is the right vulgarism? Something bodily, no doubt. How about:* "I wouldn't step on

437

your toes, Whitey. Not for anything."

The expression in Whitey's eyes worsened dramatically, became animal, in fact, and Roger's mind flashed a quick memory of the eyes of a wolverine he'd cornered in the boathouse at the Adirondack camp as a boy. "But you did step on my toe, you son of a bitch," Whitey said, and raised the ax.

Not getting through, not getting through. Roger's brain was frantically pursuing various strategies, spinning with permutations and combinations, scattering scraps and tailings of this or that scenario in the mental air — *think, moron, think* — when the door opened at his back.

Francie peered out, blinking in the light. "What's all the noise, Roger?" she said. "And I smell something odd."

"Impossible," Roger said. "It's completely odorless."

Francie's eyes adjusted to the light. She saw the second man, recognized him at once from the police photograph — Whitey something. His eyes, awful eyes, locked on hers. She looked to Roger. "What's going on?"

"Improvise," Roger said, more like a mumble, as if to himself.

"What are you talking about?"

"The chaos butterfly," Roger replied.

"I don't understand you."

Roger snapped his fingers. "But I understand you," he said, "only too well." He pointed at her, his eyes every bit as awful as Whitey's but in a different way. "There's your manipulator, Whitey, at long last. This is your big chance. The only chance you'll ever have. I can't dumb it down any more than that. Don't blow it."

Odorless? Manipulator? Butterflies? What was he saying? Francie opened her mouth to speak, but Whitey spoke first.

"I won't blow it," he said. "But she'll keep."

"No," Roger said, "that's specious reasoning, if we can even dignify it with the term. You can't possibly —"

"Shut the fuck up," Whitey said, and swung the ax like a baseball bat — Roger's eyes incredulous — swung it so hard Francie heard it whistle in the air, right through Roger's neck, the blade sinking deep into the wall. Then came a horror of spouting blood and screams, hers and Whitey's, and in that time of horror and nothing else, with the ax stuck in the wall, Francie had her chance, too, her only chance, to get away, but she froze.

The screaming stopped. Whitey jerked the ax out of the wall. He stared at her. "You're just like her," he said, "but way better."

Francie closed the robe at her throat. Was he talking about Anne? Anne's killer, talking to her like this? She shook, but felt nothing but fury. It washed away everything else — horror, fear, grief, confusion.

"Never," she said.

"What do you mean, never? I haven't even

said anything yet." He came toward her, still holding the ax, but in one hand now and low, the blade dripping.

"Never," Francie said, and heard for the second time that day the sound of her inner voice, her true voice.

"You got that wrong," Whitey said, still coming. "Like right now is when, while we got this buzz buzz happening. It's going to be incredible. Master's away and puppet plays. Fuckin' poetry."

His free hand flashed out, very quick, got hold of Francie's robe. "Don't you touch me," she said, and kicked him in the groin with every bit of strength she had. He doubled up, blocking the hall. She kicked him again, not as accurately, and got both hands on the ax, yanked it, but not free. He held on. They wrestled for it. And fell, rolling down the bloody hall, coming to the top of the stairs with him on top, the ax handle caught between them. Whitey wedged his forearm into her throat.

So heavy. So strong.

"Going to be even better now," Whitey said. "I like all the smells." He arched his back, pulled at the ax handle, forced it slowly up between their bodies, the blade slicing through Francie's robe. He gazed down at her, his face a foot away. "I'm going to come in holes you don't even have yet."

Every hair on her body stood on end. *Never.* Francie got a hand free, tore at his face, tore and tore and tore, ripping out the stitches, redoing all Anne had done, and more. Whitey screamed, jerked aside. Francie scrambled out from under him, grabbed the ax, rose, and was starting to swing it when he charged up from under her, inside the arc, caught her in the stomach with his shoulder, and she went down with him on top again, and again they were rolling, but this time down the stairs, Francie, Whitey, the ax, rolling, tangling together in — what was it? A garden hose. Francie got her hand on the hose, whipped a length of it around Whitey's neck as they fell, tried to jam it between the banisters, tried to break his neck, but he punched her, full in the face and very hard, and she let go.

Then they were on the floor in the hall, and Whitey was up first, both lips split wide, baring all his teeth. Bleeding all over, but up first, and with the ax, while she was still down — and everything had gone snowy, like bad reception.

"Nice try," Whitey said, looming over her. He raised the ax.

The hose: wrapped around his ankles. Francie rolled aside, but so slowly, as the ax came down, and pulled, but so weakly, on the hose. Whitey lost his balance, almost fell, but didn't. Francie heard the thunk of the blade sinking deep, felt no new pain. Whitey went still.

"You stupid bitch," he said.

Francie, on the floor, saw his leg, inches away, and the ax, buried deep in his thigh, and high up.

"Thought you could trip me?" he said. "With my sense of balance?"

He pulled the ax out, stood over her, started his backswing — but blood came gushing from his leg. Francie could hear the flow. He gazed down at what was happening, went white. He toppled over soon after. Francie lay on the floor as the warm pool grew around her.

Splintering sounds at the front door. Francie sat up. The door cracked open. Savard burst in, and others. They said, "Oh, God," and things like that.

He knelt beside her.

"Sorry I'm so goddamn slow," he said. "You all right?"

"No."

He took a long look at Whitey.

"Why are you looking like that?"

"I don't mean to be looking like anything." He turned to her, the savage expression still on his face. "I owe you," he said.

Francie started crying.

"Don't cry."

But she couldn't stop. She cried and cried. "Is it all right, Anne? Is it all right?"

He picked her up and carried her outside. Flashing lights everywhere. "Oh, Anne." But she said the name softly now, and soon got hold of herself.

"I can walk."

"You're sure?" He watched her carefully, his

face softened now, close to hers.

"Yes."

He put her gently down. Nora ran up from a squad car, took Francie in her arms. "It wasn't your fault."

"Whose was it?"

"Not yours, sugar, not yours."

Would she ever be able to talk herself into that?

Someone in the house said, "Open the windows."

36

Francie didn't hear from Savard until the spring, a few days after Nora's wedding; she thought she knew why he'd waited. "Read about it in the *Globe*," he said. "Were you there?"

"Of course."

"Nice time?"

"Very."

"I'm not married, myself."

There was a silence.

"Ice is breaking up," Savard said at last.

"You called to tell me that?"

"Not really. I wondered if you were interested in bears."

"I know nothing about them."

"Good. Maybe you'd come up here and take a look at something for me."

Francie went. Savard met her in Lawton Center, shook her hand. His was big and warm, full of latent strength but reserved at the same time, if she could read that much in a handshake. "You're aware of this supposed resemblance to my former wife?" he said, his gaze on Francie's face.

"Yes."

"I don't see it at all."

He drove her in the Bronco out to his cabin on Little Joe Lake. The radio was on.

"— and we're delighted to welcome a new sta-

444

tion to the *Intimately Yours* network today, KPLA in Los Angeles. My name's —"

Savard switched it off. With Em in the house: that was the part Francie still hadn't been able to understand. At that moment, the same moment she realized Savard must have had the radio on for a purpose, she remembered something Anne had said, just before asking for a surefire recipe: *He cares so much about his career.* Maybe in the end Em had come second, not first. The burning-up feeling, which had accompanied every thought of Ned since that last day in his house, was absent for the first time.

Savard parked by the shore of the lake. It was a clear, windless day, the blue sky reflecting dully off the still-frozen perimeter, brightly off the open water beyond. They got out of the car, approached the little footbridge. Francie stopped. "I'm a poor picker of men," she said.

Savard started to reply, held it inside.

"Go ahead," Francie said.

"One out of three ain't bad."

Francie laughed, her natural reaction, and she let it happen. They walked across the bridge to the cabin, where Savard paused and added, "If I'm not being presumptuous."

Their eyes met. "Let's see these bears of yours," Francie said.

Savard nodded. "But I want your true opinion."

"Everyone says that."

"They do?"

"But no one means it."

Savard went a little pale. He unlocked the door. "After you."

Francie walked into the cabin and looked around for what seemed to Savard an unendurably long time.

"So?" he said. "Good or bad?"